D0823405

"I'm Claire Campbell."

She said the words without any betraying quiver. "I hope to convince you of that fact over the next few hours."

Ben Maxwell glanced at her quickly, for the first time showing a faint trace of emotion. Surprise? Interest? She wasn't sure.

"Why did you decide it was time to come home, *Ms. Mason?*"

She smiled mockingly. "For the money, of course. What else?"

"What else, indeed," Ben murmured. "Tell me about yourself. I understand you're an artist."

"Yes, I work with glass, a family tradition, as you know. I'm really quite good, actually."

Ben's gaze rested on her face for a second before he turned away and stared out the window. "Do you have hopes of selling your creations to Campbell Crystal, Ms. Mason?"

"I don't have hopes, Mr. Maxwell. I have serious expectations. If I want to place my designs with Campbell Crystal, there's nothing to stop me. I already own the company."

She spoke quietly but the challenge of her statement resonated in the space between them as if she'd yelled it through a loudspeaker.

"Claire Campbell owns the majority of the shares in the company," he said.

She smiled. "Exactly."

Also available from MIRA Books and
JASMINE CRESSWELL

CHASE THE PAST

Jasmine Cresswell

Desires & Deceptions

MIRA BOOKS

If you purchased this book without a cover you should be aware that this book is stolen property. It was reported as "unsold and destroyed" to the publisher, and neither the author nor the publisher has received any payment for this "stripped book."

ISBN 1-55166-036-9

DESIRES & DECEPTIONS

Copyright © 1994 by Jasmine Cresswell.

All rights reserved. Except for use in any review, the reproduction or utilization of this work in whole or in part in any form by any electronic, mechanical or other means, now known or hereafter invented, including xerography, photocopying and recording, or in any information storage or retrieval system, is forbidden without the written permission of the publisher, MIRA Books, 225 Duncan Mill Road, Don Mills, Ontario, Canada M3B 3K9.

All characters in this book have no existence outside the imagination of the author and have no relation whatsoever to anyone bearing the same name or names. They are not even distantly inspired by any individual known or unknown to the author, and all incidents are pure invention.

MIRA and the star colophon are trademarks of MIRA Books.

Printed in U.S.A.

To my Mother: Welcome to America!

Footfalls echo in the memory
Down the passage which we did not take
Towards the door we never opened
Into the rose garden.
—T.S. Eliot, *Four Quartets*

Prologue

Vermont
November 1987

With infinite care, he straightened from his crouching position and peered through the cabin window into the living room. Claire hadn't bothered to close the drapes and he could see her clearly, even though none of the overhead lights had been switched on. She was sitting on a white sheepskin rug in front of the granite fireplace, arms clasped around her knees, staring into the leaping flames. The burning maple logs cast a rosy reflection on her normally pale cheeks, and burnished her blond hair to a rich auburn. He'd always considered Claire too thin and too tall, but tonight she looked so pretty he was almost sorry he had to kill her. Almost.

He shrugged his shoulders, easing the cramped muscles. His arms ached from carrying two giant cans of kerosene from the clearing where he'd parked the Jeep. He'd thought two cans would be more than enough to saturate the entire base of the cabin, but he'd run out before he got around to the fourth wall. He wasn't worried, though. The night air was crisp and cold; the fire would take hold within minutes.

He'd practiced on an abandoned shack last weekend, and the blaze had burned so hard and fierce that fire fighters had been called in from as far away as Middlebury.

Just thinking about last weekend's fire made him hot with excitement. Dozens of people had labored and sweated for hours, trying to extinguish that blaze, and all because of *him*.

God, it had been great! Clamping down on a thrill of anticipation, the watcher tucked his gloved hands under his armpits and waited for the right moment to set the fire. Rubbing the frost from his breath off the window, he peered inside the cabin and saw Jon Kaplan come out of the kitchen, carrying a bottle of champagne and two long-stemmed glasses. Yesterday had been Claire's eighteenth birthday, and she'd obviously decided that this was to be the big night when she surrendered her virginity. Kaplan was the six-foot-four dumb-ass she'd chosen to invite to the cabin this weekend, thus sealing his fate along with her own.

The watcher smiled, amused by the irony of the situation. Kaplan might be about to score big with Claire, but he wouldn't live to boast about his success.

He laughed out loud, muffling the sound in his scarf. The smell of the gasoline wafted past him on a gust of mountain air, and his skin began to prick. Not much longer now. Claire and Kaplan were really getting wrapped up in each other. In just a few minutes he'd be able to light the first match. A tight coil of pleasure twisted inside him, a strange sensation that left him feeling both sick and light-headed.

He watched Kaplan sit down next to Claire on the rug, wine and glasses cradled between his knees. Claire looked up, smiling, and an odd trick of light made it seem that she smiled straight at him, rather than at Kaplan. The watcher scowled. Suddenly he didn't feel so good. He kicked at a pile of powdery snow, angry and resentful at the emotions churning inside him. Okay, so Claire had a sweet, innocent smile. That didn't mean she deserved to live. In fact, it was all the more reason to kill her. He loathed hypocrites and Claire wasn't as innocent as she seemed. Women always insisted on confusing sex and love, and then blaming men when things didn't work out the way they expected. Goddamnit, she was no better than the rest of them. She was a whore. Her mother was a whore. All women were whores, and he hated every last one of them.

Frowning, he turned again to stare into the window. All things considered, when you got right down to it, he was doing Claire a favor by killing her. He could save her from the disillusion that would follow once she finally figured life out. Better she should die with dignity, before reality cut her dreams down to size. Or maybe he could even time the fire so that she died in the throes of her first orgasm. That way, she could go out of the world on a real high.

He saw Kaplan pour out two glasses of champagne and hand one to Claire. She took it, giggling a little as they toasted each other. Kaplan waited for her to drink most of the wine, then he leaned across and took her glass, setting it down on the stone fireplace. Having freed up both hands, he started to unbutton her sweater—without much finesse, but with considerable determination. Almost as an afterthought, he remembered to kiss her. The watcher snorted scornfully.

Kaplan's seduction techniques obviously didn't involve long hours of elaborate foreplay.

Bored by Kaplan's lack of imagination and Claire's fumbling inexperience, he lit a cigarette and puffed smoke into the shadow of a nearby pine tree. From his point of view, sex without the spice of a little sado-masochism didn't seem worth bothering about. But to each his own, he reminded himself. Hell, he didn't give a damn how she got off. It would be easier to set the fire if the pair of them got all hot and bothered, sweaty with teenage lust. That's why he'd waited. With any luck, the carbon monoxide from the fire would finish them off before they even noticed the smell of smoke, or heard the crackle of burning wood.

The night air was so cold it hurt to breathe. The watcher ground his cigarette into the snow and leaned back against the cabin wall, huddling deeper into his down jacket and wrapping his plaid mohair scarf higher around his face, so that only his eyes were left uncovered. The snow stretched out in a pristine blanket, interrupted by the moon-silvered darkness of spruce and fir trees. God, but these woods were magnificent!

No doubt about it, Vermont was a beautiful place to die.

Claire lay down on the pile of floor pillows and tried her best to feel carried away by romantic passion. Unfortunately, all she felt was tense and miserable. Jon was lying on top of her and he was heavy. Worse yet, he'd taken off her T-shirt and sweater and her arms were so chilled they were covered in goose bumps. Neither the champagne nor the blazing fire seemed to be keeping her warm.

The back of her neck prickled, giving her an uncomfortable feeling that someone was watching. Probably just embarrassment, she thought. Making love to Jon had seemed a much better idea back at school than it did right now. She shifted her hips, hoping to find a softer spot on the sheepskin hearthrug, and Jon drew in his breath on a sharp gasp of pleasure. "Yes, baby, yes. Do that some more, honey."

She wasn't quite sure how she'd excited him, but she'd read enough books and seen enough movies to know that his glazed eyes, sweaty skin and harsh moans were sure signs that he was having a great time. In fact, judging by the number of groans and the quantity of sweat he was producing, Jon ought to enjoy an earth-shattering climax any moment now.

Claire, on the other hand, was feeling more uncomfortable by the minute. She wished now that she'd drawn the drapes, so that she could get rid of the crazy feeling that she was being watched. She stared up at the wood-beamed ceiling and wondered if maybe sex got better with practice. Right at this moment, despite everything her girlfriends said about the wonders of making love, a life of celibacy was beginning to seem very appealing.

The fire was producing an interesting play of light and shadow on the overhead beams. The sputter and hiss of logs burning in the grate punctuated Jon's panting. Claire had a term paper due for French class on Tuesday morning, and she mentally planned her essay on nineteenth-century French novelists while Jon's hands tangled in her hair and his lips roamed over her neck and shoulders. Suddenly, his mouth slanted over hers in a fervent, demanding kiss. She immediately felt smothered, almost claustrophobic. "Stop!" she gasped, pushing him away and trying to sit up. "I can't breathe!"

Jon didn't look too pleased at the interruption, but he did at least give her the chance to draw in a couple of deep breaths before propelling her back against the cushions and kissing her again. This was what she'd come up here for, Claire reminded herself. Dammit, she would *not* grow up to be a frigid icicle like her mother, locked into a disastrous marriage. She would learn to enjoy sex like a normal woman or die in the process.

Abandoning her mental essay writing, Claire tried to respond to Jon's kisses with suitable enthusiasm, but the feeling of being unable to breathe was getting worse, and all she really wanted to do was get away from him.

Claire realized that she was perilously close to tears. Despite her best efforts, she felt her entire body freeze in rejection as Jon became more passionate.

His aggressive kisses abruptly stopped. "What's wrong?" he demanded, chest heaving as he sat up, visibly struggling for control.

"Nothing." She tried to smile. "This is great. You're great. Honest."

His dark eyes were still glazed with desire but, surprisingly, he wasn't willing to take her protestations at face value. He propped himself up on his elbow and looked down at her. "Hey, Claire, not that I want to boast or anything, but I've done this before, and I know when my partner's having fun. You didn't like what we were doing, did you?"

"Yes, yes..." she started to lie, but then she sat up, pulling her sweater around her shoulders and moving far enough away that they weren't touching. "No," she admitted, flushed with misery and embarrassment. "I'm sorry, Jon. I don't know what's wrong with me. I just don't seem to... I'm no good at this."

He rolled off the hearthrug, and leaned back against the sofa, breathing hard. After a while, his breathing slowed and he poured them both another glass of champagne. He held it out to her, patting the floor cushion next to him. "Come and sit here. I like to have you close."

She eyed him warily and he gave her a rueful grin. "No strings, Claire. We'll talk for a while. We don't even have to hold hands if that bothers you."

She'd always sensed a core of kindness behind Jon's macho jock exterior, which was why she'd chosen him in the first place. She got up and drew the drapes, feeling better for having blocked out the weird sensation of being watched. Breathing easier, she sat down next to him and he put his arm around her shoulders, hugging her with surprising gentleness. She hesitated for a moment, then relaxed against him. "I'm sorry," she said again. "I guess I've messed up the weekend for you."

"Hey, quit apologizing, okay? Sex isn't the only thing in life."

She smiled dejectedly. "Are you sure?"

His grin was wry. "No."

"Maybe if you want to—you know—just, like, do it... I wouldn't mind."

"But *I* would. Heck, Claire, I can wait until you feel more in the mood. You and me... Well, I guess it isn't just about sex, you know what I mean? I want us to be... like friends."

She decided it was time to warn him that she wasn't quite as naive as she looked. "That's a cute speech, Jon, but I know about your bets with the guys on the football team. I know they're all waiting to find out if you make it with me this weekend."

He had the grace to look ashamed. "Jeez, Claire, I'm real sorry, but things got kinda out of hand, you know? I like you a lot, but I'm the captain of the football team and everyone kind of expects me to behave a certain way, you know?"

"What are you going to tell them on Monday? If we don't have sex, are you going to lie so you can win your bets?"

"I'm gonna tell them to butt out," he said. "What happens here this weekend is between the two of us. Real personal." He took her hand, stroking it apologetically. "Do you want to call it quits and go back to school?" he asked. "We can if you like."

To her astonishment, Claire discovered that she had no desire to cut the weekend short. After all, she'd known about the bets before she and Jon set off from New Hampshire, so it would be hypocritical to get uptight about them now. Beneath the macho bluster, Jon was a nice guy, and she enjoyed his company. Besides, his arm felt warm and comforting around her shoulders, and she leaned a little nearer, relishing the sensation of closeness.

"No," she said. "I don't want to leave. It's beautiful up here at this time of year. The cross-country skiing will be wonderful. I'd like to stay, if you still want to."

"I want to stay," he said. His hands rubbed up and down her arms, and a tingling glow began to spread out everywhere he touched. She shivered. "Cold?" he asked.

"A little. We shouldn't let the fire go out until we're in bed."

"Stay right where you are, and I'll throw on another log. This maple wood smells great, doesn't it?"

"Mmm." She leaned against the arm of the sofa, watching through half-closed eyes as he stirred up the fire and made room for another log. They'd brought in a stack of firewood from the porch earlier in the day. It was well seasoned, but damp from the snow that had blown in under the porch roof. Maybe that's why she'd noticed this strong, almost kerosene-like smell of burning.

Jon threw a couple of logs onto the fire. They sizzled, spurting moisture droplets and belching black smoke before catching fire and beginning to burn. Jon squatted in front of the blaze for a little while, checking that everything was okay. When he returned and sat down next to Claire, his skin felt hot from the flames. She snuggled against him, relaxed and pleasantly sleepy.

"You smell of smoke," she said.

"You smell of woman," he replied huskily. He wrapped his arms around her, and when she didn't protest, he looked down with a questioning gaze. "Claire?" He crooked his finger under her chin and tilted her face upward. "I want to kiss you," he said, bending his head toward hers.

He moved slowly enough that she could easily have averted her head, but she didn't turn away, and this time, when he bent to kiss her, all their body parts seemed to fit perfectly. Her breasts weren't squashed against his chest. Her nose didn't bang into his, and their mouths met at just the right angle. His tongue pressed against her lips, and Claire opened her mouth willingly. His hand cupped her breast and a shiver rippled down her spine—a shiver that seemed to make her hot rather than cold.

"You're beautiful, Claire. I really like you." Jon spoke against her mouth, sounding young and endearingly uncertain of himself for a man who was considered the campus stud.

"I like you, too," she murmured, glad that she could say it with sincerity. "You're a kind person, Jon."

"Hey, watch it. That kind of compliment can ruin a guy's reputation." He smiled as he spoke, urging her toward the fire where the cushions waited. She followed him with only a little hesitation and he fed her the last of the champagne as he undressed her, whispering endearments. Her skin prickled with an unfamiliar pleasure as he trailed kisses over her stomach and breasts. Maybe she could learn to like this sexual stuff, Claire thought hazily. The champagne had given her a mild buzz—enough to cast a welcome veil between her actions and her critical faculties. Her body pulsed with a glow that felt like the high she got after running three miles on a sunny winter morning.

When Jon eased his fingers between her thighs, her stomach clenched tight with desire. This was better than okay, Claire decided. It was great, in fact. Maybe she wasn't going to end up in a horrible sham marriage like her parents. Maybe she was going to turn into a normal, regular person, after all.

Jon eased on top of her, thrusting hard and deep inside. She gasped with the pain of his entry, and he stared down at her in astonishment. "My God, you really *are* a virgin!"

She smiled wryly. "Not...any...more."

His breath came in short, rough gasps. "Claire, I'm sorry. I wasn't expecting... I can't hold back any longer."

"It doesn't matter." She muffled a gasp of frustration at the sudden cessation of all those intriguing prickles of desire. Jon kissed her again, moving inside her with long, powerful strokes. Just as the pain of his movements started to change into a tremble of excitement, his body convulsed and he collapsed on top of her. After a minute or two, he rolled away, propping himself up on his elbow and grasping her chin so that she was forced to turn and look at him.

"I'm sorry," he said softly.

"It's okay." She touched his cheek. "Now it's my turn to tell you to stop apologizing."

"We were doing great there for a while. Next time I'll make it good for you, I swear."

She was touched by his kindness, and willing to lie a little to save his pride. "It felt good," she said. "I feel good. Don't worry, Jon. You were terrific." At least he'd removed the tiresome burden of her virginity, and that was something to be grateful for.

He yawned, ready to be reassured. "Next time will be better, honey, I guarantee it." He pulled a soft mohair throw off the sofa and tucked it over them, although Claire realized she was feeling much warmer now than she had earlier. The cabin seemed to have gone from chilly to overly hot in the space of a few minutes.

Jon yawned again. "I don't know why I'm feeling so tired. I'm sorry, Claire, but I can barely keep my eyes open."

"Don't worry, I'm tired myself." And it was true. She was yawning repeatedly, almost as if her lungs couldn't find enough oxygen.

"We'll sleep for a couple of hours," Jon said. He coughed, then yawned again. "Gosh, I don't know what's the matter with me. Making love doesn't usually wear me out so quickly. Honest."

Claire was relieved he seemed so sleepy. She needed time to sort out her emotions, which were hovering somewhere between perplexed and totally bewildered. "Don't you think we'd be more comfortable sleeping in a real bed?" she suggested. "It smells really smoky in here. Maybe those logs were too wet."

He didn't answer—not even a mumble—and she turned to him, ready to repeat her question, but his eyes were closed and his arms flopped limply over the blanket. Within seconds, she heard his breathing change and knew he was fast asleep.

Claire's eyes drooped with heaviness, but she was too strung out to sleep. She also felt sticky and sweaty, and her head ached miserably. Her headache, in fact, was bad and becoming worse by the second.

She needed an aspirin, Claire decided; a couple of aspirin and a hot shower. She inched out from under the blanket, taking care not to disturb Jon. She picked up her scattered clothes and walked to the bathroom, relieved when she found aspirin in the medicine cabinet. She took three tablets because her headache was now throbbing with an intensity that made her want to throw up. She swallowed the pills with sips of water, grimacing at the unpleasant taste. The cabin's water supply was pumped in by electric motor from a well, and it usually tasted ice cold and fresh. Tonight, it was warm and faintly brackish.

Claire stared into the mirror over the sink, frowning as she tried to remember why she had come into the bathroom. Her head and limbs felt heavy, and it was a real effort to move, but she saw her clothes lying over the edge of the tub and decided she must have come into the bathroom to get dressed. She pulled on her warm socks, her ski pants, her T-shirt and her sweater, then looked around for shoes. All she could find was a pair of furry pink slippers, decorated with a set of cat's eyes and white whiskers. She sat down on the commode and put them on, staring in fascination at the quivering whiskers.

Jeesh, it was hot! She staggered to the bathroom window and pushed it open. The sash resisted her efforts, but she managed to ease it up two or three inches. The cool night air fanned her cheeks and she craned her neck so that her mouth was positioned in the opening between sill and window, gulping in fresh air as if she'd been deprived of it for weeks. She leaned her face against the window, closing her eyes and hoping the mountain air would blow away the nausea roiling in her stomach. Thankfully, after a while, the pounding, hammering pain inside her head began to ease.

Her headache was fading, but boy, it was hot tonight. Even the windowpane felt warm. Claire stared at the fire dancing and leaping around the edge of the cabin and wondered why the sight of the roaring flames frightened her so much. Jon had really built a doozer of a fire, she thought drowsily. But why had he lit it outside the cabin, instead of in the living room where there was a nice, safe grate?

The instant her woozy brain formed the question, she realized how bizarre it was. A second later, she understood what was happening.

Dear God! The cabin was on fire!

Claire skidded across the bathroom floor and pulled open the door. A blinding barrier of smoke rose up in front of her, thick enough to make the living room invisible.

"Jon! Jon! Wake up!" As soon as she opened her mouth to scream the warning, smoke rushed into her lungs, burning all the way down into her stomach, choking off her voice.

Towel. She needed a damp towel. The safety tip from a grade school fire drill flashed into her befuddled brain. Retching, staggering along the wall, she groped her way back into the bathroom. In the twenty seconds since she'd opened the door, smoke had poured in, filling the room with an eye-tearing, throat-rasping pall of smoke. She patted the edge of the bath until she found a towel, then wet it as best she could under the trickle of water coming from the tap. Tying the towel over her face—a much harder task than she'd expected—she ran back to the living room.

The smoke was so thick that she could see only a couple of inches in front of her and then nothing but a shifting, ever changing wall of gray. Particles of soot clogged her nostrils. Overhead, she heard the ominous crackle of burning timber. The heat was intense enough to make her break out in a sweat, but so far she could see no sign of actual flames.

Because of the cabin's open-plan interior, there weren't many walls to serve as directional guides, and she had crawled over yards of bare wooden floor before she bumped into a kitchen cabinet and realized she'd spent several precious minutes searching for Jon in the wrong direction. Biting back a sob of frustration, she felt her way along the cabinets until she reached a gap that marked the entrance to the kitchen. Controlling a surge of panic, she tried to get her bearings. The sink was behind her. She could feel the smooth surface of the fridge to her left, and the counter to her right. That meant she was now exactly opposite the fireplace in the living room, and Jon must be lying on the floor about twenty feet straight ahead of her.

She would never have believed it could be so difficult to crawl forward in a straight line. The smoke disoriented her, so that she would forget for seconds at a time which way was ahead and which way was behind. She kept her head down, staring at her hands as she placed one in front of the other, trying to use the wooden planks of flooring as a guide. She was concentrating so hard on moving forward that she bumped into Jon before she saw him.

"Thank God! Thank God!" She shook his shoulder, babbling a jumble of prayers and pleas as she strove to wake him. He didn't stir. Terrified, she pressed her ear to his lips and her fingers to his throat. She felt no whisper of breath, detected not the faintest flicker of a pulse.

"Jon! Jon! Wake up, damn you!" She shook him again, pummeling his chest. Anguish turned to rage when he refused to wake up. "Move, you stupid jock! Get your ass in gear! We have to get out of here!"

Silence. Deathly stillness.

No! He wasn't dead. He couldn't be dead. She wouldn't allow him to be dead. Sobbing, she pushed her arms under his shoulders, somehow managing to pull his limp body into a sitting position. Crawling behind him, she clasped her arms around his chest and began to drag him toward the main cabin door.

Crash! The explosive crack of sound seemed to come from everywhere around her, all at once. In the blink of an eye, a wall of fire sprang up in front of her, blocking the exit from the cabin.

How was she to get out? Dear God, what should she do now? She rocked back on her heels, resting the weight of Jon's inert body on her knees, as she tried to visualize the layout of the cabin. There was a back door that opened off the laundry room, next to the bathroom. She wasn't sure how she would drag Jon's body such a long way, but right now, it seemed their only realistic hope of escape. The kitchen was much closer, but she was afraid the window over the sink might be too narrow and too high for her to haul Jon's body through. Besides, the fire was already licking hungrily at the base of the kitchen cabinets, and she might not have time to get Jon to safety before the kitchen burst into full flame.

Claire hunched onto her hands and knees, maneuvering Jon into position on her back and clasping his hands around her neck, but as soon as she started to crawl forward, his hands fell open and he started to slide off.

"Jon, you have to hold on," she croaked, tears of frustration pouring down her cheeks. "You have to help me if I'm going to save you."

He didn't answer, of course. She'd known that he wouldn't. That he couldn't. The towel was no longer wet and she tossed it aside, trying to drag some oxygen into her seared, laboring lungs. But there was no oxygen to be had, and she turned around, readying herself for the exhausting task of heaving him back up onto her shoulders. Dear God, how was she going to get Jon out of here if he didn't even have the capacity to hold on to her?

Just as she turned to pick him up, a blazing beam fell from the ceiling, landing with grotesque symmetry in the middle of his back. Burning splinters leapt across her chest in a searing line of agony.

She screamed, instinctively vaulting out of the way as Jon's body glowed in reflected flame, before igniting with a hideous sizzle of burning flesh.

She couldn't watch. Screaming, she ran away from the loathsome roar of flames, away from the obscene ball of bloodred fire. She ran blindly, bumping into walls, clawing her way into the back corridor more by instinct than by any conscious plan to save herself.

There was no escape through the back door, which had already been transformed into a scarlet barrier of incandescent heat. She fought her way through smoke and debris into the bathroom, climbing up onto the edge of the tub and banging at the window. The warped and buckled sash wouldn't budge, but Claire was demented with the need to get away from the cabin. Stronger than the desire to save herself was the urge to flee from any reminder of Jon's hideous end. Wrapping her fist in a folded bath towel, she smashed at the panes of glass, shoving her fist through the window over and over again until there was nothing left but the bare frame. She pulled herself over the window ledge, dropping the four feet to the ground without even noticing the jump. Gasping for breath, mindless with terror, she fled from the memory of Jon's burning body.

She bolted into the woods, her pink slippers skidding in the deep snow, running until she could run no more. Consumed with shame, she leaned against a tree, her arms clasped around her waist, rocking backward and forward as her body heaved with dry, racking sobs. What was she going to say when rescuers found Jon's body? How was she going to explain away the fact that she had saved herself, but allowed Jon to die?

The snow was seeping in through her slippers, and her teeth had started to chatter with the cold. Little as she wanted to face the authorities, she clearly needed to make her way to the main road, walk a mile to her nearest neighbor, and report what had happened. The sweater and T-shirt that had seemed so warm inside the cabin were hopelessly inadequate for a November night in the Green Mountains of Vermont. The harsh reality was that she needed to get moving unless she wanted to freeze to death.

Pulling the sleeves of her sweater over her numb fingers, Claire began the weary trek out of the forest and toward the road. She was right at the edge of the clearing when she turned to give one last look at the burning cabin. What she saw immobilized her with shock.

A Jeep emerged from the woods behind the cabin and drove slowly toward the road. The driver, muffled behind a scarf and distinctive plaid cap, was no more than a bulky shadow at the steering wheel. But in the brilliant light shed by the blaze, the license plate on the Jeep was clearly visible.

ABC 4.

Claire recognized that license plate. ABC stood for Andrew Brentwood Campbell. The number four indicated the Jeep's place in Andrew's personal fleet of vehicles. As it happened, Claire knew Andrew Brentwood Campbell quite well.

He was her father.

One

The motel offered clean rooms, thirty-six channels of cable TV, discounts to senior citizens and free coffee in the lobby. Unfortunately, as Dianna Mason soon discovered, its amenities included neither adequate lighting nor spacious table surfaces.

She was accustomed to improvising, and the shortcomings of the room didn't bother her. Ignoring Hal's complaints, she dragged a battered chair to the Formica counter that stretched along the wall between the bathroom and the sagging metal clothes rack that passed for a closet. Opening her ancient suitcase, she took out a plastic travel bag of toilet articles and makeup, lining up the jars and bottles neatly along one side of the counter. "I'll wash my hands and I'll be ready," she said.

Hal Doherty viewed the room with disgust, furious that they didn't have the money to check in anywhere better. "God, how I hate Florida in summer! What the hell is Andrew Campbell doing down here at this time of year?"

"Campaigning for governor," Dianna said.

Hal hated the way she always answered questions literally. If she didn't look so damn much like Claire... He turned the air-conditioning on full blast and slung his garment bag onto the bed nearest the door. Then he wove his way around the beds and stood behind her, scowling. "There's no damn light in here. We need light, for God's sake."

Dianna gestured to the wall mirror above the counter. "At least the mirror's a decent size." Her voice was simultaneously husky and soft, a combination that made her most casual remark sound oddly sexy.

He grunted. "The mirror's no use without more light. We can't get your makeup right unless we can see your bone structure." He unplugged the bedside lamp and carried it over to the alcove, standing it on the counter between Dianna's toothpaste and a brochure advertising the local discount shopping mall. He slanted the shade at various angles and finally unscrewed it, tossing it into a corner.

"That's better." Satisfied at last with the lighting, he tilted Dianna's chin upward and stared intently at her reflection in the mirror. Then he unzipped a photograph from the pocket of his garment bag, squinting as he glanced back and forth between mirror and picture.

"Your cheekbones are all wrong," he said, stroking his mustache with nervous fingers. "My God, you don't look in the least like her! They're never going to accept you."

"Stop worrying," Dianna said. "You're forgetting that the first time you saw me at Sonya's apartment, you thought I really was Claire Campbell." She reached for her tray of cosmetics and began to apply foundation, blush and a muted gray eye shadow. After working for about ten minutes, she added a final touch of pale peach lip gloss and swiveled around to look at Hal. "Well, what do you think?"

"It's okay. More than okay." Hal squeezed her shoulder in grudging approval. "You're good with makeup, Di."

"I'm an artist, remember? I understand tricks of light and shadow, and that's all makeup is, really."

Hal wasn't interested in discussing her skills as an artist. He stared at the photo again. "Your hair's the wrong color," he said. "Dammit, Di, you're way too dark. Claire Campbell was a blonde. Your hair is light ash brown."

Dianna sighed. "We've had this conversation a dozen times, Hal. Claire disappeared almost seven years ago. She was eighteen then and she'd be twenty-five today. Her hair could easily have turned darker as she got older."

"Yeah, it could have, but maybe it didn't."

"We'll never know, will we? But the whole point is that her family doesn't know, either. Nobody's seen her for seven years."

"But they have this mental image of her as a blonde." His handsome features tight with frustration, Hal paced the narrow strip of carpet between the chenille-covered beds and the chest of drawers. The TV, bolted onto a rickety stand, stared at them balefully from the corner. "Why wouldn't you agree to have your hair dyed? Dammit, Di, a couple of hours in the beauty salon and you could have been a perfect match for her!"

Dianna shook her head, hanging on to her patience by a thread. "Only until the dye started to grow out.

If I do manage to get myself invited to stay with the Campbells, I can't spend my time worrying about whether dark roots are showing through my supposedly blond hair.''

Hal scrutinized the photo again, determined to find something to worry about. "Claire's hair was straighter than yours. And longer."

She shrugged. "Sorry, Hal. Unless you're willing to wait three months, there's nothing much I can do about 'longer.'''

Her flippant attitude infuriated him. Didn't she realize what was at stake? "You know we can't wait. That's the whole point. Andrew's found a judge in Pennsylvania who's willing to cooperate with him. In three months, Claire Campbell will be declared legally dead—"

"And all Claire's lovely money will belong to Andrew Brentwood Campbell." Dianna laughed with genuine amusement. "You're turning pale, Hal. Don't you want Andrew to get the money? He's Claire's father, after all."

"Don't joke about it," he snapped. "For God's sake, Di, twenty million dollars isn't something to joke about."

She looked at him thoughtfully, still not sure she understood him, even after almost two months of working together. "Why do you want the money so badly, Hal? If we manage to get paid off by the Campbells, what will you do with your share?"

"Spend it," he said at once. "You've never had any money, so you don't know what you're missing, but I was a successful corporate lawyer until Andrew decided to blame me for his legal problems." He looked around the shabby motel room, his nose wrinkling in distaste. "When I'm rich, I'll never stay in a dump like this again. You can bet on it."

"I can imagine what it's like to have money," Dianna said. "I have a great imagination." She picked up a comb and ran it through her hair, flicking the bangs up and away from her face without thinking about what she was doing.

"My God!" Hal said, staring at her. "That's it!"

"That's what?"

"The hair. You've got it just right." He thrust the photo under her nose, eyes alight with excitement. "See? Just then, when you were combing it—you styled it just like Claire."

"Did I?" Dianna barely glanced at the snapshot. "Put that darn picture away, Hal. I'm sick of looking at it."

"Why? She was a good-looking kid."

"She was a stupid-looking kid," Dianna said.

"She was rich," Hal said. "She didn't need to be smart."

"Given that somebody tried to burn her to death, I'd say she needed to be smarter than most people."

"I wonder what really happened to her?" Hal said. "They never found so much as a trace of her in that cabin, you know."

"If there was no trace of her remains, then she must have escaped from the fire. That's what the probate judge decided and it seems logical to me. According to you, the original probate judge said there was insufficient evidence to declare her legally dead, so I guess she's still alive, at least legally." Dianna picked up the pot of peach lip gloss and tossed it into her purse.

"You sound mighty casual about her fate," Hal said. "You'd better start praying that Claire doesn't

decide to come back and claim her inheritance right
when you're making your pitch to old man Campbell.''

Dianna's blue-gray eyes gleamed with cynical
amusement. ''Somehow, Hal, I can't believe that
prayers for help in committing criminal fraud are
likely to be answered.''

She'd noticed before that Hal had absolutely no
sense of humor. She could see him weighing her remark and deciding, regretfully, that she was right.
''Whether or not Claire died in that fire, she must be
dead by now,'' he said, looking more cheerful at the
thought.

''Why must she be dead?''

''It's obvious. If she was alive, she would have gone
back home. I mean, why would she stay away?''

Dianna shrugged. ''Maybe she has amnesia. Maybe
she just got smart and decided she had no desire to end
up barbecued. Maybe she didn't care enough about
any of the Campbells to go back home.''

''Nobody walks away from twenty million dollars.'' Hal spoke with absolute conviction. ''She's
dead, I'm sure of it.'' He popped the tab on a can of
diet Coke and drank thirstily. ''I wish I could have
gotten my hands on one of the Campbells' home
movies,'' he muttered. ''Who knows how she talked?
How she walked? What her gestures were like? You
may look just like her, but you can't possibly sound
like her—''

''We don't need to worry about any of that stuff,''
Dianna said. ''We're going to claim that my vocal
cords were permanently damaged by the smoke. As
for the rest, from what you've told me, Claire's parents never spent much time with her. How will they

know if I walk like her, or if my gestures are just like hers?''

"True. Although she and her father used to spend a lot of time together when Claire was a kid. At least, that's what everyone said.'' Hal sat down in the room's only armchair and rested his feet on the mustard yellow bedspread. "What we need to do now is go over all the background information and make sure you're ready to confront the Campbells next weekend. We can't afford to have you make any mistakes, Di. One major error and it's all over for us.''

"You've been drilling me on Claire's family history for the past six weeks.'' Dianna pushed the chair back from the counter and stood. "I have so much information floating around inside my head that sometimes I wake up in the morning and think I really am Claire Campbell.''

"Good,'' Hal said, more relieved than he wanted to admit. Sometimes he had the impression that Dianna Mason was treating his whole careful plan as some weird private joke. "That's the way it should be. Think, eat, sleep, breathe Claire Campbell.'' He swung around. "Where did you go to school?'' he barked.

She gave him the answer she knew he wanted to hear. "Linden Hall in northwestern Connecticut.'' *Claire's school.*

"College?''

"Dartmouth, majoring in art history. But I was only there for a couple of months before the fire.''

Hal gave her a brief nod of approval. She never made factual mistakes in repeating the details of Claire's past, but it had taken her weeks to stop referring to Claire as "she.''

"What happened the night of the fire?"

"I don't like to talk about it," she said, hanging her head.

Hal clicked his tongue impatiently. "No, Di, I've told you before. You mustn't refuse to answer questions about the fire."

"Why? Claire probably hates to talk about what happened that night."

"We're not interested in psychological realism," he snapped. "All we want is a convincing story for Andrew Campbell. Or, God help us, for Ben Maxwell, if we can't get straight in to see Andrew."

"This Ben Maxwell person has only been working at Campbell Industries for six years, so he's never seen Claire in his life. Why do you always sound so worried when you mention his name? How can he pose any threat to us?"

"Wait until you meet him," Hal said grimly. "Then ask me that question again. If you need to. Now, back to business. What happened the night of the fire? Who was with you in the cabin? What were you doing there?"

"It was my birthday," she said, sighing. "I'd invited Jon Kaplan to spend the weekend with me. We were good friends, and we both liked to cross-country ski—"

Hal snorted. "Honey, you can forget that line. They went up there to screw, and nobody's gonna believe any different, okay?"

"How do you know why they went up there?" she inquired mildly. "Were you with them?"

"Don't get cute, Dianna. I spent five years cross-examining claimants who pretended to be Claire Campbell—that was part of my job. I've made it my business to interview everyone who knows anything at all about what happened that night. Jon Kaplan had bet several hundred dollars that he'd get Claire Campbell into bed before the weekend was over. Claire was naive, but she wasn't dumb enough to invite the campus stud up to an isolated cabin and expect to spend the evening discussing Shakespeare's sonnets."

Dianna shrugged. "Have it your way. How's this? Jon and I went up to the cabin planning to have sex, but we never got around to it because someone poured kerosene all around the foundations and then set the place on fire."

"How come you escaped from the cabin, Claire?"

"We've been over this a thousand times, Hal."

"One more time. This is important."

She sighed. "I was in the bathroom. I smelled smoke, looked out the window, and realized the cabin was burning. I climbed onto the bathtub, pushed myself out the window and ran around to the front of the cabin, hoping to rescue Jon."

"But you didn't rescue him, did you?"

"No," she said, her voice expressionless. "The front door was burning and I couldn't get inside."

"Where was Jon's body found?"

"I don't know. I've never read an account of the fire."

"You could try putting a little emotion into that statement," Hal suggested. "Right now, you sound as if you're reciting a grocery list."

A shadow flickered across Dianna's face. "I can't bear to read about the accident, or to talk about what happened that night." Her voice shook, and she swallowed hard, turning away as if she might be blinking back tears. "It's so damn painful to remember Jon, and to know that he died for no reason except that someone wanted to murder me."

Her imitation of someone overcome by sincere emotion was convincing enough to alarm Hal. "Dianna? Hey, what's the matter, kid? Are you all right?"

She looked up at him, eyes gleaming with mockery. "I'm just dandy, Hal. Was that more to your liking?" She kicked off her shoes and sat cross-legged on the bed.

"It was much better," he said, obscurely annoyed by the ease with which she seemed able to switch moods.

She yawned. "Good. Now let's order a pizza. I'm starving."

"Wait! You can't stop there. You have to explain why you ran away, what you've been doing these past seven years—"

"I'm going to tell them the truth about what I've been doing. The whole truth and nothing but the truth. That way, when Andrew Campbell hires a regiment of private detectives to investigate my story, everything's going to check out just right."

Most of the impostors hoping to claim Claire's millions had tripped themselves up by trying to embellish their stories when they didn't need to. Hal knew they should stick as closely as possible to the facts of the last seven years of Dianna Mason's life, and yet he could feel himself starting to sweat at the prospect of opening those years to Campbell scrutiny.

"My God, we're never going to get away with this," he muttered. "I was mad to think we could pull it off. They'll demand DNA tests—"

"We can refuse to submit to testing," Dianna interjected.

"Then they'll get the probate judge to order you to comply and we'll both end up in jail."

"Perhaps not. During the time you worked as the Campbells' lawyer, how many so-called Claire Campbells tried to claim the proceeds of her trust fund?"

"Six."

"And none of them submitted to a blood test, did they?"

He shook his head. "But they were such obvious frauds, we didn't need tests in order to get rid of them."

"Look on the bright side," Dianna said. "If we get caught, I'm going to spend much more time in prison than you."

Hal's cheeks paled with a mixture of apprehension and anger. "You're not taking any of this seriously, are you? My God, there's twenty million dollars at stake, and you don't really give a damn!"

"I care," she said. "More than you know."

Dianna felt more nervous than she was willing to admit. The humidity was already high, despite the early-morning hour, and sweat was beginning to dampen the collar of her beige linen suit. Until she'd met Hal at a party, she'd worked full-time in her studio in Boston, spending most of her time dressed in baggy pants and muslin shirts. But Hal had insisted that she wear a business suit for her first interview with the Campbells, and since he was paying for her clothes, she hadn't protested. Her straight linen skirt felt like an oversize corset, and her panty hose and high-heeled sandals felt even worse. If being rich meant wearing clothes like this every day, Dianna decided there was a lot to be said in favor of poverty.

"Is Mr. Campbell expecting you, sir?" The guard at the gate sounded courteous, but doubtful. Hal was driving a Toyota Camry that had seen better days, and visitors to Laurel Manor Country Club—"Gracious Homes for the Buyer of Discrimination"—rarely arrived in anything less dignified than a small Mercedes.

Hal spoke emphatically. "Certainly Mr. Campbell is expecting us. I'm Hal Doherty and this is Claire Campbell."

Claire Campbell. The mere sound of the name was enough to give Dianna a bad attack of the jitters. Two months ago, when she first met Hal, this whole scam had seemed remarkably easy—something she could pull off without any major problems. This morning, her bravado had vanished completely. Faced with the reality of what she was about to do, she wished she were a thousand miles away from any house that contained a Campbell.

"Thank you for waiting, Mr. Doherty." The guard emerged from the gate house, carrying a portable phone. "Mr. Maxwell says you're to go through. Follow the road around the golf course, and it's the second house past the tennis courts."

"I know the house," Hal said, fingers drumming on the steering wheel. "Is Andrew Campbell at home this morning?"

"I wouldn't know, sir. I only spoke with Mr. Maxwell." The guard opened the electronic gate and Hal drove into the impeccably maintained grounds of Laurel Manor Country Club. Dianna stared straight ahead, her vision so blurred with panic that she scarcely noticed either the clusters of brightly colored hibiscus, or the smooth surface of the private road.

"We're here." The car bumped to a halt. Hal killed the ignition and turned to scrutinize her one last time. "This is it, Claire."

That name again. Dianna felt her stomach rise up in revolt. Good grief, she must have been crazy— stark, staring mad—to think she could get away with this. "I can't do it," she said. "Hal, I'm sorry, but you have to get me out of here."

"It's too late for second thoughts," he said. He got out of the car and hurried around to open her door. Overcome by panic, she started to run, but Hal grabbed her by the elbow and frog-marched her up the front steps. "You're looking at five to fifteen in federal prison if you blow it, *Claire*, so you'd better calm down and start remembering everything I've taught you." He pressed the doorbell.

A young woman, plump and dark, opened the door. She seemed to recognize Hal, for she gave him a little nod of acknowledgment. *"Buenos días, señor."*

"Good morning, Isabella. We're here to see Mr. Campbell."

"Meester Campbell, he is not available. Meester Maxwell, he is waiting for you, *señor."* The maid squinted sideways at Dianna. "And for you, too, *señorita.* Pleez to come this way."

Laurel Manor Country Club was one of Campbell Properties' newest developments, and the house was less than four years old, which meant that Claire Campbell had disappeared before it was built. Dianna could follow Hal and the maid without needing to pretend that she knew where she was going. The high heels of her sandals clicked over the marble floors, sounding thunderous in the oppressive quiet of the house. The maid stopped in front of a set of double doors, and knocked.

"*Señor,* the visitors are here!" she called out in Spanish.

"Bring them in," a mild masculine voice replied, also in Spanish.

The maid threw open the doors, and Hal strode through, beckoning to Dianna. "Come along, Claire. I want you to meet Ben Maxwell."

She stepped into the huge room, her heart thudding so hard and fast against her rib cage that she had trouble breathing. A handsome dark-haired man was seated behind a cherrywood desk, set at an angle to the shaded bay windows. In deference to the Florida heat, he hadn't put on a jacket or a tie, but his white shirt was crisply starched, and he wore a pair of formal, tailored slacks. He rose as Dianna came in, and looked at her in polite, assessing silence.

Her response to his scrutiny was an instant, visceral shiver. She'd spent her childhood learning to disguise the intimidating level of her IQ, and she'd spent her adult life learning to conceal her turbulent emotions behind a mask of cool cynicism. She had no difficulty in recognizing a fellow deceiver of expert proportions. Ben Maxwell turned his silvery gray eyes in her direction and she knew at once what sort of opponent she would be dealing with: soft-spoken, understated—and lethal.

"Hal. How are you?" Ben turned away from her and nodded in the lawyer's direction. His expression remained mild, his smile the epitome of professional courtesy, but Dianna had to clench her jaw to stop her lips from trembling with fright.

"I'm fine," Hal said, his voice sounding unnecessarily loud and blustering. "Ready to get down to business. This is Claire Campbell, as you can probably recognize, but for the past seven years, she's called herself Dianna Mason."

"Ms. Mason." Ben spoke with a neutrality that was more threatening than open disbelief. He nodded to her, then made a concise gesture indicating that she and Hal should both take a seat. Dianna perched on the edge of her chair, knees and ankles clamped tightly together, purse clutched in her hands. When she saw Ben's gaze rest for a second on her white knuckles, she drew in a deep breath and forced herself to relax. He smiled, very faintly, and she knew that he had understood the reason for her tiny movement. *Damn him.* She would not allow herself to be intimidated.

Having neatly reversed their positions, so that she and Hal were sitting whereas he was now standing, Ben leaned against the edge of his desk and shoved his hands into the pockets of his slacks. His attitude appeared casual, but Dianna knew better. Every one of his hackles was on full alert.

"Andrew has asked me to interview your... candidate," Ben said to Hal. "He also asked me to convey his apologies to you both for not greeting you personally."

"Is he sick?"

"No, he's in great shape." Ben looked at Dianna, his gaze bland. "As you can imagine, he's somewhat tired of meeting young women who claim to be his daughter."

Hal bristled. "Claire isn't claiming to be Andrew's daughter. She *is* his daughter."

Ben cocked his head in polite inquiry. "Is that so, Ms. Mason? Are you Andrew's long-lost daughter?"

The smoothness of his manner provoked her in the oddest way, perhaps because she could sense the mocking disdain that lay beneath the surface courtesy. For a wild, crazy moment, she wanted to fling the truth in his face, to stare straight into his arrogant, silvery eyes and say, *No, Andrew Campbell is not my father.* The words hovered right on the tip of her tongue, but in the end, of course, she didn't speak them.

"I'm Claire Campbell," she said, managing to produce the words without any betraying quiver. "I hope to convince you of that fact over the next few hours." As always when she was upset, her voice emerged in a low, throaty murmur, and Ben glanced at her quickly, for the first time showing a faint trace of emotion. Surprise? Interest? She wasn't sure.

Ben suddenly straightened from his lounging position against the desk and depressed an intercom button on his phone. "Isabella, would you take Mr. Doherty out by the pool and offer him some refreshments?"

"Yes, *señor.* I come."

Hal rose from his chair, looking angry. "See here, Ben, I'm not willing to be shunted off while you grill Claire about her background. I'm Claire's lawyer, her legal representative, and you have no right to demand to speak to her alone—"

"I'm so sorry," Ben said. "I certainly understand your point of view, Hal. I must have mistaken your position when we spoke earlier." He held out his hand. "Goodbye. I'm sorry we didn't get the chance to explore this matter any further."

Hal stared at Ben's outstretched hand. "What the hell are you talking about?"

Ben pretended to be startled by Hal's vehemence. "I'm not a lawyer, Hal, you know that, and I'm certainly not qualified to represent Andrew Campbell's interests if this is going to be a formal, legal conference. I agreed to meet with you this morning because I thought you wanted to work out some amicable conclusion to this situation. But if you're acting as Ms. Mason's attorney, and if you want to pursue this claim through official channels, then naturally I can't risk harming Andrew's interests by continuing this conversation. If you are treating this as a first, formal step in a complex legal process, then Andrew must be represented by a full complement of lawyers, acting under the jurisdiction of the probate court."

"You're not being reasonable," Hal protested. "We both know why you want to interview Claire alone—legal procedure has got nothing to do with it. You just want the chance to scare her into saying something she shouldn't!"

"I assure you that I have no intention of scaring anyone. And if this charming young lady is indeed Andrew's daughter, how can I make her say something that she shouldn't?" Ben smiled with every appearance of perfect amity, but his finger hovered over the intercom, ready to press the button. "What's it to be? You and your friend can leave now, or I can interview her alone. It's your decision, Hal."

"No, it's not," Dianna said. "It's mine."

Both men looked at her as if she were a performing poodle who'd jumped through a hoop reserved for another dog. She felt a minor surge of triumph in having managed to disconcert Ben Maxwell, if only for a moment.

Ben recovered all too quickly. "You're quite right, Ms. Mason. I apologize. Are you willing to talk with me without having Hal present?"

"I've no objection to talking with you for a while, but I don't know what you hope to prove. I never met you before the fire. You have no personal insights to contribute in evaluating my claim to be Claire Campbell."

"I'm not interested in hearing about your life before the fire, Ms. Mason. It's your life after the fire that I'm anxious to learn about."

That was smart of him, Dianna thought. Anyone reasonably intelligent could learn enough about Claire's past to answer a preliminary round of questions. It was more difficult to construct a credible explanation for Claire's disappearance, even more difficult to explain why she'd suddenly chosen to reappear after seven years of silence. Why would a woman walk out on twenty million dollars, and then come back, bright and smiling, to claim her place in the family?

Hal walked across to her side, smoothing his mustache, a sure sign that he was worried. She must remember to warn him about that, Dianna thought. Body language could be more revealing than words.

"Don't talk to him, Claire." Hal was almost pleading with her. "Insist on meeting with your father immediately."

"Why? My father never makes his own decisions about things like this. He'll do whatever Ben tells him."

"For God's sake, Claire, you're Andrew's daughter! You've been missing for seven years. Of course, he wants to see you! Don't let Ben Maxwell deprive you of your rights." Hal sounded genuinely horrified. One of his strengths as a conspirator was his capacity for self-delusion. Probably by now he'd almost convinced himself that she really was the missing Campbell heiress.

Dianna shrugged, feigning a confidence she was light-years from feeling. "I'll be fine, Hal. I have nothing to hide from Mr. Maxwell." The lie was so vast that she managed to deliver it in a clear voice and with an innocent expression. That was another trick she'd learned over the past few years: Never tell small lies, only big ones.

The maid knocked at the door. "If you will pleez to come, Señor Doherty. I have fruit and iced tea waiting for you by the pool."

"We shouldn't keep you waiting more than an hour," Ben said.

Hal didn't acknowledge the remark by so much as a glance. "Remember, you're doing this totally against my advice," he said, brushing past Dianna. "This man's a shark. Watch what you say and don't sign anything—anything at all."

Ben shut the door behind Hal. "Are you aware that Hal Doherty avoided criminal charges six months ago strictly because of the generosity of Andrew Campbell?"

Dianna stared straight ahead. "Hal indicated that he and Andrew had a difference of opinion about some missing money."

"Hal embezzled funds," Ben said bluntly.

After six weeks of living with Hal, Dianna could easily believe it, but she wasn't going to admit as much to Ben. "Isn't that slander, Mr. Maxwell?"

"No," he said tersely. "I have the documents to prove that it's a simple statement of fact." He sat down behind the massive desk, and reached for a thick folder. "Where did you meet Hal?" he asked.

"At a party in Boston a couple of months ago."

"What a happy coincidence for both of you."

"Yes, it was." She returned his gaze coolly. "I'd already decided it was time to come home. Hal's support provided me with the extra spur that I needed."

"Why did you decide it was time to 'come home,' Ms. Mason?"

She smiled mockingly. "For the money, of course. What else?"

"What else, indeed," Ben murmured, leaning back in his chair. "Tell me about yourself, Ms. Mason. I understand you're an artist."

"Yes, I work with glass—a family tradition, as you know. But please, don't be so formal, Mr. Maxwell. You really must call me Claire."

"Thank you, but I don't believe we're ready for that much intimacy." Ben's eyes took on an ironic gleam. "Are you a successful artist, Ms. Mason?"

Where her art was concerned, she wasn't prepared to lie, not even to placate Ben Maxwell, or to ease her way into the Campbell household. "I'm one of the most talented glassworkers in the country," she said flatly.

"And modest, too," he observed.

She surprised herself by laughing. "I'm sorry. That must have sounded obnoxious, but I'm damn good, and I get tired of pretending otherwise."

His gaze rested on her face for a second before he turned away and stared out the window. "Do you have hopes of selling your creations to Campbell Crystal, Ms. Mason?"

"I don't have hopes, Mr. Maxwell. I have serious expectations. If I want to place my designs with Campbell Crystal, there's nothing to stop me. I already own the company. A majority shareholding in that division of Campbell Industries is a significant part of my trust."

She spoke quietly, but the challenge of her statement resonated in the space between them as if she'd yelled it through a loudspeaker.

"Claire Campbell owns the majority of shares in the company," he said.

She smiled at him. "Exactly."

She could see that she'd made him furious, which had the perverse effect of making her feel much less nervous. He glanced down at a paper on his desk, then looked up, his eyes ice cold. "Shall we stop the sparring, Ms. Mason, and get down to basics? I understand that three years ago you were arrested and spent several weeks in jail. Do you have any comment to make about that incident?"

Her stomach clenched, although she'd been expecting the accusation and had steeled herself to face it. "It's true I was arrested and since I couldn't afford to post bail, I was forced to stay in jail until the public defender could persuade the D.A. to drop charges."

"You were accused of drug trafficking," he said.

"It was a mistake," she protested passionately. "I've never used illegal drugs, not even to experiment, much less to sell. I had no idea there was cocaine in my apartment that night."

"And yet twenty-five grams of coke were found in one of your sofa cushions."

"I was guilty of terminal stupidity," she said tautly, "and a rotten taste in friends. Neither of those is an indictable offense."

"But fraud is," he said softly. "And so is impersonating a dead woman in order to get your hands on twenty million dollars that don't belong to you."

She shook her head impatiently. "I wish I could convince you how little I care about the money."

"You can easily convince me, Ms. Mason." He pushed a paper across the desk. "That is a legal renunciation of all claim to Claire Campbell's estate. Sign on the dotted line and I'll be happy to believe your statement that you're not interested in the money."

"I don't want the money," she said, "but I want Campbell Crystal. My great-grandfather founded the company, and it's my heritage."

She jumped at the sound of slow applause. "Great speech, nicely delivered. You've learned your lines well." A low, cultured voice spoke just behind her and Dianna swung quickly around.

She saw a tall, blue-eyed man with gray hair and a narrow-bridged, aristocratic nose. A dozen different pictures flashed into her mind, and she recognized him at once. Andrew Brentwood Campbell.

Claire's father.

"Hello, Daddy." She had no idea where the words came from or how she managed to say them so easily.

Andrew reached out and gripped the back of the chair she'd been sitting in. "Claire?" He swallowed hard, his cheeks turning a sickly greenish white. "My God, Claire, it's really you! You've come home."

Two

"Why are you so surprised, *Daddy?*" Dianna retreated toward the window, but she wouldn't let herself dwell on the shock of meeting Andrew Campbell, and this time she spoke his name with subtle derision. "Did you expect me to stay away forever?"

"I'd given up hope of finding you." Andrew walked toward her, his movements awkward, almost stumbling, as if the shock of seeing her had jarred his reflexes to the point that familiar actions had suddenly become difficult. When there was still a couple of feet of space between them, he shambled to a halt and mopped the sweat from his forehead with a snow-white, monogrammed handkerchief. "My God, Claire, I thought you were dead. We all thought you were dead."

She smiled, regaining more of her self-control as Andrew lost his. "Sorry, Daddy, no such luck. I'm very much alive. See, no ghostly fingers. These are real." She wiggled her hand in a parody of a friendly wave, feeling a twinge of perverse satisfaction when she saw him flinch.

She hadn't expected to react to him with such visceral intensity. For the past six weeks, ever since she'd given her final agreement to participate in Hal's scam, she'd been telling herself that Andrew and the rest of the Campbell family were just obstacles to be vanquished on the way to acquiring control of Campbell Crystal. But the flesh-and-blood man wasn't easy to ignore. It was disconcerting to find that she needed to taunt him, to unbalance him, simply to keep her own emotions at a safe distance.

"You've changed a lot and yet, there's something so familiar about you...." Andrew stretched out his hand toward her face and she stiffened, not moving away, but holding herself rigidly unreceptive. His hand wavered, then fell back to his side without making contact. Relief at avoiding his touch emboldened her.

"It's been seven years since we last saw each other," she said, flicking her hair away from her face. "Of course, I've changed. I've grown up."

"And become a very lovely young woman, if I do say so myself. You're beautiful, Claire. God, you look like Evelyn. You look like your mother." Andrew's smile was still nervous, but giving voice to the trite compliment seemed to steady him, and he tucked his handkerchief into his breast pocket, looking more like the suave and distinguished figure she recognized from Hal's photos, and less like the shell-shocked man who'd greeted her.

Beautiful, just like your mother. Dianna was flooded with anger so intense that she didn't dare speak in case she said something that blew her cover. Since she couldn't think of anything safe to say, she simply stared at Andrew in hostile silence. A moment later, she realized that if she'd consciously set out to disconcert him, she couldn't have chosen a better tactic. He was a man who liked to coat reality with a shiny gloss of concealing words, and her silence left him squirming with discomfort. He smiled again, anxious to coax her into a pretense of mutual good-will, however phony.

"You may not believe this, Claire, honey, but I'm delighted that you've come home. I'm thrilled, in fact, to have my daughter—"

"Andrew, it might be wise to watch what you say here." Ben spoke mildly, but he stepped out from behind his desk, and stood between Dianna and his boss, metaphorically forming a barrier against Andrew's rash statements. His gaze skimmed over Dianna with chilling contempt. "Please remember that Ms. Mason has presented no proof to support her claims that she's your daughter."

Despite Ben's obvious scorn, Dianna found it easier to confront him than her supposed father. She lifted her chin and met Ben's opaque, silvery gaze head-on. "What documentation would you expect me to present, Mr. Maxwell?"

"An old driver's license would be nice. In fact, anything you managed to rescue from the cabin blaze. How about a family snapshot, a letter—"

"Hal Doherty has already discussed this with you. You know I don't have any of those things," she said, frustration making her voice huskier than usual.

"Why not?"

"Why not? Well, gosh, in my rush to escape from the cabin, I clean forgot to pick up my purse. Short-sighted of me, I guess, but teenagers have such weird values. Like wanting to stay alive. Like not wanting to roast to death in a flaming cabin. Gee, looking back, I can't imagine why my priorities were so messed up. No forward planning, that was my problem."

Andrew gave a crack of mirthless laughter. "Ben, take my word for it, this is Claire, all right. She always did have a tongue like a damned viper."

"Did she? I'll make a note of that for future reference." Ben actually scrawled a few hieroglyphs on a notepad before turning back to Dianna. "Your sarcasm doesn't advance your cause, Ms. Mason. Of course, I realize that many of Claire's personal documents burned, but I hoped she might have had something stuffed into the pocket of her jeans, or her jacket. Teenagers usually do."

"*I* didn't have anything in the pocket of my jeans, and *I* wasn't wearing a jacket."

Ben frowned at the subtle emphasis. "There are several other documents that would make me consider your claim more seriously than I have done so far, Ms. Mason."

"Such as what? My passport? My birth certificate? They weren't even with me in the cabin. Ask my father where they are. Presumably he arranged for my room at the college dorm to be cleaned out after... after I disappeared."

Ben's eyes turned hard as flint. "Accept that I'm not a fool, Ms. Mason, and we'll get along much better. I know that Claire's birth certificate was found when her college room was packed up after the fire—"

"Don't forget about my passport," Dianna said softly. "That was in the dorm, too. I was planning to spend Christmas in Mexico and I took it from home the last weekend I visited the family house in Pittsburgh. That was at the beginning of November, by the way."

"That's true," Andrew interjected eagerly. "Claire did pay an unexpected visit to Pittsburgh and she told us she would be spending the holidays in Mexico. I remember Evelyn and I were upset that she wasn't willing to spend the Christmas season with us—"

"You should have told me how much you cared," Dianna murmured. "You and Mother always did such a terrific job of hiding the fact that you were pining for my company. Silly me, I thought you'd be pleased to get rid of me so that you could avoid the necessity of spending the holidays together."

Bull's-eye, Dianna thought, watching Andrew's cheeks darken with embarrassed color. Since teenagers and parents almost always misunderstood each other, it had been safe to guess that Claire and her parents suffered from all the usual misunderstandings. Apparently they had. Andrew cleared his throat with visible discomfort. "Well, anyway, that's all water under the bridge. Claire announced that she was flying to Acapulco to meet some artist—"

"Fernando Velásquez," Dianna said. The name of the world-famous glassworker had been in many published accounts of Claire's disappearance and Hal had mentioned it to her several times.

"Velásquez? Yes, that sounds familiar. I'm sure that was the name Claire said." Andrew had been the nominal CEO of Campbell Crystal for fifteen years, but his interest in glass design was minimal and he obviously didn't know that Velásquez was acknowledged as one of Mexico's greatest living artists. He seemed delighted by Dianna's confident mention of the name, however, and he looked at Ben Maxwell with renewed confidence. "You see? How would she know details like that if she isn't Claire?"

"Quite easily," Ben replied. "Hal Doherty told her."

A flicker of disappointment crossed Andrew's face. "You're right, I guess." Even though he conceded the point, he sounded doubtful. "I suppose Hal knows a lot about Claire's past, doesn't he?"

"A lot," Ben agreed. "Remember, he's been interviewing would-be Claire Campbells for the past six years. Any documentable fact you know about your daughter, Hal probably knows, too. He's read all the files, and seen all the reports from the private detectives. Which is one of the reasons I'm not too interested in discussing Claire's distant past. Obviously, Hal has briefed Ms. Mason extensively and she's going to parrot the information back to us."

Dianna looked up. "Then what do you want from me, Mr. Maxwell, if not my version of the past? You were the one who brought up the subject of documentation."

"True, but I'd like to see some of the documents from the weeks immediately *after* Claire disappeared, from the time when we're not quite so sure what she was doing."

A smart move on Ben's part, Dianna thought. An interesting twist in standard interviewing techniques. But not quite smart enough for a man with his evident intelligence. This was the nineties, the cusp of the twenty-first century, and technology had tests and devices for every situation, even the validating of missing heiresses. So why was Ben wasting everyone's time asking questions that were never going to result in conclusive proof that she was Claire Campbell—or that she wasn't? Why didn't he simply cut to the chase and demand a DNA test? Even the criminal courts now accepted such testing as ninety-nine percent proof positive of paternity. Or maternity, on those rare occasions when that was in doubt.

The question had been nagging at Dianna for weeks. Hal had considered it a stroke of incredible good fortune that none of the previous contenders for the Campbell millions had been shipped off to the nearest laboratory for blood testing, and he simply hoped that Dianna would luck out, too. But Dianna had given up believing in strokes of good fortune right around the time she discovered there was no Tooth Fairy, and that Santa Claus shopped at Bloomingdale's. Given that Ben looked like the last man on earth to waste time interviewing would-be Claire Campbells when he could get guaranteed answers from a scientific test, Dianna wondered why he was messing around asking her questions and requesting documents. There had to be good reasons for his behavior, and presumably those reasons were based on the wishes of Andrew and Evelyn Campbell.

Had Claire's parents refused to agree to DNA testing? Dianna needed to know. She needed very badly to know.

In the meantime, everyone was waiting for her to speak. She shrugged. "I don't have any documents from the period right after the fire," she said, with an attempt at casualness that didn't quite succeed. This was another weak link in her story, and she knew it.

Ben smiled. "Good heavens, what a surprise!"

His sarcasm didn't fluster her as much as it would have done earlier in the interview. She reminded herself that both of them were playing with stacked decks, but maybe his hand was even weaker than her own, and she did have a trick or two up her sleeve that he wasn't—couldn't be—expecting.

"How can you begin to guess what happened to me when I disappeared?" she asked, meeting his gaze. "You're asking for documents. What if I told you there aren't any documents from the weeks right after the fire?"

"Then you'd be lying." Ben leaned toward her, his body language deliberately intimidating. "I'm not guessing, I *know* that Claire Campbell closed out her New York bank account less than twenty-four hours after the cabin in Vermont burned to the ground. If you're Claire, how about showing me your final bank statement, or a copy of some of the forms you signed that day? Any of those documents would certainly catch my attention—Ms. Mason."

Dianna forced herself not to look down, not to look guilty. "I didn't... keep... any of those papers. I was running, afraid, scared. My God, someone had just tried to kill me! I wasn't thinking about setting up a filing system for future proof of my identity. I was wondering where the hell I could go to hide."

"How about home to your parents' house? Evelyn Campbell has a penthouse apartment in central Manhattan, not five minutes' walk from the bank. Why didn't you go there? Isn't that what parents are for? To provide a safe place for their kids when the going gets too tough to handle?"

She had the feeling that he was genuinely curious, that he sensed some level of deception in the story of Claire's disappearance that nobody had yet penetrated. So she answered him honestly, with wry awareness of how easy it was to tell the truth and create a terrible lie. "I never thought of my parents as a refuge, Mr. Maxwell. Have you ever seen that apartment you're talking about so glibly? It's a cross between a museum and the film set for a 1930s drawing-room comedy. The Campbell family is—was—what you might call a tad dysfunctional.''

Andrew ran his fingers through his elegant gray hair. "Leave it, Ben. She's here now. Let's not worry about her past relationship with us."

"Fine." Ben's expression gave no clue if it cost him any personal effort to switch his line of questioning. He was damn good with that poker face of his— Dianna had to grant him that much. She watched with an odd tightening of the muscles in her stomach as he leaned back against the desk and crossed his arms.

"All right, Ms. Mason, let's get back to the interesting subject of the new bank account you set up the morning after the cabin in Vermont burned to the ground. We've agreed you were scared, and as you pointed out a few moments ago, teenagers don't do much forward planning. On the other hand, we're talking about an account that held close to a quarter of a million dollars. Even a scared eighteen-year-old might consider hanging on to some of the paperwork for that sum of money, don't you think?"

"It depends on the teenager," she said, smiling with provocative sweetness. "In my case, at that point in time, a quarter of a million dollars didn't sound like very much money. I'm an heiress, remember?"

"Poor little rich girl," he murmured. His gaze raked slowly over her, and she felt hot color burn under her skin. Good grief, why was he having this ridiculous effect on her? She'd forgotten how to blush years ago.

He lowered his head to within inches of hers. "And how does a quarter of a million dollars sound to you now—Ms. Mason?"

She drew in a quick, hard breath and told another of her big lies, this time without even a coating of truth. "It sounds like pocket change," she said, staring straight into his clear gray eyes.

Ben astonished her by stepping back and laughing with genuine amusement. "You do that aristocratic scorn really well, Ms. Mason. Congratulations. I guess you win that round."

Tamed by laughter, the predatory tension of his expression softened for an instant. Watching him laugh, Dianna felt a tiny spark of answering warmth. She had a brief, disquieting impression of how pleasant it might be to have Ben Maxwell as a friend, instead of as an opponent, but she pushed the intrusive image aside. Friendship—especially with Ben Maxwell—was a weakness she couldn't afford if Campbell Crystal was to be hers. And especially not if Andrew Campbell was to be destroyed.

"I'm not sure I understand you," she said coolly, setting their relationship back on the adversarial track she wanted it to follow. "I'm stating a simple fact. If I give you permission to offer shares in Campbell Crystal to the public, I calculate that I'll make a minimum of ten million dollars on the deal. If you combine that with the twenty-million-dollar trust fund already waiting for me, I'll be sitting on a thirty-million-dollar nest egg. I guess thirty million is the sort of sum I call real money."

All trace of Ben's laughter vanished. "If Campbell Crystal goes public, *Claire* or her legally-declared heirs will make ten million on the deal," he said softly.

She smiled at him, her eyes bright with challenge. "Yes, of course. Isn't that what I just said?"

Ben held her gaze long enough to let her know he'd accepted the challenge. Then he straightened, turning toward his employer. "I appreciate your desire to find your daughter, Andrew, and I hope that one day soon, we will. But you pay me to protect your interests, and it's my job to remind you that you can't leap to conclusions on the basis of flimsy evidence. The fact that this woman and your daughter look alike doesn't prove that they're one and the same person. Legally speaking, their similar appearance is nothing more than an interesting coincidence."

"The law is frequently an ass," Andrew said, and for once Dianna found herself in complete agreement with her supposed father. "I recognize her. She's Claire Campbell, my daughter."

If Dianna thought Andrew's seal of approval was going to win the day, Ben soon showed her she was mistaken. "Let me remind you, Andrew, that you swore we'd found Claire eighteen months ago, and the woman in question turned out to have a rap sheet longer than her arm. She specialized in showing up on the doorsteps of parents whose children had gone missing years before, exploiting their desperate need for closure—"

"That was different," Andrew countered, but he cast a sideways glance at Claire, his handsome profile shaded with new uncertainty.

Ben gave Andrew a reassuring clap on the back. Dianna was surprised to detect a hint of real sympathy and affection in the gesture. Ben Maxwell hadn't impressed her as a man capable of feeling such human emotions as sympathy. "Leave this in my hands for a couple of days," Ben said. "Let me take care of a few preliminary inquiries with Ms. Mason before you hand over the keys to the family jewel chest, okay?"

"Okay." Andrew appeared visibly relieved to have the burden of decision making lifted from his shoulders. "Anyway, I have to fly to Tallahassee after lunch. I don't have time to deal with this right now."

"Now that sounds more like the father I used to know," Dianna said. "Never let a trivial family matter interfere with what's *really* important. Isn't that right, Daddy?"

"My campaign for governor of the state of Florida is vitally important," Andrew said. "I've made promises to my supporters and campaign workers that must be kept. They've invested their time and faith in me, and now I have to pay them back."

"Of course," she murmured. "I understand completely. I'll call your secretary tomorrow. Sometime before the end of the twentieth century maybe you'll have time to write me into your schedule. 'Meet with Dianna Mason and find out if she really is my long-lost daughter.' Hey, what's the rush? We're not talking anything major here."

Andrew's lips thinned with frustration. "You left this family—" He pulled himself up short. "Claire left this family seven years ago. I think you...she... I believe Claire has a hell of a lot more explaining to do than the family she left behind. If you're Claire, what happened to you? Why did you stay away so long? Where have you been, for God's sake? Your mother has been frantic with grief and worry, and I've had detectives searching for you all over the country."

"Hey, don't sweat the little things, Daddy. I'm quite sure you spent my money on hiring those detectives, not yours."

Andrew was speechless. If Hal could hear her, he would burst a blood vessel, Dianna thought. Maybe two blood vessels. She'd never planned to follow Hal's advice about keeping a humble profile and playing it sweet and charming. She'd always thought that a display of mild hostility would be more in character for a returning runaway. After all, why would anyone hide from their family for seven years unless they were nursing some heavy-duty antagonism? But nothing she'd planned over the past six weeks, nothing she'd read in Hal's files, prepared her for the overwhelming desire to lash out that churned in her stomach every time Andrew spoke to her.

Andrew finally got a grip on his temper. He swung around to stare at her, laughing without a trace of mirth. "My God! Seven years later and we're back right where we left off, arguing about money. Your damn money."

"It's such a great subject to argue about," she retorted. "After all, there was so *much* of it until you started pouring it into the bottomless pit of your real-estate investments."

Andrew pounded his fist on the desk. "Don't you understand yet? *You* don't have any money, Claire. You have a trust fund, left to you by my brother, and I'm the trustee. I can spend that money any damn way I please. In fact, I'm legally *required* to spend the money any damn way I please—provided I think the expenditure is in your best long-term interests. And guess what? I thought it was in your best interests to invest some of your capital in land development, just as I thought it was in your best interests to hire detectives so that I could find out if you were alive or dead.''

"So now you have to hawk Campbell Crystal—my great grandfather's company—around the New York junk-bond markets to raise enough cash to keep your crummy real-estate investments afloat.''

"That's not the reason I want to sell Campbell Crystal, and my real-estate investments have resulted in a net prof—"

"You don't need to explain your business decisions to Ms. Mason," Ben reminded him. "Ms. Mason is merely one of several women who've claimed to be your daughter at one time or another, and until she proves her claim, you owe her no explanations of anything you've done, and certainly no explanation of how you've chosen to handle Claire's financial affairs.''

"That's right." Andrew shot Dianna another exasperated look, then shrugged. His mouth twisted into the rueful, self-mocking smile that had helped make him such a popular political candidate. On TV, wearing that smile, he looked like a cross between Robert Redford and Ronald Reagan—sex, good cheer and paternal protection all wrapped up in one comforting bundle. "Hell, Ben, at the least you have to admit she's different from the other women who claimed to be my daughter. She's hardly trying to sweet-talk her way into my good graces.''

"No," Ben said. "She's much too smart to do that.''

"Keep her here," Andrew said abruptly, turning toward the door. "If she is Claire, God knows we don't want her to turn tail and disappear into the

Florida swamp for another seven years. Evelyn deserves the chance to meet with her and ask her some questions."

Dianna clamped down on a rush of jittery excitement, and fixed her gaze on the floor. She'd read Andrew right. She'd made him nervous and he wanted her under his nose, where he could keep an eye on her, at least by proxy. Dear God, they were going to let her stay at the house. She was in. Inside one of the Campbell homes. Within striking distance of her goals.

"You want her to stay here?" Ben demanded, sounding amazed. "At the house?"

"Why not? She could have the cabana." Dianna could sense that Andrew was deliberately trying to sound more offhand than he felt. "Nobody's using it for the next few days, are they? All my campaign people are in Tallahassee. Are you bringing anyone from Campbell Construction down for meetings?"

"No, not this week."

"Then the cabana's going to be empty."

"I guess there are certain advantages to having her right where we can see her," Ben acknowledged, escorting Andrew to the door of his office. "Okay. I'll take care of it."

"I need five minutes with you before I leave for Tallahassee," Andrew said. "We need to talk about the Dockland project. I'm wondering if Roger's ready to fly to London and chew out the management company. He's chomping at the bit, demanding more responsibility and less administrative work."

"Fine, we'll talk. Give me fifteen minutes to see that Ms. Mason gets settled, then I'll join you on the lanai."

Andrew paused in the doorway and swung around to scrutinize Dianna one last time. "I hope you really are Claire," he said. "Because I sure as hell would like to satisfy my curiosity about why you've been hiding for the past seven years."

"I am Claire," Dianna said. "And are you quite sure you want to know why I was hiding? Secrets can be dangerous for an aspiring politician. Don't forget, Daddy, you're only four months away from the election for governor."

Ben spoke quickly, his voice quiet but his eyes colder than an ice floe in mid-Atlantic. "Are you making threats, Ms. Mason? Because if you are, I'd recommend you rethink your strategy."

"No threats," she replied, knowing she needed to be on firmer ground, and more sure of her facts, before she launched an attack on Andrew Campbell's sterling reputation. "Just a simple reminder that I'm not likely to be the only person around here who has parts of their life they'd prefer to keep hidden."

"That's an interesting admission, Ms. Mason."

"It's honest," she said. "I've done some things that I'm not proud of. Most people have, don't you think?"

"Not me," Andrew said, sounding genuinely unconcerned. "I'm certified pure of heart. My life's been put under the microscope by every muckraking journalist in the state of Florida. They've questioned any woman still living that I ever spoke three words to, hoping to prove I was an adulterous lecher. Hell, if they thought they'd get any scandalous answers, I bet those damned journalists would have dug up all the dead women I knew and questioned them, too. The truth is, after a year of searching, the slathering press hounds have come up with zilch. They've been forced to admit that in my case, what you see is what you get."

"And what's that, Daddy?"

"I've devoted the past five years to tackling the problems of land use in the state of Florida. What's more, my experience as a real-estate developer has given me good insights—good, *practical* answers—to the tough questions about the best mix of development and conservation in our fragile ecosystem. Elect me to the governorship, and we'll get job creation without destruction of our unique environment. The economy will strengthen, and then we'll be able to pay for some of the social infrastructure we so badly need."

"Great campaign speech, Daddy." With a flash of wry amusement, it occurred to Dianna that Andrew had something in common with Hal—he believed his own rhetoric. Andrew's conscience wasn't likely to be an instrument of exquisite sensitivity, and politicians were often adept at deceiving themselves along with their constituents. It wasn't going to be easy to destroy him. Self-deluded frauds were harder to trip up than outright liars.

"Thanks. I've worked hard to come up with sensible answers to some of today's stubborn problems."

Dianna wasn't surprised when Andrew took her compliment at face value. He delivered another of his Emmy-winning smiles, and his voice deepened with emotional sincerity. "If you tell the voters what you truly feel in your heart, then you can never be caught short-footed." He nodded, pleased with his parting remarks, and stepped out into the hallway. "I'll see you when I get back from Tallahassee, Cl—er, Ms. Mason."

"When is that likely to be?" Dianna asked.

"A couple of days. Thursday at the latest." He turned to Ben. "Don't forget I need five minutes with you before my plane leaves." He raised his hand in a salute, then walked down the corridor toward the rear of the house. The sound of his Gucci loafers thudding on the marble floor faded into the distance.

The silence after his departure was oppressive. It pounded against Dianna's ears, squeezing her lungs, and making sweat pool at the base of her spine. After several excruciating seconds while he stared out the window into the garden, Ben turned. Somehow, Dianna managed to meet his gaze.

"Tell me why you've chosen this precise moment to come back, Ms. Mason."

"'To come back,'" she repeated softly. "What an interesting slip of the tongue, Mr. Maxwell. Or are you accepting my claim that I'm Claire Campbell?"

He didn't answer for a couple of seconds, then he surprised her by giving a slight smile. "It was a slip of the tongue," he admitted. "You're good, Ms. Mason. Damn good. The hostility toward Andrew is a great touch, one that none of your predecessors thought of. Now answer my question. Why have you chosen this precise moment to stake your claim? Is Hal behind the timing of your arrival here in Florida? Or is it more complex than that?"

She covered her tension with the mockery that had become second nature. "Why, that's easy, Mr. Maxwell. I chose to come back at this specific moment to assist my father in his campaign for governor of the great state of Florida. I figured that the discovery of a long-lost daughter would work wonders for him in the polls. What do you think? Will the return of the long-lost Claire Campbell boost his chances of getting elected?''

Ben leaned across the desk, every line of his body radiating threat. ''What I think is that you're a dangerous woman, Ms. Mason. What I *know* is that I won't let you screw up Andrew Campbell's campaign for governor.''

''Are you offering to buy me off, Mr. Maxwell? That's an intriguing notion.''

''Don't allow yourself to fantasize, Ms. Mason. I meant only that there are important issues confronting this state right now, and we need a competent governor. A businessman with Andrew's expertise is the ideal candidate. We've had too many lawyers running politics in this state for too long. Your best efforts notwithstanding, we're going to keep the public's attention focused on the issues, and Andrew is going to win.''

Dianna laughed. ''Make sure you keep telling my father what 'the issues' are, Mr. Maxwell. How many times a day do you have to remind him that reducing the surtax on incomes over a million dollars isn't a hot topic for most Floridians?''

Ben refused to rise to the bait. ''I'm sure you don't expect me to dignify that remark with a serious response,'' he said mildly. ''Besides, Andrew has a highly competent campaign manager. He doesn't need my input to keep him in the center of the political track. So let's get down to more immediate problems. Will Hal Doherty be staying with you in the cabana?''

"How many bedrooms does it have?" she blurted out, then wished that she hadn't. She could almost see Ben filing away the information that she wasn't anxious to share a bedroom with Hal Doherty.

"There are three bedrooms," he said. "And two full bathrooms also."

"Then it would be more convenient if he stayed with me," she said. "He's my legal adviser, after all."

"Right. So he is." Ben hesitated for a moment, perhaps wondering whether to point out that her "legal adviser" hovered right on the brink of disbarment. In the end, however, he chose to continue in his previous vein of bland courtesy. He even cracked a faint smile.

"This has been a difficult morning for all of us," he said. "We seem to have gotten off to a bad start, and that wasn't what I intended. I'm sure it's not what you intended, either."

"No," she admitted. "It wasn't." She drew in a deep breath. "Are you saying that you want us to be friends, Mr. Maxwell?"

"Friends might be too much to hope for, but at least not enemies. After all, we have a common interest in bringing this affair to a positive ending, don't we?" His charm was just a tiny bit more obvious now, his smile a fraction warmer, and Dianna felt an invigorating spurt of anger. It was insulting of him to assume she could be manipulated this easily. Did he really think a few smiles from him was all it took to tame her?

"Look," he said, his voice smooth as homogenized cream. "I certainly don't want to create the wrong impression with you, Dianna. I'm not hostile to you personally, just to the situation you represent.

If you can think of some compelling reason why I should believe your claim that you're the missing Claire Campbell, then I wish you'd tell me what that is. Or show me. God knows, if you are Claire, I'm willing to be persuaded. Eager to be persuaded, in fact." He broke off, his voice roughening. "Good God Almighty! What the hell are you doing?"

"Persuading you that I'm Claire Campbell, of course." The struggle to contain her anger made her voice lower and even huskier than usual.

"By taking your clothes off?"

She continued unbuttoning her jacket. "Yes."

In an instant, all the warmth, all the charm, was wiped from his face. "Don't humiliate either of us any further," he said. "Keep your clothes on, Ms. Mason. Trust me, this isn't the sort of persuasion I was talking about."

"Isn't it? How do you know what I have in mind?" Her fingers trembled as she unfastened the final button at the waistline of her jacket. She'd been angered by his manipulative display of false charm. Illogically, she was even more angered by the swiftness with which he reverted to his previous mode of icy superiority. The emotions that had been simmering too close to the surface all morning exploded, then coalesced into a tight, hot weight in the pit of her stomach. Dammit, this interview hadn't gone as she'd expected. She felt...confused...and she wanted Ben Maxwell to feel confused, too.

She tilted forward with calculated provocation, not quite sure why she chose this method of attack, but instinctively aware that it was a good one. She pushed her jacket open, and let it slip slowly off her shoulders. Her lips parted. She hadn't intended that, either, but she recovered quickly and ran her tongue across her lips in a mocking parody of sexual invitation.

She was delighted to see that he went very still, almost as if he were fighting the impulse to lean toward her, to accept her implicit invitation. Whatever uncomfortable emotions brewed between them, he felt it, too. She opened her eyes wide, crossed her hands in front of her breasts, and kept the jacket grasped—just barely—in her fingertips. She could picture how she looked, and the very stiffness of his body told her she was having an impact on him that he didn't want, and didn't like. She smiled, not attempting to hide her satisfaction.

"What are you staring at, Mr. Maxwell?" The fingers of her left hand opened and her jacket started to slide down her arm.

"Don't! Stop this—" Ben moved with lightning speed to catch the jacket before it could slither all the way to the floor. He grabbed the lapels, pushing them together, pulling the jacket back up her arms. In his haste, his hands brushed against the skin at the tops of her breasts, exactly as she'd intended.

At the touch of his fingers against the swell of her breasts, Ben stopped, his breath cutting off as abruptly as the movement of his hands. Dianna closed her eyes, aware that she'd invited this, but no longer sure she was ready for what would follow.

The shocked silence expanded to fill one second, then another. Ben drew in a ragged breath. "What the hell . . . ?"

He opened her jacket again, pushing the two sides apart so that he could see the flesh that his hands had just touched. His mouth tightened and his eyes narrowed. Frowning, he traced a path across the scarred and puckered flesh that marked a narrow border between the top of her breasts and the slope of her chest. Dianna bit her lip to prevent herself from crying out as his fingers slipped over the crinkled skin. It was years since the scars had hurt, but the memory of the pain could still make her shiver.

Ben didn't probe beneath her sensible cotton bra to see how far the scars continued. He yanked the jacket shut and stepped back from her, brows drawn together in a furious scowl. "What happened?" he demanded. "How did you get those scars?"

"You know what happened," she said, trying to refasten the buttons on her jacket with fingers that had suddenly turned into ten wooden thumbs.

"Tell me anyway."

"I was burned."

"Where? How?"

"In a cabin in Vermont," she said. "When someone tried to murder me."

Three

Hal Doherty burst into the cabana. He felt his face break into a beaming smile when he saw Dianna, and he clapped her on the shoulder, his stomach churning with anxious delight. "Babe, I knew you could do it! You're the greatest! Hey, if you can survive Ben Maxwell and Andrew Campbell together, you can survive anything!"

Beside himself with excitement, he lunged for her, wrapping her into a bear hug that he managed to keep a hairbreadth short of sexual assault.

"Hi, Hal." Dianna disengaged herself from his arms, her complete lack of response quelling his exuberance more effectively than outspoken rejection. Jeez, but she was a ball breaker if ever he'd met one, Hal thought resentfully. In the two months since he'd spotted her at Sonya's party in Boston, she'd never given the faintest hint that she'd noticed he was a man. When he was around her, he ended up feeling like a well-trained eunuch. Most women considered him damned good-looking, so what was wrong with Dianna Mason? What right did she have to sit on her high horse looking down on him as if he'd dropped out of her mount's rear end? He quelled a rising sense of injustice. Business first, he reminded himself. At least she hadn't screwed up the all-important meeting with Ben and Andrew. He was willing to cut her some slack.

"How did it go after I was banished to the lanai?" he asked. A horrible thought occurred to him. "Hope to God you didn't sign anything, babe."

"No, nothing." She gave him one of her polite, elusive smiles. "They've already brought in our luggage from the car. Maybe you want to get unpacked?" She glanced up at the ceiling light fixture as she spoke, almost as if she was trying to draw his attention to it. Hal followed her gaze upward and saw an expensive chandelier, with dangling lusters in the shapes of dolphins and seashells. Was he supposed to love 'em or hate 'em? And who cared, anyway? He shrugged, admitting the uncomfortable truth that, nine times out of ten, Dianna's mind worked too fast for him to follow. Plunking himself down on a comfortable rattan sofa, he patted the peach-flowered cushions next to him.

"Come and sit down for a while—we can unpack later. Tell me everything that happened. Word for word. Blow by blow." He smiled, to let her know how pleased he was with her performance. For a struggling artist from a blue-collar background, she'd done well. Real well. But then, he'd never doubted her intelligence or her ability to carry off the scam—only her enthusiasm.

"Did they give you a hard time?" he asked. "Was there anything you couldn't answer? Anything we need to work on?"

She looked at him with barely controlled exasperation. "Since you and I both know that I'm the real Claire Campbell, I don't quite understand what you mean, Hal." She carried on quickly, not giving him a chance to respond. "Meeting my father again was tougher than I expected, but I guess I feel better for having faced up to him, and the memories from my past."

"Yeah, right." Hal squinted at her in puzzlement. "What's so fascinating about that damn light, babe?"

The look she shot at him this time was sharp enough to etch one of the glass bowls she was forever working on, but her voice stayed soft and honey sweet. "I was just wondering if it's a Campbell Crystal product," she said. "I wouldn't have expected the decorator to select such a fancy chandelier for a guest cottage, would you?"

"There's no accounting for taste," he said, not bothering to look yet again at the offending light. They still had three thick files of information to read through, not to mention that he'd never really had a chance to check out Dianna's social graces. God knows, she'd probably be lost if the Campbells invited her to a formal dinner and she had to cope with finger bowls and three or four different sizes of fork. He really needed to sit her down and give her some heavy-duty instruction in the life-styles of the old-money rich and famous. He shuddered to think what might happen if she met up with Evelyn Campbell before he'd had a chance to polish her table manners. The last time he'd suffered an encounter with the Empress Evelyn, she'd taken less than thirty seconds to reduce him to the point where he felt as if he'd walked before the imperial presence with his fly unzipped. As for Bainbridge, the butler who lorded it over Evelyn's household, he had no doubt the old sod would reduce Dianna to melted Jell-O in about ten seconds flat.

He leaned forward, trying not to sound impatient. "Honey, I know glass fascinates you in all its various forms, but we need to get our priorities straight. Let's concentrate on a couple of the most important things right now. Like how you're going to—"

"Oops, sorry, Hal." To his absolute amazement, she lifted her elegant, high-heeled sandal and brought the heel down onto his instep. Hard. His sentence ended in a yowl of mingled outrage and pain. "Jesus Christ, Dianna! What the hell—"

"Sorry, I tripped." She grabbed his hand without letting him finish his sentence, and jerked her head in the direction of the patio that surrounded the cabana and connected via a pathway back to the main house. "The air-conditioning gets to me after a while," she said, the mildness of her husky voice in marked contrast to her scowl. "Let's go outside, shall we?" She looked out the sliding glass door at the patio. "Boy, isn't the landscaping pretty? Where does that attractive walkway lead, I wonder?"

"To the pool and then back to the main house." Hal massaged his sore foot. Seeing that she was determined to go outside, he limped across, opened the door, and stepped out onto the patio, which was shaded from the full force of the sun by an overhanging roof and a trellis of trailing bougainvillea vines. A stand of live oak helped create the illusion of shade. Despite this, the temperature hovered somewhere in the nineties, and the humidity level felt as if it was pushing a hundred. Dianna dragged him to the very center of the patio, where there wasn't a speck of shade cast by anything. His forehead immediately broke out in a sticky mask of sweat. Sighing, he reached for his handkerchief.

"Jeez, babe, what the hell is your problem? You've earned some fresh air if you want it, but how can you stand this heat?"

"It's preferable to having our conversation recorded," she snapped. "You weren't very discreet. Didn't it occur to you that the cabana is most likely bugged? I think there might be a transmitter in the chandelier."

"Good God!" Hal's eyes widened in alarm, and he stroked his mustache with the fervor of a toddler clutching his security blanket. When he realized what he was doing, he stopped abruptly. "You're letting your imagination run away with your common sense," he said. "Bugging a place isn't as easy as they make it look in the movies. You can't do it in a hurry, and there's no reason for Andrew to keep his guest cottage wired for sound on a permanent basis. He's an arrogant son of a bitch, but he's not paranoid."

"Andrew doesn't have to be paranoid," Dianna argued. "He pays Ben Maxwell to be paranoid for him. Ben could have had the cabana bugged especially to listen in on the two of us. Why else did he agree to let us stay in Andrew's home?"

"Ben's quite capable of something like that," Hal agreed. "But he didn't know we were going to be here until half an hour ago. As I understand it, Andrew is the one who invited us."

"You're right," she conceded. "The invitation came from Andrew. But I still think you should watch what we say inside the cabana. We're vulnerable, Hal. Very vulnerable."

"You sure do have a suspicious turn of mind." He stared at her, mesmerized all over again by the enigmatic aloofness of her expression and the contrast it formed with the lush, inviting contours of her body. "Jeez, Dianna, don't you ever let down your guard?"

She smiled tightly. "Not if I can avoid it. Past experience has taught me most people can't be trusted."

"You're too cynical."

She returned his stare, eyes dancing with mockery. "Not cynical, Hal, just clear-sighted."

"You act as if the whole world was stuffed full of crooks."

"Isn't it?"

"No, of course not—"

"You know what sort of a scam we're trying to pull, Hal. Are you trustworthy? Am I?"

He turned away, not wanting to see his own lack of honesty reflected in her face. "The Campbells have more money than they can ever spend. We're just going to spread it around a little. You could say that what we're doing is social engineering without the benefit of government interference."

"Yes, you could say that." Her words mocked his self-justification. She grinned. "Gee, who'd have guessed it? We're robbing the Campbells because we're philanthropists."

He drew in a short, angry breath. "Well, whether our motives are pure or not, that's no reason for you to suspect there's a mike hidden in the light fixture."

She grimaced. "There's an aesthetic reason. That darn chandelier is so big and out of place, I can't understand why they'd hang it up there if it isn't concealing something."

"Could be they just hired a decorator with rotten taste," he suggested. "You should quit trying to find deeper existential meaning in life's heaps of dog poop."

She laughed, the sound unexpectedly lighthearted. "There is that, I guess."

Her laughter softened her face so that she looked young and astonishingly innocent. Hal shivered, despite the heat. At moments like this, she looked so much like the photos of Claire Campbell that he felt spooked. Everyone in the world might have a double, but it was eerie when you came face-to-face with one of them.

"Why are you staring at me like that?" she asked, pushing at her hair. "Do I have a smut on the end of my nose?"

"Nothing like that." No need to tell her how much she looked like Claire. Better if she didn't get overconfident. Hell, what was he so damned uptight about, anyway? Having a fake that looked too much like the genuine article wasn't exactly a major problem. In a burst of renewed goodwill, he put his arm around Dianna's shoulders. "Look, babe, now that you've delivered your warning about the hidden mikes, can we go inside? I'm melting, and you're going to get badly sunburned."

"You're right. But humor me, okay? Don't talk business in there until we've checked it out for bugs. We can search the whole place in twenty minutes."

"It's a deal." Somehow, she'd taken a couple of steps forward and shed his arm again. He followed her back inside the cabana, watching the sway of her hips as she walked across the tiled patio. Jeez, she had a great ass! For about the hundredth time, he wondered what it would be like to strip off her clothes, bury his face in the softness of her breasts, and feel her squirm beneath him on the rumpled sheets of a wide bed. Short of indulging in rape, he doubted if he was ever going to find out, and rape was definitely not his style. He liked his sex easy and a touch sentimental; definitely no hard edges.

Maybe she's gay, he thought. There was the indisputable fact that her best friend, Sonya, was an acknowledged lesbian. And it would explain why Dianna never came on to him when most women in her position would have been only too eager to curry favor by dishing out a few sexual rewards. He scowled at her retreating figure. God, if she was gay, it was a hell of a waste of a fantastic body!

Dianna stepped back into the cabana and he followed. Sighing with relief at the blast of cool air, Hal flapped his shirt until his sweaty body began to chill into dryness.

"I'm going to change into something cooler," Dianna said, giving him another of the polite, distant smiles that drove him crazy. "If visiting peons are allowed to use the family pool, I'd like to take a swim."

"Great idea. I'll join you." Lesbian or not, Hal felt himself grow hard at the mere thought of seeing Dianna in a swimsuit. Despite six weeks of almost constant togetherness, he had yet to glimpse any portion of her body between her knees and her shoulders. Even though the crappy state of their finances forced them to share motel rooms, she'd slept in enveloping cotton pajamas that looked like she'd bought them in job lots from a nineteenth-century convent. Hal was mighty tired of enveloping white cotton.

Having the hots for a woman who was part of one of his scams was nothing unusual for Hal. But his ex-wives would never believe it if he told them he'd shared a motel room with a gorgeous near-blonde for days and nights at a stretch without once making a real honest-to-God pass at her. Hal scarcely believed it himself. Jesus, what was his problem? No more Mr. Nice Guy, he thought, the refrigerated air failing to cool his frustration. Maybe he should just forget his aversion to rough sex and throw the uppity bitch onto a bed. He'd soon show her who was boss.

When you got right down to it, Dianna couldn't afford to refuse him. He knew too many of her secrets.

The Campbells' phone system was state-of-the-art electronic perfection, and the three phones in the cabana each had almost as many buttons as the control panel of a jumbo jet. A neatly printed notice attached to the receiver asked all guests to place their outgoing calls on line two. Dianna finally identified line two and managed—after some persuasion—to coax the phone into giving her a dial tone. She punched out Sonya's number, and leaned back in the cushioned wicker chair, stomach leaping in anticipation of hearing Sonya's voice. There was nothing like a guilty conscience to add spice to the simplest action, she reflected ruefully.

She was in the living room, in full view of Hal or anyone else who came to the front door of the cabana. Making the call from here rather than from the privacy of her bedroom reminded her to be careful, to watch what she said. She'd already satisfied herself that neither the cabana nor the phones were bugged, but anyone in the house could listen in to her conversation by the simple, low-tech process of picking up one of the other extensions. Fortunately, she and Sonya had prepared in advance for just that eventuality.

The phone had already rung five times. One more ring and the answering machine would click in. *Come on, Sonya, pick up the damn phone.*

"Hello. Hold on, I'll be right back."

The phone echoed with the thump of a receiver being dumped on a table or kitchen counter. Dianna grinned and her entire body went limp with the relief of hearing her friend speak. Sonya was always trying to do three things at once and the sound of her pinched, Bostonian accent precipitated a flash of unexpected homesickness.

"Okay, I'm back and dinner is saved. Sort of. Who's this?"

"It's Di. Glad you rescued dinner. How are you doing?"

"Lousy. My love life's a desert, my diet isn't working because I keep eating frozen Twinkies, and my editor—damn his miserly soul—has decided to eliminate a hundred thousand in overhead by having me do the work of three people."

Dianna laughed. "In other words, everything's much as usual."

"I'm sure my love life's worse than usual. Anyway, what's with you? It's great to hear your voice. You still in Florida with that creep, Hal? I'd expected him to turn back into primeval pond slime weeks ago."

Sonya had good taste and excellent judgment. She'd known Hal since high school, and nothing would convince her that he was a decent human being. Dianna's laughter faded. "I'm still here and so is Hal. No glimpse of pond slime, so far."

"Which motel are you at? Let me grab a pencil and write down the number."

"Actually, we're staying at Andrew Campbell's house."

"Both of you? Hal, as well?" Sonya sounded startled.

"It's more convenient this way, although I wish Hal would stop twirling his mustache and flexing his muscles, trying to convince me he'd be a great lay."

"Sweetie, stop wishing your cat was a dog." There was an infinitesimal pause, too short for anyone to register unless they were familiar with Sonya's usual rapid-fire pattern of speech. "When did that happen? The move into Campbell's house, I mean."

"This morning. A couple of hours ago."

"Have you met any of the natives? Are they friendly?"

"I've already met Andrew Campbell. I'd say he's—ambivalent. Willing to accept that I am his long-lost daughter, but needing some hard proof."

Dianna heard the soft hiss of Sonya's indrawn breath. "Want some advice from a woman who's been around the block a couple of times?"

"No, but I'm sure you're going to give it to me anyway."

"You're right. And here it is. Come home, sweetie. Today. Now. Five minutes ago."

"Sonya, you know I can't—"

"Gregory misses you. Don't screw up the great life you had just because Hal wants you to earn him some easy money."

Dianna laughed a little grimly. "I appreciate the honor of being missed by your cat, Sonya. But even the thought of the Honorable Gregory isn't sufficient inducement to bring me back up north. Not yet."

"Well, don't leave it too long, sweetie. Your plants are all dying. I can't remember to water the damn things."

I need more information, Dianna translated silently. *The leads you gave me have all fizzled out.* "Stick a reminder note to yourself on the fridge," she said. "I'm warning you, Sonya, our friendship's over if you kill off my African violets."

Translation: *I'll get some hot leads to you soon. Don't give up on finding the dirt on Andrew Campbell.*

"You're a hard taskmaster, but I'll do my best." Sonya spoke with renewed briskness. "By the way, I understand the Campbell household now boasts a fantastic cook. Her name's Sharon Kruger. Moves around from house to house wherever Andrew goes."

Had they finally managed to track down one of Andrew's mistresses? Dianna wondered. Had Sonya ferreted out the scandal in Andrew's background that the rest of the press had missed? "I'll look out for her," she said. "It sure would be great to eat some gourmet meals for a change."

"Don't let's talk about food. I'm on a diet, remember? It's rained here for the last three days. What's the weather like in sunny Florida?"

"Hot," Dianna said wryly. "But I think I can handle it."

"I wish I knew what the hell you're doing down there," Sonya said, her voice suddenly deepening. "Why have you agreed to stay at the Campbells' house, for God's sake? Sweetie, are you sure that's safe?"

Dianna blinked. This was not part of the script. In fact, most of the conversation had been far outside their pre-agreed boundaries. "You know exactly what I'm doing down here," she said. "Hal met me at your house. You know what happened between us. You know why he persuaded me to come home and claim my inheritance."

No danger in saying that, whoever might be listening. She'd been quite open about where she'd met Hal. And nobody—not Hal, not even Sonya—knew that she'd maneuvered for two weeks to set up the "chance" meeting at one of Sonya's infamous parties.

"You're wrong. I don't know why you're down there," Sonya said. "I only know why you've *told* me you're down there, and that makes no sense at all. On my optimistic days, I try to believe that what you've told me bears some nodding similarity to the truth."

Dianna stood, and her stomach immediately started churning with sick anxiety. It was only then that she realized how blissful it had been for those few moments when the churning had stopped. "Sonya, I'm counting on you. I...can't answer all your questions, but I need your help over the next couple of weeks to see me through."

"Yeah, I know." There was another one of those disconcerting pauses. "Well, we're friends, so I guess you've got it."

"Thank you. I'll be able to explain more soon." A knock sounded on the cabana door, and Dianna stopped her pacing. It was depressing to realize she was glad to have an excuse to end the conversation with the woman she considered her best friend. *Damn!* If only she'd been able to force herself to confide in Sonya before she'd left Boston.

"Sonya, someone's here. I have to go. I'll call you again in a couple of days."

"I'll be waiting. Dianna—"

"Yes?"

"Take care, okay?"

What, exactly, did that mean? "Yes, I will. Talk to you soon." Dianna hung up the phone, clumsy with confusion, and hurried over to the front door. Through the glass side panels she saw the shadowy outline of two men. "Who is it?"

"Ben Maxwell. Could we chat for a moment?"

Ben—and a companion. Obviously someone he wanted her to identify when Hal wasn't around to prompt her. The thought of pitting wits against Ben Maxwell was oddly invigorating. Dianna drew in a deep breath and opened the door.

Ben walked into the living room, followed by a young man in his early twenties. If Ben was hoping to check out her ability to identify people from Claire's past, he hadn't chosen a very good test. This young man was tall and broad shouldered, with blue eyes and thick, light brown hair, cut short at the back and swept into a carefully casual wave over his forehead. A superb example of natural good looks combined with expensive grooming, Dianna thought in silent amusement. A dominant, slightly hooked nose saved him from being merely handsome and changed his appearance into something more interesting. Altogether, he looked so much like Andrew Campbell that identifying him as Andrew's son would have been a snap, even if she hadn't seen a half-dozen photos of him in Hal Doherty's files.

"Hello, Roger," she said to him, smiling softly, her voice warm. "You sure have grown a lot."

He examined her with frank interest, showing neither Ben's controlled hostility nor Andrew's overwhelming shock. "This is very strange," he said after a long moment of silence. "I thought I'd know whether you were real or fake the moment I saw you. Somehow, it doesn't seem to be working that way. You look like Claire—and yet the vibrations aren't there. You don't *feel* like my sister. At least, I don't think you do." He lifted his shoulders in obvious bewilderment. "I'm just not sure."

She must be closer to emotional overload than she'd realized, Dianna thought, or maybe she was plain exhausted after a week of almost-sleepless nights. For whatever reason, the sight of Claire's brother precipitated a bunch of crazy emotions, chief among them an inexplicable urge to cry. She cleared her throat, shoving her hands into the pockets of the cotton slacks she'd put on after her swim.

"It's been a long time," she said, trying for a smile and not quite making it. "We've both changed a lot in the past seven years, so it's not surprising if you don't recognize me right off the bat." She had to tilt her chin quite far back to look into his eyes. She risked a smile. "The last time I saw you, you weren't much taller than me and you still had zits on your nose."

He held her gaze, then gave her a slow, friendly smile. "That's cruel," he said. "Never remind a twenty-three-year-old he once had zits. The memory is too close, and still *much* too traumatic."

She laughed, and gestured to a chair, liking his sense of humor. "Are you going to stay and chat for a while? I wish you would."

"I guess I could spare fifteen minutes out of my not-so-hectic schedule to talk with the woman who may be my long-lost sister." Roger turned to Ben. "Are you staying, Ben?"

"Sure." Ben's gaze flicked toward Dianna. "I enjoy watching Ms. Mason at work."

Dianna ignored him. She also ignored the little curl of excitement that twisted inside her when her eyes clashed with Ben's. She hunched her shoulders, ignoring him, her attention focused ostentatiously on Roger. "So tell me, kid, what have you been doing for the past few years?"

He gave an exaggerated sigh. "When I'm ninety and you're ninety-two, are you still going to call me 'kid'?"

"Probably." Her eyes twinkled. "Besides, let's get some accuracy into this discussion. When you're ninety, I'll be ninety-two and a *half*. Show proper respect for your elders, baby brother."

He looked at her, his bright blue eyes suddenly dark. "When you talk like that, you sound just like Claire. She was always teasing me about the fact that I was never going to be as old as she was, even if we lived to be a hundred."

Dianna chuckled. "I'd like to claim that as proof that I'm really and truly Claire Campbell, but honesty compels me to point out that every big sister in the world probably teases her kid brother in the same way."

"Well done, Ms. Mason." Ben's sardonic comment broke into the conversation. "You managed to make that point about two seconds before I did."

"Oh, I'm smarter than a barrel full of monkeys," Dianna countered, not bothering to turn around. "With more tricks in my repertoire, too."

Roger frowned and cocked his head to the side, scrutinizing her with almost-scientific detachment. "It's weird. Really weird. You look like her. You have a lot of the same mannerisms, at least as far as I can remember, but your voice is totally different. It's—sort of scratchy. Even the accent doesn't sound quite the same."

She ignored the comment about her accent and shook her head in mock outrage. "Scratchy! Hey, kid, the polite term for how I sound is *husky.*"

He grinned. "Whatever. Claire's voice was soft and high. Yours is low and scr— Low and husky."

Dianna felt a painful tightening at the back of her throat. She stared down at her hands as if she'd never seen them before. This encounter with Roger was even more wrenching than the meeting with Andrew Campbell, and she wasn't as well armored as she'd anticipated.

"My voice was affected by the fire," she said. "When the cabin burned, there was a lot of smoke. The doctor said I did permanent damage to my vocal cords. For a couple of weeks after... For a while, I lost my voice completely."

Roger leaned forward, tension tightening his features. "What happened to you that night? Where did you go when you left the cabin?" His detachment had vanished, and he sounded young and emotionally shaken up. "For that matter, how the hell did you get out of the cabin? I saw it a few days later—" He swallowed hard. "Well, it didn't seem possible that anyone could escape. All these years, I was never quite convinced that Claire really escaped...."

His voice trailed away and she didn't answer for several seconds. Couldn't answer. When she finally got control of her voice, she spoke in a monotone, reciting the facts Hal had drilled her in so many times.

"I was in the bathroom when the fire took hold,"
she said, not looking at him. "I climbed out the window and went to the Kerenskys' cabin, but they
weren't home. I broke into the place through the
laundry room. I was getting kind of good at climbing
through windows by that time." The feeble attempt at
humor didn't work, and she broke off, avoiding eye
contact with both men until she brought herself back
under control.

"What did you do at the Kerenskys'?" Roger asked
with quiet encouragement.

"I changed my clothes. They were charred, and wet,
and smelled disgustingly of smoke. When I took off
my sweater, I discovered I was burned all across my
chest, but I slathered on antiseptic, and swallowed a
fistful of aspirin so that the pain didn't bother me too
much. Truth to tell, I think I was in such a state of
shock that I didn't really feel the pain. I certainly
wasn't thinking or behaving rationally. I stank of
smoke, but I just grabbed some warm clothes from
Jane Kerensky's closet, found a pair of insulated boots
that more or less fit, and then I left. It never even
dawned on me I could open the front door and go out
that way. I climbed back out the laundry-room window, worrying all the time in case I ripped Jane's ski
pants."

"What happened then?" Roger prompted.

"I kept walking until I hit the highway. A trucker
picked me up. He was going to New York, so that's
where I went, too. I guess he thought I was a runaway. By that point, I must have looked pretty be-
draggled. I remember bits of powdered ash kept
blowing out of my hair into my eyes, so my face was
probably covered in smoke smuts."

Dianna had always been blessed—or cursed—with a vivid imagination. Her eyes glazed over as she talked, and she could almost feel herself inside the warm cocoon of the truck's front cabin as the miles of dark interstate highway flashed by, lights glistening on snow and frosted pavement, until the snow changed to gray slush, and the gleaming silver frost changed to the dreary mist of a New York winter morning. The scar of her old burn throbbed—not with pain, but with the memory of pain—and she rubbed her fingers across her chest in a gesture that owed nothing to artifice.

"You look as if you're remembering a bad journey," Roger said. "Did the truck driver molest you?"

"What? Oh, no, he was very kind. A wonderful guy, in fact. He tried to talk me into going into a shelter for abused teenagers. He bought me coffee and doughnuts because I didn't have any money. Then I remembered I had a bank account at National City in New York, so when we got to Brooklyn, I asked him to loan me the money for a cab into Manhattan, and he did. I swore I'd pay him back, but I didn't, of course. I lost the slip of paper with his name and address on it. I've often felt guilty about that. I wish I could tell him that I survived, that it all turned out okay in the end." Her voice dropped to a whisper. "That he saved my life..."

Ben cut into her reverie, his voice diamond hard. "Very worthy sentiments, Ms. Mason. But you did manage to remember the name of your bank in New York, and your account number, didn't you? How convenient that your shock wasn't severe enough to make you lose track of the *really* important stuff—the money."

"Yes, I've often thought that, myself." Dianna jumped up and paced over to the bar, pouring herself a glass of club soda and adding ice. "What are you angry about, Mr. Maxwell? The fact that I kept my wits sufficiently to collect money that was mine? Or the fact that you don't believe I'm Claire Campbell? Seems to me you can't have it both ways."

"Don't bet on it," he said, his voice grim. "Right now, I'm feeling ornery enough to hold several illogical resentments all at the same time."

"Come on, Ben, cut her some slack," Roger interjected. "What's gotten into you? We need to get at the truth, here." He turned to Dianna. "Were you badly burned?" he asked. "You don't look as if you have any scars."

Dianna could feel Ben's gaze boring into her back. She didn't look around. "I was burned badly enough to scar, but only in a limited area. Provided I stay away from bikinis and strapless evening gowns, I'm okay."

"I'm sorry. Perhaps you could try plastic surgery," Roger suggested.

Her hands tightened around her glass of soda. She couldn't visualize a time when she'd be sufficiently free of the past to want to have her scars eliminated. But she looked up and managed a smile. "Yes, one day I probably will. It's not a big deal for me anymore, one way or the other."

Ben remained silent, but Roger accepted her comments at face value. "I guess what surprises me the most is that you managed to get so far before you ended up in the hospital," he said. "New York is a good few hundred miles from Vermont. You must have been in the truck for hours."

Dianna shrugged. "There are a thousand cases to show that survival instinct will keep us going for a while, long after our physical strength ought to have given out. When I climbed into that truck, I'd never given a single thought to what my plans were, except to get out of Vermont. It was only when the truck driver asked me how much money I had that I realized I was penniless. At that point, I became obsessed with getting into Manhattan and accessing my account at National City before anyone thought to put a hold on it. When I'd 'liberated' my money —and that's literally how I thought of it—all my stamina seemed to evaporate. I'd escaped from the scene of the crime, and I'd rescued the wherewithal to support myself. All the adrenaline that had been keeping me going disappeared in one quick whoosh. I dragged myself as far as the bank next door, literally holding on to the walls of the building. I deposited the cashier's check into a new account, then I passed out."

"What happened then?" Roger asked, sounding worried.

"I guess the bank people called the paramedics. The next thing I knew, a nurse was bending over me in the emergency room of Manhattan General, and my arms were sprouting enough tubes and needles to supply the props for an entire episode of *M*A*S*H*."

Roger didn't say anything, but he reached out and squeezed her hand. To her horror, Dianna realized she was crying. That hadn't been part of the plan, for God's sake. She searched for a tissue, sniffing angrily. Good grief, she'd intended to play her usual role of cynical, weary woman of the world. Getting carried away with heartrending accounts of her supposed teenage suffering was definitely not part of her game plan.

"Here." Ben Maxwell handed her a wad of tissues.

"Thanks." She blew her nose, dried her tears, and carefully avoided both Ben's and Roger's eyes. "I've never talked about what happened after the fire," she said. "I'm sorry. I'm not in the habit of gushing tears."

"Dianna . . . Claire . . ." Roger stumbled over the choice of name. "Oh, hell, I don't know what to call you."

Roger's woeful complaint snapped her out of her mood of self-pity. "Ben will be very unhappy if you call me Claire, and I've gotten used to Dianna over the last few years. I'm quite happy with that."

"Okay, then. Dianna it will be." Roger gave her an uncertain smile. "What I don't understand is why you kept hiding from us. From your family. I know we weren't exactly the Cleavers, or even the Brady Bunch, but our family wasn't more dysfunctional than anyone else's. At least, I didn't think it was. We . . . you and I . . . Hell, if you really are Claire, I always thought we were good friends."

He sounded hurt, and Dianna's heart contracted in reluctant sympathy. "We *were* good friends," she said. "Roger, I didn't run away because of you. How could you believe that? I ran because I didn't feel safe. You have to remember that someone had just set fire to our vacation cabin, where I was staying. The young man with me was *killed.*"

"I understand how you must have felt," Roger said. "But when the first panic was over, surely you realized that you ought to come home? I mean, you were just a kid, trying to fend for yourself in New York City, of all places.''

''I felt safer in Manhattan than I would have felt at home,'' Dianna said. ''Someone tried to kill me. Whoever set that fire knew I was inside the cabin. How could I be sure they wouldn't try again to kill me?''

Ben and Roger exchanged glances. ''One good reason would be that the arsonist was arrested within days, and has been behind bars ever since,'' Ben said, but he spoke less aggressively than before; his voice was almost sympathetic.

Dianna twisted her hands into a tight ball. ''The *supposed* arsonist is in prison,'' she said, heart pounding.

''What do you mean, the 'supposed arsonist'?'' Ben didn't attempt to hide his puzzlement. ''Dianna, it was an open-and-shut case.''

''I was never convinced the police found the real killer,'' she said.

Now it was Roger's turn to stare at her, his bewilderment equal to Ben's. ''What are you saying, Dianna? The police got a complete confession from Ted Jenkins. They found gasoline in his trailer and ash all over his clothes. The forensic labs proved conclusively that the ash came from our cabin.''

''I'm willing to accept Ted Jenkins was at the scene of the fire at some point in time. That doesn't mean he set it.''

''Why would he confess to something he didn't do?'' Ben asked.

''It was a high-profile case. The police needed to solve it. Maybe they coerced his confession.''

"No," Ben said, shaking his head. "I'm not saying the police never bring pressure to bear, but in this instance, they did a first-class job of investigating the fire. I'm sure Hal's shown you all the reports, so you know that Ted Jenkins was an alcoholic drifter, whose first conviction for arson was handed down when he was twelve. He's a chronic offender, not too bright, and borderline sociopathic. As soon as he gets out of jail, he picks a new part of the country and goes around setting fires until he's caught and put back behind bars. He not only confessed to setting the fire that burned you and killed Jon Kaplan, he also confessed to torching at least five other cabins in the same Green Mountain region."

The roaring in Dianna's ears was so loud, she thought the inside of her head would explode. "Yes, I've read the accounts of his trial," she said. "I accept that he's a plausible villain, but his story doesn't fit the facts. He claimed he had no idea there were people inside the cabin when he set it on fire. He's lying. Nobody could have torched that place without knowing there were people inside." Her hands were shaking, and she quickly hid them by tucking them under her legs. "I was there. I should know."

"Think of it from Ted's point of view," Roger suggested gently, obviously not believing her, but not wanting to offend her, either. "He's not very bright—that's the first thing to keep in mind. Then I'm assuming the cabin lights were out, and your car was in the garage—"

"But we'd set candles on the table, and Jon had made a big fire in the living-room fireplace. It's dark up in the mountains, isolated from any neighbors, with no streetlamps for miles in any direction. The

glow of light from the fireplace and the candles must
have been visible for hundreds of yards. And if by
some amazing fluke Ted didn't see any firelight, he
must have smelled the woodsmoke coming out of the
chimney. You know how pungent that is on a cold,
clear night.''

"What you say sounds logical, but it isn't," Roger
said. "The police found a dozen witnesses who were
willing to testify that Ted had spent the two days prior
to the fire swilling whiskey at various bars down in the
village. When he's on one of his binges, everyone
agrees Ted could stumble over an invading army and
not notice anything amiss. Maybe even two armies.''

She could agree, and gloss over the whole discussion, which might be the smartest move she could
make. Or she could point out the basic flaw in their
reasoning. Dianna was scared—scared as hell—but
she'd come all this way, and it was time for her to
speak up. "If Ted was as drunk and stupid as everyone claims, how can anyone be sure he really remem-
bers setting the fire?''

"We know because he confessed," Roger told her,
not understanding.

Ben, of course, realized at once what she was suggesting. "You think someone else set the fire that night
and used Ted's alcoholic blackout as a convenient
cover."

She looked straight into his eyes and, for the first
time since they'd met, answered him with complete,
unreserved honesty. "Yes, that's what I think.''

Roger stared at them, his mouth slack with astonishment. "What do you mean? What are you talking
about? How could anyone forget setting a house on
fire?''

Dianna didn't have a chance to answer. Ben was already two steps ahead of Claire's brother. "If Ted was framed, then you're claiming that somebody set out to murder Claire, deliberately and with forethought."

"Yes. That seems an inescapable conclusion."

"Why would anyone want to kill you . . . her?" The words exploded out of Ben, clipped and harsh with urgency. "You were only eighteen, for Christ's sake. How could you have offended anyone badly enough that they wanted you dead?"

She laughed, genuinely amused that he could sound so naive, albeit just for a moment. There was even a curious sort of triumph in knowing that she'd shocked him into carelessness. For a few vital seconds, she'd made him believe she was Claire.

You were only eighteen, he'd said. *Why did somebody want* you *dead?*

Eyes alight with mockery, she met his gaze, fully in control of herself once again. "I'm surprised you should ask such an obvious question, Mr. Maxwell. Why would anyone want to kill poor little Claire Campbell? Because of the money, of course. What else? Because of my lovely, tempting, twenty-million-dollar trust fund."

Four

Dianna enjoyed her dinner with Roger at The Summer Garden, one of West Palm Beach's most expensive restaurants. By mutual consent, they avoided the charged topic of Claire Campbell's past. Instead, they talked about mundane subjects: movies and books, food and favorite wines, Roger's recent trip to Alaska. Safe, neutral topics that couldn't cut too deeply into the surface friendliness of the evening. By the time they shared a chocolate-raspberry torte for dessert, Roger had relaxed enough to volunteer some information about his job with the family company.

Dianna knew, of course, the history of the Campbells' business success. The story was the stuff of family legend, and Hal had drilled her endlessly on the details. The family fortune had been founded by two brothers, Hector and Jaime Campbell, one a carpenter, the other a glassblower. The brothers had left Edinburgh in 1890 and immigrated to the States along with a parcel of Campbell cousins. The cousins never got farther than the lower East Side of Manhattan, but Jaime and Hector worked their way north and west to Pittsburgh, where they hoped that the rapid growth of heavy manufacturing industries would ensure a constant demand for their skills.

Their optimism was soon rewarded. Removed from the constraints of Britain's class-conscious society, they discovered that in Pittsburgh, success went to the hardworking. They applied their skills, worked nineteen-hour days, and established a reputation for honesty and good service. With Scottish prudence, they married women with snug doweries, and by the end of World War I, they headed two prosperous companies with payrolls and profits that put them on the fringe of big-time success.

Hector, the carpenter, founded Campbell Construction, Builders of Fine Homes for Honest Citizens. Jaime, the glassblower, established Campbell Crystal, a diversified glass-manufacturing company. In northwest Pittsburgh, his huge factory rolled out pressed sheet glass. Across town, a smaller factory housed teams of glassblowers who prided themselves on producing lead-crystal tableware that maintained the traditions of the finest manufacturers back in the Old Country. Jaime recruited immigrant artisans from all over Europe, and set them to work creating one-of-a-kind, luxury chandeliers, and stained-glass lamp shades that many connoisseurs considered superior to Louis Tiffany's. By 1925, few brides with social aspirations considered their homes complete without a Campbell Crystal chandelier hanging in the foyer, and a set of Campbell lead-crystal glasses laid out on the dinner table.

The Campbells had become powers to reckon with in Pittsburgh society, but the brothers still had their problems. Hector, harried father of four daughters and no sons, was desperate to find a successor capable of taking over his business. Trusting the running of his company to the combined leadership of four sons-in-law was a recipe for disaster. But choosing one son-in-law as president and overlooking the other three was guaranteed to cause family strife.

Hector was still agonizing over this dilemma, when a collision between his new Daimler motor car and a horse-drawn milk cart left him with his right leg broken in two different places. Hobbled by pain and the prospect of a permanent limp, his days as an active supervisor on a building site were clearly over. The problem of finding a new manager for Campbell Construction became acute.

A happy solution was finally hit upon when Jaime—proud father of an only son—offered to buy out his brother's interest in the construction company for a million dollars in cash. The offer was modest, but Hector accepted with overwhelming relief. Stuart, Jaime's son, was the perfect candidate to run the combined Campbell companies.

Freed from the hassle of day-to-day management, Hector retired to twenty-five acres of prime land west of Pittsburgh, where he set to work building a mansion decorated with a facade of imported Scottish granite and lighted in every room with oversize Campbell Crystal chandeliers.

Stuart inherited neither his father's talent as a glass designer, nor his uncle's skill as a carpenter, but he was plentifully endowed with business sense and had an innate ability to stay one step ahead of financial trends. In 1927, at the ripe old age of thirty-two, he defied the wisdom of his financial advisers and withdrew all the company funds from the stock market. Scenting the coming crash, he bought land, and then more land. He also bought gold, diamonds, paintings by Old Masters, and virtually any tangible asset that his fellow citizens wanted to sell in their frenzy to raise cash that they could invest in the stock market.

On Black Monday, 1929, when the New York Stock Exchange slithered sixty points downward in a few frenzied hours of trading, Stuart realized that he had become one of the richest men in America.

With Stuart at the helm, Campbell Industries remained prosperous and privately owned throughout the poverty of the Depression, the turmoil of World War II, and the breakneck expansion of the booming fifties. Indomitable to the end, Stuart died at his desk, with a secretary waiting to take dictation, and a phone clutched in his hand. In 1972, his only surviving son, Andrew, grandson of Jaime, inherited the responsibility for running the family corporation and administering the family fortune.

Andrew had no interest in Campbell Crystal, which was saddled with a hopeless mishmash of product lines, and no obvious way to be streamlined into efficiency. He devoted all of his enthusiasm to developing the construction side of the family business, transforming Campbell Construction from a successful regional company into a major player in the exotic world of international real-estate development, and totally neglecting Campbell Crystal.

Despite this neglect, it took several years for the company to run itself into a state of near bankruptcy. The company's reputation was outstanding, and its craftspeople loyal, so that even determined indifference couldn't entirely wipe out its sales or its profitability. However, a decade or more of mismanagement had finally taken its toll, and Ben Maxwell's first major decision as chief operating officer of Campbell

Industries had been to cut Campbell Crystal loose and sell it as a separate company.

It was this proposed sale of Campbell Crystal that Roger and Dianna were discussing over their dessert. "What do you think of Ben's decision to put such an important part of the Campbell heritage up for sale?" Dianna asked.

Roger shrugged. "It's the right one. There are lots of reasons to keep Campbell Crystal, but they're all sentimental or personal, and the contemporary business world has no room for sentiment."

Dianna had no desire to argue with Roger, but it required some effort to resist the urge to expound all the reasons why selling Campbell Crystal was a bad idea. Roger had obviously inherited Andrew's lack of interest in the company. His knowledge of the chandelier and lamp industry was superficial; his feeling for the more rarefied world of high-priced, decorative glassware was virtually nonexistent. If he was aware of the differences between etched, carved and blown glass he gave no sign of it. Dianna doubted if he'd ever been near a glass kiln, or watched a head glassblower at work. Hungry as she was for an inside view of Campbell Crystal, she realized it was useless to ask for details from someone who had no details to give.

She resisted the temptation to probe by steering the conversation onto a new track. "How do you like working with Ben Maxwell?" she asked.

"He's a hard taskmaster, but he's reasonable, and he's always willing to listen to a different point of view." Roger's nose wrinkled in a rueful grimace. "That doesn't mean he listens to my opinion, of course. I may be the chairman's son, but as far as Ben is concerned, I'm about half a rung down the ladder from errand boy."

"Does that bother you?"

"Not really." Roger scooped the foam off his cappuccino. "When Ben joined the company five years ago, we'd completely lost any sense of direction. My father had started projects all over the globe, but he'd been bitten by the political bug, and—to put it bluntly—he wasn't spending enough time minding the store. Ben saved our bacon and we owe him big time. I sure can learn a lot just by listening to him and watching him at work."

Despite Roger's seeming accolades, Dianna sensed an element of reserve in his comments. She couldn't make up her mind whether she was picking up on hesitations caused by his reluctance to confide in a woman who might be an impostor, or whether there were genuine doubts about Ben's ability lurking behind his praise.

Roger gave her no chance to explore her uncertainties. Showing considerable social skill for a young man who'd only recently celebrated his twenty-third birthday, Roger returned their dinner-table conversation to lighter topics, appearing as anxious as Dianna to steer their talk away from danger every time it drifted toward rough waters. And there sure were a lot of shoals and reefs to be navigated, Dianna thought wryly, waiting beneath the canopy as Roger reclaimed his BMW convertible from the parking attendant. Still, they'd made it through a three-course meal unscathed, and had even taken the first tentative steps toward friendship. She was glad of that. Very glad.

"It's finally cooling off," Roger commented as they took the highway north and drove off toward home.

"Shall I open the roof or would you prefer to keep the air-conditioning going?"

"An open roof would be wonderful. Go for it."

Roger pulled over to the side of the road, fumbled with a couple of latches, pressed the release, and the hood lifted and folded with a small electronic sigh. "There's sure to be a head scarf in the glove compartment," he said, raising his voice to be heard over the sudden roar of street noise.

"No, thanks. My hairstyle's strictly wash-and-wear." The night breeze blew cool and dry against Dianna's face, whipping her hair into her eyes as they edged back into the stream of traffic. She was flooded with unexpected nostalgia for the youthful delights of a life that belonged to another woman and seemed a hundred years in the past. The smell of frangipani, mixed with exhaust fumes and the lingering heat of a hot day, assaulted her nose. She laughed aloud with the sheer happiness of rediscovering an old pleasure.

"What's up?" Roger asked. "Why are you laughing?"

"Because this feels great. I haven't done this since tenth grade when Josh Taylor stole his dad's Chrysler convertible and drove me into—" She stopped herself just in time. "Drove me downtown. We didn't go anywhere, just cruised around, convinced we were the coolest, most grown-up people ever to hit the road. It was two in the morning when we finally got back home."

"I bet you didn't feel so cool then! Parents have an annoying habit of cutting their teenagers down to size."

Roger's comment brought back other, less pleasant, realities. "I didn't get in any trouble," she said. "Nobody knew I'd gone out."

He squinted at her. "Good old Andrew and Evelyn. They weren't the hovering kind of parents, were they?"

"Strictly absentee," she said, her voice still light.

"Personally, I was always damn grateful for that."

"Me, too. I guess."

One thing about her low, throaty voice, Dianna reflected, it tended to disguise a lot of what she was really feeling. Accepting her comment at face value, Roger turned his attention back to the road, passing an elderly driver ambling along at a steady thirty. "Freakin' old fogies," he muttered. "They should be banned from the highways." He leaned back, letting the car edge up toward seventy. "Anyway, what happened to your friend Josh? Did he get in trouble?"

"Loads of it. He got grounded for a month, poor guy. His parents were the old-fashioned kind. Not like ours."

"Poor Josh."

"The truth is, I always envied him." The confession came from nowhere, blurted out before she could hold it back. "I couldn't imagine living in a house where your mom and dad would actually know whether you were home or not, but I had this nagging suspicion it might be kind of neat."

"In theory, maybe, but not in practice."

"Yes, I'm sure you're right. No kid really wants her parents breathing down her neck." Dianna cut short her reminiscing before it could get dangerous. She hadn't expected to find it so difficult to remember her role, to remember what she could safely say and to whom. She twisted around in her seat belt so that she could see Roger more clearly. She needed to keep her thoughts focused. "Anyway, that's enough about my high-living past. What about you? You hadn't even started dating when I left for college."

He twirled an imaginary mustache. "That, little lady, is all you know."

"Aha, the truth emerges at last. Everyone thought you were a cute, innocent kid, and really you were a teenage Lothario."

He flashed her a grin. "I prefer to describe myself as a bright kid who had an early appreciation for the finer aspects of living. And women are definitely one of life's finer aspects."

"I agree." She smiled back. "Women are great. Tell me about your current girlfriend."

"How do you know I have one?"

Her eyes twinkled. "It's practically a law of nature. You're smart, you're fun to be with, you're terrific to look at—" She broke off. "I can't believe I'm paying all these compliments to my snotty kid brother."

He rolled his eyes. "If I show you my new pin-striped business suit and my executive-style leather briefcase, will you stop calling me snotty?"

She chuckled. "I'm not promising anything, but I'll give it my best shot."

"Thanks. And yes, I do have a girlfriend. We've been dating for a couple of months now."

"Is it serious?" Dianna flushed when she heard herself. "I can't believe I asked that! I'm sorry. Put it down to sisterly curiosity run wild after seven years away."

"That's okay, and no, it's not serious, but she's fun to spend time with." His mouth curved into a teasing smile. "She's almost as impressed with my convertible as you were with Josh Taylor's."

"Impossible," Dianna said. "Josh and I were only sixteen when we had our great adventure in his dad's car." She sighed.

"What's that sigh for? It sounded heavy."

"I was just thinking that falling in love is much more fun when you're too young and stupid to realize what you're doing."

"Hmm. Sounds as if you've been burned—" He stopped, face stricken. "Damn, I'm sorry—"

"Don't apologize. I'm not so fragile that I disintegrate every time someone mentions a word connected with fire."

He still looked uneasy. "All I meant to say was that you sounded as if you'd been hurt by an unhappy love affair."

"Nothing so dramatic," she replied, leaning back and letting the wind blow over her in a heady stream. "But from watching my friends make themselves totally miserable, I've decided falling in love is less traumatic when you do it by instinct and hormones instead of trying to rationalize your behavior into something sensible."

"I can't believe what I'm hearing." He waggled his eyebrows in fake horror. "Are you suggesting society would be better off if we let our hormones run riot and to hell with the consequences?"

She laughed. "I guess I'm not that radical. But some unregenerate part of me still thinks falling in love is easier when you're too naive to realize the dangers of intimacy. Nobody with a grain of sense wants to bare their soul to another human being. Speaking personally, my soul is way too grungy for public display."

"Talk like that will get you drummed out of the Grown-ups Club," he said. "First rule of adulthood—Never admit that kids and teenagers do *anything* better than grown-ups."

"Tonight I guess I'm not feeling very adult. Right now, I just want to enjoy the moment, the car, the wind blowing in my face. Your company." She drew in a deep, slow breath. "It's been too long since we were together, Roger."

He glanced away from the road and their eyes met for a split second. "I think you just paid me a major compliment."

"Yes, I think I did." She covered a flare of emotion by scowling in mock annoyance. "You know, too many conversations like this would be bad news for my ego. You sound infuriatingly in charge of your life for somebody who's two years younger than I am."

"I'm a control freak," he said. "Don't you remember? If my life isn't totally organized, I go into instant cardiac arrest."

"I guess, now you mention it, I do remember something of the sort. The housekeeper in Pittsburgh was always nagging me to keep my room as tidy as yours."

"Mrs. Thompson. She was a character, wasn't she?"

"I wouldn't know," Dianna said flatly. "The housekeeper I knew was called Maureen Bailey. I guess Mrs. Thompson must have come after I left home."

"You're right, she did. They come and go so quickly, it's hard to keep them straight." Roger segued easily into their former conversation, glossing over the embarrassment of his little test. "I'm surprised you didn't hate me for being such an obnoxiously well-organized kid brother. When I was in college, I drove my roommate nuts."

"Why?" she asked, willing to pretend that he'd mentioned the wrong housekeeper by mistake, although they both knew that he hadn't. "Didn't he appreciate your tidiness?"

"Are you kidding? Tom came close to murder on several occasions. I always knew where my textbooks were, I always handed in my assignments on time, and I always had a stack of clean underwear. By the end of the first semester, he was threatening to get me fired from the fraternity if I didn't loosen up. He complained my behavior bordered on un-American."

She smiled. "He could be right. Did you turn into a temporary slob just to stay friends?"

Roger shook his head. "I moved into an apartment off campus and stashed piles of textbooks and Coke cans all over the living-room floor. That way there was enough mess for my friends to feel comfortable, and I worked in my bedroom."

"Which was probably neat enough to satisfy a Marine Corps drill sergeant."

"At least."

Dianna laughed. "Thanks for the warning. I must remember never to invite you into my workshop. You'd probably need CPR within the first five minutes. Glassblowing is a messy business and when I'm working on a design project, I tend to forget about my surroundings."

"Claire was always disorganized," he said.

"Some things never change," she replied evenly, although the way he said the name jerked her upright in her seat. This was the second reminder in the space of a few minutes that Roger wasn't taking all her stories at face value. "I'm still disorganized," she added, "although I've learned how to keep things clean, if not tidy."

"I guess that's a major improvement." Roger's expression sobered, and for the first time that evening, silence fell between them. He turned the car into the driveway leading to Laurel Manor Country Club, and waited for the security guard to open the electronic gates.

"I have to fly to London this weekend," he said. "I'm sorry there won't be any chance to spend more time with you."

"I'd have liked that, too. Is it a business trip?"

"Yes. Ben wants me to take a look at a property we own in Canary Wharf. Give him my opinion as to what we should do." Roger talked quickly, as if he hoped to fill any more gaps in the conversation before they could open.

"I'm impressed," Dianna said with perfect candor. "It sounds to me as if Ben thinks of you as much more than an errand boy."

"He has his moments, I guess. Dad bought an office building from a group of Canadian developers when they went belly-up, and Ben isn't happy with the current leasing agents we have. Peddling office space in Canary Wharf is tough, and they don't seem to have what it takes."

"Canary Wharf?" she asked. "Where's that? The name doesn't sound familiar."

"It's an isolated dockland area toward the east end of London. The British government teamed up with private enterprise to redevelop the area, but so far, the project's been a problem for almost everyone involved."

"Why choose to develop somewhere so unpromising? Or is this one of those typical government pork-barrel things?"

"How do you define pork? One person's pig fat is another person's crispy bacon. The project started out as a genuine effort to ease the overcrowding in central London. The land is potentially prime real estate, with fabulous views across the Thames River. That's why my father took the opportunity to buy into the project when the Canadian developers went under. But unfortunately, there are no subway lines in or out of the area and inadequate roads, so most of the office space remains empty. And because there aren't enough office tenants, nobody is opening up restaurants, or dry-cleaning stores, or pubs, which just makes companies even less enthusiastic about moving there because of the lack of support services."

"Sounds a mess to me."

He brushed away a moth that was fluttering around his head. "Maybe not. I'm trying to persuade Ben to open a small retail complex there, just to see if we can break the logjam. Right now, we're hemorrhaging money."

"Is that why Ben and Andrew are so anxious to sell Campbell Crystal?" Dianna asked. "Do they need to raise cash to cover their losses in the property market?"

"No, not at all. The failure of Canary Wharf has put our British subsidiary into a cash squeeze, but our parent corporation isn't in any sort of liquidity crisis.''

Roger seemed to regret his momentary burst of eloquence and he gestured with evident relief toward the impressive columns of the Campbell portico, looming at the crown of the cul-de-sac. "We're home."

"Yes, so we are." Dianna got out of the car, aware that there would be no more information forthcoming tonight on Campbell Crystal. "Thank you for a great evening, Roger. I've really enjoyed the chance to get to know you again."

He picked up on her final word. "Again?" he asked softly, following her out of the car. "Is this really *again,* Dianna?"

"Yes, it's really again," she said.

By silent agreement, they avoided the concrete forecourt of the garages, and walked around the corner of the house until they stood by a trellis at the edge of the swimming pool. She met his gaze, registering with renewed force how much he looked like his father.

"I guess we didn't know each other very well when we were kids," she said. "But we did know each other, Roger. I'm Claire Campbell and you're my brother. I remember sitting at the bottom of the stairs, waiting to meet you on the day my mother brought you home from the hospital."

"How can I be sure?" He ripped angrily at a trailing vine. "The truth is, I don't feel the connection between the two of us like I used to when Claire and I were kids. If you're my sister, why don't I feel the connection?"

"It's been seven years. The ties between us have weakened."

"What about Blood's Thicker Than Water and all those other clichés? Shouldn't I be able to look at you and know instantly if you're my sister?"

Dianna felt the tension creep back and tauten her muscles. They'd been leading up to this ever since they left the restaurant. Despite their caution in the early part of the evening, it seemed they weren't going to avoid the really difficult topics after all. Perhaps it wasn't even wise to try to keep so many explosive issues buried.

"We went to different schools," she said. "A lot of the time we lived in different houses. You spent more time with Andrew than I did." She risked a smile. "And remember, I'm two and a half years older than you. When you're a teenager, a few years can seem like a lifetime of difference."

His hand slashed at the night air. "But we're not teenagers anymore. We're both adults, leading demanding, complicated lives. The difference in our ages shouldn't prevent me recognizing you. Not now. Not now we're grown-up."

Dianna hesitated for a moment. "We're a normal brother and sister, who spent a lot of time apart. We're not Siamese twins. Why are you so convinced you ought to feel an intuitive link to me?"

"I don't know, I just do." He kicked at a decorative pebble, running his hand through his long shock of hair. Suddenly, he looked young and vulnerable, and Dianna's heart squeezed tight with emotion. He slammed his fist into the trellis, making it shake. "Damn it to hell! Surely there ought to be something special between us?" he said. "Some ingrained prick of recognition?"

"Apparently not." Her voice was husky with regret. "At least for you."

He looked up. "What does that mean?"

"You may not recognize me, but I recognized you," she said softly. "I'd have known you anywhere."

Roger's profile hardened. "Hal has lots of photographs."

His words were a blow, but she answered calmly enough. "Yes, he does, including several excellent ones taken of you last year in the Bahamas. If I were an impostor, I could easily have learned to identify you from Hal's photos."

His mouth drew tight with frustration. "You're very clever, you know? You point out just how you and Hal could have set this scam up, but somehow you manage to leave the impression that you're not working a scam at all."

"That's because I'm not."

Roger stared off into the darkness, not looking at her when he asked his next question. "Tell me something, Dianna, are you willing to have a blood test?"

Her stomach leapt into a gliding double somersault. She pressed her hand to her mouth, then quickly let it fall to her side. Why was he asking for a blood test? What did he know? What *didn't* he know? She swallowed hard.

"How do you mean?" she asked, as if she hadn't understood perfectly well. "What sort of blood test?"

"A DNA comparison," he said. "You and my father. I understand a careful DNA screening test can establish paternity with ninety-nine percent certainty."

She was shaking from head to toe. Fortunately, Roger wasn't looking at her, so perhaps he didn't know the effect he was having on her. She had to swallow twice more before her throat was moist enough to permit her to speak. "You want me to submit to a blood test that will prove whether or not I'm Andrew Campbell's daughter," she said, making it a statement rather than a question.

He finally turned and looked directly at her. "I think that would be an interesting test, don't you?"

She straightened so that she could return his gaze head-on. She felt like a butterfly pinned to a black cloth, waiting for her wings to be sprayed with fixative by an eager collector. She knew that whatever she said now was weighted with consequences, and she sought desperately for the least dangerous response. Like the butterfly, she had almost no room to maneuver.

"I don't believe it would be in my best interests to submit to a DNA comparison test," she said in the end. Her voice was so carefully neutral; it sounded as if it had been produced by a microchip inside a computer.

Roger didn't reply. Maybe he was no more ready to provoke a showdown than she was. Maybe he already knew what the DNA test would reveal. With a final assessing glance in her direction, he swung around and walked back toward the garage, leaving her standing alone and sweating in the humidity of the Florida night.

She waited, not moving, until she heard the garage door close behind Roger's car. With Roger safely inside the house, she recovered her courage. Or maybe she lost her temper. Whichever it was, she walked around the vine-covered trellis and spoke coldly into the darkness. "You can come out now, Mr. Maxwell. Your eavesdropping fun is over for this evening."

Her sixth sense hadn't deceived her. Ben was on the patio, concealed by the jutting angle of the house wall. He stood, moving with quiet steps to join her by the pool. His hair gleamed wet in the moonlight, and his tanned legs were bare beneath the short toweling robe he wore. His eyes, a chilly gray during this morning's interview, had turned smoky and unreadable in the darkness.

"You and Roger came back just as I'd finished my swim," he said, then stopped, as if unwilling to explain his presence on the patio any further.

She spared a moment to wonder why he hadn't slipped into the house as soon as her conversation with Roger had ended. He could have used the noise of the garage door opening and closing to cover the sound of his retreat and she would never have known for sure that he'd been there.

Refusing to feel intimidated—after all, he was the one caught eavesdropping, not her—she tipped her head back and looked up at him with all the bravado she could summon. "Did you hear everything you hoped for, Mr. Maxwell?"

"Listeners never hear what they're hoping for," he replied.

"Sorry. Next time, I'll remember to tell Roger I'm an impostor. I assume that's what you were hoping to hear."

"Are you an impostor?" he asked.

"No. I'm Claire Campbell. The genuine article. The one and only."

"Spoken with a convincing ring of truth," he said. "And you have such honest eyes it's almost impossible to doubt you." He smiled without mirth. "Have you ever noticed that the best liars always have the most trustworthy facial expressions?"

"Of course. That's what makes them successful liars."

He didn't reply. Instead, he raised his hand and stroked her hair, pushing it back from her face in a gesture that was almost a caress.

She jerked away. "Don't. Don't touch me." It was a major overreaction and she cursed herself for the unwitting betrayal. His eyes narrowed and his gaze dropped to her mouth. She felt her lips part in automatic response and she clamped them hastily shut, turning away from him and staring into the breeze-rippled waters of the swimming pool.

"I don't like it, either." He spoke quietly from behind her shoulder. His voice was husky, not entirely steady. He didn't touch her again, but he could probably see that she was trembling. Dianna wrapped her arms around her waist and sent silent curses into the darkness.

"It complicates things, doesn't it?" he said when she didn't reply. "A nice, placid indifference would be so much easier for both of us."

She wouldn't sink to the point of pretending she didn't understand what he was talking about—not when he must be able to see the too-rapid rise and fall of her breasts, and the flush darkening her cheeks. "You have nothing to worry about, Mr. Maxwell. I'm quite capable of separating sexual attraction from the demands of a business situation."

"Congratulations," he said, and she was astonished to hear a hint of rueful laughter in his voice.

"Unfortunately, I don't seem to be having as much success as you."

"Imagine you're a woman," she snapped. "That way you'll be able to separate your brain cells from your hormones."

He smiled. She could feel his smile, even though she refused to turn and look at him. "Right at this minute, I can't imagine anything in the world I want less than to be a woman."

For one crazy second, Dianna couldn't imagine anything in the world she wanted more than to look up and see Ben's smile. But life had taught her the hard lesson that what you wanted most always carried the highest price tag, so she drew in a steadying breath, and spoke into the middle distance. "I'm very interested in touring the design workshop for Campbell Crystal. I understand it's still in its original building in Pittsburgh. Would you be able to arrange a tour for me, Mr. Maxwell?"

"Yes, I could do that."

His response was so crisp and noncommittal, she knew it was finally safe to look at him. She turned. "Then will you?"

"Yes, whenever you tell me that your stay here in Florida is over."

He was the consummate, hard-edged businessman again, and Dianna refused to feel regret for the other Ben Maxwell, the one it would be far too dangerous for her to know. "A little going-away present, you mean?" She held out her hand and turned toward the cabana. "I'll certainly let you know when I plan to leave Florida. I don't imagine it will be anytime soon. But I appreciate your cooperation, Mr. Maxwell. Good night."

"Good night." She'd walked only a few paces when he called her name. "Dianna."

She stopped, but didn't turn to look at him. "Yes?"

"I thought you might want to know. Evelyn Campbell will be flying into Miami tomorrow. She'll be arriving here in the early afternoon."

Dianna spun around, feeling the blood drain from her face. "My mother's coming here?" she questioned. "But she hates Florida, even in the winter. She never comes here in summer!"

Ben looked at her consideringly, then spoke with the cool mockery of their morning interview. "You shouldn't underestimate your appeal, Ms. Mason. It seems that in the cause of seeing her long-lost daughter, Evelyn is prepared to push herself to the limit. She's even willing to brave the horrors of Palm Beach in July."

This morning, when she'd first met Ben Maxwell, Dianna had found his mockery threatening in the extreme. After their encounter tonight, she realized that there were many other emotions he could conjure up that were far more dangerous. Reassured by the return to their old ground, she lifted her chin and met his gaze steadily. "Then I'll have to see that I make her trip worthwhile, won't I, Mr. Maxwell?"

His mouth tightened into a grim line. "I'm sure you always give excellent value for money expended," he said and walked into the house before she could think up a suitably cutting reply.

Five

Hal was in bed—his own, thank goodness—and snoring peacefully, proving that innocence wasn't a necessary requirement for a quiet conscience. Unfortunately, Dianna's conscience was less accommodating, and she paced the bedroom in the cabana, too restless even to think of sleep.

Everything was moving too fast, Dianna thought, putting her suitcase on the bed and searching through her collection of files until she found the one Hal had prepared on Evelyn Campbell. Carrying it over to the window, she sat in a wicker chair, with her legs dangling over the arm, and opened up the slim Manila folder.

A picture of Evelyn Campbell stared up at her. Against a background of rich, hunter green velvet drapery, she stared into the camera, her forehead unwrinkled even though she was nearing fifty, her pearl choker discreetly lustrous, her straight blond hair coiffed—there was no other word for it—into an impeccable chignon. She was beautiful as well as elegant, with a bone structure that would still look good even when her skin finally succumbed to the inevitable sag of gravity. Dianna had seen the photograph at least a half-dozen times, but Evelyn's cool, aristocratic blue gaze still had the power to disconcert her.

Evelyn looked as if she'd be a formidable woman if she could ever be persuaded to step off her pedestal and engage in the nitty-gritty of life.

Hal's notes accompanying the photo were neatly typed, and informative. Dianna had often thought that if he spent one-tenth of the time and energy on gainful pursuits that he spent on get-rich-quick schemes, he would by now be a legitimate millionaire. But since pigs were more likely to fly than Hal was to settle down to honest work, her corner of the world was still safe for charlatans.

Slipping the photo of Evelyn into the file pocket, Dianna leaned back against the cushions of the chair, skimming the first page of Hal's notes, reabsorbing the familiar facts.

Evelyn Campbell, née Evelyn Henderson Duplessy. Born 1945 to aristocratic Philadelphia Main Line family. Met Andrew Brentwood Campbell at her coming-out party, and married him in 1967 right after graduation from Bryn Mawr. Couple reported to have been attracted to each other by mutual dislike of the freewheeling, free-loving life-style of many of their contemporaries. In contrast to most of their generation, both supported U.S. involvement in the Vietnam War, but although Andrew volunteered for service in the navy, the closest he came to combat duty was a six-month tour of duty in the Philippines in 1969, during which time he flew reconnaissance missions over the South China Sea. Relationship between Andrew and Evelyn has been no more than a facade for at least twenty years. Divorce has never been seriously considered, chiefly because their combined financial interests in Campbell, Inc. are too complex to unravel—note that Evelyn was a favorite of Stuart Campbell, Andrew's father, and was given five percent of the shares in Campbell, Inc. as a wedding gift. Current value of Evelyn's stock estimated at $5.2 million.

The couple maintains separate households, Evelyn mostly in New York, where she is an active participant on the boards of the symphony, the Guggenheim, and the New York Public Library. On rare occasions when Evelyn and Andrew spend time together, they meet in Pittsburgh, where Helen Campbell, Andrew's mother and the family matriarch, used to reign supreme in the family mansion, The Laurels.

The pretense of marriage seems to suit both Evelyn and Andrew very well. She supports Andrew's quest for election, and has appeared at several campaign functions, looking suitably impressed and/or adoring. No reports of arguments or open hostility when the two are at home together. Widely assumed by acquaintances that Evelyn is frigid and Andrew has multiple mistresses.

Acquaintances might assume all they pleased, Dianna thought, but so far, nobody had detected even the whiff of an extramarital love affair clinging to Andrew. Hal had worked with the man for five years and couldn't name a single woman who might have been his mistress. And Sonya, who was probably the best investigative journalist in the whole of New England, had spent six weeks searching into Andrew's private life, and come up with zilch. The man was either a model citizen, or he was damned good at covering his tracks.

Dianna knew which one of those options she'd prefer to believe, but when it came to proof of extramarital dalliance, there was none. Sonya's hint on the phone today that Sharon Kruger might be Andrew's mistress as well as his chef had been the first crack in Andrew's facade of impeccable chastity. Dianna made a mental note to visit the kitchens first thing in the morning. She needed to have a chat with Sharon Kruger. With so many balls flying through the air, she mustn't let that particular one drop.

Dianna yawned, feeling physically exhausted but still mentally wide-awake. She stood and stretched, carrying the file on Evelyn Campbell back to its resting place in her suitcase. As she put the file away, her hand knocked against the little leather jewel case that held her grandmother's locket. Slowly, almost reluctantly, she drew out the box from beneath layers of underclothes, holding it nestled in the palm of her hand. After a few moments, unable to resist, she clicked the latch. The lid flipped open and she lifted out the heavily embossed gold locket that lay inside.

It gleamed with a rich, warm lustre in the lamplight. She ran her fingers over the soft, handworked gold, admiring the skill of the worksmanship. The locket was over a hundred years old, and much too large and solid to appeal to modern tastes. In addition, with typical Victorian exuberance, the engraver had covered every millimeter of surface with leaves, flowers, vines, and abstract curlicues. In contrast to the pure, understated artistry of Dianna's glass designs, the locket was absurdly overdecorated, and yet she loved the creative enthusiasm of the unknown Victorian craftsman. Until she'd agreed to participate in Hal's scam, she'd worn the locket every day, and she missed the comforting feel of its weight around her neck.

She ran her thumbnail along the almost-invisible seam that joined the two halves, and the locket sprang apart, revealing two faded black-and-white photos, a woman on the left, a man on the right. Dianna's breath expelled in a short, involuntary sigh. Her parents. Her real mother and father.

She stared at the pictures in silence. They evoked the usual mixture of regret and confusion, spiced with a dash of anger. The psychologist had spent several months trying to convince her that the anger was healthy, a reasonable response to the circumstances of her life. Intellectually, Dianna accepted the psychologist's viewpoint. Emotionally, she still had problems accepting that she wasn't responsible for her parents' sins.

Dianna pressed the locket closed again, and shoved it back into its box, thrusting it deep into her suitcase. Irritated by her moment of sentimentality, she locked the suitcase and returned it to the dark recesses of the huge closet. She'd spent too many years struggling to overcome her past; she'd decided when she embarked on this scam that there was no longer any room in her life for nostalgia.

Enough fooling around, she muttered to herself. *Andrew is away in Tallahassee. You schemed for three months to get yourself invited into his home. You've endured six weeks of Hal's company chiefly so that you could get inside this house without anyone know-*

ing who you are. Isn't it time you took advantage of Andrew's absence to check out his room?

Once asked, the answer to the question was obvious. She might never have a better chance to search Andrew's bedroom than tonight. And since Andrew had made this house his main residence for the past five years, there was a good possibility she'd find some interesting material hidden among his personal papers. Her plan to destroy his campaign for governor was still no more than a vague outline, with all the details needing to be filled in. Sometimes it seemed that her plan didn't amount to much more than the certainty she was going to expose him to the people of Florida for the criminal he was. It was time she started finding the solid planks on which she could build her trap.

Not allowing herself any more time to stop and debate the ethics of her plan, Dianna pocketed the key to the guest cabana and walked quietly across the main living area toward the door. Hal's snoring sputtered to a momentary stop, then resumed its steady rhythm. How furious he'd be if he knew he snored with such unglamorous gusto, Dianna thought, amused. Snoring didn't fit his self-image as sophisticated lover and man of the world.

She twisted the porcelain doorknob, which was painted with shells and starfish. Whoever decorated the guest cabin had definitely gone overboard on the seashore motif. She wished, sometimes, that her eye weren't so acute, and that her visual memory were less detailed. She remembered too many things from her past with an accuracy that was painfully precise.

The door swung open on silent, well-oiled hinges. The paved path leading from the cabana to the main house was lit with ankle-high lights nestled among the foliage, too dim to disturb sleep but bright enough to point the way. Everything made easy for guests intent on petty larceny, Dianna reflected sardonically, quelling a renewed surge of guilt.

Dammit, I have no cause to feel guilty! Andrew deserves everything that's going to happen to him.

She was almost at the sliding-glass door that led into the vestibule of the main building when it dawned on her that she didn't need to debate the ethics of her plan because she didn't have a hope of getting inside the house, much less inside Andrew's suite of rooms. At this hour of night, everything was not only locked up, but alarms were most likely set that connected with the gatehouse security services, and perhaps with the police. The cabana not only provided privacy for guests, it effectively cut them off from unsupervised roaming in the main house.

"Great!" Dianna muttered, scowling at the offending patio door. Her first attempt at burglary was stymied before it began. Why hadn't she thought to check out the alarm system, or to learn the numerical code that switched it off? As a conspirator, she ranked right up there with the Three Stooges. Feeling extremely foolish, she made the trek back to the cabana. How early was the main alarm system turned off in the morning? she wondered. And could she take the risk of entering Andrew's bedroom in broad daylight? Perhaps it would be easier to find her way into his rooms during the bustle of daytime activity.

Still mulling over her options, she eased her key into the lock on the cabana door. For some reason, it jammed. As she fumbled, trying to click the tumblers, the sensation of being watched became overwhelming. A chill chased down her spine and she rubbed her arms, trying to get rid of the goose bumps pricking beneath her skin.

The unseen eyes felt as if they were drilling holes into the back of her head. She spun around, sweaty with nerves. "Who's there?" Her voice wasn't just husky, it positively croaked. She cleared her throat and tried again. "Who is it? What do you want?"

The thrum of cicadas was her only reply. A breeze shivered across the lush foliage, carrying the scent of orange blossoms and tropical heat. A tree frog croaked, but no whisper of human sound disturbed the darkness. Dianna peered into the shadows, still not entirely convinced she was alone. Something cool and damp touched her arm and she jumped, not quite managing to swallow a scream. She looked down, and a lizard returned her stare, its throat swelling and pulsing with fright. Bright green, faintly luminescent, it lurched off her arm onto a nearby bush, horrified by its encounter with warm, human flesh.

Heart still pounding, she leaned against the cabana door and forced a smile. *Freaked out by a lizard,* she reproached herself. *My God, you're in bad shape, kid.* Straightening, she put the key back into the lock, refusing to pay any more attention to the prickle at the back of her neck. The grounds were probably crawling with lizards and frogs, not to mention various other reptiles she preferred not to think about. Like snakes, for example. She was being observed, all right, but not by human eyes.

She pushed on the panels of the cabana door, and this time it swung open without resistance. Accompanied once again by Hal's snores, she strode purposefully into her bedroom, locking the door behind her. She drew in a deep, steadying breath that turned into a yawn. Her activities of the past few minutes hadn't been a total waste, after all. Between her unsuccessful attempt at burglary and her encounter with the lizard, she'd finally scared herself into sleepiness.

Despite the welcome drowsiness, Dianna forced herself to take a few minutes to brush her teeth, wash her face, and comb the tangles from her hair. She was definitely not cut out for a life of crime, she decided. Her hands were still shaking. She grimaced into the mirror, then pulled on an oversize T-shirt that had faded from bright turquoise to a washed-out blue. Time to put her overactive imagination to rest and get some sleep. Bed was going to feel wonderful.

It felt better than wonderful. The pillows were of the softest down, the sheets—trimmed with a *broderie anglaise* design of seashells—highest-quality percale. The hum of the air-conditioning was more than loud enough to cover the irritating splutter of Hal's snores.

For a few pleasant moments, Dianna hovered on the edge of sleep, her mind teetering between formless dreams and conscious awareness. When the rustle of movement came, she was so close to sleep that for a while she incorporated the sounds into her dream. Her parents had just come home from a party. Her father was pushing open the cabana door, moving silently to kiss her good-night. She drifted, languid and peaceful, letting herself sink deeper into the dream.

With horrifying abruptness, her torpor vanished and she felt herself catapulted into one of the worst of her recurring nightmares. She smelled smoke, heard the crackle of burning timber, and in her mind's eye saw the leaping flames take hold, eating into the structure of the cabana with ferocious hunger.

She fought against the power of the nightmare, refusing to accept its return. Never again, she had sworn, after two years of intensive counseling. Never again would she accept the torment of sleep that brought no refreshment. Never again would she allow her nights to be turned into wastelands of terrifying memories. Her head felt heavy and her eyes didn't want to open, but the psychologist had taught her how to force herself awake. Dianna cut ruthlessly into the dream, dragging her reluctant body into a sitting position, staggering across the carpeted floor to the bathroom, wrapped in the tendrils of her nightmare.

She moved by instinct, avoiding furniture even though her eyelids were still glued shut. Fumbling her way to the sink, she turned on both taps, splashing tepid water onto her face. "Wake up," she murmured thickly. "Time to wake up."

The water trickled down her cheeks, and across her chin, soaking into the neckline of her T-shirt. The smell of smoke was stronger now, making her gag. Why wasn't her dream fading? She pinched her cheek and saw the color come and go in the mirror. Okay, that was good. She was awake now, more or less. Why was her stomach heaving, as if she needed to throw up? Why did her eyelids still feel heavy?

Her head jerked back and her eyes shot wide open. Her heart pounded so hard and fast that the air squeezed out of her lungs in an audible squeak. She stared at her ghostly reflection in the mirror, and realized that she was peering through a light haze of smoke. Dear God, the smell of smoke wasn't part of her nightmare. *She wasn't dreaming!* She really could hear the hiss and crackle of something burning.

Dianna ran out into the living room, toward the threatening rustle of sound. The main door of the cabana was invisible behind a wall of smoke, and flames were already licking at the carpeting around the entrance. Momentarily transfixed, Dianna stared at the flames. The chemicals released by the burning carpet filled her nostrils, mingling with the pungent odor of kerosene, choking her with the memories of another time, another place, another fire. With an effort of will so tremendous that her skin broke out in a head-to-toe sweat, she turned and ran into Hal's bedroom. Incredibly, he was snoring, his mouth curved in a fatuous smile. Even in sleep, he looked infuriatingly self-satisfied.

She felt steadied by the curl of irritation that knotted in her stomach at the sight of him. It was such a normal, everyday emotion that it helped tether her to reality. *Calm down*, she told herself. *This is a small fire in a guest cabana in Florida, nothing else.*

She shook Hal furiously. "Wake up! Hal, for God's sake, wake up!"

He snorted and rolled over. She slapped his face, her heart plummeting, her body ice-cold with fear. "Wake up, damn you! We have to get out of here!"

He raised one groggy eyelid. "Whassamatter, babe? What's your problem? You want Hal to take care of you?"

"The cabana's on fire." Relief that he was alive turned rapidly to anger that he was so slow-witted. She pulled the bedcovers off, and threw a robe at him. "Get up, you stupid oaf. We have to get out of here!"

"On fire? Jesus Christ! The fucking house is on fire!" Hal shot out of bed, stumbled over the robe, grabbed his wallet from the nightstand, and dashed for the door.

"Not that way." She clutched his arm. "The front door's blocked by smoke. We can go through my bedroom. There's a sliding-glass door onto the patio."

"No time! We have to get out of here! We'll be roasted alive!" Hal was already tugging at the drapes and pushing wildly at his bedroom window. "It won't open! Jesus Christ, we're trapped!" He was white-faced with terror.

"We're not trapped. We can go out through my bedroom," she said, squeezing his hand, trying to calm him. Her voice, she noted with abstract interest, sounded cool and controlled. How odd, when her legs were shaking so much that she had to lean against the wall for support. "Hal, come with me." She tugged at his arm, and he stumbled after her, too panicked to argue.

The fire was spreading, she saw, as they skirted the edge of the living room, but they were in no immediate danger. Coughing and spluttering, she led Hal through her bedroom and out onto the patio.

Hal slumped against the trellis. "Jesus, that was a close call!" He watched smoke curl into the sky, then suddenly straightened. Now that he was out of danger, Hal was ready to play macho man. "Go over by the pool, babe, and I'll get us some help."

Yelling "Fire!" at the top of his lungs, Hal bolted toward the house, pounding and knocking on every available door and window. Ignoring his order to move poolside, Dianna stood where he had left her, in the middle of the vine-shaded patio that surrounded the cabana. Belatedly, she realized that although she had found a robe to give Hal, she herself had escaped wearing nothing but the thigh-length T-shirt and a pair of cotton panties. She still had time to rescue her clothes, Dianna realized. The patio door to her bedroom was open, and there wasn't a hint of flames anywhere except in the living room. She started to walk forward, took two or three steps, then stopped, her body convulsed by shudders. Her feet simply refused to carry her back into the cabana. Dry-eyed and silent, she wrapped her arms around her waist and stared at the burning building.

Oddly enough, from the outside, the cabana looked almost normal except for a flickering glow of orange light shining through the living-room windows. She stared at that glow with hypnotic intensity, unable to look away or even to blink.

In response to Hal's screams, lights were going on all over the main house, and people in various stages of undress began to stream out onto the patio surrounding the pool. Dimly, Dianna was aware of servants, clustered in small groups, chattering in horrified Spanish. She heard Hal yelling for someone to call 911 and Ben's low-voiced reply that he'd already called. Then she heard Roger's voice, angrily demanding to know why the fire alarm hadn't sounded.

A good question, Dianna thought, still not moving. There were smoke detectors in every room in the cabana. She'd seen them when she was checking the place for electronic bugs. Why hadn't a single one of them beeped? What was the point of a fancy electronic-alarm system if a blazing fire didn't set it off?

Her mind wasn't alert enough to come up with any answers. She let the bustle of activity ebb and flow around her, glad that nobody seemed to be paying her any attention. She thought she might just about manage to hold herself together, provided nobody spoke to her.

"Where the hell is the fire truck? What's keeping them? They're supposed to have a maximum six-minute response time! Ben, how long since you called Emergency?"

Andrew's voice. Andrew? The name echoed and reechoed inside her skull, flowing through her veins, filling her with fear. Andrew wasn't supposed to be here. He was supposed to be in Tallahassee, working to get himself elected to the governorship of the great state of Florida. Steeling herself to turn and look, Dianna swiveled around.

She hadn't been mistaken—as if she could ever mistake the mellow, aristocratic timbre of Andrew's voice. Claire's father. He was there, standing in the center of the patio, organizing the members of his household into a human chain that was scooping buckets of water out of the pool and dousing down the walls of the cabana. He was working as hard as anyone, sweating with the effort of drawing water from the pool. *Bully for Andrew. What a great guy in a time of crisis! Let's make sure the media hears what a hero he was tonight.*

Dianna shivered. It was freezing cold. Odd that it should feel so cold in Florida during the summer. She rubbed one icy foot against her shin, and then the other, before turning back to stare once again at the cabana. Despite Andrew and his pails of water, the fire had taken stronger hold. She could hear the crackle of burning wood, the pop and snap of exploding plastic. *Snap, crackle, pop.* A catchy jingle. She stared, spellbound, at the dancing flames.

"You need to move away. Sparks might start flying and you could get burned." Ben's voice spoke from behind her. She heard him—understood that he was right—but her body was incapable of complying with her mental order to move.

"Dianna." He said her name softly, urgently. She stared ahead, afraid that if she moved she would shatter, like blown glass struck too soon from the end of the pipe.

Ben's arm went around her shoulders. She found his touch oddly reassuring, but she still didn't dare to move. "We need to get away from the cabana," he repeated.

She managed to speak. "It's cold."

He gave her a swift, incredulous glance. Then he took her hands and chafed them gently. "You are cold," he agreed. "Come on, let's go and sit over there by the pool. That way, we won't be underfoot when the fire fighters arrive."

The warmth of his arm around her waist took away some of the chill, and the shivers jarring her body slowly stopped. Maybe she wasn't quite as fragile as she feared, Dianna thought. She licked her lips and found that she could produce an entire sentence if she spoke carefully. "Why are the fire fighters taking so long to arrive? What's happened to them?"

"It seems like a long time, I know, but it's only been five minutes since I called 911. But they're on their way. Listen."

She cocked her head, suddenly able to hear the clang of fire engines approaching, the wail of their sirens getting louder by the second. She swallowed, sick with relief. Help was at hand. Nobody was going to die. Not tonight. Not again. She was fiercely glad that she'd woken up in time to warn Hal. Not even Hal deserved to die in a fire.

"When did Andrew get back?" She hadn't meant to ask the question, but her mental guard was down and it just tumbled out, willy-nilly. "He was supposed to be in Tallahassee," she added, trying to explain her interest.

"His meetings finished early, and his plane was still on standby at the airport, so he came home. He arrived here a few minutes before you and Roger." Ben pushed her gently into a poolside lounger and sat down next to her, keeping hold of her hands. "It's going to be okay, Dianna," he said. "The fire fighters will have this blaze under control in no time at all. Thanks to you and Hal, we caught it in good time."

"Yes, sure. They'll soon have it under control." Reaction had begun to set in and her teeth chattered. She clenched her jaw, trying to force back the evidence of her fear. She needed to say something so that people wouldn't realize how scared she was. She didn't want—people—to realize how afraid she was.

"The smoke detectors weren't working," she said, grabbing at the first thought that floated across her mental horizon. "There are four of them in the cabana. None of them worked."

He was silent for less than a split second, but she sensed his hesitation. "You're right. That's something we'll have to look into."

"Good news, folks! The firemen are here!" Andrew's voice boomed across the patio, sounding authoritative and impressively calm. Dianna glanced toward the pool and saw a squad of fire fighters swarm around the trellis from the direction of the driveway. They looked sturdy and reassuringly efficient in waders and heavy, protective jackets. Perversely, their arrival provoked her into a fresh bout of shivering.

"Anyone inside the cabana? Anyone hurt?" a paramedic called out.

"No, we're all safely accounted for," Roger said. He caught Dianna's eye and gave her a quick, reassuring smile before turning to speak to his father.

"That's good news." The burly chief was already herding the straggling chain of amateur fire fighters in the direction of the main house. "You've done great, folks, but now we need you to step inside so that we can deploy our equipment. If you'll stay off the patio, my crew will have this situation under control in just a few minutes. Inside now, please." While the chief was speaking, his men were already unrolling yards of heavy hose, aiming the giant spray nozzles at the glowing cabana.

"Come on, we'd better do what the chief says." Ben tucked his arm around Dianna's waist and pulled her onto her feet.

She spoke through clenched lips. "I need to stay out here where I can see them working."

"No problem," he said, as if her request were the most normal in the world. "My bedroom faces directly toward the cabana. We'll be able to watch the fire fighters from there without making the chief mad at us. Look, they're killing the flames already."

He started to walk toward the house, but she didn't follow him, just stared blind-eyed at the choking black smoke billowing from the cabana. With a small, impatient sound, he marched back and put his hands on her shoulders, twisting her around so that he effectively blocked her view of the fire. Frenzied, she wriggled in his grasp but he was too strong for her. He clamped her against his chest, grasping her chin with his spare hand and forcibly preventing her from turning around.

"Dianna, the firemen have everything under control. Do you hear me?"

She stared through him, not speaking, and he lowered his voice to a soothing murmur. "Dianna, listen to me. No one's going to get hurt. It's okay. Everything's fine. The fire will be out in just a few minutes. The main house won't even have smoke damage. Now let me get you off the patio before the firemen start yelling at you. And at me, too."

At last, his words pierced the fog clouding her brain. She looked up at him, blinking dazedly. "That's better," he said, voice warm with approval. "You're back with me again, aren't you?"

She drew in a shuddering breath, then nodded. "Yes. I'm all right now."

"You're more than all right. You're terrific." His mouth curved into a smile and he gave her an approving pat on the shoulder. "Think you can walk into the house or do I have to pull a Rhett Butler and carry you?"

"I can walk." To prove her point, she strode stiff-legged across the patio, not entirely grateful for the fact that Ben had succeeded in pulling her back from the edge of her emotional precipice. There were times when emotional numbness felt a whole lot better than any of the alternatives.

Ben led her into the house through a side door, away from the main crowd of people gathered in the vestibule. "Are you sure you want to watch the firemen working?" he asked softly. "If so, my bedroom's the best place."

"Yes, I want to watch them."

Once inside his room, he dragged a chair across to the window, drawing back the drapes and the sheer curtains so that she could see out. He gestured to the chair. "Be my guest."

Ben's window afforded only a narrow glimpse of the pool and the main patio, but, as he had claimed, the cabana was directly opposite, in full view. Dianna stared at the fire fighters in silent concentration, her tension unwinding as they rapidly brought the blaze under control. There was almost no wind to whip up the flames, and just enough of a gentle breeze to dissipate the smoke into the night air. Within minutes it was evident that the cabana would survive, blackened and charred but structurally intact. The interior would be soaking wet and stink of smoke, but her clothes and belongings were all in the bedroom and might even be salvageable.

She only realized that Ben had been standing silently beside her when the fire fighters began to roll up their hoses and remove their equipment. She watched until she saw Andrew come out of the house onto the patio. He shook the chief's hand, obviously congratulating him. Feeling nauseated, Dianna turned away.

"The fire fighters did an excellent job," Ben said, breaking the silence.

"Yes."

He touched her cheek in a gesture that was at once reassuring and impersonal. "Everything's going to be okay, you know."

"Sure, it is."

"Dianna..." He hesitated for a moment. "Are you feeling all right?"

She wanted to laugh, or maybe cry, but her throat was too sore and all that emerged was a harsh, broken cackle. "I'm fine," she said, shaping the words carefully over the parched dryness of her throat. "Relatively speaking."

"What does that mean?" he asked. "'Relatively speaking'?"

"It means that I'm doing fine," she replied. "Given that somebody just tried to kill me."

The fire fighters had all gone, and everyone had returned to bed, trying to catch some rest for what was left of the night. The cabana was standing, a sodden, soot-streaked mess that would require weeks to refurbish. Unfortunately, his bedroom was on the south side of the house and he could barely see the results of his handiwork from inside his room. He had to crane his neck at just the right angle, and then he was rewarded with no more than a glimpse of a blackened corner of the cabana's living room, with its floor-length curtains fluttering, wet and ruined, in the breeze.

Still, he was pleased and excited by the drama of the night's events. The fire had been the work of a sudden impulse, but he had a talent for swift planning and creative improvisation, so he'd managed to arrange the practical details of setting the fire without much difficulty. His schedule was widely known, and didn't leave much time for taking care of personal business, but Dianna Mason's arrival had thrown everyone slightly off-center, and it had been easier than he'd expected to find twenty minutes to sneak into the guest cabana and dismantle the smoke detectors. It helped that he'd personally overseen the installation of the fire alarms and the internal security system. For an experienced arsonist, tonight's effort had been kindergarten stuff.

He'd watched Dianna's reaction to the blaze as closely as he could without drawing attention to himself, relishing the sight of her pale, taut features and the occasional glimpse of her panicky shudders. Despite the need to pretend that he was working hard to extinguish the flames, he'd been able to see that she was deeply and profoundly terrorized. Unfortunately, he hadn't been able to hang around and relish the stimulating sensation of being washed by her waves of fear.

He had Ben Maxwell to thank for that little failure. Why the hell had Ben chosen to appoint himself as Dianna Mason's protector? The guy had positively glued himself to her side out there on the patio, making it impossible for anyone else to get near without causing comment. Sometimes it seemed like Ben had an infallible instinct for sticking his nose right in the middle of other people's private business. Useful as he'd been in restoring the family fortune, maybe it was time to get rid of him. He'd never really liked Ben. Having been surrounded with straight-arrow guys all his life, he found them boring.

He paced the room, torn between irritation and the pleasant stimulation caused by the fire. He didn't have the smallest doubts about Dianna Mason's identity. He'd recognized her at once, the moment he first clapped eyes on her. Why had she chosen to come back now? he wondered. He could guess at several possible answers, and all of them meant trouble. That was another reason why he'd set the fire. It had been intended in the nature of a little friendly warning—a reminder of what happened to people who intruded where they weren't wanted.

Back off, had been his basic message. *Don't try to insinuate yourself into the family, or you'll live to regret the attempt.*

Seeing the cabana erupt in flames had been amusing, but he had to admit it wasn't a long-term solution to his problems. He prided himself on being an honest self-critic, and the truth was, he'd acted tonight with a certain degree of self-indulgence. The chances of Dianna Mason dying in the fire had been slim to none.

However, he'd delivered his warning, and it was up to Dianna to heed it. If she chose to ignore his message, then she and Hal Doherty would die. His conscience wasn't troubled by that realization. Dianna had no right to lay claim to the Campbell fortune, and Hal's ethics were intolerable to anyone with the smallest degree of moral sensitivity.

But he would have to be careful about his alibi if it became necessary to plan their deaths. No more fires, he decided regretfully. The coincidence of any more fires might cause people to start asking some very awkward questions. With so many people demanding a piece of his time, his account of his movements would hold up only as long as it wasn't scrutinized.

At the moment he was perfectly safe. Nobody suspected him. Nobody had seen him. Not even Dianna, although her instinct for survival was positively uncanny. He'd been so certain she was asleep when he crept into her bedroom. How the hell had she managed to wake up in time to drag herself out of bed *and* rescue Hal Doherty? He frowned. It was really annoying that neither of them had sustained so much as a mild case of smoke inhalation. The fire had been fun, but watching the ambulance rush victims to the hospital would have made the whole night twice as exciting.

All in all, he wasn't sorry that Dianna had decided to stake her claim. Life had seemed flat recently, despite all his efforts to inject a little excitement into his routine. Even the campaign for governor wasn't providing him with the sort of stimulation he'd anticipated. Dianna's arrival added the intoxicating spice of danger to everything he did. He always welcomed the challenge of pitting his wits against a worthy opponent. And Dianna Mason looked like the most worthy opponent he could ever hope to find.

He drew back from the window, still high on the excitement of the night. God, he'd almost forgotten how great it felt when you watched the flames of a fire you'd set creep toward their goal! He'd had an iron-hard erection ever since he'd held his disposable cigarette lighter to the kerosene-soaked towel that he'd dropped by the front door of the cabana. He stroked himself pensively. Should he let the tension build some more? Or was it time for relief?

A quiet knock at the door punctuated his thoughts. He tightened the belt of his robe, concealing his state of arousal beneath the navy blue toweling, and walked across the room, tingling with pleasure as he anticipated the probable need for evasion and deceit. Nothing stimulated him more than the feeling he was putting one over on the rest of the world. "Yes?" he said. "Who is it?"

"It's me, Sharon." Her voice was low, hesitant, the way he liked it. He'd explained to her that women should never be the aggressors, in sex or in life, and she'd cottoned on to it right away.

He covered a split second of disappointment that it wasn't Dianna, or Ben. Right now, a joust with either of those two would have been more pleasurable than sex. But it was very convenient that Sharon had arrived in time to take care of his physical needs. A good omen, perhaps? An indication that the gods were smiling on him, promising him his just rewards?

He opened the door. "Hello, Sharon. How thoughtful of you to stop by. What can I do for you, my dear?"

She glanced up at him, knowing exactly how to play the game. "I'm so scared," she said, letting her silk robe fall open so that he could see the tips of her nipples protruding over the skintight embrace of her teddy. "The fire frightened me so much that now I can't sleep."

"I'm sorry to hear that," he said, reaching out and running his finger along the edge of her teddy. She squirmed with satisfying fervor. He prided himself on the expertise of his sexual techniques, gained after years of experiment and practice, but he expected his partners to display appropriate gratitude for his thoughtfulness. "How can I help you, my dear?"

"Let me sleep in your bed," she whispered. "I'll be very, very good."

He laughed. "I'll make sure that you are, my dear." In a single fluid motion, he dropped his robe and pulled her into his arms, kicking the door shut behind them. "Don't worry, Sharon, I'll take care of you."

"I know," she said. "You always do."

Six

Tonight's blaze had taught Ben at least one truth about Dianna Mason's background: At some time, somewhere, she'd been trapped and burned in a fire. No one, not the greatest actress in the world, could have turned in the performance that she'd given out on the patio. The wide eyes and the rigid posture might have been faked, but her almost-catatonic lack of awareness of everything save the fire and the men fighting it conveyed a fear so deeply rooted that Ben had found it painful to watch.

He wondered if her other outrageous claim had also been true. Tonight, she'd said, someone had tried to kill her. Was she right? And if so, who needed her dead?

Dianna certainly believed she'd been the intended target. Ben could see that despite her desperate attempt to appear self-possessed, she was teetering on the very edge of an emotional meltdown. Her face was pale, her eyes darkly shadowed, and she looked fine-drawn with stress. At some point during the night she must have brushed her hair out of her eyes, and a streak of soot started at her right cheekbone, ran in a wavy line over her nose, then disappeared into her eyebrow. For some reason, he found the soot incredibly endearing.

Ben smothered a crazy impulse to walk across the room, sweep her into his arms, and promise her that he would always protect her from life's hazards. As chief operating officer of Campbell Industries, he couldn't afford to give in to his kinder instincts. He needed to push Dianna over the brink, not offer her comfort and sympathy. Pitching his voice so that it betrayed nothing except cold, analytic curiosity, he looked straight at her.

"Why do you think someone is trying to kill you?" he asked. "Accidents happen all the time, you know. Just because the cabana caught fire, you can't assume some wandering pyromaniac is out to get you."

He'd noticed before that pressure simply strengthened her backbone—an inconvenient trait he couldn't help but admire. In response to his curtness, she somehow managed to gather her frayed emotions and weave them into renewed defiance. Drawing herself up to her full height, she flashed him one of the sardonic glances that always inspired him with an irrational longing to fling her onto a bed and ravish her into a state of humility. Or at least to ravish her.

She swung away from him, sinking into the nearest chair and speaking with more than a hint of impatience. "For God's sake, Ben, how far do you want to stretch the long arm of coincidence? Claire disappeared after the Campbell vacation cabin in Vermont burned to the ground. Scarcely more than twelve hours after I arrive here, claiming to be Claire Campbell, the guesthouse where I'm sleeping catches on fire. Under the circumstances, wouldn't you agree that I seem to have badly rattled somebody's cage?"

"Could be, except for one rather inconvenient fact. If that fire was purposely set, the most likely arson-

ists are you and Hal. The pair of you had motive,
means and opportunity. Which, I might point out, is
damn near all an official investigator would need in
order to bring charges."

"What?" Her fatigue vanishing, Dianna jumped up
from the chair, eyes flashing, spine rigid with righ-
teous indignation. She stormed across the room, her
long bare legs flashing beneath her T-shirt. Ben tried
hard not to stare at her legs. He failed. She halted a
couple of feet away from him and plonked her hands
on her hips, unintentionally hitching up the hem of her
T-shirt another enticing and frustrating inch. Ben felt
himself start to sweat.

"I can't believe even you would sink low enough to
say that!" she exclaimed. "Hal and I nearly get murdered in our beds and you accuse *us* of setting the
damn fire! Why in the world would we do something
so crazy—so downright stupid?"

He was having a hard time remembering what it was
they were arguing about. "I didn't accuse you of setting the fire," he said, trying to collect his wits. "I
simply suggested that you and Hal were the most logical suspects."

"Why?" She sounded genuinely perplexed. "How
would firing the cabana benefit Hal or me?"

He forced his gaze away from her legs, and found
himself mesmerized by her mouth instead. He cleared
his throat, determined to focus on their discussion and
not on the fact that she had just about the most kiss-
able lips he'd ever seen. "How would a fire benefit
you?" he asked. "Here's the most obvious way. Hal
calls a meeting with me tomorrow morning, and an-
nounces—with great regret—that he had crucial documents proving your identity as Claire Campbell

packed in his briefcase. Sadly, they were all burned in the fire."

He watched the color come and go in her cheeks as she acknowledged the plausibility of his suggestion. "Hal's quite capable of doing something like that," she admitted. "But he'd simply be taking advantage of the fire after the fact. Hal's an opportunist. That doesn't make him an arsonist."

"But your claim to be Claire Campbell sure gives him a strong motive for starting the fire, doesn't it? And you, too." Ben was finding it harder and harder to remain objective, so he spoke with extra crispness. "We both know that Hal never had a single piece of solid evidence to back up his claim that you're Claire Campbell, but because of the fire tonight, I'll never be able to prove it."

"You can't pin this fire on Hal," she said fiercely, her voice huskier than ever with indignation. "He was snoring his head off when it broke out. I had to shake him hard, and yell at him a couple of times before I could wake him. He had nothing to do with what happened tonight, I swear it."

It was easy enough to snore lustily and feign deep sleep, Ben reflected, but for some reason he didn't point that out to Dianna. Maybe he'd warn her tomorrow to watch her back. For the moment, she had enough worries without wondering if her partner in crime was out to get her. "Can anyone back up your story that Hal was sleeping?" he asked. "Did anyone see you struggling to wake him?"

"Only the person who set the fire," she said. "I bet he was lurking behind the bushes, getting off on our panic. That's half the pleasure for an arsonist, isn't it?

Seeing how distraught his victims are, watching their fear as the fire takes hold."

"So I've heard." Ben poured two small glasses of orange juice from the pitcher on his nightstand and handed one to Dianna. Her hand shook as she took the juice, and he said gently, "Here, drink this, your throat must be dry."

"Thanks." She sipped thirstily. "That tastes good."

Ben nodded. "You're lucky to have woken up so quickly, given that the alarms didn't go off. What roused you? Do you remember?"

She shook her head. "I'm not sure, except that I'd never really gone to sleep. Right before I got up, I had this creepy feeling somebody was in my room, watching me while I slept, except I wasn't really sleeping—" She broke off. "Let's not waste time going over this. There's not a shred of evidence to back up my story."

"Not so far," Ben agreed. "But then the investigation hasn't begun. Who knows what the fire marshal will turn up?"

"Probably nothing. You're right. Hal and I are the logical suspects. The investigators aren't going to believe my version of events. Why should they? I wouldn't believe my story if I were the fire chief." Dianna put her glass on the tray and resumed her pacing. "*Damn!* He always manages to stay one step ahead."

"Who? The fire chief?" For a moment, Ben couldn't follow her train of thought. "Or do you mean Hal?"

She picked up a book from his bedside, then put it down again without even glancing at the title. "I didn't mean anything, I was just rambling." She smiled without mirth. "Do you hear that noise?"

"No. What noise?"

Her smile tightened. "Listen up, Mr. Maxwell, you should be able to hear it loud and clear. I think it's the jail door clanging shut behind me."

Ben had noticed before that she had this damnable knack for sounding most innocent when she admitted to the greatest appearance of guilt, but he was determined not to succumb to the lure of her husky voice and too-bright blue eyes. "You won't get any arguments from me," he said. "There's some formidable circumstantial evidence against the pair of you. For a start, we can almost discount the possibility of an outside arsonist. Not only is the house itself ringed by an electronic security fence, but there are eight-foot brick walls around the perimeter of the golf course, and twenty-four-hour security guards at both entrances. There hasn't been a single reported case of unauthorized entry since this development was opened."

"You're preaching to the converted," she said, sounding weary. "We both know this was an inside job."

Her refusal to plead her case made him angry. "Are you admitting you and Hal set the fire?" he snapped.

"You know I'm not. Just refusing to debate with someone whose mind is already made up."

He drew in a deep breath and counted to ten. "Humor me," he said. "Remember I'm just a dumb corporate suit. Explain to me how somebody managed to creep across a two-hundred-foot patio without being seen, unlock the cabana door, cut the links to the main security system, and then deactivate four smoke detectors, without either you or Hal noticing what was going on."

"That's not impossible," she said, rubbing her hand up and down her arms as if she felt chilled. "In fact, it's not even difficult. The cabana isn't locked during the day, and I'm sure dozens of people, including all the part-time domestic help, would be able to acquire a key if they really wanted to."

"Okay, but that only solves a small part of the problem. Once he's inside, how does your would-be arsonist avoid detection?"

"Easily. Neither Hal nor I was home until late tonight, so the arsonist could have made his preliminary arrangements for starting the fire during the time the guesthouse was empty. If you saw one of the cleaning crew coming out of the cabana, would you give it a second thought? Of course, you wouldn't. What if you saw a cleaning person standing on a chair, fiddling with something stuck up on the ceiling? You wouldn't even break stride as you passed by. The same goes for Roger and Andrew. The very fact that this place is so well patrolled gives everyone a false sense of security. I noticed none of the patio doors opening into the house were locked earlier today, although service crews came to clean the pool, weed the flower beds and fix the awnings."

"You make the place sound like a Grand Central Station for potential criminals."

"It certainly isn't the protected island you all imagine it to be. Have you ever noticed that the only way rich people can maintain their illusion of privacy is by pretending that service crews and domestic helpers aren't real people with eyes, ears and brains?"

"You're right," Ben said.

"What?" She stopped in mid-diatribe, bumping into a chair in her surprise.

He grinned. "You're right," he repeated. "I agree with you. Upwards of a dozen people could have tampered with the smoke detectors in the cabana."

Her skin turned an enchanting shade of pink. "Don't start sounding too reasonable, Maxwell, or I'll get confused."

"I'm not entirely converted to your point of view," he said. "I still think it's better than a fifty-fifty chance that Hal set the fire. But I'm willing to give you the benefit of the doubt."

In fact, he would have staked high odds on the theory that if Hal set the fire, Dianna hadn't been his accomplice. A triumph of hope and hormones over reason? Ben wondered. If Dianna was a criminal impostor, why couldn't she also be an arsonist?

He didn't want to pursue his own thoughts to their logical conclusion, so he changed the subject. "We shouldn't waste time second-guessing the outcome of the fire marshal's investigation," he said. "Who knows? Despite our conviction that it was an inside job, maybe he'll find evidence that the fire was started by a longtime criminal who broke into the grounds and picked the cabana at random."

"Wouldn't that be nice for all of us?" she murmured. "Just like in Vermont. A convenient scapegoat for a tragic accident. Everything swept under the rug. Ben Maxwell continues to churn out profits and Andrew Campbell stays right on the fast track to election."

Ben was impatient with her repeated attempts to portray the fire in Vermont as an unsolved mystery. "You're tying together events that have absolutely no connection. Andrew's election campaign has damn-all to do with the guesthouse catching fire. How could it? And as far as the accident in Vermont is concerned, there isn't a shred of evidence to suggest that Ted Jenkins's confession was coerced."

"Of course not," she said. "That's why it's so clever."

Ben normally considered himself the calmest and most rational of men. When he was with Dianna, however, his moods swung from benign to irritated in the space of a heartbeat. He hung on to his vanishing patience with grim determination. "Let's stick to the problem of tonight's fire, shall we? So far, we're making lots of assumptions on the basis of zero evidence. Maybe we'd do better to wait for the official report."

For a moment, she didn't reply. Then she gave a short, exasperated laugh and walked over to the window, pressing her forehead against the glass and staring in frustrated silence at the blackened walls of the cabana. "It wasn't supposed to be like this," she said at last, her voice muffled. "When I came here, I thought..."

"What did you think?"

She drummed her fingers restlessly against the windowpane. "Nothing. Nothing important. This isn't working out the way I expected, that's all."

"Scams rarely do." He realized that he wanted, very badly, for her to turn around and swear to him that she wasn't part of Hal's scam. Of course, she didn't. He already understood her well enough to know that she never defended her own integrity, or the purity of her motives. Most of the time, she seemed to delight in flaunting the sheer improbability of her claim to be the long-lost Campbell heiress.

Their bodies were reflected as blurred shadows in the darkened window and when she finally answered him, she talked to his reflection, not directly to him. "Why are you so convinced I'm an impostor, Ben?"

He opened his mouth to list some of the many reasons why she couldn't be Claire Campbell. "I'm not convinced you're an impostor," he heard himself say.

She gave him a wry smile. "You didn't mean to say that, did you?"

"No," he admitted, and their gazes met in the shadowy darkness of the window. Dianna's insubstantial image seemed to smile back at him with an expression that was wistful, almost yearning. He blinked, trying to dismiss the illusion, but it was seared onto his inner eye. When had he started to consider the possibility that Dianna Mason might in truth be Claire Campbell? he wondered. The answer came swiftly. Right around the same moment that her overwhelming sex appeal began to destroy the remnants of his common sense. He turned abruptly, pouring himself another glass of juice just so that he would have an excuse to look away, as well as something to do with his hands.

"Think about this for a minute," Dianna said. "If Claire is alive and anxious to rejoin her family, how could she prove her identity to everyone's satisfaction?"

He noticed that she referred to Claire in the third person. A slip of the tongue? Or an attempt to remove the conversation from the immediate and personal into the realm of abstract conjecture?

Infuriatingly, he wasn't sure. "There would be documents—" he started to say.

"No." From the corner of his eye he could see her shake her head impatiently. "You know that's not likely. Claire doesn't have any documents. They were burned, or they weren't in her possession at the time of the fire. We've already gone over that several times."

"Then a blood test is the only way," he said.

Her mouth twisted into a tight smile. "And if Claire doesn't want to submit to a blood test?"

He turned to look at her again—he couldn't help it. "I can't think of any reason why the real Claire Campbell would refuse such an obvious way to prove her identity."

She rubbed her fist across her eyes. "You know your problem, Ben? You suffer from a limited imagination. Your concept of human nature is strictly middle-class suburban."

What the hell did that mean? he wondered, watching as she blew onto the window, then drew a curving pattern into the mist created by her breath. C.C. She had drawn Claire's initials.

With a violent sweep of her arm, she wiped out the letters and twisted around to confront him. "Whether or not I'm Claire Campbell, haven't you ever wondered what happened to her?" she demanded. "Haven't you ever asked yourself *why* she disappeared that night and never came back?"

"Of course, I've wondered. Andrew and Evelyn spent almost two years—"

She cut him off with a fierce chopping gesture. "No, I only want to talk about you, and what you think. If I'm not Claire, then where is she? Why hasn't she come back? It's been almost seven years since the fire in Vermont. What the heck is she doing with herself?"

"Unfortunately, I'm guessing she's in a mental institution somewhere, suffering from amnesia or some other form of brain damage."

"What if she isn't?" Dianna shifted her weight from one foot to the other, as if she were too full of pent-up tension to stand still. "You saw the fire tonight. In your heart of hearts, you know it was aimed at me. What if Claire is scared? What if she's stayed hidden all these years because she thinks someone in her family is trying to murder her?"

Ben had the sudden, bizarre sensation of the ground moving beneath his feet, shifting his perspective so radically that Dianna's features slipped out of focus. As if he were viewing her through a hall of distorting mirrors, he had the bewildering impression that the woman he saw in front of him was not Dianna Mason pretending to be Claire Campbell, but Claire Campbell pretending for unfathomable reasons to be Dianna Mason pretending to be Claire Campbell. He stepped forward, instinctively reaching out to touch her, needing physical contact in order to realign his vision, to sharpen the blurred, confusing images that pranced across his inner vision.

If he'd hoped that touching Dianna would anchor him back to reality, he'd made a major miscalculation. As soon as his hand grazed her cheek, she went absolutely still, and when he tilted her head back so that he could see her more clearly, their bodies fused together in a single restless movement. Somehow, despite all Ben's good intentions, they ended up eye to eye, thigh to thigh, and damn near mouth to mouth.

Oh hell, he thought despairingly. *This wasn't supposed to happen.*

She ran her tongue over her lips and his head immediately bent lower. He jerked it up again, clinging to the tattered shreds of his self-control.

"Did my question stun you into silence?" she asked in the soft, husky voice that was calculated to drive him crazy.

What question? "Yes. I mean no." He hadn't the remotest idea in hell what they'd been talking about. He didn't much care what they'd been talking about. He only knew that her skin felt like silk and that she wasn't wearing a bra under her T-shirt. That damned T-shirt, which had been driving him out of his mind all night long. Either because it covered too much of her legs, or because it didn't cover enough. He wasn't quite sure which, and right now he didn't care. Either way, one thing was sure: He wanted to rip the damned shirt off her.

Ben fought to drag air into his lungs. He told himself that having sex with Dianna Mason was a lousy idea, one of the very worst ideas that he'd come up with in a long time. Quite apart from the fact that she would probably land a swift uppercut on his jaw if he tried to make any serious moves on her, there were a dozen other solid reasons for keeping their relationship strictly platonic. If his brain would only flip back into functioning mode, he knew he would be able to enumerate all of those good, solid reasons.

His brain, however, refused to engage in gear. His hand, meanwhile, shifted from Dianna's face, stroked impatiently across her shoulders and came to rest on the curve of her breast. He felt her nipple grow taut, and her breath expelled in a tiny, rippling sigh. Ben's entire lower body throbbed with desire. His head once again started its downward descent toward her mouth. With disastrous—or blissful—timing, Dianna tipped her chin upward. Without thinking, he crushed his mouth to hers.

In the first blinding instant of contact, Ben felt as if he was being consumed. He had never shared a kiss like this before, never experienced the sensation of melting deep into an embrace. He couldn't control the explosion of white-hot desire, the flare of passion that raced hotfooted through his veins, leaving his body vibrating with need.

"Open your mouth." He rasped the words against her lips, his tongue stroking roughly, while his hands held her captive and his knee rammed between her legs with all the sophisticated subtlety of a Mack truck on a downhill grade.

God knows why, but she didn't seem to mind his fumbling urgency. She clasped her hands behind his neck, holding his mouth pressed against hers. She parted her lips and his tongue thrust deep. *Jesus, she tasted good!* For a moment or two, Ben reveled in the supple, pliant feel of her body rubbing against his, and the hot, moist taste of her mouth, but foreplay wasn't enough—would never be enough to satisfy an aching sexual hunger that grew more demanding the longer their kiss continued.

Ben liked to think of himself as a chivalrous lover, a sensitive man of the nineties, who understood his partner's needs and never forgot that good sex required tact, mutual consideration, and lots of tenderness. But right now, he was incapable of considering Dianna's needs. Through the dark, hot blur of his desire, images flashed with compelling, intoxicating brightness. Dianna naked on his bed. Dianna, legs opening to receive him. Dianna, hot and slick, closing tightly around him as he plunged into her. Dianna, convulsed with passion, shuddering into orgasm. He could already picture how she would look when she came, with her skin flushed, her eyes closed, overwhelmed by the intensity of pleasure *he* had given her.

The images brought him right to the brink of climax, and he tensed, lifting his head away from her mouth just long enough to swing her up into his arms. She was whispering his name, her voice urgent, her body stiff—with desire. He was sure it must be with desire.

"Ben, put me down. We have to stop this."

He heard her speak, even heard the slight tremble in her voice, but he didn't hear the individual words, and he certainly didn't grasp their meaning. Like the flames that had ignited the cabana, the force of his need burned into him, laying waste his reason. Obsessed with the wish to get her into his bed, he merely heard her voice flow over him in a husky murmur that carried no threat, no warning. He couldn't stop to talk, or they would end up coupling on the floor. He wanted better for her than that. Sweet Dianna. She was so wonderfully, passionately responsive. His arms tightened about her body. God, she was magnificent!

She pummeled his chest with hard, determined force. Then she spoke again, her voice husky, a little breathless, but otherwise totally controlled. "Ben, stop this. You must listen to me."

"Yes," he lied, skirting the foot of the bed. "I'm listening, honey." The endearment tripped easily off his tongue.

"Claire Campbell died five years ago in Trenton General Hospital. I have a copy of her death certificate in my suitcase."

Ben stumbled to a halt beside the bed. He knew he'd heard something totally astonishing—totally unwelcome—but he wasn't sure what. Muscles slack with shock, his grip on Dianna loosened. She dropped out of his arms onto the bed. He stared down at her, stupid with foiled lust. "What did you say?"

She scrambled off the bed, dragging the cover with her and moving away from him before speaking again. Ben found himself staring at her mouth, watching her shape the words, as if he were deaf and needed to lip-read in order to understand plain English.

"I said that Claire Campbell died five years ago after her car crashed on the New Jersey Turnpike. I have a copy of her death certificate in my suitcase."

She stared straight ahead, making her stunning announcement without expression and without a trace of remorse. Ben stared back at her, struggling to make sense of a confession that should have been quite easy to grasp, and shouldn't have surprised him in the least.

He tried to let the meaning of her words sink in. Claire Campbell was dead, killed in a road accident. Which meant that Dianna Mason was an impostor. Just as everyone had suspected, she and Hal Doherty were working a scam.

Simple concepts, Maxwell. No surprises. Start thinking with your brain instead of your penis and you should be able to grab a hold of them.

He drew in a deep breath and then another, but his voice still came out less steady than he'd have liked. "Is this a formal admission that you attempted to commit fraud, Ms. Mason? That you impersonated a dead woman in the hope of gaining illegal profit?"

Bloody, damn ridiculous to act so pompous when he was sweating with the aftermath of unfulfilled lust. He watched as her mouth quirked into a faint smile. "I'm not sure I'd call this a *formal* admission, Mr. Maxwell."

Ben almost smiled back at her. She was tucking the bedspread under her arms and he had a spectacular, split-second glimpse of long, bare leg before she was cocooned within the folds of white woven cotton. For a moment he wanted her again with such force that he wondered if he should offer her immunity from prosecution in exchange for spending the night in his bed. When he realized what he was contemplating, he turned abruptly, shutting off his view of her, horrified at how close he'd come to violating his personal code of ethics. His opinion of people in a position of power who bought or blackmailed sexual favors was unprintable, and yet he'd nearly suggested the unforgivable. What was it about this woman that caused his brain and his balls to function as if they were damn near interchangeable?

He managed to get his lungs and his larynx functioning more or less in unison. "If this isn't a formal admission, Ms. Mason, then what is it, precisely?"

"I'm not sure," Dianna said. "Precisely. But if you repeat this conversation to any law-enforcement officials, of course I'll deny it."

"Of course." Her aggressive statement finally got his brain flipped into semiworking order, although he didn't risk turning around to look at her. "Are you expecting me to be a party to fraud, Ms. Mason?"

"I expect nothing from you," she said. "You can't be a party to fraud, because my attempt at fraud is over, voluntarily ended by me. I want to leave here as quickly as possible. I renounce my claim to being Claire Campbell. I renounce any possible right to a share in her inheritance. If you'll call me a cab, I'll be ready to leave by the time it gets here. Hal, by the way, doesn't know anything about the fact that the real Claire died in a road accident, so you have no cause to harass him."

"You're admitting that you deceived Hal Doherty as well as everyone else?" Ben asked.

"Yes, I admit that I deceived Hal Doherty. He doesn't know the truth about me." Her voice caught a little on the final word— the first sign that she wasn't quite as much in control as she'd have liked to pretend. "Now may I go, please?"

"Wait a minute. Aren't you forgetting a couple of things, *Ms. Mason?*"

"I don't think so—"

"You've attempted to commit criminal fraud," he said curtly, turning to face her. "On a personal level, you've raised the hopes of Andrew and Evelyn Campbell, and cynically exploited your looks to convince Andrew that his dead daughter is alive. You even had Roger half believing he'd found his long-lost sister. After all that, you expect me to call you a cab and offer you a free ride out of here?"

"Yes, I do." He was furious to see that she looked defiant rather than guilty. What kind of fool was he, anyway, expecting a criminal cheat to demonstrate signs of remorse?

Sickened, he walked to the phone. "I'm calling the police."

"Don't. Please, don't call." She put her hand over his, holding down the receiver. Ben flinched at the contact, and she jumped back, her cheeks flaming with hot color. For the first time, he heard a note of pleading enter her voice.

"Ben, what I've done... It isn't quite as bad as it seems. There were reasons.... I knew Claire after the fire. There were things she'd always wanted resolved.... We'd talked a lot and I made her some promises before she died. Don't... think too badly of me."

He felt a treacherous surge of hope, the yearning to believe that there might be some kind of justification for the scam she and Hal had tried to perpetrate. He killed the hope before it could take root. God knew, his judgment had been way off base from the beginning, where Dianna Mason was concerned. He didn't need to add any more misplaced emotions to the lust and regret already churning around in his gut.

"You deserve to spend time in jail," he said coldly. "Not only because you tried to steal money that isn't yours, but because you played with the deepest emotions of the Campbell family. Even if you really did know Claire—and I'm not sure I believe you did— nothing gives you the right to toy with the grief and the hopes of people who have spent more than six years searching for a missing child. What you've already done is unforgivable. What you tried to do is far worse."

Go to it, Ben jeered silently. *Mouth off enough and maybe you'll stop wishing that she'd waited until after you'd had sex with her before she dropped her bombshell.*

Her eyes went flat. "Whatever Andrew's feelings might be toward me when he hears that I'm an impostor, he'll soon remind you that his campaign for governor is more important than anything else. You don't want all the publicity that would come from having me arrested. Andrew will be the first to tell you he doesn't need that sort of media coverage. And if Andrew doesn't tell you, his campaign manager will."

"What has Andrew's campaign got to do with your fraudulent claims? He's the victim in all this, not the villain."

"Public opinion can be a strange creature. Voters want their elected officials to be supermen, not dupes and victims." Dianna took a long, hard breath and her voice suddenly sounded a little ragged around the edges. "Let me go, Ben, please. It's over. Finished. I'm paying more of a price than you'll ever imagine."

Ben knew the decision to let her go had been made minutes before and that he was demeaning himself more than Dianna by pretending otherwise. He cursed himself for every kind of fool, but he walked over to the phone. "All right," he said, his voice frozen with self-contempt. "Go and get your things. I'll call you a cab."

"Thank you." He thought he heard tears in her voice, but she turned to go and he didn't call her back. It would be crazy to call her back, and he wasn't crazy. Not completely.

The cotton bedspread made a soft whooshing noise as she walked out of his room and closed the door quietly behind her. She obviously trusted him not to call the police, trusted him to call for a cab. But he wasn't about to wax sentimental over that, Ben decided. Thank God she was gone before any real harm had been done.

He'd put her in the cab and that, he promised himself, was the last he'd ever see of Dianna Mason.

Seven

The Honorable Gregory landed on the coffee table with a resounding thump. Three years ago, when Sonya rescued him from the animal shelter, he had been a bag of bones, covered in dingy gray-and-brown-striped fur, and terrified of his own shadow. He was still covered in dingy fur, but he was now fat, and confident in the knowledge that he occupied a central spot in the universe. Sonya ascribed the beneficial changes to a combination of regular dosing with cod-liver oil, and castration; a regimen that she swore would have equally favorable effects on most of the human males of her acquaintance.

Squinting through clouds of smoke puffed from her unfiltered Chesterfield cigarette, Sonya swatted at the cat and retrieved a page of scrawled notes from under his paw. Full of offended dignity, Gregory retreated to the back of the sofa, draping his tail across the top of Dianna's head as a sign that she was still an acceptable human being, even if Sonya was in danger of falling out of grace.

Sonya read through the page of notes, then took a frustrated drag on her cigarette. "Sweetie, we're going cross-eyed trying to dredge up dirt on Andrew Campbell, and there's nothing to dredge. Much as I loathe suggesting this, are you sure you wouldn't like to accept the possibility that the guy is as pure and innocent as his publicity handouts claim?''

Dianna removed Gregory's swishing tail from her forehead. "Are you crazy? Andrew is an aspiring politician, he's a multimillionaire, and he's a real-estate developer. Right there you have three rock-solid reasons to assume he's got a past littered with skeletons."

"Normally, I'd agree with you. But, sweetie, I've been digging for nearly two months now and if Andrew Campbell has skeletons in his past, they're buried in graves so deep you'd need the Army Corps of Engineers to scoop them out. I've tried every angle, called in every favor I can think of. Hell, I even checked out his prep school reports and his college records in case he'd cheated on his exams. Nothing. I tell you, this guy is Mr. Clean with added bleach for perfect whiteness."

Dianna shook her head. "We're missing something. He's outsmarting us."

"Why are you so sure of that?" Sonya fed Gregory a chip loaded with sour-cream/onion dip. He crunched it down with an air of benevolent condescension. "Now his brother Douglas, that's a different story. Douglas wasn't even thirty when he died, but man, he'd packed some living into those few years."

Sonya sounded almost admiring—a rare feat, since she seldom praised male accomplishments. Dianna cleared her throat over a sudden lump. "What did brother Douglas do that's so special? Apart from leave Claire Campbell all his money."

Sonya's brow puckered. "How do you know he left Claire his money?" She answered her own question. "Oh, of course. Hal Doherty and his truckload of files. Yes, you're right, Douglas left Claire umpteen million dollars, which is why she has this huge trust fund and Roger doesn't.''

"I guess there's nothing remarkable about that," Diana said. "Roger wasn't born until a year or two after his uncle died. It's not that Douglas hated him, or anything. Roger simply didn't exist."

"True." Sonya lay back on the sofa, her concentration apparently devoted to blowing multiple smoke rings. "And we don't need to shed tears of sympathy for good ole Roger. Between Grandmother Helen, Mommy Evelyn and Daddy Andrew, he'll probably end up inheriting thirty or forty million bucks."

"At least. Unless Andrew blows the family fortune on his political campaigns."

Sonya sighed. "Jeez, it's a rough life for some people."

"Well, at least he isn't a spoiled brat. He seemed a nice-enough kid, what little I saw of him." Dianna took Gregory onto her lap and stroked him. He stared at her out of muddy green eyes, not quite sure whether to allow her the signal honor of getting his shedding hair all over her jeans. "Tell me what you know about Douglas," she said. "We've never discussed him."

"That's because he's irrelevant as far as Andrew's concerned," Sonya said, grinding the stub of her cigarette into the overflowing ashtray.

"Humor me."

Sonya sighed, but obliged by ticking off points on her fingers. "Douglas was two years younger than Andrew, the second child of Helen and Angus Campbell. Douglas and Andrew looked alike, but their characters must have been at opposite ends of the spectrum. Douglas got all the recklessness, and Andrew got all the quiet virtue."

Dianna snorted at the suggestion that Andrew was virtuous, but Sonya ignored her and continued with her list. "While Andrew was making a solid *B* grade, Douglas flunked fifty percent of his school courses in any given year. He quit college when he was a sophomore, at which point he'd broken most of the major bones in his body pursuing one hazardous sport or another. Andrew's a pretty fair tennis player, but Douglas was a good enough rock climber that he competed internationally, he'd sailed solo across the Atlantic, and he was a serious contender for the U.S. Olympic ski team. And that, sweetie, sums up most of what I know about brother Douglas, apart from the fact that he died much too young."

"He never got selected for the Olympic ski team, did he?"

Sonya shook her head. "Probably because he was too busy screwing the ski bunnies to make early-morning practice."

"Surely to goodness you don't approve of that! Whatever happened to man the predator, man the prowling sexual beast, man the eternal exploiter of women, et cetera, et cetera."

Sonya shrugged. "Hell, you have to admire someone who enjoyed his life so much. Besides, Douglas had principles and talent as well as all the usual male hormonal dysfunctions. He spent time in jail protesting the Vietnam War, and he'd already had a major national exhibit of his glass sculptures by the time he died." She reached for another cigarette, peered into the empty pack and crumpled it in disgust. "That should put him in your good graces if nothing else does. Doesn't anyone who works with glass automatically make it into your canon of saints?''

"It depends how good the work is." Dianna rummaged among the scraps of paper on the coffee table, trying to put them into some sort of order. "Douglas died of leukemia in 1971 when he was twenty-eight and Andrew was in his early thirties. Do you know if they were good friends?''

"Bosom buddies, despite their different personalities. But who cares? There's nothing in their relationship that you can use to bring Andrew down—which means we don't give a damn about Douglas."

So much for Douglas, Dianna thought ruefully. The Honorable Gregory condescended to roll over onto his back and expose his stomach for scratching. She complied, taking comfort in the soft feel of his fur against the tips of her fingers. "What about Sharon Kruger?" she asked. "Have you come up with anything more there?''

"Andrew's cook? She's thirty-three years old, divorced, trained at one of the finest restaurants in Chicago. She goes everywhere Andrew goes, but then he entertains all the time, so why wouldn't he take his cook with him? She's good-looking. You saw her—"

"No, I never did. She must have been out on the patio the night of the fire, but so were dozens of other people, and I never noticed her." Dianna stacked the pile of notes under a millefiori paperweight that she'd made for Sonya. "You have to remember I was in the Campbell house for less than twenty-four hours."

"I know." Sonya sighed with barely concealed regret. "Well, you did right to get out, sweetie, despite all those lovely missed opportunities for searching through Andrew's desk and so on. I never did like the idea of you going in there with nobody to look out for you except Hal Doherty. Having Hal as your protector is like walking into the lion's den with a swizzle stick as your only weapon."

Dianna laughed. "If you'd heard Hal on the phone to me last night, you'd never again compare him to a swizzle stick. He sounded more like the hungry lion, let out of the cage and on the prowl for his dinner. He threatened to sue me for breach of contract, then got hysterical when I pointed out that he wouldn't have much luck convincing a court to award damages because I refused to cooperate in bilking the Campbells out of twenty million dollars."

"It's not a joking matter." Sonya frowned. "Hal's got no money right now, and no prospects, and that can make him downright mean. I should know. He was a chiseler and a cheapskate even when we were in high school together."

Dianna felt herself blush and Sonya stared at her incredulously. "Wait. Don't tell me, let me guess. You've sent the slimy reptile a check, haven't you? You're paying the bastard off out of your hard-earned money! Your *legitimate* hard-earned money!"

"I didn't send him much," Dianna excused herself. "And he did take care of all our out-of-pocket expenses when we were in Florida."

"A few nights in a sleazy motel! Big deal."

"He bought me a lot of clothes, too," Dianna argued. "Besides, you can talk. How come you still see Hal regularly if he's such a slimeball?"

"You know why. We were in school together, right from kindergarten."

Dianna grinned. "Give it up, Sonya. Beneath that fake hard-boiled exterior, you're the softest touch in town. I bet the rest of his classmates dropped him years ago.''

''That's got nothing to do with anything,'' Sonya muttered. ''Hal and I... Hell, if you'd grown up in Wyoming, you'd understand. Our graduating class was fourteen kids and we were the only two who went on to college.'' She jumped up and went to the freezer, coming back with a fresh carton of cigarettes and a package of frozen Dorito corn chips. She tossed the chips toward Dianna, who accepted them resignedly. Sonya alternated between living on junk food and preparing haute cuisine meals that rivaled France's finest restaurants. This was obviously one of her junk-food phases and the Doritos were dinner. With great good luck, there might be eggs and bread and butter in her fridge, so that Dianna could whip up some scrambled eggs on toast before she went home and force Sonya to share it. However, past experience warned Dianna not to count on it.

In fact, Sonya's mood had been slightly off-key all afternoon. Dianna watched as she walked over to the window and threw it open, letting in a rush of hot, humid air. She lit up her cigarette and puffed smoke in the direction of Boston Harbor, her belated concession to saving Dianna from the evil effects of secondhand smoke. ''Sweetie, we have to talk.''

''We've been talking ever since I got here,'' Dianna reminded her.

''Yeah.'' Sonya avoided her eyes. ''We need to talk about this crazy obsession of yours, sweetie.''

''Which obsession?'' Dianna asked, although she knew quite well. ''According to you, I have so many.''

''Andrew Campbell,'' Sonya said, her voice abrupt. ''Right now, he outperforms all your other neuroses

by far. Di, you've got to face facts. Your attitude toward Andrew isn't healthy for you, and it's gotten to
be impossible for me. I can't justify carrying on this
research any longer. My editor loves political scandals, and he accepts I have a nose for scenting them,
so he was willing to cut me some slack, providing I
kept up with my regular assignments. But his patience is long gone. He's told me to quit wasting company time and research money on a project that isn't
going to pay off."

Sonya swung around, her plump body tense, her
dark hair dramatically framed by the billowing white
linen curtain. "He's right, Di. Unless you can give me
a good reason to keep pursuing Andrew Campbell,
I've got to stop this research and move on to something else. What I'm doing now isn't legitimate background investigation of a public figure. It's unwar-
ranted harassment. You're asking me to help you be-
smirch the character of a reputable candidate for
public office, and I can't do that. Not even for you,
sweetie."

Dianna had known this conversation was going to
happen ever since she got back from Florida the week
before. The realization that Sonya was right—at least
from her perspective—didn't make it any easier to listen to her. Dianna's stomach tightened, and her hands
balled into fists, but she knew this was a battle she
wasn't going to win. She smoothed out her hands and
fixed her face into a friendly smile.

"I understand," she said. "Of course I do. Thank
you for all the help you've given me so far. I really
appreciate it, Sonya. I know how many hours you've
put in on this project and I'll try to find some way to
repay you."

Sonya's mouth twisted with frustration. "Dammit, Di, why do you do that?"

"Do what?"

"Freeze people out with cool politeness. For God's sake, yell at me or something. Finding some way to bring Andrew Campbell down is important to you. Don't you care that I'm backing off from the chase?"

"Of course I do—"

"Well, then, try persuading me to keep at it. Or you might even try telling me what the hell this vendetta against Andrew is all about." Sonya stabbed her cigarette into the ashtray with vicious force. "How about sharing a smidgeon of the truth with me, for a change? Or haven't I earned the right to the truth yet? Why do I get the feeling that after four years, I'm still on trial as far as you're concerned? Do you think because I'm gay, there are limits to how far you can trust me?"

"No, of course not!" Dianna was appalled. "Good grief, this has nothing to do with being gay or straight, or anything else. You're my best friend—"

"And you don't trust me worth a damn."

"It's not just you!" Dianna said. "I don't trust anyone!" The urge to yell was overwhelming, but she refused to give in to it. Strong emotion frightened her, because if you felt things too intensely, you lost control. And Dianna had determined the day she left the hospital and enrolled in art school that for the rest of her life, she would always be in control.

The only way to contain her temper was to move. She jumped up and Gregory toppled to the floor, yowling in outrage. She stared down at him, panting with anger. "Sonya, you don't understand—"

"Damn right, I don't." Sonya was more angry than Dianna had ever seen her. "Try enlightening me.

Speak real slow, use nice one-syllable words and you know what? I bet I could understand a whole heap more than you think."

Dianna knew that this was the moment of truth. Unless she leveled with Sonya, their friendship was going to be under a serious strain, and might even disintegrate. She drew in a ragged breath, then another. It had been so long since she'd confided in anyone, that the act of sharing was almost physically painful. "I have a vendetta against Andrew Campbell because he tried to kill Claire," she said, speaking with cold precision. "He tried to murder his own daughter and that's why I know he isn't suited to hold public office."

Sonya's eyes narrowed, but that was her only reaction to Dianna's amazing accusation. "How do you know? Have you got proof?"

"No, I don't have proof—no written documents, or photos, or anything like that. But I'm a hundred-percent positive it's true."

"How? Why? How could you possibly know something like that?"

Dianna picked up the millefiori paperweight, staring at the kaleidoscope of refracted colors. "Because Claire Campbell told me," she said.

Sonya's breath came out in a tiny, audible gasp, but that was the only sign she gave of feeling surprise. For some reason, her face remained dark with anger. "How did you get to know the real Claire Campbell?" she asked. "You're from California, or so you told me. You've only been on the East Coast for a few years. How did you meet her?"

Dianna's mouth twisted in wry memory. "We met in the locked ward of a New York State mental hospital."

Sonya already knew that Dianna had suffered a bout of depression severe enough to put her in the hospital, so she accepted that piece of information without a blink. "If you met Claire in the hospital, presumably she was suffering from acute mental or psychiatric problems. So why do you believe her? Claiming that your father tried to murder you is an outrageous accusation to make about an outstanding citizen like Andrew Campbell. On the other hand, it's just the sort of thing disturbed young women fantasize about."

Dianna found Sonya's attitude odd, obscurely off-key in some way she couldn't quite pinpoint. Why did Sonya express so little surprise on hearing the astonishing fact that Dianna had actually known the real Claire Campbell? And why did she suddenly seem so determined to defend Andrew's reputation? Dianna twisted the paperweight around and around. It was one of the first pieces she'd made after graduating from art school, and she still loved the mysterious swirl of colored strands trapped within its crystal-clear depths. Making beautiful glass was so easy, she thought wistfully. She wished living life was half as simple. She put the paperweight down on the coffee table, searching for the courage to tell Sonya everything. Well, almost everything.

"I met Claire Campbell when I first ran away from home," she said at last. "We spent three months together in the hospital and our friendship was very intense." She smiled ruefully. "When you're confined to a mental institution, you either like your fellow inmates or you loathe them. There's no in-between. And I liked Claire a lot.''

"Liking a mentally unbalanced young woman has nothing to do with believing her wild stories about her father."

Dianna frowned, wondering if she was imagining the defensive note that seemed to have crept into Sonya's voice. "You have to accept my word for it," Dianna said quietly. "Claire was depressed, she was considered at high risk for committing suicide, but she wasn't delusional. I'm sure she told me the truth about her father. She claims he was the person who set the fire that destroyed the Campbell vacation cabin up in Vermont. She says he knew beyond any possibility of doubt that she was inside the cabin when he torched it."

Sonya continued to look disbelieving. "How come she decided to confide in you? She never told anyone else, did she?"

"I don't know. I don't think so. Maybe her psychiatrist, in private sessions."

"Why did she choose you as her confidante?"

"We were roommates in the hospital, and then we shared an apartment after we got out." Dianna hurried on with her explanation. "Naturally, when Claire arrived in the hospital a couple of weeks after me, everyone commented on how alike we were, how we could have been sisters. Anyway, the powers that be decided we should share a room, and that meant we spent a lot of time together, not only talking late at night, but in group therapy, too. Eventually, we got to be really close friends. Our backgrounds were different—she was amazingly rich, my family was amazingly poor—but we discovered that we had a lot in common one way and another. Claire was the person who first convinced me that I might enjoy working with glass. She saw that I really enjoyed messing around with the art projects assigned in our occupational-therapy sessions, and she opened my eyes to some of the possibilities that existed for working with glass."

"So where is she now?" Sonya asked. "Why hasn't she exposed Andrew Campbell herself? I should think one phone call to the media would bring her more print interviews and talk-show engagements than any one woman could handle. Not to mention the fact that I'll bet she could find a few uses for twenty million bucks of pocket money."

Dianna's emotions were too churned up, too close to the surface, after her nerve-racking past few weeks. She felt tears start to trickle down her cheeks. She dashed them away and turned toward the kitchen, unwilling to share her grief. "She's dead. She died in a traffic accident in New Jersey. I've always hoped that it really was an accident, not a horrible way for And—" She broke off abruptly. "She suffered from acute depression and she didn't shake it off as well as I did. She felt totally betrayed by what her father had tried to do. Maybe she wasn't paying as much attention that day as she should have been. The New Jersey Turnpike isn't designed for absentminded drivers."

When she turned around again, Sonya was reaching for her pack of cigarettes. "You know what, sweetie? That's a great story, told with feeling. But I don't believe a single word of it. You forgot I'm an investigative reporter—a damn good investigative reporter—and I've been lied to by the best in the business. Your status as an amateur liar is showing."

Amateur liar? The accusation would have been laughable if it hadn't been so sad. Dianna flushed. "I can't force you to believe me, or to accept that Claire wasn't lying when she claimed her father tried to murder her. If you choose to believe Andrew's publicity machine rather than my story, that's your privilege, I guess." Dianna forced herself to look her friend—her ex-friend?—straight in the eye.

"You should believe me," she said. "Everything I've told you is the truth."

Almost, she added silently. *Almost the truth.*

The argument with Sonya ended, but didn't come to a happy conclusion. After a half hour of excruciating mutual politeness, Dianna gave up and took her leave. She could only hope that before too long, Sonya's natural kindness would take over, and Dianna would be welcomed back into the fold. She had too few friends, far too few, and she couldn't afford to lose someone as warm, generous and caring as Sonya.

Sonya lived in Beacon Hill. Dianna drove home along Storrow Drive, heading for the bridge that would take her across the river to Cambridge. She drove without really being aware of her surroundings, cursing herself for her inability to take the final leap of trust and confide the truth about her past. She bitterly regretted the fact that she hadn't told Sonya everything, and yet, at the thought of turning the car around and going back to her friend's apartment to admit the whole truth, her body broke out in a cold sweat. Dianna knew that her psychiatrist would say that she was taking refuge in silence—the least healthy form of protection for the battered psyche. But silence had worked so well for so long that she was afraid to meddle with success.

Dianna pulled to a halt at the traffic light, drumming her fingers on the steering wheel, not out of impatience, but as a release for nervous tension that could find no other outlet. A horn tooted somewhere behind her, and she glanced into the rearview mirror. The car behind her was a red Mustang, and the driver had sounded his horn to attract the attention of a passing girl, who was pointedly ignoring him. The light changed to green, and as Dianna accelerated forward, she saw the familiar outline of Hal Doherty's battered Toyota following along behind the Mustang.

Not Hal! she thought, groaning aloud. *I can't bear the thought of another confrontation with Hal Doherty.* She contemplated making a U-turn and dashing for a hidey-hole—the crowded area around Harvard Square, perhaps—but she knew Hal would pursue her until he'd had a chance to rant and rave at her face-to-face, so she turned off Massachussetts Avenue and drove back to her studio, reminding herself that she was only getting the punishment she probably deserved.

Miraculously, she seemed to lose him as she turned the car into the alley alongside her studio. Unfortunately, knowing Hal, he wouldn't stay lost for long. He had the address of her studio and would soon find her again. She pressed the electronic button to raise the garage door. Although crime rates in this quieter part of Cambridge were reasonably low, she considered the expenditure on an automatic opener a worthwhile investment in her personal safety. She drove into the garage, closing the door behind her, and killed the car engine with a sigh of relief. This had been a pretty rotten day, but at least when Hal finally resurfaced, she'd be facing him on home ground.

She unlatched the car door and stepped out, clutching her purse and a sheaf of Sonya's research papers. A man stepped out of the shadows.

She started to scream, then stopped when she recognized her visitor.

"Hello," Ben said. "I've been waiting for you."

Eight

After the scene with Sonya, Dianna was definitely not up to the trauma of handling another joust with Ben Maxwell. She pushed past him, refusing to look up. "Go away," she said pettishly. "I don't want to talk to you."

"That's unfortunate. We have lots to say to each other."

"No, we don't." Dianna could hear the childish pout in her voice, but Ben set her nerve endings jangling. When she'd left Sonya's, she had felt tired and wounded, wanting only to return home and brood. She still felt on edge, but in a quite different way. Her lungs couldn't seem to catch enough air, and her pulse raced with anticipation. Bizarre as it seemed, apparently some small part of her actually enjoyed sparring with Ben Maxwell.

Dianna wasn't naive, and she wasn't willfully blind. She recognized sexual attraction when she felt it, but she was having a hard time accepting that she could experience physical desire for a man who represented a major threat to her safety.

In any case, regardless of how she felt, she couldn't afford the luxury of giving in to the dangerous pleasure of an affair with Ben. She strode across the garage, determined to ignore him. Right on the point of entering her studio, a thought occurred to her and she swung around to confront him. "How did you get in here, anyway?"

"I walked in behind your car." He showed no sign of guilt, and even less sign of going away, and Dianna scowled, annoyed with him for looking so damned self-assured, and furious with herself for noticing that he also looked impossibly sexy in a dark, open-necked shirt and loose Armani linen jacket. Right at this moment, she was definitely not in the mood for coping with a sexy man—especially not a sexy man loaded with a frightening surplus of brains and ambition.

"You wasted your time," she repeated, glowering at him. "We have nothing to say to each other. Go home, Ben. I'm sure Andrew has lots of other errands for you to run."

Ben was too smart to respond to her rudeness. Leaning back against the hood of her secondhand Saturn, he crossed his arms and smiled politely. "Andrew didn't send me. He doesn't even know I'm here. You might as well invite me in, you know."

"Why? Give me one good reason."

"I read the autopsy report on Claire Campbell. Who sadly departed this world on April 22, 1989."

Fear rippled over the surface of her skin, leaving her chilled and shaking. How in the world had she made the mistake of thinking that sparring with Ben Maxwell was enjoyable? She flattened her palms against the studio door, instinctively seeking solid support. "I trust it made interesting reading," she said, trying for bored disinterest and failing miserably.

"Fascinating reading. Poor Claire was badly smashed up, you know. Lots of crushed and broken bones, and her hands and face were both burned."

"Yes, I do know. I had to identify the body." She leaned a little harder against the door as memories crowded in. "We shared an apartment for almost a year."

"The autopsy report noted that, too. Dianna Mason, roommate, was listed as the person who'd identified the corpse. That was you, I guess?"

"That was me." She winced, hating the memories, afraid to probe to find out how much more he knew. "Look, Ben, I'm busy. Unlike most of the people you know, I have to work for a living. Does this conversation have a point?"

"It certainly does," he said. "I came all the way from Florida just to make it."

"Gee whiz, and if Andrew didn't send you, I guess you didn't get to travel in the private jet. Which means you flew in a regular, public plane for no reason."

"I don't think so," he said. His voice was gentle, his expression mild, but Dianna wanted to turn and run somewhere far, far away. "I believe I have an excellent reason to be here, and this is it. According to the coroner's report, Claire Campbell's height when she died was five feet five inches."

"That's a pretty average height for a woman." Dianna wondered if he could see how much effort it was costing her to respond with a show of polite indifference and nothing more. "Is it supposed to hold some deep and dark significance?"

The look he gave her was penetrating enough to strip the flesh from her bones. "Claire Campbell was five feet eight inches tall when she had a medical exam right before entering college. She was still five feet eight when she went with her mother to be measured for a custom-designed, full-length leather coat one week before she disappeared. But somehow, when she died in New Jersey less than two years later, she was only five feet five. Isn't that curious? Can you suggest what might have happened to her missing three inches? Somehow, she seems to have lost more than an inch a year.'' Ben gave a predatory smile. ''I'm extremely interested in your reply, *Ms. Mason.*''

''I doubt it,'' she said, turning to open the door, because if she moved, he might not see that she was trembling. ''My best guess is that the coroner goofed in taking his measurements. I'm sure it happens.''

''Could be. Except this report was prepared by a trainee, a pathologist who was still in his residency. And every measurement he made was double-checked by the county coroner. Do you think both of them goofed, Ms. Mason?''

''I've no idea, and I certainly don't understand why you're telling me all this. Maybe the coroner didn't make a mistake. Perhaps the mistake was made by a typist entering the report into the computer.''

''Perhaps.'' Ben grabbed her hand as she was about to insert the key into the lock on her studio door. ''But it could be, *Ms. Mason,* that my interest springs from the fact that I estimate your height at right around five feet eight inches. Claire's height, spot on.''

''Get your hands off me!'' Dianna didn't care anymore about the impression she was creating. She just wanted to escape into the sanctuary of her studio. Alone, without Ben. ''You're making accusations that have no validity. It's ridiculous. It's crazy—you're crazy!''

''I haven't made any accusations,'' Ben said, his voice dangerously quiet. ''What do *you* think I was suggesting, *Ms. Mason?*''

"For God's sake, stop calling me Ms. Mason in that sarcastic tone of voice!" Dianna yelled. During the entire argument with Sonya, she had never once raised her voice, but now she was shouting at the top of her lungs. And shaking, too. With fury, she told herself. Ben had absolutely no right to intrude on her privacy when she'd abandoned all claim to the Campbell inheritance. Her life was her own business, and nothing to do with him. Why couldn't he leave sleeping dogs to dream peacefully in the shadows?

Plunging her elbow into Ben's ribs, Dianna shook his hand from hers and unlocked her door. She stepped into the studio, getting ready to slam the door behind her. With any luck, Ben might be standing close enough to get his nose broken. Ha! That would reduce the perfection of his profile a bit. The thought was almost pleasurable enough to take the edge off her panic.

As soon as she stepped into the studio, Dianna glanced toward her workbench—an instinctive first reaction to being home. She looked again, then stopped dead in her tracks, forgetting all about slamming the door behind her. The breath squeezed out of her lungs in a sharp, horrified whoosh. Even Ben was blanked out of her mind as she stared in appalled silence at the destruction confronting her. Instead of four heavy lead-crystal bowls waiting to be engraved, and a series of small, faceted paperweights, all that greeted her were a hundred thousand shards of ground glass heaped in neat little piles along the center of her workbench.

"What is it?" Ben asked, crowding into the studio behind her.

It was a measure of her emotional devastation that she accepted the comfort of his arm around her waist without any protest. She gestured toward the table. "My work," she said. "I can't believe he's destroyed my work!"

Ben took in the measure of her loss in a single glance. "Who did this?" he demanded, his voice stern. "Who did this to you, Dianna?"

"Hal." She answered before she could censor herself. In normal circumstances, she would never have admitted the truth, but it had been a tough day, on top of a tough few weeks, and her defenses were spread too thin.

"Why would Hal do such a thing?" Ben asked.

"You know why." Dianna realized that she was saying far too much without filtering out the dangerous parts, but she was shocked, hurt, and too weary to stop the flow of confession. "He's mad about what happened in Florida. About Claire, and what I told you the night of the fire. This is his way of taking revenge."

"I hate to find myself defending the guy, but how can you be sure it was him? Has he threatened you?"

"Not exactly." He'd threatened to murder her, but of course she'd paid no attention to that. Maybe she should have. With cunning insight, Hal had realized that destroying her work was almost as harsh a punishment as death. "He followed me home from Sonya's house just now," she explained. "Tailing me in his car. He wanted me to catch sight of him, I'm sure." That was why he hadn't attempted to hide, or to keep five or six cars between them, she thought bleakly. He'd intended for her to spot his familiar, beat-up Toyota.

"You think that was his way of telling you who was responsible for this? That's the only reason you have for suspecting him?"

"It's typically Hal," she said, biting her lip. "This way, I know he's responsible, but I'd sound either paranoid or stupid if I reported him to the police."

"Sit here. I need to check out the rest of the place." Ben propelled her into a leather chair, lit by a skylight that glowed with late-afternoon sun. She sank into it, watching without really seeing as he searched the apartment.

"Nothing seems to be destroyed except your work," he said, coming back to her after a quick tour. "As far as I can tell, he hasn't vandalized your living space, but your equipment looks as if it may be damaged."

She glanced mechanically toward the glass blowpipes lined up against the far wall, and the furnace, which was cold and lifeless at the moment, although when she was working, the temperature in the studio could easily reach a hundred degrees. Then she let her gaze skim across the iron marvering table, used for rolling molten glass until a skin formed on the surface, and the bench with her engraving wheels. Even from this distance, she could see that the copper wheel hung at a drunken, distorted angle, and that at least two of her blowpipes had been smashed in the middle.

"He's broken some of the equipment, but it doesn't matter," she said apathetically. "All it takes to replace the equipment is money. I'll get that somehow."

As soon as she spoke, she realized she'd laid herself wide open to one of Ben's sarcastic remarks, but for whatever reason, he chose to remain silent. Tight-lipped, he walked across to the workbench and stared down at the piles of glass. "Can you reheat this and reuse it, or will you have to throw it away?"

"Throw it away," she said. "Specific projects need specific additives melted in the batch. He's smashed lead crystal and mixed it with colored glass. It's useless to me now."

Ben's mouth tightened, but he made no direct comment. "Where do you keep your dustpan and brush?" he asked. "And I need a garbage can—something solid to hold all these shards of glass. A plastic bag will break."

"I'll get what we need." There was absolutely no point in sitting around feeling sorry for herself. Hal had destroyed a month of her labor, and blighted her creative energy. So what? Other people had destroyed far more, with less cause, and she'd survived. Determined to snap out of her maudlin self-pity, Dianna got up and made her way into the kitchen, which wasn't a separate room, but a corner cut off from the main studio by a triangle of cupboards topped by a waist-high counter of dark blue granite. She stopped in front of the sink, so full of a sense of loss that she momentarily blanked out on where she kept the dustpan and brush.

She glanced around the kitchen cupboards, trying to remember. When her gaze latched onto the corner cupboard, she felt a spark of renewed vitality. Maybe Hal hadn't destroyed everything, she realized. They'd never discussed her work habits, in which he was monumentally uninterested, and there was no reason for him to suspect that she used one of her kitchen cupboards to store her finished projects. Energized by hope, she pulled open the door of her storage cupboard.

Joy filled her. A tremble started in her toes and rushed triumphantly upward. "They're here!" she exclaimed, turning to Ben, her face feeling as if it might split open around her smile. "Look, he didn't find any of these!" She gestured to the cupboard shelves, which held a half-dozen bowls and vases. She laughed, relief at their survival making her almost forget the loss of the other, half-finished pieces.

He strode across the room, his grin almost as broad as her own. "Hey, that's wonderful news," he said, high-fiveing her as he approached. "This is really great." He stopped in front of the cupboard, his expression sobering so abruptly that she wondered what was wrong.

"What is it?" she asked. "Ben, what's the matter?"

"Nothing." He cleared his throat, his gaze not moving from the shelf of her finished work. "Show me the piece you like best," he said.

She didn't have to stop and think. Reaching up, she slowly lifted the bowl that was her pride and joy, feeling a little ache of pleasure as her hands cradled the weight of it and her fingertips caressed the tiny nooks and crannies of the design she'd cut into it with loving care. A lead-crystal piece, eight inches in diameter, she had engraved the entire surface with an idealized winter scene based on memories that came from her earliest childhood. Snow-covered pine trees climbed the sides of the bowl, and a foaming creek bubbled over jutting rocks as it wound its way through the forest and around the base of the bowl. High in the night sky, stars were diamond pinpoints of light, and a full moon shone with ethereal splendor over the trees and water below.

The glass was crystal clear, without the addition of any color, and she'd created the design by roughening and cutting the surface so that opaque areas and hair-thin lines generated the illusion of depth and solid dimension. The piece was technically accomplished, but that wasn't why Dianna loved it so much. She felt that in this particular bowl she had finally achieved the artist's dream: She had managed to create something that was more than a mere representation of the Vermont woods in winter. Looking at it, she felt that she had captured the very soul of a snowy night in mountain country, when the sky seems endless and the whole world holds its breath, waiting for dawn and the gift of a glorious morning of winter sunshine. Her design depicted dark and silent night, without a single visible hint of human or animal life, but somehow it also conveyed the sense that hidden in the depths of the forest were squirrels and deer, rabbits and chipmunks, all waiting to come forth and bask in the midwinter sun.

She hadn't yet shown this bowl to anyone—not even Sonya, who was usually a trusted critic. Somehow, she was glad that Ben would be the first person to view it. She set it on the counter, standing back and feeling a nervous flutter in her stomach as he stared down at it. She knew the piece was good, felt it in her bones, but she realized that she very much wanted him to do something more than admire it. She didn't want to listen as he politely told her it was good. She wanted him to respond to it with his heart, to feel the icy purity of the night and its implicit promise of winter's end. She wanted him to feel emotion churn in his gut in the same way she had felt it when she created the etching.

He was silent for a long time. Then he reached out and slowly traced the abrasions that created the illusion of foaming white water in the icy, rippling stream. He traced the movement of the water, then stopped at the base of a tall pine tree. "There's a rabbit hiding in a burrow behind that rock," he said. "I know he's there, waiting for morning to arrive so that he can wake up and enjoy a midwinter frolic."

She was so relieved that he'd seen the life hiding within the seeming emptiness, that she had to turn away, wrapping her arms around her body almost as if she needed to defend herself against his presence. She couldn't bear to look at him, to let him see how important his reaction had been to her.

"Dianna, I'm sorry." Ben spoke from behind her, his voice thick with embarrassment. "I didn't mean to offend you. The piece is beautiful—magnificent, in fact—and I apologize for my ignorance. I've never had much opportunity to learn about art, so I just reacted instinctively to your bowl. I'm sorry if I said the wrong thing."

"It wasn't the wrong thing." She was having a damnably difficult time keeping herself from crying. Between the argument with Sonya, Hal's attempt to destroy her studio, and Ben's unexpected arrival, she felt as if she'd spent the past few hours balancing on a high wire over a pit of vipers. Her emotional state was somewhat tumultuous, to put it mildly. She was afraid to say anything more. Every time she spoke to Ben, she seemed to reveal a great deal more than was wise.

Ben reached out and rested his hands on her shoulders. She felt the warmth of his hands through the thin muslin of her summer blouse, and a ripple of heat spread out from his fingertips, circulating slowly through her veins until it touched the frozen point deep inside her where she nursed the dark pain of her memories. Guilt and pain throbbed briefly, then faded away, as if his hands moving over her skin were a balm, soothing away suffering. She gave a gasp of pleasure, a groan of despair, a cry of longing. She wasn't sure which—or maybe it was all three.

"What is it?" he asked softly. "Did I hurt you?"

The illusion of healing created by his hands was too fragile to sustain the intrusion of his voice. She winced, as if he had probed an exposed nerve in an aching tooth.

"I don't want you to touch me," she said, because that was what she knew she ought to say. "Ben, this won't work for either of us." But even as she spoke, she knew how much she was lying. Like any aching tooth, once disturbed it seemed impossible to leave the pain alone. She wanted to keep exploring the extent of her injury—and Ben's capacity to soothe.

"Trust me," he said huskily, nuzzling her neck. "I promise you this will work. In fact, my side of the partnership is already working *real* well."

Instinctively she relaxed at the note of wry humor in his voice and he drew her against him, her back to his front, so that her spine pressed against his chest and her hips rested against the hardness of his erection. Surprisingly, in view of her past experiences, the knowledge that he wanted her acted as an instant turn-on. Heat raced through her veins, and when he wrapped his arms around her and took the weight of her breasts into his hands, she wasn't sure if the shudder she felt was his or her own.

It's been so long, she thought. *That must be why I want him so badly.*

But she really didn't want to think, or to rationalize away feelings that seemed new and unique and wonderful. She wanted to escape from the constraints of her narrow everyday life and sink into the warm, scented world of physical delight. For seven long years she'd weighed every action, calculated every move, guarded every sentence she spoke. Sometimes she'd felt as if even her thoughts weren't truly free. Hadn't she earned the right to commit one act of pure, undiluted folly?

Yes, she told herself as Ben's fingers worked their magic. *Yes, yes, yes!*

This evening, for once in her life, she would give herself permission to feel and not to reason.

Perhaps Ben was smart enough to realize that if he spoke, the spell would be broken and even his enchanted touch wouldn't be enough to subdue her a second time. He always seemed so damnably in tune with her moods, so aware of the vulnerabilities she could hide from everyone else, that Dianna was scarcely surprised that he had intuitively divined that silence was his most effective means of seduction.

The boundaries of her world narrowed; time slowed. Bewitched and beguiled, trembling with new sensations, she stood passively within the circle of his arms as he rasped his thumbs across her nipples and teased them into instant hardness. He slid the zipper on her jeans downward, easing his hands inside the waistband until he could flatten his palms against the bare skin of her stomach. A sharp, sweet stab of desire cut through her lethargy, and she spun around, reaching for him, pulling his mouth down on hers, feeling an explosion of white-hot need as his kisses ravished her cheeks, her lips, her breasts, until her entire body quivered from the impact of his touch.

He finally broke the spell of silence, but it didn't matter because her body was already molten with desire. She was glowing, incandescent with heat, like glass waiting to be shaped by a master craftsman. He whispered her name, telling her that she was beautiful, telling her how much he wanted her. Her jeans were a tangled heap on the kitchen floor, her blouse had landed in the sink, but she didn't care. She could feel her body taking on new form as he caressed her, molding her into a new shape, fashioning her into another woman—a creation that was uniquely his.

The tiny part of her brain that could never entirely switch off, the guardian that had kept her safe, uttered a final, feeble warning. Dianna ignored it. Ben led her into the bedroom and lay down on the bed, pulling her on top of him. They rolled over, and his weight pressed down on her. He was hard, male, demanding. For him, at this moment, she was soft, female, submissive. She had always wondered if she was capable of feeling passion so intense that it subverted reason. Now she knew the answer: She was.

Ben moved her legs apart, and his finger slipped inside her, seeking, discovering, arousing. The lingering chill of her self-imposed isolation vanished, melted by the heat of his desire. Her universe collapsed into a single sublime sensation with Ben at its heart. He pulled her hands over her head, exposing her entire body to his gaze, then raised himself over her. He eased her legs farther apart and thrust deep inside. She felt the tremor of an impending orgasm start in her toes and shiver steadily up the length of her body. He slowed his movements, tantalizing her, teasing her, pleasuring her to a point that was almost beyond endurance.

Just when she thought he would finally bring her to the shimmering ecstasy that already danced on the horizon, he rested his weight on his hands and looked down at her, his gray eyes darker and more opaque than the most primitive glass. She clutched him fiercely, her pride forgotten. "Don't stop," she panted. "Ben, please, don't stop."

He smiled and murmured her name. Then he plunged into her in a final, climactic thrust. Her body arched beneath him, shattering into a dazzling explosion of sexual pleasure. He fell on top of her, his breath coming in great shuddering gasps.

For the space of a couple of minutes, she was almost comatose with the satiation of total physical release. When she finally managed to work up the energy to free one of her arms, she pushed Ben off her and sat up.

He spoke without opening his eyes. "Come back, honey. Don't go away. We have all night."

She balled her fist and swung it straight at Ben's jaw. "You bastard," she hissed. "You low-down, skunk-bellied *bastard*."

He opened his eyes. Wide. He sat up, rubbing his jaw. "What is it? What the hell is your problem?"

"What did you call me just now?"

Understanding dawned at once. He gazed at her out of falsely innocent gray eyes, continuing to massage his jaw. "I guess I called you by your name."

"You called me Claire! You called me that twice!"

His hair was still matted, and his forehead was damp with sweat, but Ben was fully in control of himself again. "Why shouldn't I call you Claire?" he asked, his voice suddenly turning cool. "You are Claire Campbell, aren't you?"

"I told you, she died!" Dianna took another swing at his jaw, but he was ready for her this time, and caught her fist in his hand, holding it away from his chin without much effort. She was furious at the ease with which he thwarted her.

"I know what you told me," he said.

"I'm Dianna Mason," she shouted, red faced with frustration. "I'm Dianna Mason, damn you!"

He gave her a look that was full of the most terrifying sympathy. "I understand," he said soothingly. "Do you want to tell me how that happened?"

Hal was not in a good mood when he arrived back at the run-down apartment that, for the past several months, he'd been forced to call his home. Thanks to that bitch, Dianna Mason, and her unreasonable panic over a teensy-weensy fire in the Campbells' guest cottage, it looked like he'd be forced to spend several more months living in the blasted place. He hated it. From the hideous tweed carpeting, to the kitchen with its avocado green appliances, and the bathroom with its warped white tile, its squalor was an affront to his exquisitely developed taste in luxury.

He stomped across the living room and turned on the TV. Of course, there was nothing to watch but baseball. Karl Marx had it wrong, Hal thought, flipping the channels and frowning as he watched stupid men in striped uniforms run after bouncing balls. It wasn't religion that was the opium of the masses, it was televised sports. Disgusted, he turned off the TV.

His hopes for the day were vanishing fast. He'd planned to pay a visit to his old friend Sonya. If she was in one of her gourmet-cooking moods, he'd expected to at least scrounge a decent dinner out of the visit. With luck, she might even spot him a fifty. Just as he arrived at her apartment, he'd noticed Dianna driving away. On an impulse, he'd started to follow her. They were halfway to her studio when he'd realized that he had absolutely nothing to say to her. Besides, in his current mood, he was mad enough to lose his temper, and then he might start beating her up. Hal didn't have many scruples, but he drew the line at physical attacks on women—even stupid bitches like Dianna Mason, who almost deserved to get their asses blistered. Cursing himself for a fool, he'd turned around and driven back to Sonya's.

The dinner invitation he'd been hoping for hadn't materialized. Sonya had been on the phone to one of her damned organizations that catered to queers and faggots, and she'd told him to go away and leave her alone. She'd looked really upset, which wasn't like Sonya, who was an okay woman most of the time, despite the fact that she was indisputably gay. On the other hand, she was also fat, and Hal didn't go for fat women. Since he didn't feel personally deprived by Sonya's sexual orientation, Hal was usually mellow about the lesbians who hung around her place.

But not today. Today he'd wanted company and a decent meal. Instead of which, Sonya was crying over her dyke friends and he was stuck in his depressing apartment with nothing better to do than look for-

ward to watching a rerun of *60 Minutes*. Jesus, it was
degrading to think he'd sunk this low! Hal stroked his
mustache, wondering how a man as handsome and
intelligent as he was had managed to get himself into
such a god-awful situation.

He was almost glad to hear a ring of his doorbell.
Even if it was a group of religious fanatics trying to
convert him, at least he'd have the satisfaction of
working off some of his bad temper by slamming the
door in their faces.

The doorbell ran again. "Yeah, yeah, I'm coming!" he called out as he stepped over a pile of old
*GQ*s and *Esquire*s en route to the front door. He
peered into the peephole and felt a shock of surprise,
which was followed almost immediately by a little
quiver of alarm. Jesus! Were they going to set the police on his ass, after all?

He didn't open the door but spoke through the intercom instead. "What do you want?"

Through the peephole he saw his visitor smile and
hold up a bottle of Glenlivet whiskey. "Hey, Hal, I
just wanted to chat."

He hadn't been born yesterday and he was nobody's fool. "What about?" He hadn't opened the
door, or even drawn back the bolt. "We have nothing
to say to each other."

"Sure we do. I have some questions I want to ask
you about Dianna Mason."

"Why?"

The visitor's smile never faded. "Come on, Hal.
You don't expect me to answer that out here, do you?
Why don't we share a couple of drinks, and send out

for something to eat? I know a great French bistro that will deliver in this part of town."

Food, good Scotch, and a reprieve from watching *Sixty Minutes*. The package was irresistible. Hal unlatched the door and flung it open. "Come on in," he said. "Sorry the place is such a mess." He smiled bitterly. "My cleaning crew didn't make it over today."

"That's okay. No problem." His visitor smiled. Again. He was smiling altogether too damn much, Hal decided.

The visitor cleared a space for the Glenlivet on the kitchen counter. "Where are your glasses?" he asked.

"Over here." Hal turned toward the dust-covered hutch in the corner of his living room.

The bullet hit him square in the middle of his back, severing his spinal cord and puncturing the left ventricle of his heart. He died without ever knowing what hit him.

When you had to go, a bullet in the back was a pretty good way, Hal's murderer decided, looking down at his victim. No muss, no fuss, no time to worry. Yeah, not a bad way to die, especially for a guy who'd interfered in matters that didn't concern him.

Hal's hair had blown to the side, revealing a thinning patch right on his crown. The murderer's lip curled in distaste. He loathed physical imperfections, and baldness was a major male imperfection.

He walked around the apartment, pulling out drawers and tossing the contents onto the floor. He couldn't make Hal's death look like part of a burglary, because he had no way of carrying the heavy stuff, like the TV and the stereo, out of the apartment. So he had no choice but to make it look as if this was a drug-related incident. He took a plastic bag of cocaine from his inside jacket pocket—only 250 grams, but enough to make it seem like Hal was dealing—and dropped it into the toilet tank in the filthy bathroom. According to all the movies he'd ever seen, that was one of the first places the police would look.

He returned to the living room, taking care not to touch anything and not to let his clothes brush against any of the furniture. It wasn't that he worried about fingerprints or fabric fibers, but he did worry about germs. Christ, the place stank, and it looked as if it hadn't been cleaned in months.

He cast a final glance around the dreadful apartment. Everything was as he'd planned it. The shooting and the drug setup had taken in total less than seven minutes. Now he needed to hightail it out of here and get back to Logan airport. He was expected in New York tonight, and in New York he would be. On schedule.

Sharon would be waiting for him. He smiled. The way he was feeling right now, Sharon would have an interesting night.

Putting a bullet in a man's back had none of the excitement of setting a fire, the murderer thought as he left the apartment. But then, whatever method he'd chosen to kill Hal could never provide the thrill that would come when he finally managed to put an end to the life of Claire Campbell.

Dianna Mason. Claire Campbell. With Hal taken care of, it was time to move on to bigger and better things.

He got into his car, and slid into the stream of traffic.

Enjoy yourself, Claire, while you have the chance. I'm coming to get you. Real soon.

Nine

Dianna was hopping mad. She was mad at Ben, and equally mad at herself. It was bad enough to think of Ben as a conniving bastard who'd lured her into bed just so that he could ferret out her deepest, most intimate secrets. It was even worse to think that he might consider her so emotionally fragile, so mentally vulnerable, that he felt genuine pity for her. After those months in the psychiatric ward of the public hospital when she'd struggled back to mental health, Dianna *hated* to be pitied.

Shaking from head to foot, she sprang out of bed, grabbing the sheet and wrapping it around her like a toga. With a flash of wry humor, she reflected that she seemed to do a lot of springing naked from beds when she was around Ben Maxwell.

Despite her rage, her body was still glowing from the impact of his lovemaking— No, she corrected herself. Not from his lovemaking, but from his expert sexual techniques. She wasn't going to invest their ill-advised tumble into the sack with the gloss of false romance.

Ben's expression remained unbearably kind. "Come back to bed," he said gently.

"No, thanks." As casually as she could, she tossed the end of the sheet over her shoulder and headed toward the bathroom. "But don't get me wrong, Ben. The sex was great. Super. Anytime you want a letter of recommendation, let me know."

Quick as a flash, he followed her out of bed. Except he didn't bother with a sheet. "I don't deserve that," he said, breathing hard.

She chose to misunderstand. "Don't be so down on yourself, Ben. You put on a wonderful performance."

He muttered a single, graphic expletive and stepped in front of her, blocking her attempt to make a dignified exit. Her heart started to pound, but not with fear. "Let me pass. I need to use the bathroom."

"In a moment." He grabbed her wrist and dragged her around so that she couldn't avoid looking at him unless she closed her eyes. She wasn't prepared to appear that weak, so she kept her eyes wide open and stared stubbornly at his chin.

"Dammit," Ben said, his breath still coming hard and fast. "I thought we just shared something that mattered to both of us. It sure as hell mattered to me."

"Of course it mattered to you." She blinked fiercely. "You were conducting a very important investigation. Stop pretending, Ben. I know you took me to bed so that you could call me Claire when I had all my defenses down. You wanted to watch how I reacted to...her...name."

"For God's sake, listen to yourself," he snapped, white lipped with anger. "Can't you hear how ridiculous you sound? I don't go to bed with a woman so that I can conduct sly identity checks in the middle of her orgasm!"

"Then why did you call me Claire?"

"Because *my* defenses were down, dammit, and that's how I think of you! The first time we met, you told me that's who you were!" He ran his fingers through his hair, leaving it standing up in rough, uneven spikes. It occurred to her that at this moment, Ben Maxwell looked nothing like the sophisticated businessman who'd greeted her in Florida a week earlier. On the contrary, if she hadn't known better, she'd have thought he looked very much like a frustrated lover.

She wouldn't allow herself to be beguiled by appearances. "Tell me something, Ben. If you weren't conducting an identity check, why did you take me to bed?"

He hesitated for a crucial second too long. "Because I like you," he said at last. "Because, despite everything, I think you like me. Because I find you beautiful and desirable. Because I hoped we'd give each other pleasure."

She smiled satirically, not daring to let herself be seduced by the charm of his explanation. After all, he'd called her Claire not once, but twice. In his position as president of Campbell Industries, he must meet beautiful, sexy women all the time. Why would he be swept away by her average looks and modest skills as a bedmate? "That's a great postcoital speech, Ben, and you deliver it really well. Right out of the lesson book on how to be a sensitive, caring man of the nineties."

Frustration flared in his eyes, then was replaced by the familiar sheen of cool control. "There's no point in talking to you," he said. "Half the time you're not listening, and the other half, you're too scared to hear what I'm really saying." He let go of her wrist and stepped aside. "I think you were on the way to the bathroom. Don't let me keep you."

She should have escaped while she had the chance. This argument clearly wasn't going anywhere good. Instead of keeping wisely silent, she couldn't resist one last attempt to convince him. "I'm not Claire Campbell," she said. "You're wrong about that, Ben. I'm Dianna Mason, Claire's ex-roommate."

"Sure," he replied, turning away and pulling on a pair of boxer shorts. "I believe you. One thing Andrew told me over and over again about his daughter—Claire Campbell was a courageous young woman. I guess nobody would say that about you, would they?"

This time she was smart enough not to ask what he meant. Head high, she stalked into the bathroom, slamming and locking the door behind her. Men! At moments like these, she could understand why Sonya recommended universal male castration. Right now, she was just about ready to apply the scalpel. Herself.

Dianna had found her dustpan and brush and was sweeping up piles of broken glass when Ben emerged from the shower. She'd been on tenterhooks, waiting for him to come out, and yet when she heard the sound of his footsteps on the bare concrete floor of her studio, she was flustered enough that she swept a long sliver of glass straight into her right forefinger.

The splinter sliced into her at the worst possible angle. Blood dripped everywhere. "Ouch!" She pulled out the shard, stuck her finger in her mouth and looked around for a tissue. Of course, she couldn't see one anywhere. "Darn!"

"Here." With his usual competence, Ben stepped forward, holding an entire box.

"Thanks." She extracted a couple of tissues, feeling stiff and clumsy with the awkwardness of their situation. She wondered how two people could lie together in the most intimate of embraces, and then—less than twenty minutes later—find it impossible to look each other in the eye.

"You'd better let me take a look at that," Ben said, as blood started to seep through the wad of tissue she'd wound around her finger. "You're bleeding quite heavily for such a small cut. Maybe you still have glass in there."

She glanced down at the wound, which though narrow was painfully deep and had jagged edges. It was certainly possible that a smidgeon of glass still lurked inside. Reluctantly, she extended her hand, annoyed with herself when even this prosaic act set her nerve endings tingling with the memory of how it had felt when he touched her with passion.

Ben seemed afflicted with no wayward nerve endings or titillating memories. He unwound the bloody tissue with the detachment of a physician, and gently spread apart the cut. "I can't see any glass," he said. "Run it under the cold-water tap in the kitchen, while I find some antiseptic and a bandage. Where do you keep your first-aid kit?"

"In the bathroom—the little triangular cupboard in the corner. There's a plastic case of supplies."

Ben went in search of the kit, and Dianna walked over to the kitchen sink. It was better to end the afternoon this way, she told herself, as she turned on the tap. Better if she and Ben acted like polite acquaintances instead of failed lovers. Okay, it would have been wonderful if she could have spent the rest of the night lying in Ben's arms, talking about nothing in particular, drinking wine, making love again, waking up tomorrow morning to share a pot of coffee and fresh bagels from the deli on the corner of Vine and Maple. But it was crazy to yearn for what she couldn't have. Ben was Andrew Campbell's chief operating officer and they seemed to be good friends. The sort of passionate intimacy she craved might not be possible with any man; it certainly wasn't possible with Ben. In the long run, it would hurt less if she accepted here and now that there was no scope for developing their relationship. And since they had no future, obviously it was more sensible that they cut things off before...

Her thoughts tailed away. Before what? she wondered, staring at the running water without really seeing it. And when you got right down to it, what had she done recently that fell under the heading Sensible?

Ben came back carrying the blue-and-white plastic case of prepackaged medical supplies. She turned off the water and held out her finger. From years of experience as a glassblower, she knew that even minute glass splinters could inflict cuts that took forever to heal. She wasn't surprised to find that her finger was still seeping a thin trickle of watery blood. With impersonal efficiency, Ben mopped the cut dry, covered it with a dab of antiseptic ointment, and wrapped his handiwork in a supersize Band-Aid.

"All set," he said briskly. "Anything else I can do for you before I leave? Sweep up the rest of that glass, maybe?"

"No, thank you. It's almost done. I'm used to handling broken glass. It goes with the trade."

"Right, I guess it does."

Bright smile glued into place, she held out her hand, then snatched it away before he could touch it. "Well, goodbye, Ben. I don't want to keep you."

His mouth twisted wryly. "A man of intuition might think you wanted him to leave."

Her smile wasn't holding up too well. "I think it would be best." Ridiculous of her to wish that he wasn't leaving. Insane to wish that he'd lean forward, kiss her hard on the mouth, and sweep her back into the bedroom. The sex would be great, she didn't doubt that. It was the aftermath that would be devastating.

Ben set the first-aid box on the kitchen counter. "I found this on the bedroom floor," he said, pulling her grandmother's golden locket out of his jacket pocket. "I'm afraid the clasp's broken. I guess it got caught on something."

She practically snatched the necklace from him. Good grief, how could she have forgotten she'd been wearing her locket when he tumbled her onto the bed? She ran her thumb over the tiny concealed latch that hid the photos. Had he opened it? Had he seen the pictures of her parents? She realized he was watching her intently, and she felt hot, guilty color creep up her cheeks.

"It was Claire's," she said, her voice sounding thick and unnatural. She wondered why the sort of lie she'd been telling for years suddenly seemed to stick in her throat. "She—Claire, that is—gave it to me for my birthday."

Ben merely nodded. "It shouldn't be hard to get the clasp fixed," he said. "Maybe you need a sturdier chain, though."

"Yes, the chain is a bit fragile for the weight of the locket. I'll get a replacement. I'd hate to lose Claire's final gift to me.'' That sounded better, Dianna thought with relief. Much smoother and more convincing.

Ben, unfortunately, didn't seem convinced. Without bothering to acknowledge her remark, he took a small silver case out of the inner pocket of his jacket and extracted a business card. ''This is for you,'' he said, scrawling a number on the back. ''My answering service monitors that number twenty-four hours a day, and they always know where I can be found.''

''Do they know where you are now?''

''Almost always,'' he amended, and the faintest trace of color darkened his cheekbones.

She took the card without touching so much as the tip of his fingernail. ''Well, thanks, but I'm sure I won't need it.'' She got her cheerful smile functioning again, relief that the disastrous afternoon was nearly over restoring quite a bit of her self-possession. She slipped the card into the pocket of her shirt. ''We really don't have any reason to be in touch, do we?''

Ben paused for a split second at her front door. ''I don't know,'' he said. ''I'm waiting for you to tell me.''

Dianna didn't answer. She shut the front door firmly behind him, and rammed the chain and bolt into place. Leaning against the heavy steel door, she felt secure at last. She wouldn't worry about what Ben meant by that final parting shot. With a month of her work destroyed by Hal, she had enough practical problems to keep her fully occupied without worrying about Ben Maxwell. Three of the smashed bowls had been custom ordered, and a deposit paid on them. She had some long workdays ahead of her if the replacements were to be finished by the dates she'd promised. One of the bowls was destined for a hotel dining room and the money from the sale would pay her studio rent for a month.

She put on a CD of Wagner overtures and turned it up very loud, letting her mind fill with the bombastic melodies to the exclusion of everything else. Wagner was great background music for housework, she'd found. She was humming along, getting ready to toss the final panful of glass into the trash can, when—between one crashing chord and the next—her subconscious suddenly threw up the word *tissues.*

Good God, the tissues! Mouth dry, heart pounding, Dianna dropped the dustpan into the sink and ran back to the workbench. Since the space was swept clean of glass, it took no more than a second for her to be quite certain that the bloody tissues she'd wrapped around her cut finger were no longer there.

In the garbage, she thought. *I threw them in the kitchen trash without registering what I was doing.*

She yanked open the cupboard beneath the sink and checked the trash bin. She couldn't see any tissues, although they ought to have been easily visible among the coffee grounds and empty yogurt cartons. Refusing to be alarmed, she forced herself to take the time to unfold newspaper over her kitchen floor. Then she spread the day's household trash over the paper in a thin, even layer. She found two crumpled paper towels, but not a single tissue, not even the sodden one that Ben had used to dry her cut before applying antiseptic ointment.

Dianna told herself not to panic. She *ordered* herself not to panic. She wrapped up her trash neatly in the newspaper, and returned it to the bin. Then she donned thick leather work gloves, picked up a pail, and walked back to the corner of the studio where she had left the giant garbage can holding all the smashed glass. Carefully, she began to scoop glass shards out of the can and into the pail. After ten minutes of careful sifting, she confirmed what she'd feared from the very beginning—no bloody tissues had been thrown into the trash. The tissues, in fact, were nowhere in her studio. Which could mean only one thing. Ben had taken them with him.

Wagner's *Lohengrin* Overture segued into the "Ride of the Valkyries." The drums rolled and the cymbals clashed, but Dianna didn't hear a sound. All she could think of was the fact that Ben Maxwell had acquired a generous sample of her blood.

And that he almost certainly planned to take it to a genetic-testing laboratory.

The shuttle from Boston to New York had been close to empty—an unexpected bonus—but Ben felt restless and his muscles were knotted tight with tension. Guilt, he thought wryly, was not a comfortable traveling companion.

He hailed a cab and sat back to endure the forty-minute drive into Manhattan. His cabbie was typical of the New York breed. An immigrant from somewhere unpronounceable, he drove with the demented fury of a man who had only recently escaped a war zone. Other vehicles on the road were the enemy, to be circled and outmaneuvered at breakneck speed. Potholes were minor irritations of nature, to be bounced over or accelerated around with blithe disregard for the cab's rear axle, much less for passengers. The air-conditioning wafted occasional blasts of chilled air in Ben's direction, but the floral-perfumed air fresheners stuck on various surfaces totally failed to disguise

the lingering smell of marijuana. Ben, a veteran of
New York City cab rides, leaned back resignedly, and
hoped, against all logic, that the cabbie wasn't still
high.

The driver of a thirty-foot truck beeped his horn
and simultaneously switched lanes, cutting off the cab.
The truck driver and the cabbie hurled abuse at each
other for several seconds before either of them attempted to take evasive action. With a final yelled
curse, the cabbie whipped his wheel to the right and
snaked in front of a stately Cadillac. Brakes screeched
behind them, and the cabbie flashed a wide grin into
his rearview mirror.

Deciding that he'd prefer not to watch their progress over the Triboro Bridge—they were now in the
outside lane, which didn't leave much room for mod-
ern-day gladiator contests—Ben unzipped his leather
portfolio and drew out the two plastic sandwich bags
in which he'd stored the bloody tissues he'd stolen
from Dianna. One was sodden with a mixture of blood
and water, the other was already dried out. He didn't
know which was better for the lab, nor did he know
exactly how much blood a genetic-testing facility
would need, but he figured that if rapists could be
identified from minute traces of semen, surely he had
more than enough blood here for the lab technicians
to work their scientific magic.

Ben stared at the tissues until the red stains blurred.
Then he returned the plastic bags to his portfolio,
shifting yet again on the sagging cab seat. Unfortunately, it was his conscience rather than the hot vinyl
or the broken springs that was really bothering him, so
thrashing around didn't help. He told himself that he
had no reason to feel guilty. After all, it wasn't as if

he'd cut Dianna's finger with malice aforethought. He'd simply taken advantage of the opening fate had delivered into his lap. Dianna would be furious when she found out what he'd done, but that couldn't be helped. Ben badly needed to know the truth about her identity, and he was prepared to take the flak she would undoubtedly dish out.

Even without the confirmation of a genetic test, he was ninety percent sure that Dianna was in reality the missing Campbell heiress, but he realized not many people would accept his judgment. If she was Claire, why the hell was she going out of her way to convince everyone that she was Dianna Mason?

Ben had realized the night the cabana caught fire that he was going to have to stop acting on instinct and start acquiring a solid base of facts. The first fact he needed to uncover was exactly who Dianna Mason was. Then he could wrestle with the dilemma of why she was behaving so strangely. After that, just maybe, he'd be able to tackle the problem of why the hell he'd fallen head over heels in love with her.

His feelings for Dianna were the oddest part of this crazy situation. After a youthful marriage to a college girlfriend, and a polite divorce with minimal regrets on both sides, he had devoted his energies to building his career. He'd enjoyed a couple of friendly, low-key affairs, but seventy-hour workweeks didn't allow much time for meeting interesting women, and no time at all for developing deep, meaningful relationships. He certainly wasn't accustomed to feeling passionate concern for a woman whom logic dictated he shouldn't even like.

In Florida, when he saw Dianna for the first time, his reaction had been intense, primitive and overwhelming. He'd wanted her. The image of her spread-eagled on his bed had been immediate and graphic, mind-blowing in its erotic details. Nothing that had happened since their first meeting had changed his response. Every time he saw Dianna, he wanted her. Worse, when she wasn't around, he worried about what she was doing and how she was getting along. He was actually jealous of Hal Doherty, for Christ's sake!

Ben cordially disliked untidy emotions. He disliked behaving irrationally even more. If he knew the truth about Dianna's past, he ought to be able to understand her better; which, in turn, might help him to reassert control over his feelings. He might even get some inkling as to why he had this overwhelming compulsion to make love to her every time they came within a ten-foot radius of each other. Ben was getting mighty tired of feeling horny every time a picture of Dianna Mason—or was it Claire Campbell?—flashed into his mind. Hell, he was thirty-five, not fifteen.

This visit with Evelyn Campbell should be the first step toward discovering the truth about Dianna's past. By some miracle, Evelyn had not only been at home when he called from Logan airport, she'd actually agreed to see him as soon as he could catch a plane to New York. So here he was, at eight o'clock on Sunday evening, hoping he'd survive the cab ride to Evelyn's midtown Manhattan penthouse, and hoping even more fervently that Evelyn would agree to give him a sample of her blood to take to a genetic-testing lab.

Ben tried to decide exactly what he would say to convince Evelyn that genetic testing was the best way to solve the mystery of Dianna Mason's past. Of the half-dozen previous claimants to the Campbell fortune, only one had managed to persuade Ben that she might be the long-lost Campbell heiress. Ben had quickly decided that it was a waste of everyone's time to hire a private investigator to check out the details of the claimant's story. Why speculate on her true identity, when the issue could be resolved simply by sending blood samples to any one of a dozen genetic-testing laboratories scattered across the country?

To his astonishment, both Evelyn and Andrew had been reluctant to agree to the necessary tests. Ben had tried to persuade them that the only certain way to establish the woman's identity was to submit samples of her DNA for genetic comparison with the DNA of her supposed parents. Both Evelyn and Andrew had insisted that they would agree to a parental blood-match test only as a last resort.

Despite the Campbells' reluctance, Ben would have persisted in advising genetic testing, except that Roger had trapped his would-be sister in a dozen inconsistencies within an hour of meeting her, and insisted that they turn her over to the police. A fingerprint search by the FBI confirmed that Roger was right in his suspicions. The impostor was a twenty-eight-year-old woman named Doreen Palek, who had a record of similar scams stretching back into her early teens. With Doreen exposed as a fraud, the whole question of genetic testing had become irrelevant and Ben had never learned why Andrew and Evelyn resisted the idea so strongly.

"East Sixty-eighth and Madison." The cabbie careered to a halt outside the canopied entrance to the building that housed Evelyn Campbell's penthouse apartment. Ben handed over a couple of bills and climbed out onto the sidewalk. His cabbie accelerated away to an accompanying screech of tires and crashing of gears.

The doorman recognized Ben and nodded politely. "'Evening, Mr. Maxwell. Mrs. Campbell, she expecting you. She tell me already you coming."

"Give her a ring to let her know I'm on my way up, will you?" he asked, slipping the doorman a couple of bucks.

"Yessir, I do that right now."

Ben stepped into the elevator, which had smoked-glass walls and a carpet that said Sunday in beige embroidery on a royal blue ground. Ben had never been able to decide if the daily change of carpet was to impress visitors with the fact that the building possessed seven elevator rugs, or if it was supposed to be a reminder for those owners whose wealth weighed so heavily on their minds that they had a problem recalling tedious details like what day of the week it happened to be. He suspected the latter.

An elderly man in a black jacket, gray waistcoat and pin-striped trousers was already standing in Evelyn's private lobby when the elevator glided to a halt on the eighth and top floor, waiting to greet Ben. Bainbridge had been with the Campbell family for a quarter of a century, and Ben had known him ever since he started working for Campbell Industries six years earlier.

On first meeting Bainbridge, Ben, who'd never before encountered a real live butler, had decided the man was slightly more intimidating than God. Now, several years and a dozen meetings later, Ben was more sophisticated and not nearly so easily impressed. Hell, no! These days, Bainbridge didn't scare him more than the Pope and an entire college of cardinals.

Ben cleared his throat and resisted the impulse to tug at his collar. "Good evening, Bainbridge." In another few years, Ben thought he might work up the courage to ask the man his first name. In a century or so, he might have the courage to use it.

"Good evening, Mr. Maxwell."

"It's a lovely evening, isn't it? Mild for this time of year." With Bainbridge, Ben had discovered it was easier and quicker to observe the proprieties. Any attempt to rush straight to business simply prolonged the delay.

Bainbridge inclined his head in a slight nod of approval. "It is indeed, sir. We've been fortunate with the weather this month. May I relieve you of your briefcase, or would you prefer to keep it with you?"

"I'll keep it, thanks. I may need some papers I have in there. Is Mrs. Campbell ready to see me?"

"She is indeed. Mrs. Campbell has ordered a light supper to be served in the terrace room. If you'll go through, sir, I'll see that it's sent in at once. I believe the cook has prepared cold poached salmon, to be followed by a fresh fruit sherbet."

"It sounds delicious, thank you." Ben was conscious of the honor of being allowed to show himself into the terrace room, unsupervised by the butler. He gave the man a quick parting nod and walked away.

Ben's footsteps rang out on the marble floor of the hallway. Evelyn heard him coming, and glided to the door of the terrace room to greet him, preceded by an elusive hint of Joy perfume. Severely elegant in a tailored dinner dress of navy blue silk shantung, she held out a fragile, exquisitely manicured white hand. "Ben, you're a few minutes earlier than I expected! Your plane must have been on time, thank goodness."

"The plane was on time, and the traffic into the city from La Guardia was moving quite fast." Ben shook hands, thinking what an amazing contrast there was between Evelyn's cool elegance and Dianna's sensual, almost-lush beauty. Could they really be mother and daughter? At this moment, it scarcely seemed possible. Evelyn suggested that they go outside, and he followed her over to the French doors that led onto the huge balcony.

"The view from up here never ceases to amaze me," he said, stepping outside and breathing in the scent wafting from a dozen waist-high pots of geraniums and old-fashioned carnations grown especially for their perfume. "It's spectacular."

"Manhattan on a summer night has a magic all its own," Evelyn agreed. "We've had just enough rain this summer to keep Central Park green and flourishing. I'm sure that makes a difference to the quality of the air in this part of town. Ah, here comes Consuela with our supper. I suppose we'd better eat inside or we'll be devoured by midges and mosquitoes."

The maid silently deposited several covered dishes on a table by the French doors that was already set for two. As the maid left the room, Bainbridge entered carrying a bucket of iced Dom Pérignon, the only liquid, other than Earl Grey tea, that Ben had ever seen Evelyn drink. Bainbridge set the silver ice bucket next to the table, poured two flutes of champagne and bowed politely toward Evelyn. "Is there anything else I can bring for you, madam?"

"No, this is splendid, thank you."

The butler bowed again and withdrew. Evelyn gestured to Ben, indicating that they should both go inside. She then managed to consume a full five minutes in an agonizingly courteous serving of cold salmon, iced asparagus with hollandaise sauce, and wafer-thin slices of whole-wheat bread and butter. Ben was hungry, but hearty eating in Evelyn's presence seemed too crude to be contemplated, so he served himself tiny portions, nibbled on a limp asparagus stalk, and vowed to order himself a giant pizza as soon as he could get across to Third Avenue.

The food, Ben discovered, looked much better than it tasted. Six months earlier, Bainbridge, in a unique display of temperament, had refused to remain in the same household as Sharon Kruger. On the evidence of tonight's meal, Ben concluded that Evelyn had paid a high price for the privilege of being browbeaten by her butler. He couldn't imagine why Bainbridge had taken such an immediate dislike to Sharon, who seemed pleasant and easygoing, as well as a superb cook. The butler had offered no excuse other than that Sharon received phone calls from her men friends at all hours of the day and night, disturbing the household.

Ben would have thought that problem easily resolved. Installing a private phone line would be a small price to pay in exchange for the glories of Sharon's cooking. Still, Evelyn didn't look as if she spent much time swooning over chocolate-fudge cookies, so she probably hadn't even noticed the loss.

This was the first time Ben had ever shared a meal alone with Evelyn Campbell, although he'd met her frequently at Andrew's political dinners, and at charity fund-raisers. Ben knew his boss so intimately that he was occasionally astonished by how little he understood Andrew's relationship with Evelyn. As Evelyn toyed with her salmon and discussed the latest exhibition of medieval religious art at the Met, Ben found himself thinking about her not simply as Andrew's wife, but as a woman in her own right. With astonishment, he realized that after six years and some forty meetings, he knew nothing about her, other than the bare facts of her biography.

Gazing around the overfurnished room, he wondered why on earth someone who hadn't been born until the end of World War II chose to run her Manhattan apartment as if it were a Philadelphia estate in the 1920s. Quite apart from the British butler and the freezing formality of the decor, Evelyn herself had the sort of old-fashioned manners that precluded any possibility of honest discussion or relaxed laughter. Watching her play the hostess, it was not only impossible to imagine her as the mother of Dianna Mason, Ben thought, it was impossible to imagine her as *anyone's* mother. Andrew was a courageous man to have undertaken the daunting task of impregnating her. Ben couldn't begin to imagine what it would be like to take such a flawless icicle to bed.

It was almost as if Evelyn could read his thoughts. She flashed him an ironic glance and put down her champagne glass. Ben actually felt himself blushing. Mockery danced briefly in her extraordinary blue eyes—the first flash of life he'd spotted all evening—and his breath caught in his throat. At that moment, for a split second, she had looked so much like Dianna that the resemblance had been uncanny.

Evelyn rested her fork on the edge of her plate. "Well, we seem to have totally exhausted the subject of the inadequacy of modern art, so perhaps we should move on. What did you need to see me about, Ben? You sounded as if it was really urgent."

"It's about Dianna Mason," he said. "I went to see her today at her studio in Boston."

Evelyn dabbed at the corner of her perfectly clean mouth with a spotless linen napkin. "I understood that Ms. Mason had declared herself to be an impostor."

"She did." Ben put down his champagne. "I'm not sure I believe her."

Evelyn might be an icicle, but she wasn't in the least slow on the uptake. "If Dianna Mason is really my daughter, Ben, can you suggest any reason at all why she might hesitate to reclaim her heritage?"

"Yes," he said bluntly. "I think she's afraid."

With great care, Evelyn aligned her antique silver knife next to her antique silver fork. "Afraid of what?"

"She believes someone is trying to kill her." Until he answered the question, Ben hadn't realized how thoroughly he understood Dianna's behavior.

"Is she right? Is someone trying to kill her?"

"Possibly." Ben found the concise questions bothersome in their lack of emotion. He pushed back his chair, unable to tolerate the confinement of its spindly gilt legs and padded velvet arms. "She's convinced the fire in Vermont wasn't set by Ted Jenkins."

"The police seemed sure they had the right man."

"I know they did." Ben tossed his napkin onto the table, feeling the frustration spiral tighter and tighter in his gut. "But then there's the fire that broke out when Dianna was staying with us in Florida. What caused that?"

"I spoke to the fire marshal. I understand he believes that either Hal Doherty or Dianna herself was responsible for setting the fire."

"Dianna didn't set it," Ben said. "I'd stake next year's operating profits to a dozen doughnuts that Dianna had nothing to do with setting that fire."

Evelyn lifted her shoulders in a delicate gesture that was almost a shrug. "From everything Andrew has ever told me about Hal Doherty, he's quite capable of doing the deed without any help from anyone."

"I know, and I agree with Andrew—in theory." Ben rubbed the muscles at the back of his neck that had somehow become snarled into a twisted knot of pain. He leaned across the table, looking straight into Evelyn's eyes. For a moment, before she managed to screen her feelings, he saw pain, so naked and intense, that he flinched.

"What is it?" he demanded, forgetting to be polite. "Evelyn, what do you know? There's something you're not telling me, isn't there?"

"Of course not." Evelyn once again appeared cool and utterly possessed. But Ben was no longer deceived and his frustrations boiled over. What the hell was it with these Campbells? Why did he need to dig and grovel to extract every tiny nugget of information?

"Shall I tell you what I think?" he said. "I believe Dianna Mason is Claire Campbell, your daughter. What's more, I think you'd better come down out of your ivory palace and pay her a visit."

Evelyn got up and walked over to the balcony. It was an indication of her turbulent state of mind that she didn't offer so much as a single murmured word of excuse for leaving the table. "If she is Claire, where has she been and why has she chosen this precise moment to return?"

"I don't know the answer to either of those questions, not exactly. Do you want to hear what I'm guessing may be true?"

She didn't turn around. "Yes."

"I think Claire Campbell and a young woman named Dianna Mason met in a psychiatric hospital not too long after the cabin in Vermont burned down and Claire disappeared. I think they probably looked somewhat alike, enough so that they could have been sisters. They made friends in the hospital and when they were released, they decided to share an apartment." Ben paused and Evelyn slowly turned around.

"Go on," she said. "What happened next?"

"One of them died in a car accident," Ben said.

Evelyn's hands clasped and unclasped. "Which one?"

Ben looked her straight in the eye. "An interesting question," he said. "I believe it was Dianna Mason. The death certificate says it was Claire Campbell."

"Why? How did the mistake happen?"

"Because the survivor, whoever that was, identified the victim, whoever that was. The women looked similar, the body was pretty smashed up. They were both runaways. Why would anyone question the identification?"

"Papers. Papers in the car wreck."

Evelyn was speaking with the appearance of calm, but Ben suddenly realized she'd been delivering these odd, curt questions and answers because she wasn't capable of forming longer sentences. Looking at her more closely, he saw that she was clinging to her self-control by her fingernails. Beneath her makeup, her skin was gray, and her body seemed about to explode under the stress of holding itself upright. With a sense of overwhelming shock, he realized that Evelyn Campbell—the socialite icicle—was a woman of tightly controlled emotions, rather than a woman who lacked all feeling.

"Evelyn," he said gently. "If this is distressing you—"

"Papers," she said through gritted teeth. "There must have been documents in the wrecked car. How did the survivor take care of the papers?"

"I don't know," Ben admitted. "But the two of them lived together, and Claire was pretty smart." He thought of how fate had played into his hands when Dianna cut her finger. "Maybe it was sheer chance," he suggested. "Maybe Dianna grabbed the wrong purse when she went out in the morning. That sort of thing does happen."

"You're making the details fit together," Evelyn said tightly. "But the big picture makes no sense. Why would Claire Campbell choose to become Dianna Mason? We're back at the beginning, right where we started, asking the same question."

The answer came to Ben like the glare of a spotlight on a battlefield, illuminating bumps and hollows and crevices that previously had appeared as a flat stretch of inhospitable ground. "No, we're not," he declared. "Of course, we're not! Don't you see? Claire was afraid the car crash was another attempt to kill her. So she provided the murderer with the victim he wanted. She gave him Claire Campbell. She identified the battered body as Claire Campbell and took on the identity of Dianna Mason."

Evelyn was silent for a very long time. "I want to meet this young woman," she said at last.

Ben drew in a quick, triumphant breath. "You shall," he said. "Very soon. But first we need to be absolutely sure that my guesses are right, and that the woman calling herself Dianna Mason is really Claire Campbell."

"Don't you have that somewhat backward, Ben? Until I've seen her, you have absolutely no way of knowing who she is."

"That's not quite right," Ben said. "Even if you see her and decide she's your daughter, that doesn't constitute proof. These days, I doubt if any court in the land would accept your word when there's a death certificate saying Claire Campbell died. Besides, you have no reason to subject yourself to that sort of emotional trauma. I have a much better way to test the truth about Dianna Mason." He unzipped his portfolio and drew out the plastic bags with their stained tissues. "These are samples of Dianna's blood," he said, speaking too quickly but afraid Evelyn would cut him off with the same irrational refusal she'd given before. "If you would agree to provide me with some of your blood, I could send the samples to a reputable genetic-testing lab and they would provide us with a definitive answer on Dianna Mason's heritage. I understand they can identify parents and children with better than a ninety-nine percent certainty."

He'd hoped for agreement. He'd steeled himself for refusal. In the event, she asked him a question he hadn't anticipated. "Did this woman...Dianna... Did she willingly give you this blood sample?"

For a split second, Ben considered lying. In the end, a lifelong habit of honesty won out. "No," he said, wondering if the truth was going to prove fatal to his plans. "She cut her finger on a piece of glass and I took the tissues without her knowing." Some demon of integrity compelled him to add, "She'll be furious when she finds out what I've done."

Evelyn plucked a carnation and held it to her nose. "It's a funny thing," she said. "I loved Claire more than anyone in the entire world. She was the center of my universe. And she's probably the only person in our family who never realized that."

Ben wondered what that confession had to do with his request for a blood sample. He didn't dare to ask. Evelyn had turned away to stare out into the darkness of Manhattan. She didn't move. At times she scarcely seemed to be breathing. For almost a full minute Ben could only watch the rigid line of her shoulders. Then she swung around and looked him squarely in the eye.

"I'll give you a blood sample on one condition."

"What is that?"

"You're not to tell Andrew what we're doing."

He was astonished by the request, but the tilt of her chin positively forbade him to ask questions. "Very well," he said. "It's a deal."

She smiled faintly. "Come into my bathroom," she said. "I imagine I'll be able to find a sterile razor blade."

Ten

The kiln had been turned off a couple of hours earlier and the temperature in the studio had finally dropped to a mere ninety degrees. Dianna poured herself a tall glass of iced tea and returned to her workbench. She was dirty, tired, hungry, and sticky with half-dried sweat. She was also as close to happy as she ever came these days. Four lead-crystal bowls sat on the bench, gleaming in the late-afternoon sun. One had a bubble in it, two were fractionally lopsided. But the largest one, some fifteen inches in diameter, was absolutely perfect. Dianna smiled every time she looked at it.

The bowl was going to be decorated with an etched scroll of hummingbirds and wildflowers. She'd already taken all the photographs she needed to serve as the basis for her design, so tomorrow, first thing, she would start to mark out the design on the belly of the bowl, using special wax crayons. Lead crystal was relatively soft and easily cut, and as soon as her copper engraving wheel was repaired, she'd be able to cut the design into the surface of the glass. Eric, a neighborhood metalworker, had promised to fix her wheel sometime today. He'd probably stop by with it tonight. If not, she'd pick it up in the morning and, with any luck, the finished piece would be ready to present to the bank at the end of next week. Dianna fingered the smooth, fragile lip of the bowl and grinned. There was no feeling in the world to compare with the glorious sensation of a successful, productive day in her studio.

Except making love with Ben Maxwell.

Dianna's smile faded instantly, and she pressed the ice-misted glass of tea to her hot forehead. Memories of Ben Maxwell had been officially banished, and she was annoyed with herself for letting one intrude. Her euphoria fled, to be replaced by a familiar mixture of dread and reckless anticipation. It was all very well to create an illusion of safety by hiding in her studio and working doggedly on her assignments, but the real world kept beating on her safety shield. Soon her past was going to explode into her present, and the blast was going to rock a lot of lives. She wondered—often—if she would survive the explosion. She sometimes had the feeling that she'd been bucking the odds for years, and her luck was beginning to run out.

When she'd approached Hal Doherty two months earlier, she had chosen a course of action that she knew held danger. She realized now that despite all her attempts to be both clever and cautious, by the mere fact of turning up on Andrew's doorstep, she had set in motion a chain of events over which she had no real control. Clearly, Ben was planning to take the tissues he'd stolen to a genetic-testing lab. He would need blood from either Evelyn or Andrew to use as a comparison, and the question that haunted her was, whose blood would he request? And would either Andrew or Evelyn be willing to cooperate?

Before going to Florida, Dianna had blithely assumed that her safety was not seriously at risk. If the going got too hairy, she would simply expose Andrew for the fraud he was. Now she wondered how she could ever have been so naive. Andrew, like any other wounded and cornered animal, had proven repeatedly that he would lash out with deadly aim if he saw his ambitions leaking away in a blaze of unfavorable publicity. If she decided to go ahead and expose Andrew, she would have to move swiftly and secretly. Even so, her life would probably be on the line. Alternatively, she could forget about revenge, forget about justice, forget about her family, and retreat back into the safety of her anonymous life-style. Except that she might not be able to find anywhere shadowed and obscure enough to hide herself. From now on, every knock on the door would have the power to set her heart pounding.

She poured the dregs of her tea down the sink, staring blindly as the melting ice cubes rattled down the drain. To compound her problems, she was no longer sure that she wanted to see Andrew stand trial for murder. At eighteen, the world had been full of black-and-white absolutes. Nowadays, her moral landscape seemed drawn in a thousand shades of murky gray. Andrew's arrest and conviction would hurt many people—among them, Evelyn and Roger, who had committed no crimes. On the other hand, the people of Florida deserved to know that one of their candidates for governor was a murderer. She had hoped that Andrew would be defeated in the primaries, but he had sailed to an easy victory. And now all the polls showed that Andrew was marching toward a landslide victory in the November election. Didn't she have a duty to tell the voters what she knew?

The front doorbell rang just as she was making her way across the hallway to her bedroom. That must be Eric with the engraving wheel, she thought, her spirits reviving marginally. She padded across the tiny stretch of tiled floor, her thonged leather sandals flopping as she walked. She squinted into her peephole—and saw Andrew Campbell.

She must have conjured him up with the intensity of her thoughts, Dianna reflected ruefully. She wanted to hate him with full, undivided force, but she never managed to pack all her feelings into such a simple and tidy box. Stomach churning, she watched as he paced her courtyard. He looked nervous, she decided, although he was immaculately dressed in a lightweight mohair suit, teamed with a tie bearing a logo that commemorated the twenty-fifth anniversary of his naval service on board the aircraft carrier *Spirit of Freedom.*

Dianna's lip curled. Andrew was big on not-so-subtle reminders that during the Vietnam War he'd volunteered for active duty while most of his contemporaries had scurried to take cover in Canada, or in cushy positions with the National Guard. In Florida, with its large contingent of retired military people, his service in the navy went over *really* well. His opponent in the campaign for governor was always floundering around, trying to explain why he'd been studying law in a comfortable graduate school, while Andrew had been stationed in faraway Subic Bay, making patrol sweeps of coastal Vietnam, and generally keeping the South China Sea safe for decent, God-fearing Americans. Evelyn had given birth to Claire while Andrew was on active duty overseas. One of the more impressive photos in Andrew's PR kit showed a shyly smiling Evelyn holding up three-month-old Claire to be kissed by the returning "warrior."

Andrew pressed the doorbell again and Dianna opened the door, leaving the chain in place. "What do you want?"

He looked at her almost pleadingly. "Just to talk," he said. "Please, Claire, we really do need to talk."

It was one thing to face Andrew when they were both surrounded by other people. It was quite another to invite him into her home. Alone. Just the two of them, with no witnesses. Dianna might have been rash in her behavior recently, but she wasn't totally heedless, and Andrew's presence on her doorstep filled her with a healthy dose of fear. She started to close the door. "We have nothing to say to each other. Nothing."

He stuck his foot between the jamb and the door. "Claire, please. If you don't tell me what I did to hurt you, I can't put it right." To Andrew, a New Englander of Scots ancestry, pleading didn't come easily. He was flushed with the discomfort of expressing his feelings. "I loved...love...you, Claire. What happened? Why did you run away? Even if you don't care about me... Well, you hurt your mother terribly, you know. She was absolutely devastated when you disappeared."

She was blazing with rage, choking on his hypocrisy. "How dare you ask me that? How dare you come here, pretending that I'm the one who caused Evelyn pain? You make me sick—sick to my stomach—because I know what sort of a man is really hidden behind that smooth facade of yours!"

He blanched. "Is that what this is all about? I know I'm not perfect, and I haven't been the best of husbands, but I'm not sure you have the right to fling that in my face. Evelyn and I have reached an understanding—''

She was shaking so hard that she really thought she might throw up. "Get your foot out of the door," she said. "Don't come near me again, or I'll call the police. And how will that look in your campaign publicity, Mr. Would-Be Governor? Andrew Campbell Arrested For Harassing Young Artist. It's an eye-catching headline, although I can think up several others that would be a hell of a lot more damaging. And they're all true, too."

"Claire..." A car drew to a halt outside her courtyard, brakes squealing. Andrew straightened. "Someone's coming to see you."

Dianna glanced across the courtyard. "Sonya!" she said in relief, watching her friend stride toward the house. She took off the chain and opened the door wide. With Sonya as a witness, she had no more reason to fear Andrew. "What's up, kiddo? You were driving like a bat out of hell."

Sonya took her cigarette from her mouth with a hand that shook visibly. She glanced toward Andrew, but didn't seem to see him. She certainly gave no sign that she recognized him as the man whose past she'd been researching for the past several weeks.

"It's Hal Doherty," she said, her voice hoarse. "He's dead."

"Dead?" Dianna repeated the word as if she had never heard it before. "How can he be dead? I saw him yesterday afternoon. He was fine then."

"Yeah, well, I guess that was before he let some joker into his apartment who put a bullet in his back."

Dianna felt the world spin around her in a dizzying circle.

Dear God in heaven, please not another death to pile onto her already overburdened conscience. She blinked, trying to focus, and her gaze landed on Andrew.

"Who killed him?" she demanded, her voice strident.

Sonya took a deep drag on her cigarette. "The police think it's drug related. I told them Hal's not into drugs. He gets off strictly on women and booze. Which reminds me, I need a drink. Invite me in, sweetie, and point me toward the hard liquor."

"Of course, come in." Dianna gestured to usher her friend in, and realized Andrew Campbell was still standing on her doorstep, although he'd moved off to the side. She couldn't cope with Andrew right now, she simply couldn't. Dear God, he was utterly ruthless, totally without moral scruples! The sickening possibility occurred to her that he'd come to tell her that Hal Doherty was dead and to gloat over her reaction. She shuddered, not sure what to do. If she made too many wild accusations, she was going to find herself locked up in a mental institution with friendly nurses offering her pills every couple of hours. Dianna was well aware that her history of mental instability acted very much against her if she ever needed to stack her credibility up against Andrew's.

"Sonya," she said shakily, as her friend walked by. "This is Andrew Campbell. He's just leaving. Andrew, this is Sonya Harvey, a political reporter for the Boston *Globe*."

Sonya half turned, her expression arrested. She held out her hand, studying Andrew with an oddly intent scrutiny. "It's good to meet you, Mr. Campbell. I've been following your campaign for governor with interest."

Andrew shook her hand, his expression grave. "I wish the circumstances of our meeting had been different. Hal Doherty worked in my organization for over five years and I'm very sorry to hear that he's dead. The violence in our cities these days is truly shocking, and the drug problem is absolutely out of control."

Dianna simply couldn't let him get away with mouthing such easy platitudes. "Cut the campaign speech," she said. "Where were you yesterday evening, Mr. Campbell? In Boston, perhaps, somewhere near Hal's apartment?"

"In Boston?" Andrew gave a credible performance of appearing stunned by her implicit accusation. "Are you suggesting... You can't be suggesting... that I had anything to do with Hal Doherty's murder?"

Sanctimonious bastard, Dianna thought, wanting to cry and not sure why. "You had plenty of reasons to dislike him," she said. "Far more than most people know."

"Di!" Sonya murmured, sounding shocked. "Steady on, kid." The news of Hal's death must have knocked Sonya for a total loop, because normally she'd have been pursuing Andrew like a terrier after a rat. Not because she really suspected him of committing murder, but just on the general principle that politicians always have something to hide that reporters ought to be pursuing.

Andrew turned pale beneath his tan. "It's okay. I understand that... Ms. Mason... is upset. I certainly didn't find Hal Doherty a likable person. But I don't kill people I dislike. Otherwise there'd be a trail of dead bodies scattered around the country in my wake."

"Perhaps there is," Dianna said, brave enough to challenge him, now that Sonya was right there listening.

Andrew gazed at her thoughtfully. "And perhaps I have reason to be grateful for my horrendous campaign schedule," he said. "Fortunately, my entire day yesterday was programmed to the minute. Whatever time poor Hal Doherty was shot, my alibi is rock solid. I was in Florida yesterday, and then in the early evening I flew into New York City for a dinner with the mayor. If I was alone for ten minutes, it's as much as ever."

He wasn't a stupid man, and lying about something as easy to check as his schedule would be stupid. Dianna felt a totally irrational flare of relief at the knowledge that Hal might not have been killed by Andrew Campbell. Maybe she didn't have to add the guilt of Hal's death to all the other burdens she carried. Perhaps she should stop putting herself at the center of everyone's universe and not leap to the conclusion that Hal had been murdered because of his association with her. The police might be right about a failed drug deal. *Please God, let the police be right.* Hal could have been killed by an irate drug dealer, or even a burglar. Or how about one of his ex-wives? Lord knew, he had enough of them, all with darn good reasons for loathing him. Dianna allowed herself to hope.

Andrew turned to go, and Sonya said goodbye. "It was a pleasure to meet you, Mr. Campbell. Good luck with your campaign."

"Thanks." He flashed her one of his most engaging smiles. "I'm not used to hearing such sincere good wishes from journalists."

Sonya shrugged. "I've read your position papers. I think what you say makes a lot of sense, especially about the need for finding ways to protect the environment without destroying decent-paying jobs."

Andrew nodded. "I've spent a quarter of a century as a real-estate developer. I've learned that there are usually ways to build commercially successful projects without bulldozing every tree and draining every marsh in the vicinity. I want to persuade special-interest groups to stop shouting at each other and start listening. Sometimes the noise level gets so high on controversial issues that the voice of moderation gets drowned right out."

"Like gays in the military?" Sonya suggested. "There's an issue that seems to generate a lot of noise and not much light."

"Yes, indeed." Andrew's smile was in full working order. "But I confess that's not a subject I've devoted much time to. We politicians have to pick our causes, you know. Otherwise we end up being half informed about a dozen subjects and masters of none. I feel I have special insights into the subject of development and the environment because I've spent my working life dealing with just that."

Sonya took a long, deep drag on her cigarette. "In view of your own service in the navy, I would have thought that gays in the military would be something you had strong opinions on."

"No," Andrew replied. "It's not. I believe we should leave military policies to be decided by our military leaders, and by our commander in chief, of course. Goodbye, Ms. Harvey. I've enjoyed talking to you, but I need to get back to my hotel before my campaign manager sends out a search party."

Andrew let himself out of the iron gate that separated Dianna's small courtyard from the road. A Cadillac with smoked-glass windows drove out of the alley and glided to a halt in front of Sonya's car. Andrew let himself into the front seat of the Cadillac, next to the driver. Sonya watched the limo drive off, then sighed and stalked into the studio. "Where's the booze, kid? I'm gonna bug out if I don't get a drink soon."

Dianna opened her cupboard. "I only have vodka and a bottle of brandy that's been hanging around since last Christmas."

"Vodka sounds wonderful. On the rocks, with a twist of lime."

"It's terrible news about Hal," Dianna said, handing Sonya her drink and pouring herself a weak mixture of vodka and tonic. "Nobody deserves to end up with a bullet in their back. I'm so sorry, Sonya, I don't quite know what to say. You've known Hal for a long time. This must be dreadful for you."

"Yeah, one way and another it's been a bitch of a week. Hal was a creep, but he was kind of my creep, you know what I mean? When we first hit college, we saw each other through some tough times. Let's face it, two kids from Wyoming, we had a lot to learn. Hell, I didn't even know I was gay until I got to college, and then I damn near freaked. Hal spent a lot of

time holding my hand that first year. *Aw, shit.* Why
did he open his stupid, friggin' door?''

Sonya didn't usually spend time reflecting on her
sexual orientation. Obviously, hearing of Hal's death
was affecting her deeply. Even her exchange with Andrew Campbell had been oddly off-key. Dianna would
have expected her to pursue him about his policy on
land use, where he was potentially vulnerable because
of his company's history of aggressive development.
Instead, she'd thrown him an open-ended question
about gays in the military, which Andrew hadn't even
pretended to answer. What's more, she'd let him get
away with the evasion.

Sonya sipped her vodka, too restless to sit still.
''What was Andrew Campbell doing on your doorstep?'' she asked, stopping in front of the four new
bowls, and stroking the largest one admiringly. ''This
is a hell of a handsome piece, by the way.''

''Thanks.'' Dianna decided this wasn't an appropriate moment to tell Sonya that she suspected one of
Hal's last acts had been to sneak into her studio and
smash up a month's worth of work. ''And I don't
know why Andrew came to visit me. He said he
needed to talk to me.''

''Do you really think he knows something about
Hal Doherty's murder, or was that just a random accusation you hurled out because you can't stand the
guy?'' Sonya directed her question to the workbench.
For some reason, she seemed anxious to avoid meeting Dianna's eyes.

''I was angry,'' Dianna admitted. ''I was lashing
out. But I think he's perfectly capable of arranging
Hal's death if it happens to seem expedient to him.
You see, I know he's already committed murder.'' She

stirred her vodka and tonic with her finger, realizing the conversation was heading straight back to the subject that had precipitated her argument with Sonya yesterday.

Sure enough, Sonya picked up the threads of the previous day's discussion. "You think he's capable of murder because you believe the story Claire Campbell told you. You believe that Andrew burned down the cabin in Vermont, knowing she was inside."

Dianna drew in a shaky breath. "Yes. I'm convinced he tried to murder Claire."

"What was his motive? Did she tell you that, too?"

"Money," Dianna said succinctly. "Claire's money was left to her by Andrew's brother, Douglas. Under the terms of the original trust, the entire fund reverts to Andrew as soon as Claire dies."

Sonya crunched an ice cube. "Why does Andrew need the money? He's already rich."

"You can never be too rich if you want to be president of the United States," Dianna said. "Twenty million dollars would make a swell start to Andrew's campaign chest."

Sonya gulped the last of her drink in a single swallow. "A man has to be pretty sick to try to murder his own child."

"Sick, or very ambitious."

Sonya swung around, holding up her glass. "I need another of these," she said. "May I?"

"Help yourself. Sonya... About yesterday... I owe you an apology. You were right. I wasn't telling you the whole truth, but there are reasons why I didn't, and why I still can't. But I told you the absolute truth about Andrew. I know he tried to kill Claire. What's more, I don't think he's a reformed character. I suspect he set fire to the guesthouse in Florida because he was afraid I was Claire come back to haunt him. That's the reason I left Florida—I was scared that Andrew Campbell would kill me.''

Sonya drowned her ice cubes in vodka. "I hear you," she said. "And you can't go to the press with any of this stuff, because nobody will believe you.''

"You didn't believe me," Dianna said. "And you've known me for years. If you think my judgment is screwed up where Andrew's concerned, why would any self-respecting reporter believe me? I spent six months in a mental hospital and now I want the world to believe one of America's most popular political candidates tried to commit murder.'' She smiled bitterly. "Maybe I should approach the *National Enquirer.* They could print my accusations right next to their story about Big Foot saving newborn twins abandoned in the forest.''

Sonya made her third tour of the studio. Her second neat vodka was disappearing fast. "Look, what happened yesterday wasn't quite what it seemed. I was mad at you because that was easier than being mad at myself. You weren't telling the whole truth, but neither was I.''

"You weren't telling the truth?" Dianna looked up, puzzled. "But we weren't talking about you.''

Sonya's smile was weary. "Yes, we were, sweetie, although you had no way of knowing it.'' She set the empty glass down on the workbench and stared at the photos Dianna had taken of hummingbirds drinking sugar water from a feeder. When she looked up, Dianna was astonished to see the gleam of tears in her eyes.

"Do you remember last summer? My mother was dying of breast cancer, and I went up to Wyoming to stay with her."

"Yes, of course I remember."

"I was with my family for two weeks," Sonya said, reaching for her cigarettes. "I guess they were the worst goddamned weeks of my entire life."

Dianna's voice softened in sympathy. "Losing your mother has to be dreadful."

"Yeah, well, I guess for some people it's worse than others." Sonya puffed nervously. "Mom was so damned happy to see me. She couldn't talk much, so she saved her breath for the really important stuff. Like asking me when I was going to get married and give her some grandchildren. I told her my brother had already given her three terrific grandkids. She told me it was my kids she'd always wanted to see."

Dianna's heart lurched in sympathy. "Gosh, I'm sorry, Sonya. That must have been really hard for you to hear."

Sonya gave a laugh that contained not the smallest trace of mirth. "You want to know what happened? I decided that since my mother was dying, maybe it was time for us to tell each other the truth for a change. So I did. I told her that I would like very much to have a baby, but I didn't know if it would ever happen because I was gay, and I wasn't sure how I felt about lesbians who deliberately set out to become single parents. And I worried even more how my kid would feel when I had to explain that Daddy was an unknown donor from a sperm bank, and Mommy had passed out like a Victorian maiden the only time she tried to have sex with a man."

Dianna could see that her friend was on the verge of breaking down. "What did your mother say?" she asked, as gently as she could.

"She didn't exactly say anything." Sonya screwed up her eyes, but not in time to prevent a couple of tears from escaping. She swiped at her cheeks. "Damn! This vodka's making me maudlin."

"It must have been hard for you to tell her the truth," Dianna said. "On the other hand, she was from a different generation and she lived all her life in a small town with old-fashioned values. I expect she found it hard to listen."

"That's sort of an understatement," Sonya replied. "In fact, when I finished my little speech, Mom simply closed her eyes and turned her face to the wall. She never spoke directly to me again, although she did find the energy to tell the hospital staff that I was never to be allowed into her room under any circumstances. The next time I saw her was at the funeral. Dad looked at me as if I were something the barn rats had vomited up, and my brother took me to one side and yelled at me for twenty minutes because, as he put it, I was so determined to fling my perverted sexuality in my mother's face that I couldn't even let her die in peace. My sister-in-law followed up with the suggestion that I'd be doing my family and the state of Wyoming a major favor if I never came back. Nobody in the family has spoken to me since."

Dianna put her arms around Sonya and hugged her. "I'm so sorry, Sonya. Why didn't you tell me? I knew your mom's death hit you hard, but I never knew how much garbage you were trying to get through."

"I guess some things hurt too much to talk about," Sonya said. She reached for a tissue and blew her nose. "Hell and damnation, and all those other good cusswords. Right now, I'm not sure who I'm crying for. You, or me, or Mom. Or maybe even Hal, the old slimeball."

"Maybe for your brother and your father," Dianna suggested quietly. "Think of how much they're losing by cutting you out from their lives."

Sonya sniffed. "I'm sure they don't see it that way, but thanks, kid. You're a good friend. If I have another vodka, may I pass out on your sofa tonight?"

"Be my guest. Here, let me get it for you." Dianna fixed her friend another drink. "Enjoy it, kiddo, because there's no more. Unless we start on the Christmas brandy."

"Three drinks ought to be enough for a modest hangover. Cheers." She sipped in silence for a minute or two, then sighed. "You're too goddamned understanding, Di. You're supposed to ask me why I suddenly broke loose and told you the sob story of my mother's deathbed."

Dianna perched at the other end of the sofa. "Okay, why did you?"

"Because it's extremely relevant to you and your pursuit of Andrew Campbell."

Whatever she had expected to hear, it wasn't that. Dianna shook her head in confusion. "Sorry, you lost me. What's Andrew got to do with all this?"

Sonya stared into the depths of her drink. "I guess my experience with Mom taught me that people should be allowed to keep their secrets. Since society refuses to accept homosexual behavior, people who are gay should be able to stay in the closet if they want to. Confession isn't always good for the soul. You ought to be able to sympathize with that viewpoint.''

"I do, to a certain extent. Unless the secrets are concerned with something illegal, or dangerous.''

"All secrets are dangerous,'' Sonya said flatly. "Haven't you realized that? If you go on *Oprah* and confess to sixty million TV viewers that you made love to a gorilla, nobody cares. If you're ashamed of the fact that in sixth grade you cheated on Miss Hepplewhite's spelling test, and you keep that a secret, everybody in the whole world will condemn you when the facts come out.''

"I suppose that's true." Dianna spoke gently, so anxious to find out what Sonya was trying to tell her that she didn't relate the argument to her own behavior and the secrets she clung to with such stubborn determination. "Sonya, you're procrastinating. What's any of this got to do with Andrew Campbell?''

Sonya set her glass down so hard that vodka and ice sloshed over the side. "Check his military record,'' she said, her voice hard.

"His military record?'' Dianna repeated. "What for? Sonya, he won a Purple Heart, he was honorably discharged. There's nothing there. A million reporters must have checked those records.''

"Look again,'' she said. "Cross-check Andrew's files with the court-martial records for Lieutenant Jordan Edgar III. Read between the lines and tell me what you come up with.''

Dianna's stomach gave a lurch either of excitement or of fear. "Are you telling me there's something in the court-martial record of this lieutenant that will derail Andrew's campaign for governor?"

"I'm sure of it," Sonya said. "Sweetie, I can positively guarantee it."

Eleven

Ben had shut his door and turned off his phone in an effort to clean his desk at the end of a too-long day, when Roger poked his head into the office. "Can you spare five minutes?" he asked. "We need to talk about my trip to London."

"Of course. Come in. I've been meaning to get back to you all day, but it's been one crisis after another." With only the smallest of mental sighs, Ben cleared a space on his desk and swiveled around to face his computer screen. "So how was your trip?" he asked, as he clicked his mouse through a couple of prompts and pulled up his file on the Canary Wharf project. "Bring me up-to-date on what you did."

Roger grinned, hooking a chair with his heel and pulling it up to the desk. "I'm assuming you don't want to hear about the dancing girls I brought up to my hotel room, or the all-night session in one of London's most exclusive gambling clubs where I lost a hundred thousand on a single turn of the dice."

"Sorry, no time for the interesting stuff." Ben smiled back. "How about a few boring details on how we can stop leaking money on the Canary Wharf project?"

Roger leaned forward, instantly all-business. "I arrived at Heathrow early on Monday morning and went straight to our London offices. I worked with our people there, trying to get a handle on the problems from their perspective. Then on Tuesday, I went out to Canary Wharf to visit our properties. It's even more difficult to get there by public transport than we thought, by the way. I spent the next three mornings discussing various options with Gerald Hughes, who's the director of the rental operation out at the Wharf, and three afternoons working alongside the supervisor who handles day-to-day management of the property. She's a woman. Maggie Mitchell.''

Ben consulted his computer screen. "We're using Beavis & May. They're one of the largest property-management companies in Europe and it says here that Gerald Hughes has twenty years of experience in commercial real estate.''

"Yes, and my professional opinion is that Gerald and his company both suck. At least, for our purposes.''

Ben raised an eyebrow. "Any particular reason why?''

"Several.'' In brief, succinct terms, Roger listed half-a-dozen areas in which he'd found the existing management ineffective. "But there's one major reason why I decided we have to replace them,'' he concluded.

"What's that?''

"They're conservative to the point of paralysis. Every suggestion I made, every change I proposed, Gerald or Maggie would look at me pityingly and say, 'I'm sorry, Mr. Campbell, that can't be done. You just don't understand the London property market. We don't do things here like you do in America, you know.''' Roger shook his head in disgust. "They were so blasted smug, all of them. If they were achieving outstanding success, I could understand that they might not want some brash college kid to come in and tell them their business. But given that they're running our properties at less than thirty-percent occupancy, I think they ought to welcome a few helpful suggestions."

"I agree." Ben spoke crisply. "We can't work with people who won't listen to our ideas. We certainly can't work with people who reject our ideas simply because they're new. Have you checked our contract terms with these people?" He tapped a few keys on his computer. "I don't have the agreements entered into my data base, but I assume we have decent escape clauses written into our contracts?"

"Ironclad. Our lawyers did us proud. We can fire them, no problem. Shall I set the process in motion?"

Roger made no effort to hide his eagerness to fire the existing management and Ben didn't need much imagination to visualize how the sessions in London must have gone. He could picture the stuffy, middle-aged Brits doing their patronizing best to put the brash young American in his place. But even if Roger wanted retribution chiefly because his youthful ego had been wounded, Ben didn't doubt that Beavis & May needed to go. Ben had intended all along to fire them unless they presented Roger with an innovative plan to reverse the current losses. In fact, Roger's trip to London had been designed to give him experience in assessing a complex situation within a short time-span, rather than to provide Ben with crucial information. However, Ben had no intention of letting Roger know that his trip had been more in the nature of a training exercise than a genuine fact-gathering mission. There were only so many buffets a young ego could take.

"Let's get our replacements lined up before we finally fire Beavis & May," Ben said, swinging his chair around from the computer. "Any recommendations as to who we might use?"

"I'm working on it. I had one meeting with a company called Harrington Associates, and that went pretty well. The company's just been formed and the partners are all young, but they have impressive backgrounds, and they're keen to innovate. At least they don't think that the way it worked in 1950 is the ultimate answer to problems in the nineties."

"Maybe I should take a quick trip with you to London and check them out," Ben said. "Youth and enthusiasm are all very well, but day-to-day property management needs administrative skills and practical know-how as well as entrepreneurial spirit."

"Well, sure, I realize that," Roger said, his voice cool. "Naturally I did some checking on Harrington Associates and I would certainly take their practical expertise into account before I finally recommended hiring them. There's no need for you to make the time to fly all the way across the Atlantic and back when you're so busy, Ben. No reason at all."

In other words, butt the hell out of my deal, Ben thought in silent amusement. He admired Roger's get-up-and-go attitude, but the younger man lacked the experience to make snap judgments about something as complex—and potentially costly—as the Canary Wharf project. However, convincing an eager twenty-three-year-old that he wasn't seasoned enough to handle a deal on his own was a delicate matter, and

Ben rapidly weighed and discarded various options. Despite the fact that Andrew neither requested nor expected special treatment for his son, Ben was always aware of the fact that Roger would one day inherit the company and that he needed to learn how to conduct an international negotiation.

"You've done a great job so far," Ben said finally. "I appreciate the fact that you didn't come back with a wishy-washy report that hedged and fudged and got us nowhere. You were decisive and informed, and I like that."

"Thanks. Does that mean I get to conclude the deal myself?"

"Yes, you can negotiate the deal," Ben said slowly. "But I get to come along as observer. If you don't screw up, I'll keep my mouth shut and the deal will be entirely your baby."

He could tell that Roger was disappointed, but Ben was the boss, and Roger was smart enough to know it. "Okay," he said. "I'll talk with your secretary. Between the two of us, we'll check out a few alternative dates, and get back to you so you can make the final decision on when we make the trip."

"Great. Tell my secretary to clear a couple of days soon, won't you?" Ben punched a few keys on the computer and grimaced. "The cash-flow graph for Canary Wharf looks like the diagram of a guy doing a swallow dive."

"So what else is new?" Roger stood, pushing his chair into the corner. On the point of leaving the room, he hesitated, swinging around in the doorway. "I hear you went to Boston over the weekend," he said. "You paid a visit to Dianna Mason."

Ben looked up, not quite sure why he wished that particular piece of news hadn't leaked. "Who told you that?"

"I called Mother from the airport when I landed in New York on Sunday night. What's the big deal? Mom was sounding very mysterious and wouldn't say much, except that you were still investigating Dianna's claims. I thought that was all over. When I left Miami for London, she'd just declared herself Impostor of the Week and was running for cover in Boston before you guys could get around to having her arrested."

"That's true," Ben said. He debated for a second or two, wondering how to balance Evelyn's right to privacy with Roger's right to know the truth about what had happened in regard to a woman who might well be his sister. The truth was bound to come out in the end, Ben decided, and Roger deserved to know what was going on. "I think Dianna was lying," he said, as unemotionally as he could. "I think she's your sister, Roger. I think she's Claire."

Roger was silent for a long time, then he wrinkled his nose. "You know something? That's kind of creepy."

"What does that mean?"

Roger shrugged. "I'm not sure. It's just an expression of how I feel, not something logical." He leaned against the credenza, spreading his hands in a gesture that was at once vulnerable and pleading. "I mean, if she's Claire, why is she doing this? I don't understand a single, solitary thing going on in her mind right now. How can my own sister feel so...so damned *alien?*" He rubbed his forehead, kneading at the bridge of his nose. "Hell, are you sure she's not tricking you, Ben?"

"As sure as I can be without objective proof of her identity."

Roger shoved his hands into his pockets, his expression darkening. "What are we going to do, Ben? We can't go on like this. We have to find out the truth. My mother may look like she's the most self-possessed woman in the world, but she's much more vulnerable than she seems, and Claire's disappearance freaked her out. Every time one of these blasted frauds turns up, she allows herself to start hoping all over again."

"That's the whole point. I don't think Dianna Mason is a fraud."

Roger scowled. "Then what the hell is she playing at? I mean, it's...spooky...having a woman out there who may be Evelyn's daughter—and my sister—but nobody knows for sure."

Roger looked young and confused and Ben felt a surge of sympathy. "I know this must be damned difficult for you—"

"Difficult? It's impossible!" Roger looked up pleadingly. "Help us, Ben. How can we stop this dragging on for weeks, with no resolution? My mother's mental health won't stand too much more of this uncertainty."

"It's already taken care of," Ben said. "I sent blood samples to a genetic-testing laboratory this morning. They'll get the samples tomorrow and they're promising me a definitive result by next week."

"My father agreed to give you a blood sample?" Roger said, sounding amazed.

"Why wouldn't he?" Ben asked.

"Oh, no reason. He's always refused in the past, that's all."

Roger spoke with convincing casualness, and most people would have been deceived. But Ben had trained himself to read the body language of the people who worked for him, and he'd worked with Roger for more than a year. Why was Roger so surprised at the prospect of his father agreeing to a DNA comparison? Should he tell Roger that Evelyn had provided the sample, when she had obviously chosen to withhold that information? Ethically, he'd already screwed up quite enough over this whole issue of genetic testing. If Evelyn wanted to keep silent until the test results came through, he probably ought to respect her wishes.

"Dianna Mason is a more convincing candidate than any of the other young women who showed up on the Campbell doorstep," Ben said, avoiding a direct response. "The test results will probably come through on Monday, so we aren't going to be kept in suspense much longer."

"Next Monday?" Roger asked. "Holy hell, I'm sure that's going to create a stir if they turn out to be positive. What do you think it will do to Dad's campaign for governor?"

"I imagine it will give him another big boost in the polls," Ben said. "Everyone loves missing-children stories with a happy ending."

"Yeah, they sure do." Roger turned away, his eyes full of emotion. "Well, keep me posted, won't you, Ben? Jeez, this still doesn't seem quite real. Claire's been gone so long.... We didn't see all that much of each other, but she was such a terrific big sister.... I can't wait to have her back home again...."

"Don't count on it too much," Ben said, putting his arm around Roger as he walked him to the door. "After all, we could be running hard in pursuit of a very wild goose."

"Do you think that?" Roger asked.

"No," Ben said reassuringly. "To be honest, I think on Monday we'll have proof positive that your sister and Dianna Mason are one and the same person."

"Weird," Roger said, shaking his head. "Totally weird."

Dianna emptied an overflowing ashtray, and shuffled papers until she cleared a space on Sonya's desk. Her friend returned, carrying two files, both relatively slender.

"Here you are," Sonya said, slapping the folders onto the desk. "The one with the red label contains Xerox copies of all the information I could find on Lieutenant Jordan Edgar III. The one with the green label has biographical data on Andrew Campbell for the same time period."

Dianna took the files, her stomach churning with an emotion that she recognized as dread, not excitement. Looking at the bland Manila folders, she was overwhelmed by a superstitious fear that if she opened them, many lives would be irrevocably changed. But change was what she wanted, wasn't it? Change, retribution, justice. Noble goals—so why did she feel so damned *dirty?*

"If you don't want to read the files, I can take them away," Sonya said.

"No, I want to read them." Dianna drew in a deep breath, and smoothed her hands over the file labeled

Lieutenant Jordan Edgar III. "If I have questions, where will you be?" she asked.

"In the kitchen," Sonya answered dryly. "Drinking coffee, eating aspirin, and wondering if I've done the right thing. Jesus, I hope you haven't made a mistake, Di. I hope to God Andrew Campbell really is a murderer, because nothing less would justify what I'm helping you to do."

"Rest easy," Dianna said, her resolve returning. "He is."

"Yeah, well, if it was anybody else in the world but you, I'd be wondering." Sonya padded over to the door. "Happy reading, kiddo. Jeez, I can't make up my mind whether to throw up now, or wait until you hand that material over to the media."

"I'd wait," Dianna said. "It's always possible that I won't find anything I can use."

Sonya didn't bother to reply and Dianna opened Lieutenant Edgar's file with hands that she was pleased to note were entirely steady. She read through the brief biographical note with cool detachment. Jordan Edgar III. Born 1941, educated Groton School and Princeton University. Graduated summa cum laude in 1962 and followed family tradition by volunteering for the navy. His father, Jordan Edgar II— nothing as commonplace as Jr. for the Jordan Edgars—was at this time a rear admiral, who had served with distinction as a submarine captain during the Cuban Missile Crisis.

Lieutenant Edgar apparently didn't acquire or inherit his father's passion for naval service. He completed his two years, and was honorably discharged, still a lieutenant jg, after a career that seemed remarkable only for its plodding mediocrity. He entered Harvard Law School in the fall of 1965, still a relatively young man of twenty-four.

Dianna turned the page to the next sheet with more interest than the bare facts appeared to warrant. Andrew Campbell had also attended Groton, and he'd graduated from Princeton in 1962, just like Jordan Edgar. He had then worked in the family business for almost three years, before entering Harvard Law School in the fall of 1965. She had never heard any previous mention of Jordan Edgar's name, but it was hard to believe that he and Andrew had been strangers to each other when their early lives had followed such similar paths.

The sixties was a restless, turbulent decade, and Jordan Edgar had soon found himself caught up in the sweep of history. As the Vietnam War intensified, and casualties mounted with horrifying swiftness, the protests on college campuses escalated. Rear Admiral Edgar, a Harvard alumnus, visited his alma mater in the spring of 1968 and attempted to defend government policy and military operations in Vietnam. He could scarcely have picked a worse moment for his speech. The recent Tet offensive by the North Vietnamese had exposed failures at all levels of the U.S. command, and Rear Admiral Edgar was shouted off the platform by angry young people who didn't want to find themselves dying in the rice paddies of Southeast Asia for a cause almost nobody believed in.

Amid loud student cheering, the leader of the Black Panthers—antiwar protests and civil-rights campaigns sometimes got confusingly jumbled—sprang up onto the stage where the rear admiral had tried to speak, and symbolically burned a U.S. flag.

According to the *Crimson,* Harvard's student newspaper, Andrew Campbell was the only student who even attempted to speak up in support of Rear Admiral Edgar. When Andrew tried to point out to his fellow students that, under the First Amendment, even unpopular or foolish speech was protected, he was driven from the stage by a barrage of hurled debris. The tone of the report suggested that the *Crimson* heartily approved of this violent form of student censorship.

A photo accompanying the original article showed lots of grungy, long-haired students, wearing tie-dyed shirts and carrying flowers, shrieking ecstatically as the flag burned. On the far-left side of the photo was a small group of young women with neatly combed hair, wearing white blouses with perky lace collars and carrying a banner with lettering too small to read. Sonya had circled the face of one of the women.

"Evelyn Campbell, née Duplessy," she had noted in the margin. "Married Andrew Campbell two months after this miniriot, in July 1968."

Sometime during that summer, while Andrew and Evelyn were enjoying a honeymoon in Europe, Jordan Edgar III made the decision to return to active service with the navy. In October, he was assigned to the aircraft carrier *Spirit of Freedom,* which was based in the Philippines, with a home port in Subic Bay.

Dianna paused in her reading, staring at the pages in front of her with blurred eyes. Andrew Campbell, as she knew without bothering to check the other file, had volunteered for active duty early in the fall of 1968, right after he returned from his Parisian honeymoon. After a few weeks of basic training in Virginia, he had been awarded a temporary commission and assigned to a junior command on board the *Spirit of Freedom*. He had left the United States on February 15, 1969. He hadn't returned until a year later, when his daughter Claire was almost three months old. He still had almost another year to serve, but he wasn't sent abroad again. Posted to a desk job in Virginia, and cushioned by plenty of family money, he'd served out the last few months of his tour of duty in relative comfort, living in a spacious rented house with his wife and baby daughter.

When Andrew launched his campaign for governor, Evelyn Campbell had granted a rare personal interview to Miami's NBC affiliate. In response to a question about how it had felt to give birth to her first child while her husband was thousands of miles away, Evelyn told the reporter that she had been "relieved" when Andrew volunteered for active duty in the navy. Relieved, she had explained, because he recognized his duty and wasn't afraid to put himself at risk in order to fulfill it, despite opposition from his family and virtually all of his college friends. With a serene smile, Evelyn had suggested that if the people of the state of Florida elected Andrew as their governor, he would always recognize his duty—and strive to do it. The interview had boosted Andrew's standing three points in Miami-area political polls, and Evelyn, who for years had rarely spent more than a day or two a month in Andrew's company, suddenly became a fixture at his side on important campaign stops.

Dianna realized her detachment had vanished completely as she read, and that she was trembling. She took a sip of ice water, and turned back to Jordan Edgar's file, struggling to remain impartial as she read on. Either because naval commanders were getting

killed at a fast clip—Vietnam, like other wars, was
great for rapid promotion—or else in recognition of
his earlier service to his country, Lieutenant Edgar—
junior grade—was promoted to the rank of full lieutenant shortly after arriving in Subic Bay.

His successful climb up the career ladder lasted less
than six months. In the late spring of 1969, with more
than half a million American men fighting and facing
death in Vietnam, the navy took time out to relieve
Lieutenant Edgar of his command. He was accused of
the crime of indulging in repeated homosexual activities with an unknown, unidentified partner. Because
he refused to name his lover, an Article 32 investigation under the Uniform Code of Military Justice was
hastily conducted. The investigation unearthed all the
evidence it needed, and more. In August, 1969, a
general court-martial was convened.

Lieutenant Edgar had no realistic hope of pleading
not guilty. The prosecution produced damning photographs, showing him indisputably engaged in what
the prosecuting officer coyly termed "unnatural acts."
Jordan Edgar's fate seemed sealed, but the authorities were obsessed with uncovering the name of his
partner in perversion. Lieutenant Edgar's lover was
obviously a shipmate, and almost certainly a fellow
officer, since the photographs had been taken in the
lieutenant's cabin when the ship was at sea. The trial
rapidly degenerated into a witch-hunt for Jordan's
partner.

Jordan's homosexuality had first been suspected by
Lieutenant Bruce Trenton, his cabin mate. Bruce was
an Annapolis graduate from South Carolina who believed in the United States Navy, his God, and his
country, in that order. With unfeigned horror, Bruce

told the court-martial judges that, in his opinion, homosexuality in the navy was a more deadly threat to national security than the North Vietnamese armies. In response to questioning, he sadly confirmed that, despite weeks of snooping, he was quite unable to pin a name on Jordan's lover. Naturally, the trysts had taken place only when Bruce was on duty. Naturally, both Jordan and his partner had used great cunning to keep their relationship secret.

Determined to root out perversion before it contaminated the entire ship, Bruce had rigged up his camera with help from his commanding officer. Unfortunately both of the would-be detectives were inexperienced photographers and the camera, aimed randomly through a crack in the shutters covering a porthole, had never managed to capture any identifiable pictures of the elusive lover— The panel of judges, with no sense of irony, ruled that blurred photos of tumescent "lower portions of the anatomy" could not be used as a means of identification.

The judges asked repeatedly if Jordan wanted to make things easier for himself by naming his partner. He refused either to admit his guilt, or to name his lover. In retribution, the judges imposed the maximum sentence, and Jordan was stripped of his rank and hauled off to military prison on the naval base in Guam, where the taxpayers of the United States could enjoy the satisfaction of paying for ten years of his incarceration.

The rear admiral, Jordan Edgar's father, took the news of his son's conviction very badly. Unable to stand the shame of his son's disgraceful behavior, he pleaded ill health, retired from the service, and killed himself in a convenient car accident shortly after sentence was imposed on his errant son.

On hearing of his father's death, Jordan Edgar III slashed his wrists with a knife he'd honed from the slats of his prison bed. More efficient in this than he'd been in his other endeavors, he managed to bleed to death before anyone found him, thus saving himself nine years of hell, and the taxpayers nine more years of expensive prison maintenance.

The master sergeant in charge of the cell block was reprimanded for failing to find the knife, but casualties in the Vietnam War had reached a hundred thousand, and the death of one imprisoned ex-officer scarcely registered as a blip in the monthly statistics. The naval file on the case of former Lieutenant Jordan Edgar III was officially closed. His body was released to the family and he was buried privately, with only his mother and two sisters in attendance.

As a footnote, Sonya had scrawled a notation to the effect that Bruce Trenton was promoted to full commander in July of 1970 and given a posting in Hawaii—not exactly a hardship assignment. Trenton enjoyed continuing success in his career and retired with the rank of vice admiral in 1986. He was now a consultant to a prestigious think tank in Washington.

Dianna pushed her chair away from the desk, leaning back and stretching cramped muscles. She reached for the green-tagged file, then pushed it away unopened. Every day for the past three months she had hoped that Sonya would find something that could be used to destroy Andrew Campbell's campaign for governor. The silver bullet she'd craved was now lying in front of her, waiting to be picked up, but she was finding herself oddly reluctant to load the gun.

Not because of any lingering fondness for Andrew, she assured herself. Her concerns were all because of Jordan Edgar. The Edgar family had suffered enough—far more than enough—because of stereotyping and prejudice. Was Jordan's mother still alive? Dianna knew she would have to find out before she made any final decisions. She hated to think that, in her need to bring down Andrew, she might open painful wounds and bring back memories that Jordan Edgar's family had every right to keep buried under the soothing blanket of time.

But first, before she worried about the Edgar family, she needed to confirm that Sonya had somehow managed to identify Andrew Campbell as the man Jordan Edgar had given his life to protect. She forced herself to open the green-tagged file and read its contents, line by line.

The information was circumstantial, but damning. Sonya had unearthed a dozen previously unremarked links between Andrew and Jordan. The two of them had lived in the same dorm at prep school and been partners on the tennis team and in the debating club. When Jordan was serving his first tour of duty in the navy, Andrew always seemed to turn up wherever Jordan was taking leave. He'd even flown out to Hawaii for a vacation when Jordan was stationed there for a couple of months.

More damning still was a telling photo, clipped from the society pages of a Pittsburgh newspaper. The photo showed Andrew Campbell on the night of his betrothal to Evelyn Duplessy. Dianna vaguely remembered seeing the picture before. Evelyn, elegant in a royal blue satin evening gown, leaned on Andrew's arm and smiled prettily into the camera. At first glance, it seemed that Andrew had turned toward his fiancée and was smiling down at her. Looking more closely, Dianna realized that Andrew wasn't gazing at his prospective bride. He was, in fact, staring across the room at a lone figure poised on the edge of the crowd: Jordan Edgar III, resplendent in full-dress naval uniform.

By the time she'd finished reading the file, Dianna was convinced Andrew Campbell had been the lieutenant's lover, and she was sure any other unbiased reader would reach the same conclusion. Sonya hadn't unearthed any startling new facts about Andrew. Most of the dates and details she had recorded were well-known to lots of other journalists. Sonya's insight had been to rearrange the established facts, and align them with the sad record of Jordan Edgar's too-brief career.

The only piece of information previously unknown to Dianna was the fact that Lieutenant Andrew Campbell jg had suffered from battle fatigue after two months of patrolling the coastal waters off Vietnam. On October 25, 1969, two weeks after the death of Jordan Edgar III in his prison cell—which was just about time enough for news of the death to circulate on board ship—Andrew had collapsed while at sea. A sympathetic captain had arranged for his transfer to a military medical facility in Okinawa, where Andrew had spent a month recuperating before being flown back for another two months of active duty on board the *Spirit of Freedom*.

Andrew himself had been very clever, Dianna decided. Instead of trying to gloss over the details of his military record, he had harped constantly on his year of service aboard the *Spirit of Freedom*. Journalists assumed he was angling for the votes of retired military personnel, and yawned through his speeches about the trials and joys of life in the navy. In their determination to avoid pursuing the obvious, journalists had been led right down the garden path. Nobody asked Andrew tough questions about his military career. Nobody probed to find out if there was anything hidden behind the insipid details of his official service record. Instead, investigative journalists were scurrying around all over Florida trying to identify the secret women in Andrew's life.

Heck, Dianna thought, *Andrew probably stirs up all those rumors about his extramarital affairs himself. Maybe he even takes Sharon Kruger everywhere he goes just so that people can whisper and wonder if his glamorous cook warms his bed as well as his dinner plates.*

She'd read all that she needed and more. Dianna closed the files and walked into the kitchen. Sonya was sitting on a bar stool drawn up to the counter, using a limp straw to stir the ice melting in her glass. Dianna had the impression that she'd been sitting on the stool for the past half hour, stirring without drinking.

"I read the files," she said flatly.

Sonya continued to stir her drink. "So. Now you know all about Andrew Campbell's nasty little secret."

"Sad little secret," Dianna replied without thinking. "What happened to Jordan Edgar is dreadful. It's horrible to think that Andrew stood by and said nothing while his lover was hauled off to jail."

Sonya looked up, her mouth twisting into a crooked smile. "Yeah, well, what are you gonna do about it, kiddo? If you take the information in those files to the media, you know what will happen."

Unfortunately, Dianna could imagine all too clearly. The issue of gays serving in the military rumbled near the surface of public life, an unresolved issue that grated on a lot of people's nerves. Jordan Edgar's tragic story would generate a lot of heat, a lot of tension, and very little constructive discussion.

Dianna frowned. "One thing I know for sure. The homophobes are going to have a field day."

Sonya smiled austerely. "True. But on the other hand, you'll have achieved your purpose. Andrew Campbell will be toast the day that story breaks. He'll be history as far as the race for governor is concerned."

"That's true, but I wish we could do this some other way," Dianna said. "I don't want Andrew Campbell to become governor of Florida. He's not suited to hold public office. But that's because he's a murderer, not because he once had a homosexual relationship with Jordan Edgar."

Sonya went back to stirring her ice. "Yeah, well, the end justifies the means and all that good stuff. Since he's guilty of one thing, what does it matter if the public condemns him for something else?"

"Not much, I guess." Extraordinarily, Dianna found herself wishing that Sonya hadn't presented her with the two files, hadn't provided her with the material that made Andrew's downfall possible. She had a sick certainty somewhere deep in her gut that no good could ever come of exploiting people's prejudices— not even for the noble cause of destroying Andrew Campbell. So many people would be hurt. *What about Evelyn?* she thought. *My God, what will Evelyn do when this story breaks?*

"Is Mrs. Edgar still alive?" she asked abruptly.

"Mrs. Edgar?"

"Yes, you know, Jordan's mother. The rear admiral's wife."

Sonya pulled a tray of ice from the fridge and slammed it onto the counter, popping ice cubes with a noisy crack. "Mrs. Edgar died last year. I don't know anything about his sisters. They're married, but I don't know who to, and I didn't waste time tracking them down."

Jordan's sisters had disappeared and his mother was dead. Which meant that she couldn't be hurt by anything that Dianna chose to reveal to the media. Andrew, on the other hand, was very much alive. What's more, he had set the fire that killed Jon Kaplan, he had probably engineered the car crash in New Jersey, and even if he hadn't murdered Hal Doherty, the recent fire in Florida suggested that he was willing to kill again if he felt threatened. With a record like that, he was clearly unfit to hold any public office, much less the office of governor.

Dianna stared down at the files she was holding. Right here, clutched in her hands, was information that would destroy Andrew Campbell. Why was she holding back? Dammit, she'd waited years for this moment, and she wasn't going to wimp out because she didn't like the method she would have to use to bring him down. Sometimes the end really did justify the means.

Dianna drew in a deep breath and forced herself to meet Sonya's eyes. "Okay, I'm going to make this material public. Do you want to break the story, Sonya?''

Sonya laughed, a grating sound that rasped across Dianna's soul. "No, thanks, kiddo. I think I'll pass on this one. Gay bashing isn't precisely my style. For obvious reasons.''

Dianna didn't press the issue, although she had a suspicion that Sonya's career would be significantly advanced if she took the story and ran with it. "In that case, I'm going to try for maximum impact and go for a revelation on prime-time TV. Andrew has an interview with Steve Sterne next Monday on *Newsmakers*. It's a big deal for him because it will be a national broadcast as opposed to a local Florida transmission. I'm going to see that Mr. Sterne gets the information contained in these two files, with the salient points all highlighted for his reading convenience. I assume he'll use the material, at least to press Andrew for some answers on issues like homosexual rights, which he has always avoided in the past.''

"Yeah," Sonya said. "That seems real likely. With the research staff he has on call, by Monday he'll probably have found love letters from Andrew to Jordan, or something equally damning.'' She stood, her face pale to the point of transparency. "Now, if you'll excuse me, kiddo, I'm gonna take a few minutes to retire to the bathroom and throw up. Not only do I hate to toss a fellow gay to the lions, the hell of it is, Andrew Campbell strikes me as a nice guy.''

"A lot of murderers do," Dianna said tersely. "Not all of them go around foaming at the mouth and swinging an ax.''

Sonya swung around, leaning against the door-jamb for support. "Tell me the truth, Di—I think I've earned it. Is Andrew Campbell really your father?"

Dianna paused for no more than a heartbeat. "No," she said, her smile bitter. "Andrew Campbell is not my father. I swear it."

Twelve

Revenge, Dianna decided sadly, needed to be taken swiftly, and enjoyed hot and steaming. If you allowed your passions and your hatreds time to cool, retribution had a bitter taste. She watched Andrew's interview with Steve Sterne—massacre would be a more accurate description—with her heart pounding against her rib cage, and her breath squeezing out of her lungs in tight, uneven pants.

Andrew was a veteran of televison interviews, and an accomplished public speaker, but Steve Sterne was famous for an interview technique that stopped just short of outright belligerence. Which was one of the reasons she had approached him with her information, Dianna reminded herself; but she quickly began to wish she'd chosen someone a little less brutal.

Steve cut Andrew no slack, and gave him no chance to prevaricate. He attacked from the opening seconds of the interview, starting off with a couple of hard-hitting questions about legislation pending in Florida pertaining to homosexual rights. While Andrew was still trying to stumble and equivocate his way around those, Steve led straight into the issue of Andrew's personal code of ethics and his relationship with Jordan Edgar.

Andrew made the disastrous mistake of pretending not to recognize the name. "Jordan Edgar, did you say?" He managed a smile that looked only a bit nervous. "I'm sorry, Steve, I don't quite remember..."

"You went to the same prep school, Mr. Campbell. You were in the same grade, slept in the same dorm for five years, and then you both went on to Princeton where you majored in political science. Both of you."

"Oh, yes, of course. How could I forget?" Andrew was a campaign pro. He realized he'd made a near-fatal mistake and he struggled to regain the ground he knew he was losing. "We played on the tennis team together. Jordan was my partner during our senior year at Groton. Heck of a tennis player. Wonderful guy." Andrew smiled straight into the camera, but Dianna saw a bead of sweat break out on his forehead and trickle toward his collar. She wondered how many other viewers had noticed the same thing.

Steve Sterne turned to a side camera, temporarily cutting off Andrew's image. He gazed toward his unseen audience with passionate-seeming sincerity. "We thought that a lot of potential voters might be interested in Mr. Campbell's friendship with Lieutenant Jordan Edgar," he said. "So we did a little research here at *Newsmakers* and we managed to find Jordan Edgar's sister, Christine. With Christine's help, we've put together a picture history of Jordan Edgar's life."

Steve swung back to address Andrew, who was caught by the camera mopping his forehead with a snowy white handkerchief. "In case your memory's slipping again, Mr. Campbell, I'd like to remind you that Jordan—Lieutenant Edgar—came to a very unhappy end while he was serving on board the *Spirit of Freedom*—the same ship as you, by the way.''

Andrew mumbled something incoherent—Dianna caught only the words ''great crew, great ship.'' Steve Sterne told the viewers to stay right where they were, because he'd be back after a short commercial break.

Dianna muted the sound and watched without really seeing as a cup of coffee steamed onto the screen, and the Energizer bunny thumped across a Scottish landscape. *Smile,* she told herself. *Be happy. This was what you wanted. Andrew squirming in the hot seat, while the voters of America look on.*

Yeah, said a little voice, *but I didn't expect the program to be quite this grim, and Steve Sterne quite so . . . so gloating.*

Why not? He's always this way, and you knew it.

Well, I certainly never expected Steve Sterne's research team to find one of Jordan's sisters! Good grief, they've only had Sonya's material a few days. I mean, a movie, for heaven's sake! Nobody could have figured they'd put together a film.

Liar. You knew damn well that Steve would force a dramatic confrontation one way or another. Jordan's sister is the absolutely logical person for his research team to go after. If Sonya had wanted to break this story, she would have done the same thing, and you know it.

The researchers must have been working twenty-four hours a day, Dianna thought, pressing her knuckles to her mouth as the commercials stopped and Steve's face smiled once again into the camera.

She used her remote control to turn up the sound. Steve welcomed back the viewers and the film biography of Jordan Edgar's life started to roll. Dianna watched, almost in a trance, as the now familiar story was played out. His editors had done an incredible job of splicing Christine Edgar's home movies with professional film clips from the turbulent days of Vietnam and the antiwar protests. Visually, the story was a masterpiece, mingling color and black-and-white film in a collage that seemed to add unbearable verisimilitude to the sad little tale.

With a sickening sense of inevitability, Dianna saw that the editors had selected only those home-movie shots of Jordan that included Andrew somewhere in the same frame. The two men were usually standing close, although they rarely touched. In one brief scene, Jordan flung his arm around Andrew's shoulders. Affection and camaraderie radiated from the silent pictures.

Perhaps viewers would accept that Andrew and Jordan were just friends, Dianna thought. Nothing in these movies proved that they were anything more than good buddies. When she realized what she was thinking, she had to turn away from the television for a few seconds to recapture her control. What in the world was happening to her? She surely wasn't hoping—she *couldn't* be hoping—that Andrew would survive this ruthless exposé?

The entire film probably lasted no more than five minutes. During the final sixty seconds or so, a voice-over commentary told the story of Lieutenant Edgar's court-martial. The narrator, without emphasis, explained that Jordan's refusal to name his lover had led to the imposition of the maximum possible sentence. The film ended with a still photo of Jordan Edgar in full-dress uniform. An unseen female identified herself as Christine Wallenstein, Jordan's younger sister. In a voice thick with emotion, she added the final chilling facts about Rear Admiral Edgar's death and Jordan's suicide in a military prison on the island of Guam.

When the camera returned to the studio, a middle-aged woman was just joining the set and taking a seat across from Andrew. She looked at him with loathing, her body tense with barely controlled dislike. Seemingly oblivious to her presence, Andrew stared straight ahead, a stone figure, deep-frozen in pain.

"This is Christine Wallenstein, Jordan Edgar's sister," Steve Sterne said into the camera, introducing her to the audience. He turned back to Christine. "You must feel that your brother's suicide was a tragic waste of a good man's life."

"Yes, Steve, that's exactly what I feel. My brother was a wonderful, warm, caring human being, but he was literally persecuted to death."

"Under the letter of the law as it applies to military personnel, the sentence given to your brother was entirely just. What's your opinion? Do you think the military authorities, and the navy in particular, handled his case fairly?"

"Of course not. Until the policy was changed in 1993, hundreds of people were dismissed from active duty every year for homosexual activities, but they didn't get sent to prison. At worst, they were court-martialed and given a dishonorable discharge. Hundreds more were allowed to remain on active duty and serve their country, quite often with the implicit approval of their commanding officers. My brother was made an example of for one reason only."

"What was that, Christine?"

"He wouldn't name his partner," she said angrily. "It's a not-so-secret dirty little secret that the navy brass are always terrified of homosexual relationships developing among the officers on board a ship, especially in wartime. My brother wouldn't name his lover, and the captain couldn't bear to think there was another gay loose on his ship, prowling the gangplanks waiting to jump on decent, heterosexual American boys. So my brother was sacrificed to placate the fears of a prejudiced captain and a bunch of neurotic admirals."

"Do you think it would have made things easier for your brother if his partner had come forward?"

Christine fought back a sob. "Of course, it would. That's the whole point. My brother was willing to face a prison sentence to protect his lover. But his lover was such a coward, he didn't even have the guts to step forward and admit his part in what had been going on. If they had both confessed, I'm sure neither of them would have received prison sentences."

"I can see you have a lot of angry feelings, Christine, and I'm sure our viewers will understand why." Steve Sterne leaned forward, his body language promising support and comfort if she would only trust him. "The military judges never did find out the name of your brother's lover. The record of Lieutenant Edgar's court-martial gives no hint as to who that man might have been. But you're his sister—his favorite sister, as I understand—and he may have confided in you. Did he?"

"He didn't write me a letter or anything like that," she said. "He didn't need to. I know who his lover was. I've always known."

Tension tautened Steve's profile, making him appear even more photogenic. "Knowing the truth, you've kept silent all these years. Why?"

Christine shook her head, as if she herself didn't quite know the answer to that question. "Jordan was dead. Nothing would bring him back to life. Besides, he'd been willing to go to jail to keep his lover's name secret. It seemed like the least I could do was follow his wishes."

"But now you've changed your mind and you're going to speak up. Is that right, Christine?"

"Yes. My mother died last year and I've been thinking about this issue of gays in public life a lot lately, and I've decided silence only makes the problem of homophobia worse. The American public needs to recognize that a lot of the people they admire are gay, but that doesn't mean anything in and of itself. There are brave, wonderful men who are gay, like my brother. And then there are cowardly, deceitful gays, like his lover."

"And so you've decided to put a name to the mystery man who was your brother's lover. And you're going to reveal that name tonight, here on this show."

"Yes, I am." Christine turned slowly until she was facing Andrew. Their eyes met. Their gazes locked. "My brother's lover was Andrew Campbell," she said, her voice clear and steady. "They'd been lovers for years. At least since college, and probably since high school."

Dianna's head jerked back. The blood roared violently in her ears. She swallowed a great gulp of air and stared wide-eyed at the screen. Steve Sterne leaned back in his chair. Despite years of experience as a TV journalist, he couldn't quite conceal his triumph. This was a major coup of investigative journalism, and he knew it. Circling in for the kill, he twisted around to confront Andrew.

"Do you have anything to say in reply to Mrs. Wallenstein's accusations, Mr. Campbell? Were you the mysterious homosexual lover that Jordan Edgar died to protect?"

The stone facade of Andrew's face cracked, and then crumbled. He looked with desperate pleading toward Christine. "Jordan begged me to keep silent," he said. "But I shouldn't have listened to him. There's nothing I can say to excuse my behavior, except that I'm sorry for what happened—desperately sorry. If I could go back and do things over differently, believe me, I would. Your brother was a wonderful man, and I loved him." Andrew stopped abruptly, covering his eyes with his hand. He pulled out the concealed mike from inside the lapel of his jacket and walked off the set, leaving the camera to pan over his empty chair.

Steve Sterne quickly segued into another commercial break and Dianna drew in a long, ragged breath. It was done. Andrew Campbell had been publicly discredited, not simply because he'd once had a homosexual love affair, but because he had stood by, silent and passive, while his partner suffered all the consequences of their relationship. Andrew had finally been paid back for his sins.

So why wasn't she celebrating? Dianna wondered bleakly. This was a genuine, honest-to-God triumph. After tonight, she could pretty well count on the fact that Andrew Campbell's career as a public figure was over. He was destroyed. Ruined. Finished. Andrew's many victims were avenged at last.

She ought to be deliriously happy.
She wondered why she was crying.

He was angry—so goddamned mad at the ruin-
ation of his plans—that he couldn't stop shaking.
Sharon was full of sympathy, repeating mindlessly
how dreadful it was and how the people of Florida
would probably understand. In the next breath, she
was moaning about how sorry he must be, and that the
scandal would take years to be forgotten.

Sorry? What a laugh! He wasn't sorry, he was *furious.* The governorship of Florida had vanished in
one twenty-minute broadcast, exploding in a nuclear
holocaust of TV-generated publicity.

And not only the governorship was lost. The presidency of the United States was now no more than a
hopeless pipe dream. The moral climate of the country might be more liberal today than it had been a
decade earlier, but Boris Yeltsin had more chance of
being elected president than someone tainted with the
tar brush of homosexuality. He was so fucking mad he
wanted to stand in the middle of the room and howl
with anguish like a wounded dog.

He paced his bedroom in the Pittsburgh house, just
enough in control of himself to refrain from picking
up one of Evelyn's antique vases and smashing it
against the wall. Christ Almighty, he'd worked so
hard—it just wasn't fair for some jerk of a TV inter-
viewer to come along and snatch away the prize!

He'd *counted on* that governorship as part of his
overall game plan for winning nomination to the
presidency a few years down the road. He wanted to
be president of the United States. He deserved to be
president. He had all the necessary qualifications. He

was a certified genius. He worked hard. He came from a good family and he would never consider taking a bribe....

Sharon was curled up against the pillows, watching him with a hint of wariness. No wonder, after the revelations on TV tonight! He stormed over to the bed, one of those antique Italian monstrosities with a curved headboard and a damned footboard you banged your knees on every time you got up to go to the bathroom. He scowled down at her, and she looked up at him, not quite managing a smile. Was she imagining him lying in bed with some queer? he wondered, sick with humiliation. Hell, he'd show her he was a red-blooded American male! There was nothing of the friggin' pansy about him, and she'd better remember that!

"Move over," he ordered curtly.

She scooted to the other side of the mattress, her blond curls bobbing on the lace-trimmed pillows. She was looking a bit haggard tonight, he noticed. There were lines around her eyes, and her eyebrows were ragged where she hadn't taken the time to pluck them. She was thirty-three years old, and at this moment she looked every day of her age. Maybe it was time to get rid of her. She was a fine cook, of course, but he wasn't all that interested in food and he really preferred his women young; young and slender, with a touch of the virgin still clinging to their bodies. Unfortunately, these days, virgins were pretty hard to find—at least, if you confined your activities to girls who were over the age of legal consent. And he wasn't dumb enough to run the risk of blackmail from some underage chick with a grasping, low-minded protector. No, sirree. He was way too smart to set himself up for that sort of a problem.

Sharon reached across the bed and stroked her hand tentatively down his belly. She might as well have hit him with a fillet of wet fish for all the effect it had on his libido. Jesus, he was limp as a piece of yesterday's lettuce. Obviously, he needed someone a bit more exciting than Sharon to grace his bed. What was the use of a woman who couldn't arouse him?

"Don't," he said, taking her hand and laying it across her stomach. "I'm thinking."

"About the TV show tonight?" Sharon asked, accepting his rejection without comment.

"What else?"

"I still can't believe what happened," she said. "Don't you think it's kind of strange...? You know, creepy...?"

"I think many things are strange. What, precisely, are you talking about?"

"Well, the fact that Steve Sterne knew where to go to find out all that unfavorable stuff about Jordan Edgar and..."

He hated to think about the interview, much less to talk about it, but she'd made a valid point. He clasped his hands behind his head and stared angrily at the ceiling. "Steve Sterne is an investigative journalist with a huge research staff that's trained to muckrake."

"I know, but—"

"If he was the sort of guy who spent the entire program chatting about land use in the Florida Everglades, how the hell do you think he'd keep his viewers? The campaign manager should have known we were being set up, and he should have refused the invitation to appear."

For once Sharon wasn't willing to accept his opinion in docile silence. "I'm sure the campaign manager... I'm sure everyone expected a hard-hitting interview," she said. "But there are dozens of controversial issues in this campaign, most of them a lot more current than the Vietnam War and how gays were treated by the military brass back in 1969. I mean, why did Steve Sterne suddenly decide to send his research people chasing around looking for scandals in Jordan Edgar's backyard? All that stuff happened twenty-five years ago, for heaven's sake. Sterne would never have wasted his resources unless he knew he was going to find something."

She might be a faded blonde with a depressing crop of wrinkles, but sometimes she could be quite smart. He rolled over, running his fingers absentmindedly around her nipples.

"You're right," he said, rewarding her with a couple of halfhearted licks on the swell of her breasts. "Dammit, my brain must be parked in a side alley tonight. Why didn't I realize that? Obviously somebody tipped Sterne off. Now I wonder who the hell that could have been?"

Sharon arched appreciatively against him, holding his mouth pressed to her flesh. "How about Evelyn?" she suggested, sounding nervous. "After all, she's the most likely person to know about... you know."

Sharon was right to sound nervous, but this time he decided to forgive her. She knew he didn't like her to mention Evelyn's name. After all, Evelyn was her employer and it wasn't appropriate to speak of her when the two of them were lying in one of *her* beds, getting ready to screw.

Could it have been Evelyn? But why now, after all these years of compliant silence? He would understand much better if this had happened right after Claire disappeared—

"Ouch!" Sharon wriggled on the bed. "Careful, honey, you're hurting me."

"Sorry," he said, his mind miles away.

Claire, he thought, with a grimace of triumph. Good Lord, how could he have been dumb enough not to recognize Claire's sticky fingerprints all over tonight's disastrous performance?

He cupped Sharon's breasts, burying his face in their softness. Then he kissed her nipples where he'd accidentally pinched her, and murmured a few more meaningless words of apology. She wasn't a bad sort, he decided, as she gasped and undulated beneath him, and sometimes sex with her helped to get his tumbled thoughts into a better order. Her thighs parted, and she pressed against him. He felt himself grow gratifyingly hard.

Claire, he thought, letting the name resonate inside his head until it rang loud and clear as a church bell on a winter morning in Vermont. Claire Helen Campbell, alias Dianna Mason.

It really was time he killed the bitch.

And this time, he'd make sure he did it right.

Dianna tossed restlessly, unable to find any position that felt comfortable. There was nothing like a guilty conscience, she decided, for making the padded coils of her innerspring mattress feel harder than rocks. When the doorbell rang, she experienced a quick, jarring moment of shock, followed by a spurt of relief. At this point, sleep was obviously a lost cause and she welcomed the excuse to get up and think about something—anything—other than Steve Sterne and his interview with Andrew.

Pulling on a pair of sweatpants, she padded to the front door. She squinted into the peephole and saw, almost without surprise, that Ben Maxwell was pacing up and down the length of her doorstep. He was scowling. So what else was new? An angry or supercilious glare seemed to be Ben's permanent expression where she was concerned.

She opened the door, fighting a mixed bag of emotions, chief among them the realization that, scowl or no scowl, she found him too damned attractive for her peace of mind. "Hello, Ben," she said, keeping the door chain firmly in place. To barricade him outside? Or to stop herself from welcoming him in? "This is an odd hour to come calling."

"Sorry, but it's been a hell of a night," he said wearily. "I've been with Andrew and Evelyn and couldn't get away. Let me in, please. We need to talk."

She hesitated only for a moment before unlatching the chain and walking into her studio. She didn't watch to see if Ben followed, but she heard the front door close behind him and she swung around at the sound of his voice. "Did you see Steve Sterne's show tonight?" he asked without preamble.

"Yes."

"That's all you have to say? The show didn't provoke even a smidgeon of sympathy for Andrew as far as you're concerned?"

She stroked the rim of one of her bowls, subconsciously seeking the reassurance of feeling the hard, crystal purity beneath her fingertips. Glass was so uncomplicated, she thought. If it was sufficiently flawed, it shattered. If it was pure, you could see right through its perfect transparency.

"What do you expect from me, Ben? Why did you come here? I've told you often enough how I feel about Andrew. He's not qualified to hold public office, and the voters needed to know that. I can't feel regret for what happened tonight. Steve Sterne held up a mirror and showed the public who Andrew Campbell really is."

Ben stared at her for a moment in stunned silence. Then the weariness in his eyes gave way first to disbelief and then to savage anger. "My God! It was you! You're the person who passed that farrago of lies and innuendo to Steve Sterne! Jesus, why didn't I even think of that!"

"It wasn't lies," she said, stepping back from the sheer blazing heat of his anger. "It was the truth. My God, can't you see it was the *truth!* Andrew's service career was dark and dirty, based on deceptions. He let Jordan Edgar go to jail, and yet he's had the unmitigated gall to spend the last twenty-five years boasting about the glories of his time in the navy, and how he volunteered to protect his country during the Vietnam War. Andrew *deserved* what happened tonight. He deserved all of it."

"Are you sure?" Ben asked, white lipped. "Does Andrew's relationship with Jordan Edgar somehow mean that the combat patrols he went on off the coast of Vietnam weren't dangerous? Does it mean that because he loved Jordan, he didn't volunteer to defend his country? When Andrew signed on for a tour of duty in the navy, there's no way on earth he could have known he would be posted to the same ship as Jordan Edgar. He volunteered to serve his country out of patriotism and a sense of duty. What happened after he got posted to the *Spirit of Freedom* reflects a hell of a lot worse on the navy brass than it does on him. Since when did you get appointed judge and jury of Andrew's moral worth?"

Ben's contempt was the final straw. Her control snapped. "When he tried to kill me!" she yelled, her body heaving with dry sobs. "When he let Jon Kaplan burn to death, and when he arranged for the brakes on Dianna Mason's car to fail! Or maybe when he tried to burn me and Hal Doherty to death in Florida!" The dry sobs turned into an explosion of wet, noisy tears. "I guess it must have been one of those times when I appointed myself judge! And I don't regret what I did. Or would you like to have a multiple murderer smiling and sweet-talking his way into being governor of Florida? And maybe trying for president next time?"

She pushed past him, so shaken by the turmoil of her emotions that she literally could only think in straight lines. She wanted to go to her bed and curl up under the protection of the covers. Ben was blocking the entrance to her bedroom. It never occurred to her to walk around him, or to ask him to step aside. She simply reached up and pounded on his chest, expecting him to read her mind and know that he should move.

Instead, he grabbed her hands, twisting around and forcing her back against the angle of the wall between the workbench and the window. "Claire, calm down, for God's sake! What are you talking about?"

"Don't call me Claire! I'm not Claire! I'm not! I'm not! I'm not!"

He looked down at her, eyes flat. "The blood test says that you are. That's one of the things I came to tell you. I ran a DNA comparison of your blood with Evelyn Campbell's. You'd better get used to being called Claire, because that's your real name."

The blood test. So the tissues he'd stolen had finally given him the proof he'd been searching for. He'd had no right to pry into her private business, she cried silently. She reacted instinctively, not stopping to ask herself why she felt this desperate need to counter his words with physical blows. She knew only that she felt a scorching, consuming rage because he was forcing her to confront the ultimate, inescapable reality of who she was. Pain burned inside her, fierce as alcohol poured onto a bleeding wound. She couldn't stand the pain, so she turned it outward and hurled it at Ben, lashing out and aiming her knee directly at his groin.

Some instinct must have warned him what was coming. He twisted just in time to catch most of her blow on his thigh.

"I'm bigger than you," he said, panting. His body weight held her legs pressed against the wall, preventing her from aiming any more kicks. "Do you want to find some other way to settle this argument?"

For answer, she balled her fists into tight knots of fury and swung wildly at his jaw. He defended himself by the simple method of pinning her hands above her head and ramming her harder against the wall. His body pressed against hers, his flesh touching hers from chest to knee. She could feel his erection thrusting stiff and aggressive against her belly and realized that what she felt pounding beneath her own rage was the same compelling throb of sexual desire. She gave a tiny gasp of horrified recognition, and Ben immediately went totally and utterly still.

She closed her eyes, shaken by the surge of sexual hunger that roared through her. This was why she'd provoked the fight, she realized. She'd wanted to drown her distress in a mind-numbing act of hot, violent mating. She should have known better than to try to provoke Ben into playing the part of her ravisher. He simply wasn't the sort of man who would allow her to sublimate complex feelings in a mindless, clawing tumble on her bed. She drew in a shuddering breath and felt some of the raging urgency go out of her.

"You can let go of me," she said.

His hold slackened, but only marginally. "Will you promise not to throw anything? These bowls of yours are way too beautiful to be destroyed."

Her breath was coming a bit easier now. "I won't throw anything," she said. "I won't even try to hit you."

He smiled faintly. "I guess our relationship is taking a dramatic turn for the better." He relaxed his hold, still looking wary as she slid her hands down the wall and let them hang limply at her sides. When she didn't move, he smoothed her hair out of her eyes and looked at her with renewed gentleness.

"Okay," he said. "It's time for us to talk. Why do you believe that Andrew Campbell wants to kill you?"

There was an ache in her throat that wouldn't go away, but she found it strangely comforting to tell someone the truth at last. "Because I'm not his daughter," she said. "And because, when my father died, he left me all of his money."

Thirteen

Before Claire finished speaking, Ben knew he didn't want to hear what she had to say. Her words blew over him, colder than an Arctic wind, and he frowned. His brain was too weary to fumble its way around pieces of information that didn't seem to fit together. He sorted out the two pieces of the puzzle that seemed clear: Claire genuinely believed Andrew Campbell was a murderer, and Ben didn't want to consider that she might be right.

She'd said before that she suspected Andrew of trying to kill her, but Ben had never been able to take her accusations seriously. He'd worked with Andrew for six years, and relished ninety-nine percent of the experience. Like every other person in the world, his boss was an imperfect human being, but Ben had found him intelligent and hardworking, with a mellow sense of humor and a tolerance for the foibles of the human race.

Andrew's integrity had seemed rock solid, although his relationship with Evelyn was odd, to say the least, and the revelations on tonight's Steve Sterne show did nothing to make their marriage more comprehensible. Had Evelyn known her husband was gay?

Were more of Andrew's lovers waiting to step out of the closet and reveal themselves on national TV?

Ben couldn't begin to guess, but he'd always felt an offbeat sense of kinship with Andrew over his screwed-up marriage. If Cheryl, Ben's ex-wife, had gotten pregnant, he suspected they would have stayed together for the sake of the child, and their relationship would probably have degenerated into the same sort of hollow shell as Andrew's marriage to Evelyn. Cheryl had been six months younger than Ben, but about a decade more mature in her emotional development. The further away he got from their divorce, the more Ben realized he owed Cheryl a huge debt of gratitude for calling a halt to their marriage before either of them could hurt the other too badly.

Ben walked over to the sink, splashing cold water onto his face. It was two in the morning, he saw, glancing at his watch. He'd been up since five and was beginning to feel battered. When he turned around, Claire was still standing propped up against the wall where he'd left her. Under the harsh overhead lights of the studio, the skin beneath her eyes looked bruised. However bad he was feeling, he guessed she must feel a thousand times worse. For all her superficial bravado, it couldn't have been easy for her to watch her father humiliated in front of several million viewers.

"We need to talk," he said kindly. "But you look worn-out. Maybe the sofa in your bedroom would be more comfortable for you?"

She gazed at him with just a trace of her old-Dianna mockery. "Don't patronize me, Ben. My mind isn't crumbling under the stress of acknowledging that I really am Claire Campbell. I told you Andrew tried to kill me because that's the simple truth, and sitting on a comfortable sofa isn't going to change that, however much you wish it would."

In a subtle way, he had been patronizing her, Ben realized, and he should have known Claire would see straight through him. "You're right," he said. "I didn't understand what you told me, so I decided *you* must be tired and confused. I'm sorry."

She scowled at him, then gave a puffy little sigh of frustration. "Damn you, Ben. You have the most annoying habit of being reasonable just when I'm enjoying getting mad at you."

She looked utterly adorable when she scowled, but Ben decided he'd be *real* smart not to tell her that. Perching himself on a stool, he looked at her with as neutral an expression as he could muster. "Explain to me again why you think Andrew wants to kill you," he said. Even as he spoke the words, he thought how absurd they sounded; how crazy. "The concept just doesn't compute for me, Claire, and that's the honest truth. I would have staked my last dime on the idea that Andrew was incapable of murder."

"Then you would have lost," she said.

He shook his head. "Basically, I have so much respect for him that my thought processes cut off every time you make the accusation. Andrew's my employer, but in some ways, he's like a second father to me...."

"I loved him, too," she said, then stopped, as if the admission made her angry. She shook her hair out of her eyes, lifting her head to stare at him with angry defiance. "There's nothing very complex or mysterious about Andrew's motives," she said. "Like I told you, he hates me because I'm not his daughter."

"How can you believe you're not his child?" Ben wasn't all that great at spotting family likenesses, but even he could see that her nose, the shape of her forehead, the slant of her cheekbones, were all exactly like Andrew's. "Claire, the resemblance between the two of you is so strong it's remarkable!"

"Why shouldn't it be?" she said with a breeziness that didn't quite come off. "It's not surprising if there's a family resemblance. My father was Douglas Campbell, Andrew's brother."

My father was Douglas Campbell.

Her quietly spoken words sounded loud in the cavernous space of the studio, but they rang inside Ben's head with the pure chime of newly recognized truth. So many facts shone in a clearer light, once he held up the blazing torch of that simple insight.

Douglas Campbell was her father.

"How do you know?" he demanded. "Did Evelyn tell you that? Did Andrew? Douglas had leukemia. He must have been sick by the time you were born, so you didn't hear it from him. You were just a toddler when he died."

He could see that she misinterpreted the reason for his questions. She assumed from their staccato urgency that he was rejecting her statements, rather than hungrily seeking details to round out their truth.

"There's no chance of a mistake, Ben. I was seventeen when I learned who my father really was, and my source of information was impeccable. Of course, I didn't discuss what I'd learned with Andrew or Evelyn."

"Why not?" he asked.

"Why not?" She shot him an incredulous glance. "You've met Evelyn many times, so you must know what sort of a facade she presents to the world—"

"Cool and formal," Ben agreed. "But she's your mother—"

"And I assure you she has never been any more forthcoming with me than she is with the rest of the world." Claire's voice cracked, and her brows drew together in a quick frown. As usual, she seemed cross with herself for betraying emotion.

Poor kid, Ben found himself thinking. *She's spent the past seven years of her life training herself not to feel what she wants to feel.*

"Evelyn wasn't a bad mother," Claire said, as if she was trying to be fair. "In many ways, she was an excessively perfect mother. She allowed me to pursue my own interests, choose my own school, select my own friends. She expressed polite interest in everything I did, and praised me lavishly when I achieved success, even for something quite trivial. But she never let me get close to her, or to see a glimpse of anything behind that public image of immaculate, groomed beauty and aristocratic dignity. I was as neurotic and insecure as any other seventeen-year-old. Surely you can see how impossible it was for me to ask Evelyn if it was true that she'd carried on a mad, passionate affair with her brother-in-law?"

Ben had to concede that the task wouldn't have been easy. He risked a small smile of sympathy. "I guess I can understand it might have been a tad difficult. But if Andrew and Evelyn didn't tell you the truth, then who did?"

Claire shifted the bowls on the workbench, automatically rearranging them so that the cuts in their surface refracted a maximum rainbow of colored light. Ben thought he saw tears shimmering in the corners of her eyes, but when she spoke, her voice was crisp, with no trace of tears.

"My grandmother told me," she said. "Gran was dying of ovarian cancer, and she insisted on being brought from the hospital to the old family house in Pittsburgh. She announced that she intended to meet her Maker lying in a decent bed, without tubes rammed up her nose, and needles stuck into her arms."

Affectionate laughter warmed Claire's face. "Actually, what she said was a great deal more graphic than the version I've just given you. Grandmother was one of those people who never called a spade a spade if she could think of a way to call it a bloody damn shovel."

Ben smiled. "I've heard lots of great stories about her. I understand she was a somewhat-feisty lady."

"I think that's one of the polite euphemisms Grandmother would never have used about herself. She often said she was stubborn as a mule, and not quite as refined! She was probably the richest woman in Pittsburgh, and so she was always at the top of everyone's invitation list, despite her outrageous behavior. She used to take a wicked delight in going to a fancy tea intended to benefit some super-respectable charity like widows of church ministers. And once she was there, she'd write a huge check for the respectable widows, on condition that everyone coughed up for prostitutes dying of syphilis, or scholarships for divorced mothers who wanted to go to college. She recognized battered-woman syndrome at least a generation ahead of her time, and single-handedly founded a shelter for abused women in south Pittsburgh. That's remarkable when you remember she achieved all this in the days when everyone believed a wife's place was with her husband, no matter how badly he treated her.''

Ben nodded. ''Andrew has often told me what a truly remarkable and wonderful woman she was. He loved her almost as much as you seem to.''

He cursed himself as soon as the words left his mouth. The mention of Andrew's name was enough to take all the light and warmth out of Claire's eyes. ''Did he?'' she asked coolly. ''Personally, I've always found Andrew's real feelings hard to determine. Anyway, I guess all this reminiscing about my grandmother is irrelevant. You want to know how I found out Andrew isn't my father.''

''I'd like to hear that part of the story,'' Ben agreed.

''It's quite straightforward, really. A couple of days before she died, Grandmother sent for me. She ordered the nurse out of the room, and told me she had something to give me. She was completely lucid at the time, although I could see she was weak and in excruciating pain. It was years later before I understood that she must have denied herself morphine just so that she could be clear-minded enough to talk to me.''

Claire stopped and cleared her throat. ''This is what Gran gave me,'' she said, reaching behind her neck and unfastening the clasp of a necklace that was hidden beneath her sweatshirt. When she finally held out her hand, a heavy gold chain dangled from her fingers. "Take it," she said to Ben. "Open the locket."

Ben saw that she had handed him the same old-fashioned locket that he'd found on the floor of her bedroom the night they'd made love, although it now had a new, stronger chain, just as he'd recommended. He'd wanted to open it then, but he'd resisted the temptation. Stealing the tissues for the DNA test had seemed a big enough invasion of Claire's privacy for one night. Now he ran his thumbnail along the almost-invisible seam of the locket and pressed at the indentation. It sprang open, revealing two black-and-white pictures, both apparently cut from snapshots.

The picture on the left-hand side he recognized as that of a much younger Evelyn, although she laughed into the camera with a sparkling animation he'd never seen in any of her posed studio portraits. The other picture was of a young man, somewhat like Andrew in looks, although less classically handsome. He had strong, dynamic features and a smile that seemed to challenge the world with its self-confident energy. He also looked dramatically—astonishingly—like Claire.

Ben studied the pictures in silence for a full minute before looking up. "Is this Douglas?" he asked.

Claire nodded. "Douglas Campbell," she said. "My father."

Her words rippled across the silence that stretched momentarily between them. "Your grandmother told you explicitly that Douglas was your father when she gave you this locket?" Ben asked.

"Yes. She said that when he died, Douglas had been carrying that picture of my mother in his grandfather's watch case, together with a picture of me, taken on the day I was christened. His dying wish to my grandmother was that she should tell me the truth about my parentage whenever she thought I was old enough to hear it.'' Claire managed a shaky smile. ''Grandmother said that she wasn't at all sure I was mature enough to hear the truth, but unfortunately, God took the eternal view, and he was speeding up her preferred timetable. She implied that if she'd been in charge, things would have been managed a great deal more efficiently.''

Ben smiled. ''I'm sure they would have been. Did she explain how Evelyn and Douglas got involved with each other?''

In the abstract, Claire's account of her parentage was believable, but he found it almost impossible to picture Evelyn conducting an adulterous affair with her husband's younger brother. Good God, the idea was profane, Ben thought. Rather like casting doubt on the moral integrity of Mother Teresa.

''Grandmother made their affair sound quite logical,'' Claire said. ''She explained that Douglas had been away in the Himalayas trying to climb Mount Everest when Andrew got engaged to my mother. Douglas came back just in time for the wedding, literally forty-eight hours before the ceremony took place. Apparently he fell in love with Evelyn at first sight. On the morning of her wedding, he tried to persuade her to call off the ceremony, telling her she was making a dreadful mistake, that she'd live to regret it, that she should come with him to Chile, and work off her inhibitions climbing in the Andes.''

"And of course she wouldn't hear of canceling her wedding." Ben spoke with certainty. He could—with gargantuan effort—visualize Evelyn falling in love with Douglas. It was beyond the bounds of his imagination to picture her calling off her wedding with three hundred guests already on hand, and the Episcopal cathedral decked out with satin ribbons and bouquets of nuptial roses.

"Of course not." Claire smiled wryly. "My mother is everything my grandmother wasn't."

"The pattern card of punctilious behavior," Ben murmured.

"That's an excellent description," Claire agreed. "Even I can be objective enough to understand where Evelyn was coming from, and to sympathize with why she's the way she is. Her parents were both from blue-blooded Philadelphia families who'd lost all their money, but were determined to cling to the appearance of gracious living. She'd been force-fed rules of decorum and noblesse oblige along with her baby cereal, and she was convinced that good breeding inevitably led to a certain code of behavior. The Duplessys never changed their outward life-style, even when money was so short that the servants were the only people in the household eating decent food."

"It never occurred to her parents to fire the servants and order themselves a few pounds of steak?" Ben asked, thinking of the formal splendor of Evelyn's Manhattan apartment and realizing she hadn't shaken off the strictures of her upbringing even now, when she was fifty years old.

"Of course not." Claire's voice expressed the same mixture of exasperation and wry admiration that Ben himself was feeling. "But in marrying my father, she knew everything was going to change for the better. Her parents were going to retire to Cape Cod, and Evelyn was finally going to have the means to back up all the elegance her parents had been forced to scrape and scrimp and darn near starve themselves to maintain. Given her background, given what was at stake, how could she possibly have thrown away marriage to my father in exchange for the promise of love and illicit passion from a young man whose entire life was one long record of fleeting fancies and noncommitment?"

"I can see it would have been difficult for her," Ben said. "But I also admit I'm impressed by the empathy you can feel for your mother. I'd have expected you to condemn her for being so dishonest with herself about her own feelings."

Claire grimaced. "You're hearing the benefit of about a hundred sessions with an expensive therapist. I wasn't always this benign."

"Three cheers for therapy?" Ben suggested.

She laughed. "I guess so." When Claire laughed like that, Ben found himself thinking of forbidden words like *forever*, and *serious*, and *committed*. Words that he'd spent the past ten years keeping carefully separated from the word *relationship*. He gulped, and to cover the swooping sensation in his stomach, spoke with extra briskness. "At the moment, we have Douglas passionately in love with your mother, and we have Evelyn unwilling to break her engagement, or to call off her wedding. So far, there's not a hint of illicit sexual passion between Evelyn and Douglas. How did your grandmother explain your arrival on the scene?''

"She simply said that Evelyn and Andrew soon found out that being good friends wasn't necessarily an ideal basis for marriage. My parents took one of those old-fashioned wedding trips through Europe, staying for weeks in Paris, then going on to the south of France, and stopping off in Rome and Florence before flying home. I'm guessing that the honeymoon was pretty much a disaster, at least in sexual terms. My grandmother only said that within days of getting back to the States, Andrew volunteered for the navy, and a couple of months after that, he got shipped off to the Philippines. You know what happened next, at least as far as Andrew's concerned."

Ben's breath hissed out between his teeth in a long, slow exhalation. "My God! Are you telling me that your grandmother knew Andrew had been involved in a homosexual relationship with Jordan Edgar? Is she the person who told you about their affair?"

"I have no idea what Gran knew about Andrew and Jordan Edgar," Claire said, her voice rough. "My grandmother may have guessed something of what was going on, but she certainly didn't give me even the smallest hint about Andrew's sexual preferences. She simply said that while Andrew was away at sea, my mother fell as passionately in love with Douglas as he still was with her. She sort of indicated that they became lovers within days of Andrew shipping out to the Philippines. Grandmother did say that they planned to ask Andrew for a divorce as soon as he returned from active duty. For obvious reasons, they didn't want to send him a Dear John letter while his life was at risk." Claire's sentences were getting choppier as emotion kept threatening to intrude.

"So why didn't Evelyn ever ask Andrew for a divorce?" Ben asked, struggling to make sense of a situation that still seemed incomprehensible. "Or did she? And did he refuse? In the circumstances, a divorce would have seemed the best solution, don't you think?"

"It might have been," Claire said bleakly. "Except that right around the time Evelyn realized she was pregnant, Douglas found out that he had leukemia. Survival rates for leukemia victims in the early seventies were nothing like as good as they are nowadays, and it was soon pretty clear that Douglas wasn't going to live very long. My grandmother says that—quote—'everyone' decided it would be better if Evelyn stayed married to Andrew."

"And—quote—'everyone' expected Andrew just to accept the situation?" Ben asked in amazement. "His wife's been cuckolding him with his younger brother, and he just smiles and accepts the resulting baby as his own?" Belatedly, he realized that his comment wasn't very tactful, considering that the "resulting baby" was actually Claire.

"I never understood that, either," she said, wrapping her arms around her waist to cut off a shiver. "But I think I finally understand what must have happened."

"Finally?"

She stared at her row of glass bowls. "I only found out about Andrew's affair with Lieutenant Edgar recently. That helped to explain a few things."

"You think so? Yes, I see what you mean." Ben spoke his thoughts out loud. "Andrew comes home from the Philippines, full of remorse and guilt over the tragic ending of his affair with Jordan Edgar. Meanwhile, your mother is equally full of remorse over her affair with Douglas. They strike a deal. She'll forgive him for Jordan, if he forgives her for Douglas. Jordan is dead, and Douglas is dying. The two survivors turn to each other for mutual support."

"Something like that," Claire said, with an attempt at lightness. "Best of all, that way everybody got to keep their dirty linen wrapped away in a nice dark closet. Except for one minor inconvenience. I was born ten months after Andrew shipped out to Subic Bay, and according to my birth certificate, I weighed in at a bare six pounds. Not exactly a bouncing, overdue baby."

Ben shrugged. "I don't suppose Evelyn or Andrew worried much about that minor discrepancy. Lots of first babies are born late, and Evelyn's so slender, why would anyone expect you to be big? People question early births, not late ones. If you'd been born six months after your parents were married, there might have been a few whispered remarks, especially given the circles Evelyn moved in. But you said yourself, Andrew shipped out to the Philippines right after your parents came back from an extended European honeymoon. What could have been more natural than Evelyn returning pregnant from her honeymoon?"

Claire shrugged. "You're obviously right, because as far as I know, there was never even a whisper of scandal about my birth, and Evelyn's reputation remains more pure than driven snow."

Ben felt as if he were piling facts one on top of each other, like some crazed statistician who kept hoping one more figure, one more survey, one more set of analyses, would make the mystery of life suddenly comprehensible. "So now everything is explained except the problem that started this entire conversation," he said.

She glanced up, puzzled. "What's that?"

"Why do you think Andrew is trying to kill you?" His question dropped into the quietness of the room with the force of an explosion, and she literally flinched under its impact. He crossed to her side, grabbing her hands and squeezing them tightly in an effort to make her see things from his point of view.

"Claire, absolutely nothing that you've told me suggests a reason for Andrew to turn homicidal maniac on the day you reached your eighteenth birthday. On the contrary, he seems to have known you weren't his child virtually from the day you were born. You said you loved him once.... Doesn't that mean he treated you well? That you enjoyed each other's company? Why would he wait eighteen years before deciding he couldn't stand the sight of you?"

"Money," she said tersely. "Douglas left me his shares in the company, and several million dollars, as well—all in some sort of a trust fund, with Andrew as sole executor. On my eighteenth birthday, Andrew lost some degree of control over the money. Under the terms of the trust, I got to participate in all the decisions and he couldn't invest money without my approval. And on my twenty-fifth birthday, I got outright control of everything. Don't you see? As soon as I turned eighteen, Andrew didn't have control of my money anymore, and he needed it, to cover his losses in the real-estate market.''

Ben took her into his arms, gathering her against his chest and stroking her hair. "Claire, listen to me. I know you don't quite trust me where the finances of Campbell Industries are concerned, in part because you don't want to see Campbell Crystal sold. But I wish you'd put your emotions aside for a minute, and hear what I'm saying. The truth is, honey, that Andrew doesn't need your money.''

"Then why are you selling off Campbell Crystal? My great-grandfather founded that company, and it was always considered the jewel in the Campbell crown.''

"Times change,'' Ben said. "Markets alter dramatically. We're selling off Campbell Crystal because it doesn't form a logical part of our core business anymore. Because there are no worthwhile synergies between chandeliers, fancy crystal tableware, and real estate. Because, until you came back, there was nobody left in the family who had the smallest interest in owning a glass-manufacturing company. It's definitely not because Campbell Construction is desperate for cash. In fact, of the divisions, the real-estate company is far more profitable than Campbell Crystal. And far larger, too, in terms of overall revenue.''

"How can that be?'' she protested. "The property market crashed all over the country right around the time I was turning eighteen. Every time I picked up a newspaper, I read another article about the savings-and-loan debacle and the glut of office space and the desperate plight of real-estate developers.''

He grinned, shaking his head. "If you read it in the papers, you should have known it was only half-true. It is a fact that the commercial property market took a severe plunge in the late eighties, particularly in a few states like Texas and New York. But Andrew had already diversified into domestic real estate and environmental planning, both of which boomed in many areas of the country. Campbell Construction rode out the dip in property sales a lot better than most of our competitors, and we've been going great guns for the past two years. Claire, believe me when I tell you there has never been any time when Andrew needed the money in your trust fund to bail him out."

"You're the president of his company. You have to say that."

"Don't take my word for it." He tilted her chin up, forcing her to look straight into his eyes. "Use some of the spare cash lying around in your trust fund and hire a top-notch auditor. You can pick whatever auditing firm you want and send them in to study the accounts for the past few years. I'll open the books—and your own auditors will come back with the news that Campbell Industries is a profitable enterprise, with sound underlying finances. They'll also tell you that Campbell Crystal is the least profitable division of the corporation."

If he had hoped that she would be converted to a belief in Andrew's innocence, he was doomed to disappointment. Her shoulders sagged and she suddenly looked unbearably weary, but her certainty about Andrew's guilt never wavered. "If it's as you say, Ben, then I can't give you a reason why Andrew suddenly decided that he wanted me dead." She pulled away from him, her expression steely. "All I can tell you is that I know he's tried to murder me on at least three occasions."

She made the accusation sounding more sad than angry, and Ben realized he had to stop defending Andrew and listen to the evidence Claire had—or thought she had—against her father. "Tell me about these murder attempts," he said.

"Is there any point?" she countered. "Will you listen? Or are you just going to keep explaining to me why I'm a hysterical female with an advanced case of PMS?"

"I promise to listen with a totally open mind."

She hesitated, as if still not quite sure it was worth her time to try to convince him. Then she spoke slowly, almost painfully, as if hating to remember. "The first time he attempted to kill me was on the night of my eighteenth birthday," she said. "That's when Andrew set fire to the cabin in Vermont. As you know, he killed Jon Kaplan, but I escaped."

"And you know that Ted Jenkins was not only arrested for setting that fire, he freely confessed to the crime," Ben said.

She smiled at him, her eyes sad. "Open mind, Ben?"

He sucked in a quick breath. "Sorry, it's just that I don't see—"

"But I did see," she said. "That's just the point. I saw Andrew Campbell right outside the cabin."

He stared at her, openmouthed with shock. "You saw Andrew the night the cabin caught fire? How? I mean, when?"

"I saw him right after I'd escaped from the fire," she said wearily. "When the flames started to take hold, I happened to be in the bathroom, but I knew Jon was asleep on the sofa in the main living area. As soon as I realized the cabin was on fire, I tried to crawl into the living room so that I could wake Jon up and get him outside. I managed to get back into the living room all right, but I couldn't wake Jon. I think...I think he must already have died of smoke inhalation. Then a burning ceiling beam fell on him."

Ben saw that her hands were clasping and unclasping, and he gripped them loosely, massaging his thumb over her knuckles, trying to offer her comfort, even as he realized that some memories were simply too grim to heal smoothly.

"Is that when you saw Andrew?" he asked, wanting to take her mind away from the horror of Jon Kaplan's death. "And does he realize you saw him? Do you think that's why he wants to kill you?"

"I don't think he realizes I saw him. We were too far away from each other to make eye contact."

"But you were close enough to be sure that it really was Andrew you saw?"

"Close enough for that," she agreed desolately. Despite the warmth of the summer night, her hands were icy cold, as if she were reliving the horrors of the bitter Vermont cold. "I didn't see Andrew until I was outside the cabin. I ran away from the fire toward a little cluster of evergreens that borders the west corner of our property. I stopped and rested for a moment, in the shelter of the pines, and something— maybe the noise of the car engine starting—made me look back toward the cabin one last time." She stopped abruptly. "That's when I saw him."

"He was getting into a car?"

"No, he was already in the car. He was driving away from the fire in his Jeep. Not fast. It didn't seem fast, anyway. I had this horrible impression that he was hunched over the steering wheel, laughing."

Ben felt a great surge of relief. If this was the evidence she'd been nursing against Andrew all these years, it was pretty flimsy. He took her hands and tucked them against his chest. "Claire, don't misunderstand, but I have to ask this. How can you be sure it was Andrew driving the Jeep? It was dark. You were upset. God knows, you had every reason to be upset—"

"Don't try to convince me I didn't see what I know I saw," Claire argued, tugging away from him. "The Jeep had one of Andrew's personalized license plates. ABC 4. The light from the fire clearly illuminated the numbers."

"I'm sure you saw Andrew's Jeep," Ben said. "But how do you know Andrew was driving it?"

"I'd seen Andrew drive that Jeep a thousand times, and the driver *looked* like Andrew. He was male, the right height, and he was wearing one of Andrew's plaid golf caps with a matching scarf." Ben didn't say a word, but she must have sensed his mental reservations, because she tossed her head angrily. "If it looks like a duck, quacks like a duck, and swims like a duck, then why would anyone believe it's a chicken?"

"You don't have to believe you've seen a chicken," Ben said. "But maybe a mechanical duck?"

"I don't know what that's supposed to mean," Claire replied.

"Well, let's just pretend for a moment that Ted Jenkins set the fire. Is it possible, do you think, that he could have driven Andrew's Jeep and worn a hat and scarf like the one belonging to Andrew? Plaid caps and scarves aren't exactly Andrew's exclusive property."

"It's a possibility," she conceded. "But who would have given Jenkins the keys to the Jeep except Andrew?"

"I don't know—"

"Exactly. In which case, if you're determined to pin this on Ted Jenkins, it simply means that Andrew wanted me killed, but to maintain his alibi, he hired a drunken drifter to do his dirty work for him."

"Hold on a minute! There are a dozen reasons—maybe a hundred reasons—why Andrew might lend someone the keys to his Jeep without also handing out instructions to commit arson!"

Claire paced in angry frustration. "I love your definition of an open mind, Ben. If Andrew loaned the Jeep to Ted Jenkins for some innocent reason, then why the hell hasn't he ever stepped forward to say so?"

Her question stopped him dead in his mental tracks. *That's a reasonable question,* Ben thought, feeling shock burn through him as fiercely as if he'd trodden on a live wire. A reasonable question for which he had no answer—or at least no answer that he liked. Despite all that Claire had told him, he couldn't believe that Andrew was capable of trying to murder the woman he'd raised as his daughter. But was he capa-

ble of concealing facts that displayed him in an unfavorable light? Could Andrew have had dealings with
Ted Jenkins that would have caused embarrassment if
they were known? Based on the evidence produced
during Steve Sterne's TV show, Ben acknowledged
that Andrew had shown himself quite capable of
moral subterfuge when it was expedient. Reluctantly,
he admitted as much to Claire.

"Andrew may have covered up his dealings with
Ted Jenkins out of embarrassment rather than because they were criminal," he said quietly. "I guess a
man who let his lover face a court-martial alone
wouldn't hesitate to conceal irrelevant, but awkward,
details concerning his relationship with an accused
arsonist. That makes Andrew morally weak, but it
doesn't make him a murderer."

He could see that Claire acknowledged his point. A
gleam of something akin to hope shone briefly in her
eyes and then was extinguished. "I might believe Andrew had nothing to do with the fire in Vermont if it
weren't for the fact that I'm nearly sure he killed
Dianna Mason in the mistaken belief that he was killing me."

"I've read the police files on the death of Dianna
Mason," Ben said curtly. "The authorities treated it
as a routine traffic fatality."

Claire looked at him almost with pity. "I never said
that Andrew Campbell was stupid," she said tightly.
"Only that he was a murderer. Don't you think it's
stretching the long arm of coincidence too far when
Dianna Mason—who looks like me and was driving
my car—dies on the New Jersey Turnpike as the result of a freak accident? And all this just a couple of

days after a private investigator tracks me down and says he's been working for my father for two years, and that Andrew will be thrilled to know that I'm alive and well and living in New Jersey?''

Ben couldn't think of anything to say. Up until a few hours ago, he might have suggested that Dianna Mason's death was strangely timed, but life was made up of random accidents and bizarre coincidences. Tonight such logic seemed feeble, almost escapist. Claire was right: There did seem something sinister about Dianna's death, but at this distance in time, how would they ever uncover the truth?

"Do you remember the name of the investigator who claimed to be working for your father?" he asked finally.

She nodded. "He said his name was Daniel Webster, and he showed me a New York State license. At the time, I wondered why any parent would want to name their child after a dictionary. In retrospect, I guess I've concluded that the name and the license were false. He never tried to get in touch with me again, that's for sure."

Ben's frustration boiled over into a burst of impotent anger. "Dammit, Claire, what you say seems to tie together into a neat case against Andrew, and then I remember who it is that we're talking about! You're asking me to believe that *Andrew* is a cold, calculating killer. A terrifying example of the Dr. Jekyll and Mr. Hyde syndrome! Good God, I've worked side by side with the guy for six years! Do you really expect me to believe he's an honorable, pleasant man by day and a crazed predator by night?''

"I don't know what I expect you to believe," she said, her voice scratchy with fatigue. "I sometimes don't know what I believe myself. Everything you've said tonight, all the excuses you've invented for Andrew, I'd already invented for myself. I spent six months in the psychiatric ward of a hospital getting myself to the point where I could think about the fire in Vermont without dissolving into hysterics. I'd even reached the point where I was willing to admit I might have been mistaken about Andrew. After all, what had I seen that night in Vermont? I'd seen Andrew's Jeep, driven by a man who looked like Andrew." She smiled bitterly. "'Hey,' I said to myself, 'maybe the duck was a chicken, after all.' Then Dianna Mason died. And as far as I was concerned, the chicken had turned back into a duck."

Ben felt a chill settle somewhere deep inside—a chill of reluctant doubt. "The fire in Florida..." he said, and then couldn't bear to put his suspicion into words.

"That was kind of the finishing straw," Claire said. "I'd hoped that Andrew wouldn't recognize me when I turned up with an obvious fraud like Hal Doherty in tow. The smoke had changed my voice, and I'd made several subtle alterations in my appearance. I figured he'd think I was just one more impostor after the Campbell family fortune."

Ben smiled wryly. "You were fifty percent successful," he said. "You convinced me."

"Unfortunately, you weren't the person I wanted to convince." She almost managed to return his smile. "I thought maybe I could get back inside the family homes and scout out the lay of the land, perhaps even find some sort of proof of Andrew's nefarious activities before he got rattled enough to risk another attempt on my life.'' She laughed with a noticeable lack of mirth. ''Well, I guess I calculated that one all wrong. Did you notice how as soon as we met, Andrew went out of his way to tell me that he'd have known me anywhere, and that he was absolutely sure I was Claire Campbell? That was his way of warning me off. When I didn't take the hint, he torched the guest cabin, just to make sure I got the message.''

Ben muttered a few curses under his breath. It didn't advance the discussion much, but it sure was better than standing around admitting how utterly helpless he felt. Could they go to the police? Not unless they wanted to look like total idiots, he decided. Ted Jenkins was serving time for the Vermont fire, Dianna Mason had died in a traffic accident, and the fire marshal in Florida was more likely to indict Snow White than he was to bring arson charges against Andrew Campbell.

Claire, as always, seemed to guess what he was thinking. ''It's frustrating, isn't it?'' she said. ''Are you beginning to understand why I passed Steve Sterne that information?''

The hell of it was, he did understand. He looked at her, and his heart missed a beat. Claire was tall, and she was strongly built, but tonight she looked so weary, so vulnerable, so *fragile*, that he was overwhelmed by the urge to offer her his protection. His eyes met hers with the tenderness of an embrace.

''This has been a hell of a long day,'' he said, ''and it's beginning to feel like an even longer night. I'm bushed. Could we go to bed, do you think?''

It wasn't until she blushed that he realized how she must have interpreted his remark. What the hell, he thought. Wasn't that what he really wanted? To go to bed with Claire. At this moment, he couldn't imagine anything in the world that would feel better than sinking onto the bed next to her, and losing himself in the magic of her lovemaking.

She eyed him warily. "Ben, do you think I'm crazy?"

He started to laugh, and then realized that for a woman who had spent six months in a locked psychiatric ward, the question was not one to be answered jokingly. He bent down and put his hands on her shoulders. "No," he said. "I don't think you're crazy. I think you're talented, and smart, and very much in touch with your own emotions. I also think you're unbelievably sexy."

"Thank you," she said.

He cleared his throat. "Not that I'm a coward, or lacking in macho spirit, or anything, but if I kiss you, am I likely to get socked in the jaw? That does seem to be our usual pattern."

She looked up at him, eyes gleaming with hidden laughter. "Try it and find out."

He linked his hands around her waist, then touched his lips to hers, gently, but with the promise of passion.

She leaned against him, her body flowing into his, her mouth soft and welcoming. "Make love to me," she whispered.

Fatigue vanished. Like a flare exploding into the darkness of the night sky, he felt desire erupt deep inside him. He slanted his lips hard against hers, his kiss hungry and seeking. "Oh God...Claire."

Her hands slid down his spine and clutched feverishly. "Oh, yes...Ben. Yes."

As far as Ben was concerned, the conversation made perfect sense. He swept her into his arms and carried her into the bedroom. What the hell, he thought, kicking the door shut behind them. He'd always wanted to play Rhett Butler.

Afterward, lying beside her in a state somewhere between comatose and ecstatic, Ben realized that those forbidden words were creeping into his head again.

Committed. Long-term. For a moment *love* even darted out from behind a barricade, before it scuttled back into terrified obscurity.

The worst of it was, Ben thought, that the words were all beginning to sound amazingly attractive. *Claire. Relationship. Committed.* Hell, the more he said them, the better they sounded.

Claire. Love. Marriage.

No point in frightening himself to death. He closed his eyes.

Fourteen

Claire—she was trying to think of herself that way again, after nearly five years of banishing the name from her consciousness—paid off the cab outside the familiar apartment building on Madison Avenue and walked into the lobby. The doorman on duty was new and didn't recognize her.

"Yes, miz. Can I 'elp you?"

"I'm Claire Campbell." It was the first time she'd said the words without any mental reservation, and the effect was disorienting. She gave her head a slight shake. "I'm here to see my mother, Mrs. Andrew Campbell."

"Yes, miz. Pliz wait. I tell 'er." The doorman looked dubious. *Perhaps he suspects I'm an impostor,* Claire thought with wry humor. She walked over to the elevators and waited while the doorman placed his call.

The doorman put down the phone. "You can go up now, miz. Pent'ouse floor." He pressed a button at his desk and the elevator doors slid open. She stepped inside, the doorman's gaze boring into her back. The rug at her feet told her it was Wednesday. She was glad to know that she and the rug agreed.

Stop it, she commanded herself silently. *You're only making these snide mental comments because you're terrified to let yourself think about meeting your mother.*

The elevator glided to a halt on the eighth and top floor. She'd steeled herself for the worst, but as the doors opened, she saw that she'd stiffened her spine to no purpose. Evelyn was nowhere in sight. Instead, a familiar much-liked figure waited to greet her in the foyer.

"Bainbridge!" She ran and hugged him before she could censor her spontaneous rush of pleasure. "It's so great to see you! You're looking wonderful!"

The butler didn't exactly melt into a puddle of warm chocolate, but he came pretty close. His cheeks flushed pink, his eyes misted, and he had to clear his throat half a dozen times before he trusted himself to speak. "Thank God you're back! Welcome home, Claire. We've all missed you something shocking."

He so far forgot his dignity as to return her hug, patting her back, and making little clucking noises that Claire found oddly cheering.

She found a tissue and blew her nose hard. "It's good to be home, Bainbridge." And, at that moment, it was. How could she have stayed away so long? How could she have given Andrew the power to cut her off from so many people she loved? Filled with a new confidence, she tucked her arm through the butler's and followed him into the apartment, making appropriate oohs and aahs of approval every time he showed her some minor improvement or alteration in the decor.

"Your mother will be down in just a moment," he said, when they finally reached the drawing room.

"Er...good. No hurry. We've waited so long for this...." Claire's ramblings tailed away in a hiccup of nervous laughter. The truth was, she didn't mind how long Evelyn took to put in an appearance. Somehow, she didn't think their reunion was going to proceed as smoothly as the one with Bainbridge. Glancing nervously around the room, she spotted a white damask cloth laid over a small side table and grinned, her momentary gloom lifting.

"The tablecloth looks promising," she said. "What are you serving for elevenses, Bainbridge? I hope it's one of your specials."

The butler had kept up several British customs in his kitchen, including the habit of serving milky coffee with imported English biscuits precisely at eleven. Some of Claire's happiest childhood memories involved half hours perched on a kitchen stool listening to Bainbridge's stories while she munched buttery Scottish shortbread and drank "coffee" that was basically flavored hot milk.

"I daresay I might be able to find some jam tarts," Bainbridge replied, and Claire smiled, almost hearing the implicit childhood condition: If you're a good girl.

"My favorite," she said softly. She looked at Bainbridge, her eyes suddenly swimming in tears. "Thank you," she added.

"Whatever for?"

"For being so kind. For welcoming me home."

He appeared flustered with pleasure for a moment, then he frowned and looked at her sternly. "You shouldn't have stayed away," he said. "No matter what 'appened up in Vermont, you should have let your mother know you was all right."

Bainbridge rarely made grammatical errors. Claire knew it was a sign of deep emotion when he slipped up and allowed his Cockney accent to intrude. What could she say to him? That she'd stayed away because she was afraid her supposed father was trying to kill her? That she was still afraid for her life even now, because the closer she got to Andrew Campbell, the easier it would be for him to arrange another accident? No, of course she wasn't going to burden Bainbridge with any of that grim information.

She picked up the silver sugar tongs, then returned them carefully to the Queen Anne bowl, which was filled with hard cubes of crystalline light brown sugar. "I would have come back earlier if I could," she said at last. "Honestly, Bainbridge, I didn't . . . want . . . to stay away."

"Better late than never, I suppose." Bainbridge's voice was gruff. "But don't you go running off again without telling your mum where you're going, and that's an order." The butler stopped abruptly, and gathered himself together, almost visibly donning the mantle of dignified old family retainer. "I hear Mrs. Campbell coming downstairs now, miss. I'll be back with the elevenses in a few minutes."

Bainbridge might be in his seventies, but he obviously had acute hearing. Claire had to strain to hear her mother's footsteps. Since this was a penthouse apartment, there was a small upper floor that had been converted years earlier into a boudoir—she could think of no other word—for her mother. Evelyn had always spent most of her spare time there. Doing what? Claire wondered, never having paused to ask herself that question before.

Evelyn's footsteps tapped lightly across the marble hallway. Claire found she was holding her breath, the lump in her throat so huge that she literally had to swallow before she could find room to draw in any oxygen.

For a split second, the footsteps stopped and the drawing room filled with silence. Then Evelyn stepped across the threshold, standing just in front of the doorway, a cool vision in pale blue linen and darker blue leather accessories. She smiled a polite, restrained smile. "Hello, Claire. Welcome home."

"Hello, Mother." Claire stood rooted to the spot. Her skin flushed with heat, then rippled with cold. There were so many things she wanted to say to her mother, but her mind was a blank, and her throat felt so dry she wasn't sure she'd ever be able to speak again. Dammit, she'd been able to hug Bainbridge, who terrified half the world with his nineteenth-century-butler routine. Why in the world couldn't she cross a few feet of carpet and kiss her mother?

Evelyn advanced into the drawing room. Not many women in their fifties could brave morning sunlight, but Evelyn's perfect bone structure compensated for the fact that the skin around her eyes was now etched with fine wrinkles, and her forehead was no longer an unblemished expanse of perfect white skin. Claire, for some reason, was fiercely glad that her mother hadn't resorted to a face-lift to hide the natural signs of aging.

Of course, she didn't dare tell her that. Passing personal comments about Evelyn was rather like informing the queen of England that you liked her new haircut. Claire watched her mother's progress across the room in a silence that rapidly became thick with embarrassment. *Oh God, this is dreadful! I've got to say something.*

Desperate, she blurted out the first thing that popped into her head: "Bainbridge is serving jam tarts for elevenses."

"Is he? How...how delicious." Evelyn looked shocked, as well she might. After seven years, she'd probably hoped that her daughter would come up with a more interesting topic for discussion than the food being served for midmorning snack.

"Did you have a good journey down from Boston?" Evelyn lost no time in getting their conversation back onto a more acceptable track. "I'm so glad you were able to come for this brief visit. You're looking well, Claire."

"Thank you. So are you. As elegant and beautiful as ever."

Evelyn gave a tiny smile. "You're very kind to say so."

That covered the journey, their health, and their general appearance. The next topic looked as if it might be the weather. Surely to God they weren't going to end up discussing the weather? Claire turned toward the door, hoping against hope that Bainbridge might arrive with the refreshments. No such luck. She shot a covert glance toward her mother and saw to her amazement that the lace handkerchief Evelyn held was becoming more mangled by the second. The incredible realization flashed across Claire's mind that her mother might be silent not out of disapproval, but out of nerves. Was it possible that Evelyn the Ever-Gracious was apprehensive?

"Mother?" she said, taking a tentative step forward. "Mother, are you all right?"

"Of course I'm all right." Evelyn's reply was cool, with an overlay of arrogance. She turned away, but Claire could see that her shoulders were shaking.

"Mother?" She decided to risk advancing another step closer. "What is it? Won't you tell me what's the matter?"

"What do you think is the matter!" Evelyn exclaimed, not turning around, her voice tight with fury and self-loathing. "I'm hopeless at this, utterly useless! I've been up half the night, inventing things for us to talk about, trying to make sure I say the right thing." A tatter of lace fell from the handkerchief. "Oh, *damn!* Why can't I just hug you, and sob out my relief on your shoulder, and worry later if maybe I'm making a fool of myself?"

"Sounds like a great plan to me," Claire said, her heart beginning to thump like a renovated steam engine. She closed the gap between herself and Evelyn, touching her mother tentatively on the elbow. "Mom? I could sure use one of those hugs you mentioned."

"You could?" Evelyn turned around, her lips quivering, her exquisite blue eyes bright with tears. "Dear God, I thought I'd never see you again. I can't believe you're here, in the same room. It's so wonderful!" She opened her arms, then let them drop to her sides, still not quite able to abandon a lifetime of training and inhibitions.

She was terrified of being rejected, Claire realized. Terrified of forcing an embrace on her daughter that wasn't truly wanted. "Oh, Mom!" she said, leaning forward and snuggling her face against Evelyn's soft cheek. "It's so great to be back."

The familiar scent of her mother's Worth perfume filled Claire's nostrils, and she felt tears spill over and drip down her nose. She sniffed, and her tears dissolved into woeful laughter.

How typical. Evelyn weeps, and her dazzling blue eyes become more dazzling. I cry, and my nose starts to run.

"I missed you, Mom," she mumbled, catching her breath. "Gosh, I really missed you."

"It's been a nightmare, but you're home now." Evelyn's arms tightened around Claire's waist. "You can't imagine how dreadful it's been, meeting all those impostors, telling oneself not to hope, knowing that they would almost certainly turn out to be frauds—"

"I'm sorry," Claire said, thinking how banal the words sounded. "Mom, truly, I didn't mean to hurt you—"

"At least you're back now." Evelyn gave a little laugh that was almost girlish in its relief. "Oh, Claire, I know it seems trite, but I want to pinch myself to make sure I'm not dreaming!"

"No need for pinching," Claire said. "I'm really here."

"Yes, you are. And I'm so happy, and here's Bainbridge, right on cue, with the elevenses." Evelyn moved over to the table, her steps quick and energetic. "Something smells delicious," she said to the butler.

"I have your midmorning coffee, madam, and some jam tartlets. I hope you'll both find them to your

taste." Bainbridge was firmly back in his role of loyal
nineteenth-century servant, but Evelyn wasn't in the
least put off. She simply smiled at him with the ease of
an old friend.

"I'm sure they'll be wonderful, Bainbridge. As always."

"Thank you, madam." The butler bowed. "I will
leave you to pour the coffee, madam."

Claire laughed, so happy that she made no effort to
guard her tongue. "Bainbridge, you're such a phony.
If I didn't know better, I'd swear you learned all that
faithful-family-retainer stuff watching old Charles
Boyer movies."

A swift glance flashed between Evelyn and the butler, then he smiled politely and handed Claire a cup
and saucer of her mother's favorite Limoges china.
"Charles Boyer is French, miss, and I don't believe he
ever played the role of a butler. Certainly not the role
of an *English* butler. He wouldn't have been up to
that, not by a long shot." Bainbridge indicated that
the discussion was over by giving a nod of his head
that wasn't quite a bow, and quietly withdrawing.

Claire watched him go with a hint of dismay. "Oh,
Lord, what did I say? I think I've hurt his feelings."

"Not at all," Evelyn said briskly, sitting down at the
table and picking up the heavy silver pot. She poured
out the premixed brew of coffee and hot milk. "Bainbridge just likes to put us all in our places from time
to time. He really hasn't come to terms with the fact
that he's working for Colonial upstarts, so every now
and then he pounces on the opportunity to remind us
that we're inferior beings who lack the elegance of
mind to appreciate his superb butlering skills."

Claire laughed, sitting down opposite her mother and helping herself to a jam tart. The pastry was warm and flaky, the strawberry jam thick with sweet berries. She closed her eyes and munched contentedly. "Mmm...these are heavenly. As good as I remembered. Maybe even better." She licked her fingers with sudden appetite, having been much too jittery to consume any breakfast.

"Have another. Help yourself. They are good, aren't they?" Evelyn was using a silver cake fork—of course. She took a final tiny bite, then set down her fork and dabbed at her clean mouth with the corner of her napkin. Then she stirred her coffee for several seconds, although she'd added no sugar.

"Claire, I have to know," she burst out. "Why did you run away?" The fact that the spoon dropped with a clatter into her saucer as she asked the question indicated the extent of her emotional turmoil. "Claire, what happened? How could you have stayed away so long? Your father and I missed you so much. My God, we were *frantic.*"

Claire ignored the reference to Andrew. "I was scared," she said, with perfect truth. "The fire at the cabin frightened me. Perhaps I didn't react quite rationally."

"I understand that." Evelyn leaned forward, her breath shallow, and coming too fast. "I understand that after a major trauma, people often behave strangely, go into shock for a while. But Claire...you stayed away for seven whole years!" She broke off, her gaze slipping uneasily downward. "Claire, I'm your mother. Can't you bring yourself to tell me what kept you away?"

She's asking but she already knows, Claire thought, and the tarts she'd just eaten roiled uneasily in her stomach. *She knows that I ran away because of Andrew. Because of her husband.*

Claire picked up a fork and pushed edgily at the crumbs of her jam tart. It was time, she decided. Time to start unraveling the cocoon of lies that had been invented to protect her, and had ended up nearly getting her killed. Deception hadn't kept her safe. Maybe it was time to try total honesty. She smoothed out her table napkin and put it carefully alongside her plate.

"It's all very complicated," she said.

"Start at the beginning and keep on going," Evelyn urged dryly. "We have all day."

Claire drew in a deep breath. "Grandmother told me about my father," she said. "About you and Douglas and how you fell in love. About how the two of you had an affair that ended up producing me."

A dark flush stained Evelyn's cheeks. "I see," she said. "I often wondered if your grandmother had told you. Now I know." She folded her napkin into a neat rectangle. "Andrew and I had planned to tell you the truth sometime after your eighteenth birthday, but of course we never had the chance."

Claire said nothing. She stared at her plate and Evelyn sighed softly. "Does it make it easier to forgive any of us if I tell you that Douglas and I fell so deeply in love it seemed for a time that the normal rules of behavior just didn't apply to our love affair?"

"I don't know," Claire said painfully. "Isn't that what all adulterers think? That the normal rules of behavior don't apply to them?"

Evelyn's flush disappeared, leaving her stark white. "Yes, I'm afraid you're absolutely right. All I can say is that I was very young, and very naive, and Douglas was the sort of man who comes along once in a lifetime. My upbringing hadn't equipped me to cope with the situation in which I found myself. My parents belonged to a class and a generation that genuinely believed well-brought-up women didn't feel sexual passion." For a moment her eyes gleamed with wry self-mockery. "Douglas aroused feelings in me that were totally outside the realm of anything I'd been taught to expect—outside anything I'd read about, or even dreamed of. So I had to invent my own rules as we went along. Not surprisingly, I didn't do a very good job of it."

For some reason, Claire found herself thinking about Ben, but she forced the intrusive images away. She had managed to spill pastry crumbs all over the tablecloth, and she occupied herself with scooping them up and returning them to her plate. She cleared her throat. "You'd made promises to Andrew when you married him, and he was away fighting for his country when you embarked on your affair with Douglas. Didn't your marriage vows mean anything to you? Or to Douglas, for that matter? After all, Andrew was his brother." And why the *hell* did she care about Evelyn's promises to Andrew? she asked herself.

"Of course, my promises to Andrew mattered," Evelyn said. "But during our honeymoon, he'd told me—" She cut off abruptly. "Sometimes life isn't quite as morally simple as we're taught when we're children. I can never regret the fact that you were born, or that I loved Douglas. Or even that we gave in to our passion and had an affair.'' She smiled, her gaze soft with memories. ''You're so much like him, you know, in so many ways.''

Claire avoided the plea in her mother's eyes. She knew that she'd inherited her father's love of working with glass. She wondered what other, less desirable, characteristics she'd inherited from him. An inability to make long-term commitments? A need to be the center of attention? A tendency to melodrama? She scooped the pastry crumbs into the middle of her plate, concentrating on making a perfect pyramid.

Evelyn sighed. ''For what it's worth, when Douglas was dying of leukemia, you were probably the greatest source of joy in his life. The knowledge that you existed, and that you were such a happy, healthy child, made his own suffering bearable.'' Her voice became husky. ''Your father was a remarkable man, Claire. I wish you could have known him.''

Claire had always realized that it would be difficult to discuss the subject of her illicit conception with her mother, but she had never confronted the full reality of just how difficult it would be. Despite all the relaxing of sexual standards in society generally, the acceptance of moral imperfections in her own mother still went against the grain. In her heart of hearts, Claire clung to the immature belief that *women* might have affairs, but *mothers*—and especially her very own mother—would never indulge in anything so embarrassingly carnal. She knew her attitude was irrational, but nothing much about the mother-daughter relationship was amenable to logic, and this was proving no exception.

"I was angry when Grandmother told me what had happened between you and Douglas," she admitted.

"Because I'd failed to live up to your expectations?" Evelyn asked.

"No." The truth came out in a rush that probably surprised Claire more than it surprised Evelyn. "I was angry with you because Andrew wasn't my father. I loved Andrew."

"And I'd taken him away from you," Evelyn said quietly. "I'd taken him away and given you a dead person in his place. Is that how you saw it?"

"At first," Claire admitted. "Then later, after the fire, I didn't care anymore. I was glad Andrew wasn't my real father." She stopped, unable to go on.

"I don't understand," Evelyn said, looking genuinely puzzled. "Why would the fire make you love Andrew any less?"

A tiny spiral of rage began to twist and turn through the morass of Claire's churning emotions. "Don't pretend," she said hoarsely. "For God's sake, Mother, don't keep on protecting him just because he's your husband and you feel guilty about cheating on him. You can't protect him now. Not anymore."

"How am I protecting Andrew?" Evelyn asked. "I kept quiet about his affair with Jordan, that's true—" She broke off. "Claire, what are we talking about?"

The smell of lukewarm coffee was suddenly nauseating. The elegant drawing room began to blur around her, and Claire squeezed her eyes shut. "Mother, don't make me say it," she pleaded. "I don't think I can say it. Not to you."

"You must," Evelyn said, and her voice no longer sounded gentle, but implacable instead. "Tell me why you think I'm protecting Andrew. Tell me why the fire in Vermont drove you out of the house for seven years."

"Because Andrew was trying to kill me!" Claire said. Except that she didn't *say* anything. She yelled, the effort of bringing the words out over the lump in her throat making control of her voice impossible. She'd flung the same accusation at Ben on more than one occasion. She'd been making the accusation silently, inside her head, for over seven years. Somehow, the sense of betrayal never seemed to get any less.

Andrew, how could you have done this to me? she cried silently.

Evelyn turned sheet white, but she didn't say anything. They stared at each other, two figures in a frozen tableau, with only the ticking of the Louis XVI clock on the mantelpiece to remind them that they were still living, breathing human beings who would have to cope with the problems caused by Claire's accusation.

Claire recovered first. She pushed away from the table, her mouth dry and her head aching. "I'm sorry, Mother. You asked me to tell you the truth, but I guess you didn't really want to hear it."

"Claire, you're so wrong! I did...I do want to hear the truth, and I'm glad to hear at last why you stayed away for so long. But how could you believe something so horrible about such a good man! My dear, Andrew loves you every bit as much as he would if you were his biological child. You know he's never shown the slightest preference for Roger, rather than you."

"Of course not," Claire said, her voice thick with irony. "Andrew is such a noble, forgiving man that he doesn't care in the slightest that I'm a walking, talking reminder that his wife betrayed her marriage vows with his younger brother."

Evelyn flinched, but she didn't lose her control. "In many ways I think Andrew is both noble and forgiving," she replied, her voice carefully level. "However, I don't think it's appropriate for me to stand here and make excuses for Andrew on his behalf. You owe it to yourself and to Andrew to confront him with your suspicions and to lay them to rest, one by one."

"What a good idea!" Claire said, rocked by a bitter sense of betrayal. Why in the world had she expected her mother to believe her when nobody else did—probably not even Ben? "I can just visualize the conversation now— *Daddy, is it true that you set fire to the cabin in Vermont and tried to kill me?*

"'Me? Try to kill you? Good heavens, little Claire, where did you get that silly idea? Of course I didn't try to kill you, honey.'

"Gee, well, that's a relief, Daddy. I guess I just imagined seeing you drive away in that Jeep of yours—"

"What are you talking about?" Evelyn interrupted. "Are you actually suggesting Andrew was in Vermont the night the cabin burned down? If so, you're wrong. Quite wrong."

"I'm not suggesting it," Claire said. "I'm stating it. I saw him, outside the cabin, in his Jeep with a personalized license plate. ABC 4."

"You may have seen one of his cars," Evelyn said tightly. "But you didn't see Andrew driving it. Your father was in Pittsburgh that night. He called me from the house to let me know about the fire, and about the fact that the fire fighters believed you might have escaped—"

"How do you know Andrew called from Pittsburgh?" Claire asked wearily. "Because he told you that's where he was calling from? He could have used a credit card and phoned from virtually anywhere in the United States and you'd never have known the difference. Mother, I know what I saw."

"The housekeeper was at the house with Andrew—"

"Did you ever check with her to confirm that Andrew was really in Pittsburgh the night of the fire?" Claire asked.

"Well, no, of course not." Evelyn appeared disconcerted. "Naturally, there were a hundred more important things on my mind. We were trying to help the investigators discover how the fire had started. We were desperately trying to locate you. We were doing our best to console poor Mike and Michelle Kaplan, Jon's parents.... Why would I even consider the possibility that Andrew was lying to me?"

"Precisely," Claire said huskily. "And that's how he almost got away with murder."

"Knock, knock!" Roger's voice spoke from the doorway. "May I come in? I'd sure like to say hi to my long-lost sister!"

"Roger!" Not surprisingly, Evelyn sounded relieved as well as pleased to see her son. "Come in, and join us. I wasn't expecting you, but what a nice surprise."

Roger came into the drawing room and gave his mother a swift kiss on the cheek. "Ben arrived in the office at the crack of dawn this morning, so I decided to let him take care of the family fortunes while I hopped on a plane and joined the family reunion." He smiled, turning to give Claire a quick, slightly awkward hug. "Welcome home, sis. It's been too long."

"Thanks. It's great to be back." She squeezed his arm, delighted to see him, not just for his own sake, but because his arrival had so successfully lowered the tension level between herself and Evelyn. Swept by vague but fond memories of their shared childhood, she gave him another hug. "Gosh, Roger, I've missed having you around to fight with these past few years!"

"Same here. Every guy needs at least one older sister to drive him crazy." Roger stepped back and scrutinized her intently. "I suppose I can see traces of the sister I once knew, but only just." He shook his head. "Damn, Claire, I wish I could say I'd have known you anywhere, but the honest truth is that I figured almost from the moment we met in Florida that you were an impostor."

Claire laughed. "Yes, I rather got the impression that you'd decided I was out to get my thieving fingers on the Campbell fortune."

He grinned. "Hey, somebody had to protect my sister's interests, you know."

"Thanks for looking out for me." She tugged affectionately at his tie. "Your outfit is impressive, Roger. Really sharp. I like the power tie, too."

He flexed his biceps in a mock preen. "This is my killer business suit," he said. "Seven hundred bucks and counting. Saved for occasions when I need to walk into the room and knock 'em dead.''

"Who was the intended beneficiary of all this sartorial splendor?" Evelyn asked, giving him a smile. "Not us, I gather, since you came here on the spur of the moment."

"No, this was in honor of Dad and the campaign team," Roger said, his expression sobering. "I'm flying on to Palm Beach this evening for a meeting with all of them. The news from Florida isn't good, I'm afraid."

"Andrew said when he left that he would invite the entire team to the house for an in-depth evaluation of where they stand," Evelyn said. "They're trying to determine the effects of that wretched Steve Sterne interview on voter opinion in Florida."

"Yes, they've been working twenty-four-hour days, taking phone polls and all that sort of thing." Roger cleared his throat. "Dad asked me to join him because he's decided he'll probably have to withdraw from the race."

"Oh, no!" Evelyn's mouth tightened in distress. "I can't believe something that happened a quarter of a century ago can destroy Andrew's campaign when he's worked so hard to serve the public interest."

Roger shuffled his feet, and Claire realized that her brother was finding the discussion acutely embarrassing. And why wouldn't he? She hadn't thought about Roger's feelings when she'd plotted Andrew's downfall. Belatedly, she acknowledged how difficult it must be for a young man to learn that his father was gay, or at least bisexual. Damn! In retrospect, there were so many innocent people whose needs and feelings she hadn't sufficiently considered in her obsession with punishing Andrew.

"Homosexuality makes the American public uncomfortable," Roger stated, looking none too comfortable himself. "The latest poll results are in and they're—uh—pretty disastrous for Dad."

"Initial reactions don't always hold," Claire reminded. "The trend might reverse."

Roger shook his head. "So far, each survey shows that the trend is continuing downward."

"It's such a shame," Evelyn said fiercely. "Andrew made one mistake, a long time ago, and that's wiping out everything he's done since. His practical knowledge of sound land development is unsurpassed in this country. He would have been a wonderful governor, particularly in a state like Florida where land-use issues are so important."

"And you'd have made an even more terrific governor's lady," Roger added.

"To be honest, I never had much interest in that particular role, so I feel no personal sense of loss whatsoever. Besides, I've always felt I work better behind the scenes."

Roger drummed his fingers on the top of a console table. "What do you think, Mother? Is there any point in trying to persuade Dad to carry on with the campaign?"

"Not unless he personally feels a burning need to continue," Evelyn replied. "Let's face it, he'll be hounded by the press unless he withdraws and they'll probably do their usual expert job of trivializing the difficult choices he had to make when Jordan Edgar was court-martialed." She stared at the coffeepot, obviously not seeing it. "Poor Andrew, I must call him."

"Why not come with me to Florida instead of calling?" Roger suggested. "Dad could use all the support he can get right now, and it would quell some of the more disgusting gossip if you appeared with him when he makes his resignation statement."

"I could, I suppose, but Claire and I were planning to spend the day together." Evelyn sounded doubtful.

"Don't worry about me," Claire said. "I'm not going anywhere except back to Boston. You should go to Florida if Andrew needs you." *Why not?* she thought sardonically. *Let's all rally around the poor victim, who hasn't done a thing to bring this situation down on his own head.*

Evelyn still appeared torn, but Roger was persuasive, and eventually she agreed to visit Claire the following week in Boston, and forgo the meeting she had scheduled for Thursday with the trustees of the Metropolitan Opera, thus clearing the way to fly with Roger to Palm Beach.

Claire felt none of the triumph that should have been hers. Hands clasped in her lap, she listened to the conversation, realizing she was hearing her mother and brother discuss what amounted to the deathknell of her father's political career. She'd wanted to destroy Andrew Campbell in the most public and humiliating way she could think of. It seemed she had succeeded. So why was success leaving her feeling more than a little sick?

Be careful what you wish for, because the gods may grant your wish. Proverbs and sage old sayings had an annoying habit of revealing their wisdom when it was too late to pay attention.

She looked up and found her mother gazing at her questioningly. Claire's cheeks flamed with guilty color and she stirred uneasily in her chair. Was Evelyn wondering who had supplied Steve Sterne with his devastating information about Andrew? Worse yet, had she guessed the truth? Claire could imagine few things that would be more painful than admitting to Evelyn that she had been the person who set Steve Sterne sniffing on the trail of Andrew's tragic relationship with Jordan Edgar. What would Evelyn say if she learned that her daughter, Claire Helen Campbell, had deliberately set out to destroy Andrew's career?

Fortunately, whatever Evelyn was guessing or thinking, she decided not to broach the subject of Steve Sterne's sources. "Why don't you come with us to Florida?" she said. "I'm sure Andrew would be delighted to see you again, and the pair of you have a great deal to discuss."

"Oh, no," Claire answered quickly. "I don't want to confuse the issue when Da—when And—when he has so much else on his mind. The two of us will have plenty of chance to talk later." She tried for a bright smile. "Besides, I really ought to get back to work. My studio was vandalized a couple of weeks ago, and a lot of my inventory of crystal bowls was destroyed, so I have a heap of catching up to do."

"That's terrible!" Roger exclaimed. "I had no idea you'd had a problem. And you're so talented, too. How could anyone destroy work as beautiful as yours?"

"I'm envious," Evelyn said, turning to Roger. "When did you get a chance to see Claire's work? That's a treat I'm still looking forward to."

Roger smoothed back the long lock of hair that had a tendency to fall forward into his eyes. "Actually, I haven't seen Claire's work. My admiration is strictly secondhand. Ben seems to think Claire is the most talented artist since Michelangelo." He flashed a glance toward Claire, and smiled teasingly. "Even allowing something for the exaggeration of a man in love, I guess she must be pretty hot stuff."

Evelyn raised an eyebrow, but she was much too tactful to make any direct comment about Ben's role in Claire's life. "Well, now I'm looking forward to seeing your work more than ever," she said. "Ben doesn't give praise lightly."

"Don't expect too much," Claire said, abashed by the compliments and trying to make light of her pleasure. "Ben's second-favorite artist paints pictures of Elvis on black velvet." She was secretly thrilled to hear that Ben was so impressed by her work that he'd enthused about it to Roger. On the other hand, she was still so uncertain of her own feelings toward Ben that she wished Roger hadn't been quite so quick to reveal their involvement. Come to that, she wondered how he'd found out. Ben hadn't struck her as the sort of man who would parade details of his personal life around the office. Were their feelings for each other so obvious that they couldn't be hidden? It was a disconcerting thought.

"It's always so worrying when a random act of violence like this occurs," Evelyn said. "I hope you reported what happened to the police, Claire, because you never know when one of those crazy hoodlums is going to start smashing you up instead of a piece of your crystal."

"I'm not at all at risk," Claire said. "I know who did it, you see, and it wasn't exactly a random attack." An unexpected streak of loyalty to Hal Doherty's memory kept her from speaking his name. The guy was dead, she thought. Let the memory of his sordid crimes die with him. "He's learned his lesson by now, I'm sure, and he won't be trying any mean little tricks like that in the future, I'm quite certain of that." Since Hal was dead, she could afford to be dogmatic.

"I hope you changed your locks, at least," Roger said.

"Oh, yes," she lied. "They're changed."

A light tap at the open door warned them of the butler's return. "Would you like me to clear the tray away, madam?"

"Yes, thank you, Bainbridge."

"The jam tarts were delicious," Claire said. "I don't know how I survived so long without them."

Bainbridge smiled indulgently. "I'm glad you enjoyed them, miss." He picked up the tray and gave a polite nod to Roger. "Good morning, Roger. Would you care for me to bring you some fresh coffee?"

"No, thanks. I never could get used to that brew you serve." Roger chuckled. "I guess Sharon's spoiled me with her cooking. Visits to Dad have been a real pleasure recently."

The butler deftly added Claire's plate to the heavy tray. "I'm sure Sharon has spoiled you," he said austerely. "From what I understand, she's a very fine cook." He turned in the doorway, and spoke to Evelyn. With the addition of a wing collar and a pair of white gloves, he'd have looked like the butler from *Upstairs, Downstairs* come to life. "How many people will be staying for lunch, madam?"

"All three of us," Evelyn said. Roger started to protest about leaving for the airport, but she cut him off with a polite shake of her head. "No, Roger. I'll come to Florida with you, but not until I've spent at least another couple of hours with my daughter. We have a lot of catching up to do."

"Of course," said Roger. "Nothing is more important than making time for you to chat with Claire." He smiled, totally unaware that his words could be interpreted as carrying a slight edge. For a split second Claire thought he looked amazingly like his father. Then he crooked his arms, offering one to his sister and the other to his mother, and the illusion of likeness vanished.

"Shall we brave the humidity and go out onto the balcony?" he suggested. "There's something splendidly decadent about sitting in midtown Manhattan, way above the traffic, surrounded by flowers and trees."

Evelyn chuckled. "Until now, nobody has ever called my balcony *decadent*," she said. "It casts my potted palms in a whole new light."

Roger raised her hand and kissed it with considerable flair. "That's what sons are for, Mother. To help you see situations in a new and more exciting light."

Evelyn pressed the tips of her fingers affectionately against his cheek, sat down on a white wicker chaise longue, and turned eagerly to Claire. "Now," she said. "We have an hour before lunch. Tell me about yourself. I want to know everything that's happened in the past seven years."

Roger gave an irritated exclamation. "Give her a break, for heaven's sake! No daughter wants to tell her mother *everything* that's going on in her life."

Evelyn smiled and reached for Claire's hand. "All right. I'll settle for the expurgated version, suitable for doddering, middle-aged parents."

"Where do you want me to start?" Claire asked. "Seven years is a long time."

"We already know you went to New York, and withdrew money from one of your bank accounts. One of the private investigators we had working for us found out that you'd been taken to the hospital and treated for burns, but after that we lost track of you. Tell me what happened after your burns healed and you were released."

Claire grimaced ruefully. "I managed to survive three weeks on my own, and then I checked into the psychiatric ward of a hospital in New Jersey."

"Why New Jersey?" Roger asked. "Any special reason?"

"None. I just happened to be there when I realized I was on the brink of going totally nuts. The nightmares were so horrible that I couldn't bear to lie down and close my eyes, and after twenty-one days virtually without sleep, I was beginning to have what the admitting psychiatrist politely termed 'psychotic incidents.'"

Evelyn gave a quiet murmur of sympathy and Roger walked over to the corner of the balcony, staring out over Fifth Avenue and Central Park.

Claire was still talking about the apartment she'd shared with Dianna Mason when Bainbridge returned to announce that lunch was served.

And Roger was still looking out over Central Park.

Fifteen

Ben called from Pittsburgh at lunchtime on Friday, and promised to be in Boston that night. Claire had given up trying to pretend indifference in her feelings toward Ben. She just hoped that she didn't sound quite as pathetically eager to see him as she felt.

"By the way," Ben said as he was hanging up. "Watch the evening news tonight. Roger called a few minutes ago to let me know that Andrew's going to announce his withdrawal from the race for governor sometime this afternoon. The networks may carry something."

By means of diligent channel flipping, Claire managed to catch Andrew's speech on all three major networks. Flanked by Evelyn on his left, and with Roger hovering sympathetically in the background, Andrew delivered a brief, dignified statement expressing regret that he wouldn't be able to serve the people of Florida, and gratitude for the continuing support of his wife, family and friends. He declined to answer questions, and refused all requests for interviews.

The withdrawal of a candidate for state office didn't usually merit such broad coverage on the national news, but Andrew had not only been touted as a prospective presidential candidate, he also seemed to have hit a collective nerve in the national consciousness. Larry King scheduled an immediate interview with Jordan Edgar's sister, and even PBS weighed in with a heavy-duty report on the remarkable divergence between the way citizens behaved in private life, and the behavior they demanded from candidates for public office.

"Great," Claire muttered, switching off the television and roaming her studio in a state of prickly nervous tension. The doorbell rang, just as she was deciding that the faceted paperweights she'd made the day before were the ugliest things she'd ever seen. She scowled. The last thing she needed right now was Ben Maxwell complicating her life. She would send him away. She would tell him they couldn't see each other again. She would tell him they had nothing in common. She'd been out of her mind to think they might be developing some sort of a meaningful relationship. She flung open the door.

"Hello," Ben said, his gaze flying to meet with hers. He held out a single rosebud, its cream-and-pink petals nestled tantalizingly among feathery fern. "I thought that if anybody was likely to own the perfect vase for this, it had to be you."

"Th-thank you." She couldn't say anything more because she felt an absurd impulse to burst into tears. Drops of moisture were beaded on the furled bud, and a faint, old-fashioned scent wafted to her nostrils. The emotion that ripped through her as she took the flower was so fierce that it hurt. Panicked, she realized that it was already too late to protect herself, even if she found the willpower to send Ben away. Banishing him wouldn't keep her safe because the damage was already done. Somehow, while her attention had been occupied elsewhere, she'd committed the cardinal folly of falling in love.

She stared at him, wide-eyed with fear. Love and perfidy were so inextricably mixed in her experience that she could already feel the ache of his impending betrayal.

"What is it?" Ben asked quietly.

"Nothing." She managed a smile. "Come in. I must find a vase. This rose is so lovely."

He followed her into the kitchen, closing and locking the front door behind him. He took the bud from her and laid it in the sink. "We'll find a vase later," he said softly. "Right now, we have more important things to do."

She'd experienced sexual passion before, and she'd learned how to find physical enjoyment while keeping her emotions safely guarded. But when Ben took her into his arms, he undermined all her carefully nurtured defenses. His kiss was searching, tender, even hesitant, and she wanted it to last forever. She clung to him, drowning in the bittersweet pleasure of feeling so secure, so cherished, even while her brain kept yelling out the warning that she'd never been in greater danger.

"I love you," he said. "God, I love you."

The words made her feel warm and shivery—a warning signal, if ever she'd felt one. She pulled away, hating to be so vulnerable, terrified that she might murmur something she'd regret before her emotional shields had time to lock into place.

"Don't," she said jerkily. "Honestly, Ben, you don't have to say things like that."

He framed her face in his hands. "I know I don't have to say it," he said. "But I want to." He kissed her tenderly on the end of her nose. "I love you, Claire Campbell, and to prove it, if you want me to wait five whole minutes before I take you to bed, I guess I could manage it." He grinned. "Hey, nobody will be able to claim our relationship is just about sex."

She drew in a shaky breath. This was better. Sex was much easier to talk about than love. "Why sacrifice?" she said, proud of the casual smile she managed to toss off. "I'm no more anxious to wait five minutes than you are. You're a great lover, Ben, as I've told you before."

He shook his head. "Claire, honey, I thought we'd settled this a while ago. Tell me that you're not sure if you love me. Tell me that you're not ready to make a commitment. Tell me that you have too many unresolved issues in your life to think about a long-term relationship. But don't trivialize what we have by pretending there's nothing more between us than great sex. We both know that's a lie." He brushed his thumb gently across her mouth, smiling. "Not that the sex isn't terrific, mind you. I wouldn't want you to think I don't appreciate the fabulous sex."

She drew in a shuddering breath. "I'm afraid," she said, horrifying herself by the stark admission.

His hold tightened. "I know, honey. But running away isn't going to solve your problems. You've been running for seven years, and look where that's gotten you."

"Here," she said. "With you."

He chuckled. "True. And that's a great reason to stop running. Maybe you've arrived at your destination."

She wanted to call him names, tell him he was an arrogant bastard, leaping to ridiculous conclusions. Somehow the anger wouldn't come. She went hot, then cold, then hot again. She'd been running for so long, she'd forgotten to consider the end of her journey. "But, Ben—"

"No more buts, honey. My five minutes of self-control were up thirty seconds ago." He didn't bother with any more attempts to persuade her, just kissed her and swung her up into his arms. "Have you noticed I'm getting damned good at this?" he said, carrying her into the bedroom. "Rhett Butler, eat your heart out."

She'd noticed, all right. She'd noticed that where sexual activities were concerned, Ben's technique could best be described as all-around fabulous. He laid her down on the bed, shucking off his shoes and tugging at his tie as he stretched out beside her.

His fingers brushed along her cheekbones. "You're so beautiful," he said, his voice throaty, his eyes dark with desire.

Claire told herself that the compliment was just one more example of his expertise at seduction, but her defense system seemed to have collapsed, felled by a single rose, and she turned to him, helpless to hide what she was feeling. "I...want you," she whispered.

He smoothed her hair out of her eyes, his hands simultaneously gentle and taut with desire. "I'll never betray your trust, Claire,'' he said. "You know that, don't you, honey?"

Until that moment, Claire hadn't realized how heavy a burden of skepticism she carried around with her, day in and day out; a permanent barrier between herself and everyone she met, even a dear friend like Sonya. Lying in Ben's arms, listening to the husky timbre of his voice, she felt her skepticism begin to thaw around the edges. The fear that had been a constant part of her life ever since the Vermont fire seemed to vanish beneath his touch, like a film of ice dissolving to reveal the warm, pulsing emotions beneath. She had already learned the hard lesson that the consequences of living a lie could be devastating. Suddenly she understood the flip side of the coin: The truth was no less potent for being kept silent. She reached out her hand and cradled it against Ben's cheek.

"I love you," she said, not sure whether to laugh or cry because in the end it was so easy to say the words. "I love you, Ben Maxwell."

He covered her hand with his. "Thank God," he said.

Claire lay with her head snuggled comfortably on Ben's shoulder, watching a stray moonbeam illuminate a crack in her ceiling. She was blissfully, actively engaged in doing nothing at all, except thinking that maybe the aftermath of making love was almost as wonderful as the act itself.

"I found Daniel Webster," Ben said.

"Daniel Webster?" Claire blinked as the moon disappeared behind a cloud and the ceiling crack disappeared into darkness. "Daniel Webster!" She sat up so fast, two pillows slid to the floor. "You mean you found my Daniel Webster? The detective?"

"That's the one. He's a private investigator, licensed by the state of New York, and he occupies a very swish set of offices on the West Side, with a great view of the park."

"How did you find him? Did he tell you anything?" Claire's drowsiness had vanished completely. She leaned forward, ready to pounce on Ben's every word.

"Finding him was easy. I hired another investigator from a major firm, and he reported back within a couple of days. Persuading Webster to talk was more difficult."

"Aren't there rules of client confidentiality? How did you persudade him to confide in you?"

Ben shrugged. "I took a risk and called him up. I told him I was Andrew Campbell and that I wanted to tie up a few loose ends in connection with the search for my daughter."

Claire's heart pounded like a jackhammer. "What did he say? Did he acknowledge you—Andrew—as a former client?"

Ben reached out and pulled her back into the crook of his arm. "Yes," he said, his hand restraining her when she jerked in reaction. "Webster remembered the case well, because he was so sorry about the tragic outcome. As far as he's concerned, you see, he did a great job of locating Claire, and then she died before Andrew had a chance to see her again."

"It must have been very upsetting for him," Claire said dully. "On the other hand, I guess from our point of view this is a great find. You've finally unearthed some proof that I'm not totally crazy to suspect Andrew of trying to kill me."

"It seems that way on the surface," Ben said.

She heard the doubt in his voice, and pulled away from him, rolling over to switch on the light. "What?" she asked. "What other explanation is there, unless you want to believe that Dianna Mason died in a tragic accident?"

"If you think about it, I believe you'll agree there are a couple of rather strange aspects to Andrew's dealings with Mr. Webster," Ben said. "For example, I managed to extract the information that Webster had never met his client in person, and that he'd mailed all his bills to a post-office box, and the only phone number he'd had for Andrew was monitored by an answering service."

"I don't find that surprising," Claire said. "What other choice did Andrew have? He couldn't let the bills come to the house. Evelyn might have seen them, or if he sent the bills to Pittsburgh, his secretary or the housekeeper might have asked awkward questions."

"That's true," Ben agreed. "But it's not what I meant. I don't find it strange that Andrew directed the bills to a post-office box, or that he didn't want Webster calling the house. But I find it very strange that Andrew used his real name. He'd taken such pains to cover his tracks, and yet—inexplicably—he was stupid enough to give a private detective his real name. Why?"

Claire's mouth was bone-dry. "Well…if he'd called and said his name was John Smith, maybe Daniel Webster wouldn't have been willing to investigate."

"Why not? There's nothing illegal in looking for a missing person, provided Webster didn't have reason to believe that the so-called John Smith intended harm."

"Then that's it. Andrew couldn't think up a reasonable story to explain his interest, so he had to tell the truth."

Ben shook his head. "It won't wash, honey. Here's a list of reasons, right off the top of my head, any one of which would be good enough for Dan Webster. I'm the bank manager, I'm her boyfriend, I'm a distant cousin, I'm an old school friend, I'm her mother's lawyer, I'm Claire's lawyer and we need to wind up the trust. Andrew's a smart man, with a wide range of sophisticated business interests. If he'd wanted to hire an investigator and keep his identity secret, he'd have known exactly how to go about it."

Claire could feel truths and certainties that had been part of her life for years slipping away. She grabbed for them, needing the security of familiar suspicions, familiar hatred. "Then he deliberately revealed his name," she said. "Maybe he had some reason why he wanted the detective to know who was really hiring him."

"What reason?" Ben asked.

She searched long and hard for a reason and came up with nothing. "I don't know," she admitted. "But there must be a reason. What's your theory?"

"A simple one," Ben said. "Andrew didn't hire Daniel Webster, and the man who did, protected his own identity by throwing suspicion in Andrew's direction."

"Someone else?" Claire questioned, her voice hoarse with disbelief. "You think someone else, not Andrew, hired Daniel Webster?"

"Yes."

"But then...that means someone else killed Dianna Mason, not Andrew."

"Yes." Ben turned to her, taking both of her hands and holding them tightly. "Claire, this is going to be difficult for you, but it's very important. If Andrew didn't try to kill you, who did? Who else hates you enough to want you dead?"

"I don't know," she whispered. "Nobody. There can't be anyone else. I've always known it was Andrew. It has to be Andrew...."

"Think again," Ben said grimly. "Think hard. Your life may depend on it."

He'd smiled all through the TV interview, looking as if he didn't care, looking as if his ambitions weren't being flushed right down the toilet with every word that was spoken. Goddamn it! He was sick to death of smiling in public, while the rage built inside him, churning and boiling and grinding so that he couldn't sleep, couldn't eat, couldn't even enjoy Sharon's nighttime visits anymore.

He walked out onto the patio and stuck his feet into the pool. Jesus, it was hot tonight! There was one consolation—at least he could spend more time in places that really appealed to him.

Unfortunately, he couldn't leave just yet. Not until he'd taken care of Claire, who was beginning to set too many disturbing wheels in motion. Evelyn had asked him about Maureen Bailey, the housekeeper in Pittsburgh who'd been working at the house on the night of the fire. He'd passed off the question, of course, but for all her cool smiles, Evelyn wasn't easily deceived. Now that her mind had been opened to the possibility that all was not as it seemed on the surface, she'd dig and burrow until she found out the truth.

Until he closed the issue by getting rid of Claire. Why the hell did she have to live in Boston? How the hell was he supposed to establish an alibi when he had to fly to goddamned Boston to kill her?

What he needed to do was simple, really. Fire. He would light the fire that would finish the job he'd started seven years earlier.

In his mind's eye he could already see the glow of the flames. He smelled the smoke, and felt the heat.

He heard the patio door open behind him and turned to see who was there. "Sharon," he said. "I didn't know you were still up."

"I was waiting for you to come home," she said, letting her robe slide suggestively off her shoulders.

He no longer found her even mildly seductive. "Go to bed," he said curtly. "I'm not in the mood for company."

She wasn't smart enough to do as she was told. "What's wrong, honey?" she asked, sitting down beside him and dangling her feet into the water.

"Didn't you see the news?" he said.

"Well, I know it's sad and all, but when you get right down to basics, it doesn't really affect you, does it? You've got your own life to lead, outside of politics. And life goes on, doesn't it?" She uttered the cliché as if it were the wisdom of the ages, reaching up to stroke his cheek with her hand. Her nails were painted bright red, and the polish was chipped at the tips. He turned away in disgust.

"Let's go swimming," she said, holding out her hand and trying to coax him into the water. "Come on, it's a lovely night for a swim."

She was asking for it, he thought, so he might as well give it to her. She slithered out of her robe and jumped into the pool, laughing, pretending to scream as the cool water covered her naked breasts. He dived in after her, catching her ankle and pulling her under. He counted to sixty, watching her struggle.

When she was in a state of real panic, he pulled her back to the surface and held her against the side of the pool while she coughed and spluttered and gasped her way back to breathing normally.

"That wasn't funny!" she exclaimed. "My God, you damn near drowned me! What's gotten into you?"

"Nothing," he said, jumping out of the pool and holding out his hand to yank her out after him. He was revitalized by her panic and he felt energy pump through him. "Come on, let's go to bed."

"I don't feel in the mood anymore," she said, shivering as she bent down to pick up her robe.

"But I do," he said softly. He circled his hand around her wrist and hauled her into his bedroom, dragging her over to the bed.

"Stop it!" she cried, tumbling against the pillows in a sprawling heap of body parts. "You're frightening me! Let go! Will you listen to me? Stop it—I mean it— or I'm going to scream!"

"I'm sure you're much to smart to scream," he said. "You're too smart for that, aren't you, Sharon?"

She started to cry—strangled little sobs that finally aroused him after everything else had failed. "I'll make you feel better," he said, holding her wrists pinned over her head as he plunged into her. "Smile, damn you! You know this is what you want. This is what women always want. You're whores, all of you, however goddamned pure you look on the surface."

"Don't do this!" she wailed. "My God, let me out of here! You're hurting me!"

He didn't listen. Instead, he took a pillow and put it over her mouth so that he wouldn't have to hear her screams.

Her eyes rolled backward in her head, and she fainted. Probably from fright. The stupid bitch.

He found the sudden silence very erotic.

Sixteen

Over the hum of her engraving wheel, Claire registered that the phone was ringing. When she was working, she usually just let it ring until the answering machine clicked in, but this morning she was more than ready to be distracted. She switched off the engraving wheel, shoved her protective glasses high onto her forehead, and grabbed the receiver a split second before the answering machine picked up.

"Hello," she said.

"Hello, Claire, this is your—father."

Her hand tightened reflexively around the receiver, and she glared at the phone. *We both know my father's dead,* she wanted to say, but she had heard the uncertainty in Andrew's voice, the note somewhere between defiance and entreaty with which he claimed the relationship, and her throat closed up. She blinked fiercely, trying to control her churning emotions.

Sometimes she felt like a kidnap victim, locked in a dark closet, who learns to love her kidnapper, because he is the only one who opens the door, lets in glimpses of light, and brings her food. She knew what he'd tried to do to her, and logically she realized she ought to hate him. And yet she couldn't, because happy childhood memories kept intruding. Memories of rambling walks through the Pennsylvania country-side when the ground was strewn with autumn leaves; sandcastles built on hot Florida beaches, Saturday mornings perched on Andrew's desk at the office, taking pictures of her hand on the Xerox copying machine while he brought her cans of Coke in a giggling conspiracy against her mother, who insisted children ought to drink only milk and fruit juice.

Too damn many memories, Claire thought.

"Why are you calling?" she asked, her tone of voice aggressive from the effort of repressing her feelings. "What do you want?"

"I want us to meet," Andrew said. "Preferably soon. This evening, if possible. Claire, these misunderstandings between us have gone on way too long, and I blame myself for not forcing a meeting earlier."

"You were busy," Claire said, falsely polite. "With your campaign schedule, and all."

"At least I don't have that problem anymore."

"Every cloud has a silver lining," Claire said sweetly.

There was a tiny pause before Andrew replied. "I would have served the people of Florida to the very best of my ability," he said quietly. "But that's not why I called. I'm in New York with your mother, at the apartment. We've been talking a lot—things we should have discussed before.... Anyway, the long and the short of it is that Evelyn's told me why you disappeared...about what you think happened the night of the fire—"

"You mean, how I saw you driving away from the cabin?" Claire interrupted angrily. "How you left Jon and me to burn?"

"Honey, I wasn't there, so you can't have seen me!"

Claire gritted her teeth. "Has she told you how clearly the flames illuminated you? I saw you, all right. I watched you drive away at full speed, without a single backward glance. You set the fire, and then you drove off, leaving me and Jon Kaplan to die inside the cabin."

She heard Andrew draw in his breath on a sharp note of distress. For a long moment there was silence, then he cleared his throat and spoke with some of his former briskness. "Evelyn's explained what you *believe* you saw, and that's just one of the things we need to talk about—"

"You tried to kill me," Claire accused, with deliberate brutality. Good grief, she wasn't going to feel guilty at stating the simple truth. She had excellent eyesight, and she knew darn well what she'd seen. "Did my mother also tell you that I don't believe Dianna Mason's death was an accident?"

"Yes, Evelyn told me everything." Andrew cleared his throat again, sounding close to tears. "Claire, you must see that we need to talk and resolve these questions before they destroy us all." His voice cracked. "I may not be the ideal father, and God knows I'm not the wonderful, happy-go-lucky man my brother was, but I love you, sweetheart, and I've always thought of you as my own, very dear daughter. We've got to straighten out the terrible mess we've gotten ourselves into. Claire, we loved each other for so many years. Surely we deserve a better ending to our relationship than this swamp of ugly suspicion?"

Claire realized she was crying. She shoved the protective work glasses higher on her head, wiping away the tears with the heel of her hand. What if Andrew was speaking the truth? she wondered. What if he hadn't been driving the Jeep? She had been coping with niggling doubts about Andrew's guilt for days now, and since Ben's revelations two nights earlier, her doubts had swelled into a critical mass.

Could she have been mistaken about the *meaning* of what she saw on the night of the fire? She didn't doubt that she'd truly seen Andrew's Jeep, with its customized license plate. That image was etched in acid on her soul. Nor did she doubt that the driver had been dressed in Andrew's favorite plaid cap and muffler. But she was willing to concede that she'd been too far away—and too shocked—to make a positive identification of the driver's facial features. It was possible that Ted Jenkins had stolen the Jeep from the airport parking lot, where it was often left. He could have worn Andrew's distinctive cap and scarf simply because they were inside the Jeep and he was cold. As for his motives in setting the fire, maybe he'd burned the cabin because it was there, and he was a compulsive arsonist. He hadn't noticed the lights inside the cabin, or the people, because he was an alcoholic, and his mental faculties were zonked with liquor.

Claire had made it her business to read the report of his trial, and she knew that Jenkins had freely admitted his guilt. Why was it so difficult for her to accept that he was telling the truth? The simple explanation, she reminded herself, was very often the correct explanation.

But even if Andrew hadn't been involved in arranging to burn the cabin in Vermont, many mysteries remained. For example, who had hired Daniel Webster?

If it hadn't been Andrew, who had given Andrew's name to the detective, and why? Who had killed Dianna Mason? Or was her death just a terrible accident? More recently, who had set fire to the guest cabana in Florida? Not Ted Jenkins, that was for sure, since he'd been locked up in prison for the past seven years . . . hadn't he?

A chill feathered down Claire's spine when she suddenly thought of all the debates she'd seen recently on television about the early release of criminals, even violent murderers, because of prison overcrowding. My God, was it conceivable that Ted Jenkins had been released?

She spoke quickly. "Dad—Andrew—do you know if Ted Jenkins is still in jail?"

"I'm sure he is." Andrew paused for a moment. "At least, I suppose he is," he amended doubtfully. "I haven't checked, of course, but I always assumed they'd let us know when he was released. Maybe I'm wrong. I guess he might have been paroled without any of us knowing. Why do you ask?"

"Because of the fire at your house in Florida," she said. "Do you think it could have been revenge on the part of Ted Jenkins?"

"It hardly seems likely," Andrew replied. "At the time of his arrest, he had an advanced case of alcoholic dementia. He wouldn't have been mentally capable of tracking me down to Palm Beach, however badly he wanted to wreak revenge."

"There's no booze in jail," Claire reminded him. "At least not enough to keep his brain pickled. If he's sobered up, maybe his wits have returned."

"True, but why would he hold a grudge against me, or anyone in our family? The police found him and arrested him. We had nothing to do with it."

"Still, can you check where he is and what he's doing?" Claire asked, then wondered how the conversation had taken this surreal turn. Why in the world was she asking Andrew to check on the status of his own alibi?

"Certainly. A couple of phone calls should do it." Andrew sounded more cheerful. "Does this mean you're willing to see me tonight? It would be a worthwhile meeting for both of us, I'm sure."

"I don't know. I'm very busy." Logically, Claire accepted that she owed herself and Andrew the chance to talk honestly, one-on-one. Emotionally, it wasn't so easy to confront the past. In some ways, she knew that what she'd been doing for the past few years was the equivalent of trying to live her life with a cesspool stuck smack in the middle of her studio. However hard she scrubbed and disinfected the surroundings, the toxic waste at the core of her existence reached out and contaminated everything. Wasn't it time to end the poisonous absurdity? she asked herself. If the darkness at the heart of her life could no longer be hidden, wasn't it time to confront that darkness? To face the light, whatever it might reveal?

Claire drew in a shaky breath. The words she was about to speak sounded so normal, so mundane, and yet they were so excruciatingly difficult to say. "Do you want me to catch the shuttle to New York? I guess I could do that sometime this afternoon. I'd be at Mother's apartment before dinner. We could talk, I guess. There's not much harm in talking."

"No," he said at once. "Let's do this the other way around. I'll come up to Boston and see you. I think this discussion would be easier if you were on home ground and there was nobody present but the two of us. We need to thrash these problems out honestly, without your mother locked in the middle, trying to adjudicate between the two of us. This is between you and me, Claire, and nobody else."

All the old doubts immediately rushed back. "You and me? Just the two of us—alone?" she said mockingly. "I don't think so, Andrew. If you don't want Mother involved in this, I'm willing to meet you in my studio this evening, but I sure as heck plan to have witnesses around for the meeting."

"If you think that's really advisable—"

"I think it's essential," she said coolly. "I'm very attached to the prospect of surviving our meeting."

For the first time, Andrew sounded angry. "For God's sake, Claire, to suggest that I would harm you in any way is ridiculous— No, worse, it's obscene—"

"Ben Maxwell will be here," she said, cutting him off. "And just to make doubly sure that you don't plan anything fancy, I intend to let my friend Sonya know that you're coming. You remember Sonya Harvey? The two of you met on my doorstep when she came to tell me that Hal Doherty had been killed."

"I remember. She's an investigative reporter with the Boston *Globe*."

"Right. And, trust me, she wouldn't allow my death to go unexamined, however accidental it appeared. If I fall from a window, or my car crashes, you can count on being suspect number one in an all-out murder investigation."

There was a momentary silence on the other end of the phone, then Andrew spoke with unmistakable weariness. "I can't believe that you feel it's necessary to take those precautions," he said. "My God, Claire, don't you have any idea how painful it is for me to hear your mistrust expressed so savagely?"

"Don't you have any idea how painful it was for me to know that my supposed father had tried to kill me?" she retorted.

The silence vibrated with tension. "We seem to be going in circles," Andrew said finally. "Perhaps we'd better not talk any more until we're face-to-face. I'll see you this evening, Claire. There's some information I need to collect before we meet, but I should be able to make it to your studio around eight at the latest. We'll talk then." He hung up the phone before she could reply.

He broke the connection almost as if he was afraid of what hurtful thing she might say next. For a moment, Claire was filled with regret and she caught herself wondering if she'd spent the past seven years of her life hiding from the wrong person. Then she pushed the thought aside. Before she'd accept that Dianna Mason had died in an unfortunate car accident and Ted Jenkins had set the fires in Vermont and Florida, somebody would have to produce some darn convincing evidence. When she thought back over the conversation, reflecting on precisely what Andrew had said, she realized that although she had several times flat-out accused him of attempting to murder her, he had never once responded with a flat-out denial of her charge. Why not? Was it because some odd quirk of his New England conscience kept him silent?

Engraving was out of the question. Claire started to clean up her workbench. Given the muddled mood she was in right now, she was more likely to cut off a chunk of finger than complete a satisfactory design. She tugged off her work glasses and tossed them onto the bench, then reached for the phone and dialed Ben's office number in Pittsburgh. It was amazingly comforting to know that Ben would be arriving in Boston tonight, and would be around to share the burden of her meeting with Andrew. Still, she couldn't wait so many hours to talk to him. She needed to talk with him now. Maybe it would ease some of her confusion if she let him know that Andrew would be visiting tonight.

The number she dialed was supposed to connect directly with Ben's office, a personal line not answered by his secretary. After several rings, she was just about ready to accept that Ben wasn't at his desk, when the phone was answered.

"Ben Maxwell's phone," said a male voice.

"Roger? Is that you? This is Claire."

"Claire, how nice to hear from you." Roger sounded polite, as always, but she got the distinct impression he was in a hurry. "How's everything with you? Okay, I hope?"

"Fine," she said. "But I need to speak with Ben, if he can spare a moment."

She could almost see Roger's teasing smile. "Sorry to rain on your parade, big sister, but he's in a meeting with a couple of our project managers. Anything I can do to help out?"

"Could I leave a message for him? It's fairly important or I wouldn't bother you. I can tell you're busy."

"Sure, no sweat. I have a pencil and paper. Fire ahead."

"Andrew is in New York with Evelyn and he's coming to meet with me tonight." All the better if Roger was aware of the situation, Claire thought quickly. Maybe she was grossly misjudging Andrew, and maybe she wasn't, but she preferred to be safe rather than sorry. After all, Andrew had insisted on coming to see her in Boston, rather than accepting her suggestion of flying down to Manhattan. In fact, come to think of it, she only had Andrew's word for it that he was staying in Evelyn's apartment. If he was lying, Evelyn might not even realize that her husband had arranged tonight's meeting. In any event, the more people who knew Andrew was planning to visit the studio, the safer it would be for her.

"Is that the whole message?" Roger asked.

"Not quite. Ben said he'd try to arrive at my place by nine o'clock tonight. Tell him if he can make it any earlier, I'd sure appreciate it."

"I'll do that," Roger said. He hesitated for a moment, and she could almost hear him debating between the press of business and his need to talk to her. In the end, he compromised. "Look, Claire, there's a lot of stuff we have to talk about, you and I. When the cabin burned down...when you disappeared... Well, I was only fifteen, and a pretty immature fifteen at that. But I think we could help each other a lot if we talked honestly about some of the situations in our family—"

"I'd love that," she told him. "Roger, anytime you can spend a weekend with me, I'm on. You name the date, and I'll clear my calendar. Boston's a great city to visit, and I'm sure we could have a wonderful time together."

"That would be terrific," he said. "Or you could fly out to Pittsburgh. In fact, you should definitely come here to Pittsburgh. I'm sure you'd love to see the old house again. Dad keeps threatening to sell the place, and I keep talking him out of it." He broke off, and she heard the sound of another phone ringing. "Claire, it's a madhouse around here today. I've gotta go. But we'll be in touch soon, okay?"

"Sure. Go take care of that phone," Claire said. "Bye, Rog. We'll talk next week."

She felt more cheerful after her chat with her brother, brief though it had been. Inspired with a sudden determination to get the truth out on the table in all her relationships, she decided to go visit Sonya at the office rather than relying on a phone call to impart the news that Andrew was paying a visit.

She drove from Cambridge across the river to the *Globe* offices, taking the inevitable traffic jams in stride. Rolling down her window, she ignored the gas fumes and admired the pretty day. A cool breeze was blowing in off the harbor, sending high clouds scudding across the sky and lifting the pall of humid summer haze. She stopped at a Thai restaurant at the corner of Henderson Street, buying a selection of her favorite shrimp-and-vegetable dishes. Finding a parking spot after only five minutes of circling, in itself a minor miracle, she made her way up to the cubicle off the main newsroom that served as Sonya's office.

"Hi! Nice to see you, kid." Sonya greeted her with a surprised smile and a cloud of smoke. "Come on in," she said, removing three empty cans of root beer and a stack of books from a chair and onto the corner of her desk so that Claire could sit down.

"Can you take time for lunch?" Claire asked. "I brought us some carryout stuff."

"Dianna, honey, I can always find time to eat." Sonya cleared a pile of old newspapers from her credenza, sniffing appreciatively. "Lordy, Lordy, you're a woman of exquisite taste. I see the beautiful white boxes of the Thai Garden restaurant peeping out of that bag."

"Spiced garlic prawns, pea pods with walnuts, and caraway rice," Claire announced, arranging the cartons on a stack of napkins.

"The pathetic rumbles of my empty stomach must have reached out to you." Sonya found the plastic plates and bundle of forks. "What brings you to the city, Di?"

"Andrew Campbell called this morning. He plans to pay me a visit tonight. He wanted it to be just the two of us. Andrew and me, alone together, eyeball-to-eyeball."

Sonya paused in the middle of serving herself from the steaming packages. "Why's he coming? To bitch about the Steve Sterne show?"

"No, I don't think so. To be honest, I got the impression that Andrew's withdrawal from the race for governor isn't the most important thing on his mind right now."

"Then what the heck does he want?"

"He wants to talk about the fire in Vermont, and a whole bunch of other things from the past."

"That's odd." Sonya speared a prawn. "Why does he feel the need to discuss old family history with you, of all people? Do you want me to come and play chaperon?"

"No, thanks. But I did want you to know he's coming." Claire crunched a sautéed pea pod, then tried for a smile. "If you hear a report that my body was fished out of the harbor wearing concrete shoes, please don't believe it was suicide, will you?"

Sonya leaned forward, her smile fading. "Look, Di, this is no joking matter—"

"I know it's not. And I have something to tell you." Claire put down her fork and laced her fingers tightly in her lap. "I'm not Dianna. I'm Claire. Claire Campbell. Dianna Mason died five years ago in that accident on the New Jersey Turnpike."

"My God!" Sonya choked on a bite of food. She swallowed, then swallowed again. "Dianna Mason died in a car accident? But you told me that it was Claire Campbell who died. Hell, you showed me her death certificate!"

"I know. But Dianna looked like me, and since I was the one doing the identification, it was quite easy to say she was Claire Campbell. Dianna's only relative was a brother in California, and he didn't even come to the funeral. Ben Maxwell was the first person ever to question that death certificate."

Sonya stared from Claire to her food, and then back again. "Do you want to tell me why you decided to kill yourself off, metaphorically speaking, and then assume another woman's identity?"

Claire unlaced her fingers. "For the obvious reasons, actually. I wanted to disappear. I thought if Claire Campbell was dead, it was a fairly safe bet that people would stop trying to murder her."

"Sounds like a crazy scheme to me."

"It worked."

Sonya shoved aside her plate of food and reached for a pack of cigarettes. She lit up with shaking hands. "I'm having trouble taking this in. You're not Dianna Mason, starving artist. You're Claire Campbell, heiress to umpteen million dollars."

"Claire Helen Campbell, that's me." She laughed nervously. "Heiress in the flesh, so to speak. Certified by an official blood test."

Sonya glowered at the ashtray. "So if you're Claire Campbell, what was all that bullshit you fed me the other day? I asked you point-blank if Andrew Campbell was your father, and you swore to me that he wasn't."

"I'm sorry," Claire said. "In fact, I told you the literal truth, but I knew you'd misunderstand what I was saying."

Sonya blinked. "Wait a minute, can we backtrack here? You're Claire Campbell, but Andrew isn't your father?"

Claire pushed her plate away. "That's right. That sums up the situation in a nutshell."

"My God!" Sonya stared at the ceiling, puffing busily. "You were adopted? No." She shook her head, answering her own question. "You look too much like Evelyn. Evelyn *is* your mother, right?"

"Right." Claire smiled wryly. "You're being uncharacteristically tactful, Sonya. Yes, my mother had an affair, and yes, I'm the result."

Sonya coughed around a lungful of smoke. "Roger," she said finally. "Isn't he Andrew's kid, either?"

"Oh, yes, of course he is! My biological father died several months before Roger was conceived, let alone born."

Sonya cocked her head. "He died?"

"Yes." Claire looked up and met her friend's eyes. "My father was Douglas Campbell," she said.

"Douglas Campbell, of course!" Sonya's breath came out in a puff of understanding. "Great guy," she offered, putting her hand briefly over Claire's. "I'm sorry, sweetie. That's inadequate, but I don't know what else to say."

"There's nothing else you *can* say," Claire replied. "Douglas died a long time ago. I'm sorry I never knew him, but it's a fairly impersonal sort of regret."

"Was Andrew a cruel stepfather?" Sonya asked. "Is that why you're so mad at him?"

"On the contrary." Claire smiled tautly. "Until he started trying to kill me, I guess you could say Andrew was a great substitute dad."

Sonya stubbed out her cigarette. "You're still convinced he's behind the fire, and the car accident that killed Dianna?"

Claire nodded.

"I don't understand what you've been trying to do," Sonya said. "When you met Hal Doherty at my party, why didn't you tell him you were the real Claire Campbell? Good Lord, the guy spent two months coaching you day and night to play the part of the woman you really are! Jesus, do you have any idea how bizarre that is! Why the hell didn't you tell me what was going on?''

"I couldn't—"

"I think I'm offended. Dammit, we're supposed to be friends. I thought you trusted me.''

"We *are* friends. I do trust you.'' Claire leaned forward. "Please don't be offended, Sonya. I just couldn't confide in you, and if you think about it for a while, you'll understand why.''

"I am thinking. And I don't understand.''

"After so many years of being Dianna Mason, it seemed as if clinging to that identity was the only thing that kept me safe.''

"Then why the blazes did you agree to work that stupid scam with Hal Doherty? If you wanted to remain Dianna Mason, why walk into the heart of the Campbell clan claiming to be Claire? And if you suddenly had a burning urge to reclaim your true heritage, why didn't you walk up to the front door and say, 'Hi, folks! Good news—your long-lost daughter is home.' For God's sake, you're legit. What the hell was that ridiculous masquerade all about?''

"Staying alive,'' Claire said.

Sonya tossed her short hair impatiently. "By walking right back into the home of the man you suspected of trying to kill you?''

"It seemed logical at the time,'' Claire stated wryly. "I was working on the assumption that Andrew is a selective murderer, rather than a homicidal maniac.''

"What's that got to do with your decision to work a scam with Hal Doherty?''

"There've been dozens of claimants to my inheritance over the past seven years," Claire explained. "And at least six would-be Claire Campbells who looked enough like me to get personal interviews with Hal Doherty, or Ben Maxwell, or even a family member. None of those impostors died. They all lived to get arrested and charged with fraud. I concluded that Andrew didn't want a trail of murdered Claire Campbell look-alikes littering his doorstep, so casting doubt on my own identity seemed to be a very good way to keep myself protected."

"Sweetie, that's the most dumb-ass reasoning I've ever heard."

"But it worked, didn't it? I'm still here. And Andrew isn't on track to become governor of Florida, in large part thanks to your information."

"Yeah, well, I'm not sure that I want to be thanked for the role I played in that debacle," Sonya said. "If Andrew's a murderer, I'm all in favor of letting him fry, but the fact that he's gay doesn't seem to me to disqualify him from public office."

"I know," Claire said, troubled. "I guess this is a case of the public making the right decision for the wrong reasons."

Sonya stacked the nearly full cartons of food back into the brown-paper sack. Then she looked up, examining her friend's face. "You know, I guess I'm not all that surprised to hear you really are Claire. The feelings you had for Andrew Campbell were just too strong to be secondhand, passed on from a roommate. You hated him with the sort of intensity we can only manage to conjure up for members of our own family when they betray us."

"Spoken with real feeling," Claire murmured.

"Yeah." Sonya straightened from stuffing discarded plates into her overflowing garbage. "I had an amazing phone call last night. My brother called from Wyoming."

Claire looked up quickly. "Not bad news?"

"Not really. He called about Hal Doherty. He knew Hal well, of course. They'd played on the football team together, although my brother was almost three years older than Hal."

"You must have been pleased to hear from him. Is that the first time you've spoken to each other since your mother's funeral?" Claire asked, cautiously probing what she knew was delicate ground.

"Yes. Apparently there's going to be a memorial service for Hal over Labor Day weekend. My brother suggested I might like to stay at his house if I went back for the service."

"I'm so glad he invited you," Claire said. "That's terrific. It doesn't make up for the rotten things he said when your mother was dying, but at least it's a start."

"Yeah." Sonya shrugged, trying without much success to hide her relief. "He has the cutest kids you'd ever want to meet. I was having a hard time accepting that I might never see them again." She shoved her hands into the pockets of her cotton skirt. "The hell of it is, however much your family drives you crazy, it's tough to cut them out of your life."

"I know," Claire said. "Boy, do I know what you mean." She touched her friend lightly on the shoulder. "I'll keep you posted on what happens at my meeting with Andrew tonight."

"Do that," Sonya said, her moment of sentimentality over. "And keep your eyes peeled, kiddo. I don't have many millionaire friends, so I'd like to bum a few fancy dinners off you before you end up floating in Boston Harbor."

Claire actually found herself laughing. "Hey, with friends like you around, I need never wonder if I'm loved for my money or my own great personality."

"Just watch yourself, sweetie," Sonya said. "Remember, I'm really looking forward to those dinners."

Dashing between meetings, Ben stopped at his secretary's desk to pick up his phone messages. "Anything important?" he asked, shuffling through the pile of yellow slips, all stamped Urgent.

"Just the usual emergencies on three continents," Nancy replied, smiling.

He smiled back, then glanced down at his watch. Almost three o'clock. Another one of those days crammed so full that it seemed over before it began. "Anything I need to handle right now? I'm already late for my meeting with Sanchez."

She shook her head. "Everyone should be able to maintain their present state of crisis until Monday."

"No personal calls? Messages?"

"No, although I believe there was a call for you—" She broke off as the phone started ringing again and she reached to pick it up. "Ben Maxwell's office."

Ben heard the low murmur of a female voice on the other end of the phone. Not Claire's. He could recognize Claire's husky, enticing tones at twenty paces. He turned to go. Sanchez, the project manager for the retirement complex in Daytona Beach, had been waiting all afternoon to see him. Nancy stopped him as he was about to step out into the hallway. "Ben, I think you should take this call."

"Who is it?" he asked, turning back into his own office. "Sanchez has a plane to catch. I can't give anyone more than two minutes."

"She says it's personal. She won't tell me her name, but she's obviously calling from a public phone and she sounds frantic."

Claire, Ben thought, grabbing his phone. My God, he'd been mistaken about his capacity to recognize her voice. What had happened? What was wrong? "Hello, this is Ben."

"Can anyone hear us?" a woman's voice asked.

"No, nobody." Ben let out a sigh of relief. His caller wasn't Claire, after all. "This line doesn't go through the main switchboard," he assured the woman.

"Is Roger there?" The question was asked so softly, he could barely hear it. He frowned, sure he recognized the voice of his caller, even though he'd never heard her sound so nervous . . . so *raw*. Why the heck was Andrew's personal chef calling him? And why did she sound nothing at all like her usual competent self?

"Roger isn't here," Ben said. "I promise you this line's secure. Nobody can hear what you have to say except me. Is this Sharon? Sharon Kruger?"

"Don't say my name!" Her voice rose into a panicked squeak. "I'm in Miami airport, and I'm about to catch a flight to Mexico. Five more minutes and I'm outta here."

"Tell me what's bothering you," Ben said, sneaking another glance at his watch and trying not to feel impatient. "Is there some way I can help?"

"Not me. You can't help me. I finally wised up." Even over a thousand miles of optic-fiber phone wires, he could hear the mixture of bitterness and hysteria in Sharon's voice.

"Don't hang up," he said, sensing that she was poised right on the verge of cutting the connection. "Sharon, what is it? If you don't tell me, I can't help."

"It's not me who needs help," she said. "I've got fifty thousand dollars in my bank account—more cash than I've ever seen in my life before, and boy, did I earn it." She gave a tight, ugly gasp, somewhere between a sob and a gulp of laughter. "You wanna know how I got it?"

"Yes, I would like to know."

"Roger gave it to me," she said, the words tumbling out in a frightened rush. "Roger paid me off so that I'd leave the country and not tell anyone he damn near killed me two nights ago."

"Roger nearly killed you?" Ben shook his head, feeling dull and stupid with shock. What in the world did Sharon mean? Her accusation seemed so absurd, it was almost incomprehensible.

"Yeah. Spoils the image of hardworking, all-American, holier-than-thou Roger Campbell, doesn't it? He put a pillow over my face and damn near choked me to death." Sharon laughed mirthlessly. "Sex with him was always a bit kinky, but that was okay. I put up with all his weird stuff because I was dumb enough to think he might marry me. Was that stupid, or what? Then a couple of nights ago, he went over the edge. Right over the edge. He almost drowned me, then he raped me...."

Ben breathed a little easier. He was shocked by Sharon's revelations, and he certainly took her accusations of rape seriously. But there was a difference between rough sex that got out of control, and attempted murder. "Do you need medical help?" he asked. "Sharon, if we're going to straighten out this mess, you need to tell me what happened. The whole story. Draw in a deep breath, and start over, from the top."

"There's no time," she said. "Besides, I can take care of myself. But the Campbells have been good to me, especially Andrew, and I don't want Roger to mess everything up for the family. I decided I ought to warn someone, and I could see you'd fallen in love with Claire...Dianna...whatever her name is—" She broke off. "They're calling my flight. I've got to go! I have to get out of Florida...away from him—"

"Sharon, settle down for a moment." Ben fought to keep his own voice level and reassuring. "Listen to me, Sharon, you still have twenty minutes at least before the flight leaves, which is plenty of time to tell me why you called. What is it you think we should know? Something else about Roger?"

"Yeah, something else about Roger," Sharon said, with mocking emphasis. "He's going to kill Claire, I'm sure of it. The crazy bastard needs to be locked up before he does someone a serious injury."

Sharon's accusations exploded inside Ben's head. *Roger was trying to kill Claire.* He fought to hang on to his cool, to speak coherently, to ask intelligent questions.

"Sharon, don't hang up! How's he going to kill her? When? How did you find out?" He barked his questions into the phone. His only response was a dial tone. "Sharon!" he shouted, jiggling the receiver rest, his last vestige of calm vanishing. "Sharon, dammit, give me the rest of the story!"

The phone responded with a bland continuation of the dial tone. He slammed the receiver into the cradle and ran to the door that separated his office from Nancy's. He flung it open. "Where's Roger?" he demanded.

"I think you just missed him. He said he had an appointment—"

"Here? Inside the office building?"

"I don't know—"

"Call security. Search the building. If he's here, I want to know it. This is an emergency. Find Roger. Top priority." Ben strode back to his desk and flipped his Rolodex file to Claire's number in Boston.

You're overreacting, he told himself, punching in the numbers. Sharon had sounded on the edge of a breakdown, and he needed to take her wild accusations with a giant pinch of salt. God knows, she wouldn't be the first person to lash out with false accusations when a relationship broke up. She'd admitted that she'd hoped to marry Roger. Frustration and hurt feelings could be driving her to stir up trouble.

That was all very rational, Ben thought. So why the hell was his stomach heaving and his legs shaking?

Claire's line gave back a busy signal. Pressing the redial button, he tried again. The phone still gave him a busy signal.

That was no reason for panic, Ben told himself. If Claire was talking on the phone, she was obviously fine. With determined calm, he dialed the long-distance operator.

"I need to speak with the person at this number," he said, reciting Claire's number. "I keep getting a busy signal."

"I'll try the number for you, sir. Right away."

Ben waited, sweat gathering at the base of his spine. The operator returned, professionally cheery. "I'm sorry, sir, but my equipment does show a problem with that number. I'll report it to the engineer—"

"What sort of a problem? Is the phone off the hook? What's going on?"

"Nobody's talking on the line, but I can't really diagnose problems from here, sir, we need to send out a technician. But it does seem to be a problem in the outside line—"

Ben slammed down the phone, and strode out of his office, no longer even attempting to conceal his worry. "Any word from security? Anyone seen Roger?" he asked Nancy.

"No sign of him in the building," she said. "I think he mentioned he was planning to spend the weekend at home, catching up on paperwork. Ben, is there something wrong—"

"I'm leaving for Boston on the next flight," he said. "I'm going to Claire's studio. If Andrew happens to call, tell him where I've gone, will you?"

"Of course—"

"And if you find Roger, leave a message for me at the airport."

"Yes, certainly, I'll do that. What about Mr. San-chez?" But she spoke to Ben's back.

For some unfathomable reason, Claire decided that it was important to look her best for her meeting with Andrew. At six o'clock, two hours before she could realistically expect either Ben or Andrew to arrive, she had already showered and dried her hair, and put on her makeup. After frowning for several minutes over the modest contents of her wardrobe, she selected a pair of cotton pants and a white muslin blouse that she cinched around her waist with a silver belt of Navaho design, studded with chunks of turquoise. She swept her hair up into a loose twist, added exotic dangling earrings and decided, on viewing the finished effect in her bedroom mirror, that she looked aggressively artsy-craftsy. She wasn't sure whether to be amused or dismayed by her need to stake out such an obvious claim to an independent identity. Her clothes would tell Andrew quite clearly that he was dealing with Claire the almost famous glass designer, rather than Claire the Campbell heiress.

She was wandering somewhat aimlessly around the living area in her studio when the doorbell rang. Her heart beat fast with momentary fear, then steadied. Andrew wasn't totally crazy. He wasn't going to at-tack her when he knew he would be the prime sus-pect. Still, she hoped to God it was Ben who'd arrived early, rather than Andrew. It would be so much easier to confront her supposed father with Ben at her side.

Her visitor turned out to be neither Andrew nor Ben. Instead, she opened the door to find Roger standing on her doorstep, a small airline travel bag slung over his shoulder.

"Roger!" she exclaimed, smiling with extra enthusiasm to make up for the fact that she wished he had been Ben. "Well, this is a nice surprise. Come on in."

"Thanks." He stepped inside and she closed the door after him. "I don't think you're going to be so happy when you hear my news," Roger said. "Ben isn't going to be here this evening, Claire, not until midnight at least. He's sent me as a stand-in, if I'm acceptable."

"More than acceptable. It's great to have you here," she said, genuinely pleased to have the protection of his presence. She covered a rush of disappointment at Ben's absence by giving him a quick, sisterly hug. Then she ushered him ahead of her into the tiny living area in a corner of her studio.

"Did you just fly in from Pittsburgh? Was it a crush?" she asked.

"A total zoo. You know what planes are like on a Friday afternoon."

"Miserable," she agreed. "Are you hungry? Can I make you a sandwich or something?"

"No, thanks. But a drink would be great."

"Sure, coming right up." Claire gave an embarrassed laugh. "This is strange, isn't it? Here I am, playing hostess to my own brother, and I have no idea what you like to drink."

"I'm easy," he said, grinning.

She returned his smile. "That's good news. Okay, I have a bottle of Chablis in the fridge, plus I have Coke, diet soda, or fresh lemonade. Take your choice."

"The lemonade, please," he said. "It was a rush to catch the plane out of Pittsburgh and I still haven't cooled off."

"Loosen your tie, and let me hang up your jacket."

Roger immediately tugged off his tie and tossed it over the back of a chair, unfastening the buttons at his collar. "Thanks, that feels a lot better. I won't bother with my jacket." He got up and wandered over to her workbench, running his fingers admiringly over her display of faceted paperweights.

"It's fascinating how the cuts are refracted differently depending on where the paperweight is positioned relative to the light," he remarked. "These are lovely, Claire."

"Thanks." She was gratified by the compliment. "Half the pleasure of working with faceted glass is developing an interior design that's going to make interesting refractions." She poured two glasses of lemonade and walked over to hand him his.

"I'm sure it must be an absorbing hobby," he said, sipping thirstily. "This is delicious, by the way."

"I'm glad you like it. Fresh lemonade is one of my favorite drinks at this time of year." In the interests of peaceful family relations, Claire decided not to tell him that calling her work a hobby was monumentally insulting.

He set his glass down and looked intently at the bowl she'd been engraving that morning. "This is another interesting design," he said. "More abstract than most of your work. I really liked that stemmed goblet you made with the ivy-leaf design."

"This pattern's much more abstract," Claire agreed. "But it's not entirely geometric. The main motif is based on the shape of a rose petal."

Roger bent down to examine the bowl more closely. "So it is. I can see that plainly now you've pointed it out, but I'd never have noticed on my own." He laughed deprecatingly. "I'm afraid you got all the artistic talent in this family, Claire. Along with most of the money."

She stared back at him, her eyes blank with shock. She swallowed hard, the lemonade suddenly acid in her mouth. "Wait! How did you know that the design on this bowl is more abstract than most of my work? How did you know about my stemmed goblet with the ivy-leaf design?"

He turned slowly, his smile bright. "I guess Ben must have described it—"

"No, that's not possible." Claire struggled to speak composedly. "Ben never saw that bowl. It was smashed by the time he paid his first visit to my studio. All my work had been destroyed."

"Had it?" Roger seemed unruffled by her stuttering agitation. "Now let me think. How else could I have seen that bowl, I wonder?"

His mockery was barely concealed by his pretense of puzzlement. Claire set her lemonade on the counter, shivering with shock, outrage and a desperate sense of betrayal. "You saw the goblet because you were here, in my studio," she said huskily.

"You know, I think you must be right." Roger smiled again, and this time his mockery was blatant. "I must have been here, in your studio, in order to see your pretty bowls."

"And you smashed them," Claire said. "It wasn't Hal Doherty who destroyed my work. It was you!"

"Right again," Roger said. "It was me."

"But why... My God, why?"

"I can't believe you need to ask," he said bitterly. "All my life I've had to live in your shadow. The big sister who was adored by everyone. The big sister who had the twenty-million-dollar trust fund. The big sister who had inherited Grandpa's artistic talent, so that nobody seemed to notice or care that I was twice as smart as you." He crashed his fist down on the counter, his face crumpling in lines of bitter frustration. "And you were a bastard, damn it! You weren't even the real Campbell heir. It should have been me, not you! Andrew should have loved *me!*"

"I'm sure he did," Claire said.

"Right. We're real close," Roger said bitterly. "And now the stupid dumb-ass has gone and ruined my political career."

"How did he do that?" Claire asked cautiously, edging backward toward her phone.

"By getting caught out in his sordid affair with Jordan Edgar, of course!" Roger snatched the receiver and held it up to her ear. "Is this what you're creeping toward, big sister? You don't think I'd be crazy enough to leave you with a functioning phone, do you? I cut the lines as soon as I got here."

Claire realized that what she felt was sheer, unadulterated terror. "Roger," she whispered. "What are you going to do—"

She never finished her question. Roger lunged for her, grabbing her around the neck and immobilizing her by the pressure of his forearm against her windpipe. She felt the breath squeeze out of her lungs, leaving a burning pain in her chest. She tried to ask him what he was doing, what he wanted, but his arm choked off speech. She looked up, but all she could see was the side of his face, and the stubble of his beard.

She felt the prick of a needle in her arm, the unmistakable sucking and fizzing sensation of a liquid being injected into her vein.

Red dots floated in front of her eyes. Roger's nose melted into his chin. His chin flowed into his shirt collar.

Roger, she thought. Roger was driving the Jeep that night in Vermont.

He's going to kill me.

The red dots exploded.

Her eyes closed.

Seventeen

She was sweating from the heat. In the distance, she could hear the murmur of powerful waves lapping onto the shore. The sound should have been peaceful, but it wasn't. Claire felt tension winding tighter and tighter inside her as she listened to the roar of the ocean.

She had been lying on the beach too long, and the sun was burning her skin. She felt sick with the intensity of the heat, and her body ached when she tried to move.

Claire knew that she ought to get out of the direct light of the sun, but she didn't have the strength to move. She dragged her face along the ground, trying to find a cool spot on her beach mat without actually exerting herself to lift up her head. Even that limited movement was enough to send nausea shooting up from her stomach, and her muscles howled in protest.

The pain sent her retreating into the comfort of semiconsciousness. She was so disoriented and dopey that for a long while she lay still, subliminally aware that she would die if she didn't move, but lacking either the desire or the energy to save herself.

The heat was truly unbearable, Claire thought. With excruciating slowness, another coherent thought took shape inside her woozy brain.

She wasn't sunbathing on the beach. She was in her studio.

The realization frightened her, although she couldn't imagine why. She let the fear wash over her, mingling with the pain and the nausea. Feeling fear required too much effort, so she wouldn't feel it. On the very edge of drifting back into peaceful darkness, another thought formed, although it wasn't really a thought, more an overwhelming sensation of dread.

Roger.

His name echoed inside her head, setting off bells that clanged loudly with the warning of approaching doom. She knew that it was vitally important to move, to sit up, to throw off the deadly, enticing drowsiness, but she couldn't.

Roger.

With an effort that made sweat break out all over her body, she opened her eyes.

She saw concrete floor. So, she thought, as her eyes drifted closed. She'd been right. She wasn't lying on the beach. She was in her studio.

Roger.

Not at all sure why it was so terribly important to make the effort, Claire forced her eyes open again. She was lying on the floor of her studio, her hands and feet bound with tape. She responded with an instinctive gasp of horror. Except that no sound came out of her mouth because it, too, was covered with tape.

The need to throw up was suddenly acute, but some residual instinct for self-preservation warned her that she simply couldn't afford to give in to the need. With her mouth sealed by tape, if she vomited, she would choke and could easily die. Closing her eyes, Claire waited until the dizziness passed. Then, with extreme care, she risked opening her eyes for the third time.

This time it took her mere seconds to orient herself. She was lying under her workbench, facing the small furnace in which she heated the silica compounds that would eventually become molten glass. The furnace had been lit, she realized, and it was roaring full blast—a sound that she had interpreted in her semiconscious state as the crash and swell of ocean waves.

The temperature in the core of a glassmaking furnace could easily reach a thousand degrees and more; and lying this close, it was uncomfortably—unbearably—hot. But her furnace was new, well insulated, and equipped with all the latest safety devices. A series of thermostats and exterior locks ensured that the dangerous fire could never blaze out of control. She might get heatstroke, Claire thought, but Andrew or Ben would be here before too long, and they would rescue her. She was safe.

Unless the furnace exploded first.

With the calm that came from accepting that she hovered on the razor edge of death, Claire considered the fact that her furnace, new and well designed as it might be, was not equipped to withstand the effects of a deliberate attempt at sabotage. Roger had trained as a civil engineer and spent much of his youth messing around on building sites. Along the way, he had probably acquired all the knowledge he needed to enable him to dismantle a thermostat, and disconnect the other controls aimed at preventing her furnace from dangerously overheating. What better way to arrange the murder of his half sister than to have her die in a tragic accident? He had probably removed the various safety devices, reconnected the thermocouple, turned the furnace up to full power, and then run—no doubt to establish himself a rock-solid alibi for the moment when the furnace blew up.

Which, Claire decided, was likely to be sometime very soon, judging from the temperature in her studio. Any minute now, one of the pipes that connected the kiln to the power supply was going to melt at a joint. Gas would leak into the room through the faulty coupling, and what followed would be a conflagration large enough to blow up her studio, and half the rest of the street, besides. No wonder Roger hadn't worried about investigators finding drugs in her bloodstream, or tape binding her feet and wrists. If she was still lying here when the furnace blew, there'd be no need for a coffin at the funeral service. The coroner's office would be picking up charred fragments of her body for weeks to come.

Like hell, Claire decided, energized by a lifesaving burst of fury. She'd be *damned* if she was going to lie here and wait to be blown to smithereens.

Deciding to save herself was easy. Choosing a way was more difficult. She soon discovered that she was bound too tightly to have the flexibility in her elbows and knees to scoot across the floor. Nor could she roll to the front door, because there wasn't room to maneuver herself around the workbench without bumping into the boiling-hot furnace. There was nothing for it, she decided; she would simply have to cut through the tape, which wasn't too much of a problem if she could only reach one of the many sharp implements on the surface of her workbench.

Panting and sweating, choking behind her gag, she twisted onto her stomach and humped her knees under her. Forehead resting on the floor, hips stuck up into the air, she tried to suck oxygen into her lungs through her nose. Her stomach heaved in protest, and she immediately stopped moving.

You will not *vomit,* she ordered herself. *You will stand.*

For a while it seemed as if her stomach and legs would both refuse to obey instructions. After several excruciating seconds, the nausea faded enough for Claire to tuck her toes inward and, with a rocking motion, lever herself up high enough to clutch on to the seat of her work chair. With the chair as a support, it took only another thirty seconds or so to rest her chin on the edge of the workbench and haul her body semi-upright. She sobbed with relief when she saw the specially designed, heavy-duty scissors she used for cutting molten glass lying in their accustomed spot next to her engraving wheel.

Fumbling, frantic with haste now that the possibility of salvation was at hand, Claire grabbed the scissors. There was no way to angle them so that she could cut the tape binding her wrists. Instead, she pried the scissors open and poked very gently at the tape sealing her mouth. When she found the slit of her lips, she eased the thick blade of the scissors inside and ripped gently from right to left, allowing her mouth to open. The tape remained stuck to her face and hair, but at least now she could breathe through her mouth as well as her nose. She savored the small triumph by gulping in several quick mouthfuls of hot, tinder-dry air.

With the danger of throwing up significantly reduced, she slashed at the layers of heavy-duty electrical tape wound around her legs and ankles. It seemed that the roar of the furnace was getting louder, and she guessed that the temperature in the studio had climbed to somewhere near a hundred and twenty. Sweat poured off her body, and the scissors kept slipping in her slippery, bound hands, but she poked, incised, jabbed and cut, blessing the strength of the blades as she gradually sawed through the tape.

By the time the final layers separated, she was almost blinded by sweat, and nearly fainting from the heat. She ran to the front door, simultaneously crying and laughing with the relief of knowing that she had saved herself, that she had defeated Roger by guts, ingenuity, and sheer dogged determination. She grabbed the door handle and pulled.

Nothing happened. The door didn't budge.

No sweat, she told herself. *Don't panic.* She ran to the door leading into the garage. She twisted the handle. The door remained stubbornly, obstinately shut.

She ran back to the front door, pulling and tugging, a hairbreadth away from full-blown hysteria. The doors were her only exit route. Her studio was at ground level, but the windows were all covered with sturdy iron grills to discourage burglars, and if she couldn't open the door, then she was trapped.

Tears streaming down her cheeks, she beat out her frustration against the panels of the door. They were literally scorching hot, and she realized that the steel plate around the lock must have expanded with the heat so that the door was now warped, and too big for its frame. Great. She understood the problem, but she had no way to solve it. To open the door would require heavy pressure from the outside. She needed someone with a crowbar, or perhaps a hammer, to literally smash the door free of its frame.

Claire battled the temptation to slide down into the soothing comfort of unconsciousness. What was the point of fighting anymore? Roger had won. She was going to die.

I'm sorry, Andrew, she apologized silently. *God, I'm really sorry I misjudged you so badly.*

She closed her eyes and thought of Ben. Now, when it was too late, she was aware of a yearning regret for all the pleasures they hadn't shared, for all the discoveries they would never make together. She wished she could see him one more time. Not to tell him that she loved him, but to tell him how much she *liked* him, and how much she enjoyed his company. Going to bed with Ben was wonderful, but staying out of bed was wonderful with him, too. She wondered if he liked Vivaldi, or the Rolling Stones, or both. She wondered if he was any good at Scrabble. There were so many important things that she would never know about Ben.

The realization was unbearably sad. Her thoughts slipped out of shape, drifting away into warm, smothering darkness.

When she heard the pounding on the other side of the door, it took her a minute or so to realize that the noise was not just a figment of her delusions but an actual, physical reality.

"Claire! Are you there? Open up, honey! You must let me in! What's going on? For God's sake, open up!"

"Ben?" She pulled herself up off the floor and leaned against the door, not caring about the heat burning her cheeks, crying with the relief of hearing his voice. "Ben, I can't open the door. It's jammed."

"I understand. I'll push. You pull."

"No good," she said. "You need something to smash the lock and break the vacuum. The door's expanded in the heat. Hurry, the furnace in my studio is going to blow."

He didn't waste time asking for explanations. "Lock the handle in the open position. Then stand back, but don't move away too far from the door. Do you understand?"

"Yes." She turned the handle in the direction that would normally have opened the door, and twisted the little knob to hold the latch in an open position. "Done," she said.

"I have a rock from your front yard," Ben said. "I'm going to smash the lock, okay?"

"Yes."

She heard the crash of stone hitting wood. The door vibrated, but didn't open. Ben pounded again, and then again. The door shuddered, then swung inward with such force that he and the rock both tumbled inside the hallway.

He cast one swift look toward the blazing furnace, then he grabbed her bound wrists and pulled her out into the yard. "Come on," he said. "The extra oxygen we've just let in is going to send that furnace sky-high."

Her legs would barely hold her upright, let alone carry her across the bumpy, paved courtyard. Ben stopped and swept her up into his arms. He'd traveled about a hundred yards down the street when the explosion came. He threw Claire onto a neighbor's lawn and spread-eagled himself on top of her.

When the thunder of the blasts finally stopped, he looked down at her anxiously. "Claire, darling, are you all right? Are you hurt?"

"I'm fine." She blew a blade of grass off her nose, and peered at him through a tangled mass of sweaty hair and dangling electrical tape. "Do you play Scrabble?" she asked.

"Scrabble?" He looked startled, then his mouth curved into a smile. "Absolutely," he said.

"Good," she said, and promptly fainted.

When she came to, the paramedics had strapped her to a stretcher and were loading her into the ambulance. Ben was standing right beside her, and Andrew was leaning over her, his face a bleak mask of anguish.

"I'm sorry," she said, squeezing his hand. "Dad, I'm so sorry."

"My God, Claire, we should be apologizing to you," he said. "You have nothing to be sorry for, nothing at all." He patted her hand, awkwardly comforting. "They're going to take you to the hospital, check you out, pump some fluids into your system. You'll feel much better by this time tomorrow, honey."

If the fear hadn't been so recent, if she hadn't been feverish with pain, she would have watched her words more carefully. As it was, the accusation tumbled out in stark condemnation. "Roger tried to kill me," she said. "Not just here, but the other times—in Vermont, in New Jersey."

"I know," Andrew said, his mouth twitching in a spasm of pain. "Dear God, Claire, I don't know what to say to you."

Ben stepped forward and rested his hand lightly on her forehead. "The police are looking for him, Claire. He won't get away, and he won't hurt you ever again, I promise."

"I'm counting on you," she said, and closed her eyes, floating away into sleep.

Roger switched off the morning news broadcast, and sat in his car, ice cold with the shocking awareness of failure. The bitch wasn't dead, and the police had put out an all-points bulletin authorizing his arrest. If he'd tried to leave Boston, and if he hadn't been smart enough to rent a car at the airport yesterday using fake ID, they'd probably have arrested him last night.

What was the matter with Andrew? Roger wondered, his stomach clenching with a bitter sense of betrayal. How the hell could he have let Claire tell her vicious, lying stories to the police? Claire wasn't his daughter, and yet he showered his love on her. Didn't he care that Claire was a bastard, a usurper, a whore like her mother? A half-baked artist who would run Campbell Industries into bankruptcy if she ever got the chance?

And Ben. Who could've figured Ben? Roger had worked his ass off just so that the guy would look good, and what happened? The stupid, ungrateful nincompoop went and fell in love with Claire!

Roger drummed his fingers against the steering wheel, knowing what he had to do, and savoring the secret knowledge. Then he leaned across the car and opened the glove compartment. His 9 mm Smith & Wesson gleamed at him in welcome. When all else failed, he thought, a man could always count on his gun. With a quick check to make sure that it was properly loaded, Roger tucked the gun into the inside pocket of his jacket. Then he got out of the car and walked briskly across the parking lot toward the hospital.

The lobby smelled of coffee and hummed with the bustle of early-morning activity. He bought flowers at the gift shop before walking over to the inquiry desk and asking for Claire. The hospital apparently liked to make it easy for murderers and other visitors. A volunteer at the desk obligingly looked up Claire's room number and gave him directions.

Third floor, west wing, number 327. Take the elevators with a purple stripe on the doors. "Nice flowers," she said.

"Very nice," Roger agreed, and thanked her politely for helping him.

A nurse gave him a sweet smile as he stepped into the elevator. She was young and pretty, and on another occasion, he might have made her day a bit brighter by striking up a conversation. Today, he ignored her. Hell, after so many unsuccessful attempts to kill Claire, he didn't have much to smile about. It was amazing to think that an inferior person like Claire could have foiled his brilliant efforts on so many occasions. But not today, he thought, striding along the corridor in the direction of room 327. Not today.

The door to her room was open. He peered inside and saw at once that she wasn't alone. Ben was with her, looking rumpled enough that he probably must have spent the night sleeping in the chair beside her bed. For a moment, Roger was flooded with a despair so profound, so far-reaching, that he felt paralyzed. Then he understood how he would have to overcome the problem of Ben's presence, and the despair left him, to be replaced with a wonderful sense of peace. Soon it would all be over.

He took the gun out of his pocket, and hid it carefully behind the bouquet of flowers. He walked into her room.

Ben saw him a split second too soon and threw himself over the bed, dragging Claire and half the bedclothes onto the floor. "Roger, don't do it!" he yelled. "For God's sake, don't do it!"

Roger tossed the bouquet aside. He raised the gun and aimed at the crumpled heap hidden behind the bed, but his hand was shaking and even when he squeezed the trigger he knew he'd missed. Had he planned to miss?

"Roger, don't!" Claire's voice. "Please don't do this!" He heard her frightened plea at the same moment as he heard footsteps running from the nurses' station toward the room.

He raised the gun again, his finger stroking the trigger. Ever since Claire had come back, ever since he'd seen her in Florida, he'd known in his heart of hearts that it would come to this.

The nurse was at the door, he could see her white jacket out of the corner of his eye. He swung around to face her. She screamed and he heard the eerie wail of an electronic siren. She must have pressed some sort of emergency panic button. Funny that they should all be panicked when he finally felt at rest.

Roger bent his arm and slowly swung the gun around until it was pointed toward his face. He opened his mouth, put the barrel of the gun into the opening and pulled the trigger.

Epilogue

The White House Rose Garden
One year later

Bainbridge rose to his feet as the President and First Lady stepped out of the White House into the glare of midsummer sunshine. Applause rippled through the audience and Bainbridge deigned to add a few judicious claps. Truth to tell, he'd been naturalized years ago, and he was mighty proud of being an American. But he would never let on, because that would ruin the illusion he'd spent years striving to create. Evelyn Campbell had hired him when he hadn't known where his next meal would come from, and he owed her the best. And in the profession of butlering, the best meant playing the part of a snooty Brit who wasn't impressed by the rituals of American democracy. Bainbridge caught a reporter's eye, and adjusted his expression into one of suitable condescension.

Of course, Evelyn had realized within a couple of days of hiring him that he was a complete fraud. Thirty years ago, Bainbridge had been an actor, usually out of work, and his only qualification for the job was the fact that he'd played the part of a British butler in a short-lived television soap and a half-dozen off-Broadway plays. Instead of firing him, Evelyn had stuck by him, until he'd become almost as good at the real job of butler as he was at playing the part. He was delighted to know that her life was finally taking a turn for the better after the tragedies of the past few years. Her grief and guilt over Roger's death had lasted for months. In fact, the entire family had barely been re-covering from the trauma of Roger's suicide when Claire and Ben got married over the Christmas holi-days.

But now it was time to move on to happier things. TV cameras whirred as Andrew Campbell, the newly confirmed Secretary of the Interior, stepped up to the bank of microphones, ready to be sworn in to office. Behind him, Bainbridge could see the smiling faces of Claire and Ben, happily married now for almost eight months.

Bainbridge permitted himself a fond nod of ap-proval as Evelyn, supremely elegant in navy blue silk and pearls, held out the Bible that Hector and Jaime Campbell had brought across the Atlantic more than a century earlier. Andrew placed his hand on the worn cover and repeated the oath of office, his voice firm and strong.

Andrew's speech following the swearing-in was short, barely more than a few sentences promising to follow environmentally sound policies that took into account the diverse needs of local economies. Smart man, Bainbridge thought dryly. Everyone agreed with the principle, and nobody wanted to hear the compli-cated specifics. The reporters would rather eat straw-berries and drink punch than listen to a new cabinet official deliver a twenty-point oration.

Andrew and Evelyn joined the President and First Lady to mingle with the invited crowd of lobbyists and interest groups, but Claire and Ben broke away from the crowd of friends and dignitaries to walk over to Bainbridge. He stood, and Claire linked her arm affectionately through his. She was totally unimpressed by his haughty, raised eyebrows, of course, but Bainbridge was amused to note that Ben still seemed appropriately intimidated.

"Good morning," Bainbridge said austerely. "It's a pleasure to see you both looking so well."

"You, too, Bainbridge. Wasn't that a great ceremony?" Claire was marching them all toward the serving dishes of strawberries and cream. "The confirmation hearings were a bit hairy when they kept skating around all that personal stuff, but Dad is going to do a super job, I know he is."

Bainbridge relented, and patted her hand. "I'm sure he will, my dear. The fact that the Sierra Club and the Chamber of Commerce both endorsed him shows what an excellent record he has."

Ben handed them each a bowl of strawberries. "Evelyn's looking positively radiant," he said. "Thank God."

Bainbridge coughed. "I believe she and Mr. Campbell are looking forward to establishing a residence in Washington. Mrs. Campbell is such a superb hostess, I'm sure their dinner invitations will soon be the most sought-after in town."

Claire laughed. "With you in charge, they wouldn't dare to be anything but the most sought-after."

"Thank you, Mrs. Maxwell. I appreciate the compliment."

"Oh, Bainbridge, don't be such an old fogey." With the unconscious assurance of a woman who knows she is well loved, Claire leaned back against Ben's arm. "Remind me to send you a set of the new Campbell Crystal glasses for Mom's new house. I've been working on the design eighteen hours a day, and I think we've finally got it right."

"I'm sure you have, Mrs. Maxwell. Your mother and father have shown me some of your work, and it's exquisite."

Claire actually blushed. "Thanks, Bainbridge. Praise from you is really worth something." She turned to Ben, who looked down at her with so much love in his eyes that Bainbridge was hard-pressed to maintain his expression of sober decorum. Ben gave an almost imperceptible nod, and she drew in a tiny little breath of excitement. "Ben and I have something to tell you," she said.

"And what's that, Mrs. Maxwell?"

"We're going to have a baby." It was Ben who answered. He tightened his arm around Claire's shoulders, his grin stretching nearly from ear to ear. "In January," he said. "Right around the New Year."

A baby! Bainbridge felt a surge of pure, unadulterated delight. To hell with dignity, he thought, and gathered Claire into a jubilant hug. "That's wonderful," he said. "Simply wonderful. I'm so happy for you both."

Claire laughed, the joyful sound sweeping away the shadows of past grief. "Yes," she said. "We think it's wonderful, too."

Compelling Debut Author

TAYLOR SMITH

Catapults you into a world where deception is
the rule

Guilt by Silence

In the flash of an eye, Mariah Bolt's world came
crashing down. Confronted by the destruction of her
family and too many unanswered questions, she's
determined to prove that her husband's accident was a
carefully planned attempt at murder. As she probes
deeper into what really happened, she realizes that she
can trust no one—not the government, not her husband,
not even Paul Chaney, the one person willing to help
her. Because now Mariah is the target.

Available this June at your favorite retail outlet.

MIRA The brightest star in women's fiction

MTSGBS

Over 20 million copies of her books in print

Sandra Brown

They were stranded, in danger and they were

TWO ALONE

(previously published under the pseudonym Erin St. Claire)

The only woman to board a charter flight to the Northwest Territories, Rusty Carlson feared she was the only survivor after its fateful crash. But when rugged Cooper Landry regained consciousness she was grateful that now she wasn't alone. The odds were against them surviving in the dense terrain, but they had more than luck—they had each other. As Rusty and Cooper fought for survival, they discovered that the toughest fight of all was the battle of their hearts.

Don't miss TWO ALONE, this June at your favorite retail outlet.

MIRA **The brightest star in women's fiction**

MSBTA

New York Times Bestselling Author

LINDA LAEL MILLER

How much passion is too much?
Look for the answer in

USED-TO-BE-LOVERS

Breaking up is hard to do...especially if the biggest
problem is loving each other too much! With the ink
barely dry on the divorce papers, Sharon and Tony
were on the brink of rekindling the passion that first
brought them together. Were they crazy? Or was this
their last chance to right yesterday's wrongs?

Discover how it turns out, this May at your favorite
retail outlet.

MIRA The brightest star in women's fiction

MLLM2

New York Times Bestselling Author!

HEATHER GRAHAM POZZESSERE

Brings you a mesmerizing tale of a time in Eden with

STRANGERS IN PARADISE

Alexi and Rex were strangers who found that they had more in common than simply being neighbors. They were each running from their past, and hiding from their memories. But when someone began stalking Alexi, Rex vowed to protect her. The only danger Alexi sensed, however, came from Rex himself.

Visit your favorite retail outlet this May to find out if paradise really exists.

 MIRA The brightest star in women's fiction

MHGP3

New York Times **bestselling author**

BARBARA DELINSKY

Takes you to a world of crime, wealth and
passion this May in

THROUGH MY EYES

Jill Moncrieff had walked away from the stifling
world of wealth and privilege to escape painful
memories. But when a close friend was falsely
accused of a crime, she knew the only way to
help was to hire a hotshot lawyer from her old
world. Attorney Peter Hathaway was a big-city
lawyer who embodied everything Jill hated, but
he was the best man for the job. Although he
threatened her loyalty to her husband's memory,
she found him unforgivably alluring…and found
herself unforgivably tempted.…

MIRA The brightest star in women's fiction

MBD2

Bestselling Author

Introduces you to the woman called

Everybody loves Red—whoever she is. A haunted
teenager who defied the odds to find fame as a top model.
A pretty face who became a talented fashion photographer,
A woman who has won the love of two men. Yet, no
matter how often she transforms herself, the pain of Red's
past just won't go away—until she faces it head on....

Available this July, at your favorite retail outlet.

 MIRA™ The brightest star in women's fiction

MESR

New York Times Bestselling Author

JAYNE ANN KRENTZ

Sometimes having too much money can be a curse.

Full Bloom

Emily Ravenscroft is a woman who doesn't need her
wealthy, overbearing family to tell her that money can't
buy love. Her problem is finding a man who can't be
bought. And Jacob Stone might just be that man—provided
Emily can survive the unwanted advances of a bitter
ex-fiancé....

Available this July at your favorite retail outlet.

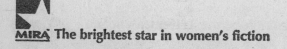

MIRA The brightest star in women's fiction

MJAKFB

If you love the romantic style of

JASMINE CRESSWELL

Then order now to receive another thrilling story by
one of MIRA's rising stars:

#66040   CHASE THE PAST $4.99 U.S. ☐
                                   $5.50 CAN. ☐

(limited quantities available)

TOTAL AMOUNT	$
POSTAGE & HANDLING	$
($1.00 for one book, 50¢ for each additional)	
APPLICABLE TAXES*	$_____
<u>**TOTAL PAYABLE**</u>	$_____
(check or money order—please do not send cash)	

To order, complete this form and send it, along with a check or money order
for the total above, payable to MIRA Books, to: **In the U.S.:** 3010 Walden
Avenue, P.O. Box 9077, Buffalo, NY 14269-9077; **In Canada:** P.O. Box 636,
Fort Erie, Ontario, L2A 5X3.

Name:_____

Address: _____City:_____

State/Prov.:_____ Zip/Postal Code:_____

*New York residents remit applicable sales taxes.
 Canadian residents remit applicable GST and provincial taxes.

MJCBL1

MIRA